Copyrighted Material

Ruins of the Galaxy Copyright © 2019 by Variant Publications, Hopper Creative Group

Book design and layout copyright © 2019 by JN Chaney

This novel is a work of fiction. Names, characters, places, and incidents are either products of the author's imagination or used fictitiously. Any resemblance to actual events, locales, or persons, living, dead, or undead, is entirely coincidental.

All rights reserved

No part of this publication can be reproduced or transmitted in any form or by any means, electronic or mechanical, without permission in writing.

Version 2.0

1st Edition

RUINS OF THE GALAXY

CHRISTOPHER HOPPER
J.N. CHANEY

VARIANT PUBLICATIONS

LAS VEGAS, NV • NEW YORK, NY

JOIN THE RUINS TRIBE

Visit ruinsofthegalaxy.com today and join the tribe. Once there, you can sign up for our reader group, join our Facebook community, and find us on Twitter and Instagram.

If you'd like to email us with comments or questions, we respond to all emails sent to ruinsofthegalaxy@gmail.com, and love to hear from our readers.

See you in the Ruins!

STAY UP TO DATE

J.N. Chaney posts updates, official art, previews, and other awesome stuff on his website. You can also follow him on **Instagram**, **Facebook**, and **Twitter**.

He also created a special **Facebook group** called "JN Chaney's Renegade Readers" specifically for readers to come together and share their lives and interests, discuss the series, and speak directly to me. Please check it out and join whenever you get the chance!

For updates about new releases, as well as exclusive promotions, visit his website, jnchaney.com and sign up for the VIP mailing list.

https://www.jnchaney.com/ruins-of-the-galaxy-subscribe

Stay Up To Date

Enjoying the series? Help others discover the Ruins of the Galaxy series by leaving a review on **Amazon.**

CONTENTS

Chapter 1	1
Chapter 2	11
Chapter 3	23
Chapter 4	33
Chapter 5	37
Chapter 6	49
Chapter 7	59
Chapter 8	71
Chapter 9	77
Chapter 10	93
Chapter 11	107
Chapter 12	121
Chapter 13	129
Chapter 14	133
Chapter 15	145
Chapter 16	161
Chapter 17	171
Chapter 18	183
Chapter 19	191
Chapter 20	197
Chapter 21	211
Chapter 22	223
Chapter 23	235
Chapter 24	245
Chapter 25	257
Chapter 26	269
Chapter 27	275
Chapter 28	289
Chapter 29	297
Chapter 30	309

Chapter 31	319
Chapter 32	329
Chapter 33	341
Chapter 34	355
Chapter 35	371
Chapter 36	385
Chapter 37	407
Chapter 38	419
List of Main Characters	429
Join the Ruins Tribe	435
Stay Up to Date	437
Acknowledgments	439
About the Authors	443
Author's Note	445
The Night of Fire	451

DEMONS AT WAR

Chapter 1	483
Chapter 2	501
Chapter 3	511
Chapter 4	527
Chapter 5	535
Chapter 6	549
Epilogue	559

For the Renegade Readers. Your support has meant the world(s) to me.

—J.N. Chaney

---

*To my wife for holding my hand in the void.
I'd be lost without you, Jenny.*

*And to Jim Krisher and Douglas Ort, my two
snow markers in the whiteout.*

—Christopher

1

"I know you wanna bust out your bikini, Flow, but mind telling me if you see any hostiles yet?" Magnus asked over a private channel on TACNET.

"Negative, LT," Flow replied. "A city of fifteen million Jujari, and we ain't seen splick."

"Your mama raise you to talk like that, Sergeant? Or are you just pissed you can't go swimming?"

"I'm pissed I can't see anything to shoot yet."

"Copy that." Magnus touched his MAR30's safety out of habit.

Magnus and his Charlie Platoon of fifteen operators had set security on what was one of the worst danger areas he'd ever been assigned to. The landing platform they stood on was forty stories up the side of a composite sandstone skyscraper in the center of Oosafar, and it jutted out like a waiter's silver platter. The sun's heat was punishing, pushing their armor-cooling capabilities to the limit and threatening to cook the men before any objectives were reached. While his platoon controlled the perimeter of the pad, a sea of buildings surrounded them, each rife with potential sniper nests or heavy blaster emplacements. Magnus couldn't shake the feeling that his unit was being served up as some Jujari chief's main course. They were, to put it in Marine speak, hanging out like dogs' balls.

"You don't really think this is about peacekeeping, do you, LT?" Flow asked.

"Not any more than you do. Since when has Recon been tasked with security? Plus, these dogs have alliances with five other systems and a fleet to match. No way they asked the Repub here to surrender all that after three hundred years of resisting us. Something smells off."

"Copy that," Flow said with a sniff.

The higher-ups had tried to assure Magnus that this mission was critical to Republic progress. And maybe it was. But Magnus and his platoon were stuck babysitting sycophants in a chemical reaction of politics and cults waiting to go nova. It was just a matter of time before one of his Marines got killed in the name of progress, and that was not what he'd signed up for.

"You know, I hear they bleed their prisoners for weeks," Flow said. "Some ancient ritual sacrifice or some splick. 'Living blood' they call it. You think that's true?"

"Don't know, don't care, Flow." Magnus looked over the platform's edge. It was a long way down. "If we don't accomplish the objective, we're dead anyway."

"How's that?"

"The Jujari drain us of our blood or the major drains us of our stripes. Either way, we're done. But I'll take my chances with the hyenas."

"Copy that, LT," Flow replied with a chuckle.

"Just own the field and keep your eyes peeled for our bird."

A gust of wind blew up from within the city and buffeted Magnus's men. He turned to see them covering their respective fields of fire with their MAR30s. The sooner they could get off this platform the better.

"Heads up, LT," Flow said. "I'm picking up an inbound Regent-class cruiser."

Magnus looked skyward and flicked his eyes through menus in his heads-up display. A blue targeting reticle latched onto a square of empty sky and showed Repub designations fed from the orbital convoy overhead, including the shuttle's code name, Falcon One. He let his eyes focus on the marker until his helmet's artificial intelligence zoomed in. The AI's neural-sensor suite was responding quicker than before. *Nice update.* Magnus reminded himself to thank the battalion's coders when he got back.

The sky expanded in his HUD, filling his field of view with a static-laden image of a diplomatic shuttle. Even from this distance, Magnus could make out the Order of the Luma's insignia on the ship's large vertical stabilizer: a single maroon flame within an unbroken circle. Magnus cringed. *Blasted peacemongers.*

"Those are our assets," Magnus said, wondering if Flow could hear the disdain in his voice.

"Roger that," Flow replied. "Don't act too happy about it, LT."

Magnus switched off the private channel with Flow and opened a direct line to Alpha Platoon's leader and CO for the op.

"Go ahead, Lieutenant," came Captain Wainwright's baritone voice.

"We've got eyes on Falcon One, Captain."

There was a pause. Magnus knew Wainwright was reviewing the HUD data. The captain was a legend in the Recon and one Magnus was proud to serve under. Alpha Platoon was charged with security for the Republic ambassador and his envoy, while Charlie was tasked with the Luma emissary. According to the mission plan, Wainwright was fifteen minutes ahead of Magnus's platoon and already topside at the meeting location.

"Copy that," said the captain. "You're all green."

"Roger, Captain." Magnus signed out. He surveyed the landing platform again and brought up a unit channel. "Look alive, Hunters. Shuttle inbound, ETA is three." Magnus watched his HUD as each platoon member confirmed unit readiness with green affirmation icons.

The private channel chirped. Flow was calling again.

"Go, Flow," Magnus ordered.

"LT, I don't wanna beat this to death, but this is *splick*. We're three-sixtied. Hell, they're probably covering our undercarriage too, and we can't do a damn thing about it. The way I see it, the only thing good about this place is that we don't have the squirts like we did in Caledonia."

"Wait, you mean that time we were crapping our brains out in a honeymooner's paradise?" Magnus replied. "Nah, don't remember anything about that."

Jokes aside, Magnus was just as frustrated as Flow. Their position was begging for an ambush. Oosafar's urban environment was perfectly suited for veiled attacks from nearly every angle. Where any other world would have had solid windows in its buildings, the Jujari hung white curtains and had a low-level force field to keep out the elements. The fabric billowed in the late-afternoon wind, moving like ghosts in and out of a thousand cave entrances, and the constant motion provided the ideal concealment for an enemy on the move.

"Which desk jockey you think approved this op without reading the fine print?" Flow asked. "Feels like they're playing Terberian roulette with us, ya know? The problem is—"

"The house always wins," Magnus finished.

"Yeah, exactly. Only this house wants to kill us."

Flow was just talking splick. It was how they all processed the tension before a fight. But there was some truth to his words too.

"A neutral planet certainly would have been a smarter choice," Magnus said. "But no one expects jockeys to have street smarts."

"Copy that, LT." Flow looked at his MS900 sniper blaster. "So, that request for overwatch never went through?"

Magnus knew Flow would much rather be in a perch somewhere, picking out targets with his weapon. Command had asked for overwatch positions but was refused access since the Jujari would not permit outsiders to tread in ceremonially clean parts of the city. As a compromise, they provided "unrestricted access" to building files, which, as it turned out, were a joke. *They have every known descendant of the first mwadim inked in blood on tanned gorangi skin*, Magnus thought wryly, *but they can't keep track of how many floors are in their structures. Perfect.*

"Negative," Magnus said. "Brass said the Jujari wouldn't allow us access. Something about us desecrating sacred ground with our unclean feet."

"I'll have you know that I wash my feet daily, LT," Flow said.

"And that's exactly what I told Colonel Caldwell." The idiom *telling Colonel Caldwell* had become a joke around the unit, inspired by Magnus's familial and combat connections with the famed commander. It was Colonel Caldwell who'd gotten Magnus and his three best noncommissioned officers, dubbed the Fearsome Four, a shot at Recon Indoctrination School. "Clean feet, I said. None cleaner. Pretty sure that's the only reason he let you attend RIP with me."

"And what were Cheeks's and Mouth's excuses?"

"Good looks and muscle," Magnus replied. "The Four have to stay well-rounded, but don't tell them I said that."

"And what does that make you, LT?"

"I'm the brains, Flow. Always the brains."

Magnus's pulse quickened as his armor's cooling system suddenly increased power consumption. It was fighting to keep its occupant comfortable under the sun's oppressive heat. Magnus was sweating enough to fill his reclamation bladders every few minutes. He could even feel his short beard soaking up sweat. He'd maintained a beard since he graduated from RIP, taking full advantage of the elite unit's more permissive grooming allowances, but now it was annoying him. If it hadn't been for his helmet's air-treatment capabilities, he wasn't sure which would smell worse, his body or the capital city.

While the men in his unit continued to scan every building with their helmets' thermal imaging, tagging occupants with yellow indicators, Magnus cycled through the icons, checking floors and rooms against shoddy city records gifted to the Republic because of the "momentous exchange."

"Let's just keep the emissary safe, let all the jockeys have their fun, and then get off this desert rock. Keep your eyes open and call it in. Own the mission, own the field."

"OTF. Copy that, LT."

Magnus closed the channel and turned from observing the buildings to see the Luma shuttle on final approach, matte gray and resembling a ferret—its slender crew module the animal's neck and the command bridge cantilevering up and away like a head. The shuttle had a single vertical stabilizer in the aft and a narrow bridge window above the nose. Its engines vectored toward them to bleed off speed in a hotter-than-usual landing. Apparently, the pilots were as apprehensive as the Hunters.

"SITREP," Magnus called over TACNET to his team leads, asking for a situation report.

"Good here," Mouth said.

"You know," Corporal Miguel Chico said, "normally, I'm

good for rolling in the sheets, but I don't care if I ever see another set again."

"Can it, Cheeks," Flow ordered.

"Copy."

As one, the Marines braced themselves against the sand that blasted their helmets. The stuff had found its way into every crease in their armor, and they'd been on planet fewer than thirty minutes. The armor's mag boots engaged, sensing slippage, as the shuttle's thrust threatened to push each Marine off the platform. Magnus's body vibrated, absorbing the ship's ferocious energy. As soon as the landing gear touched down, however, the pilots killed the engines. It felt as though someone had shut off a midsummer Dustoovian cyclone just by flicking a switch.

The Hunters in the platoon scanned their respective fields of fire with their MAR30s. This was the time for an ambush. Magnus looked to the ship's hydraulic ramp as it lowered to the platform, awash in a swirl of white steam. The blue-uniformed flight steward came down the walkway at somewhere between a run and a walk, betraying just how nervous he was. He spotted Magnus, tapped the top of his head, then waited for the reply.

"We good, Flow?" Magnus asked.

"Still green, LT."

"Copy. Bringing out the assets. Eyes up, Hunters." Magnus took a deep breath. *Professional. Be professional.* For as much as the Jujari repulsed him and as much as the Republic's bureaucracy annoyed him, neither compared to how much he loathed the emissaries about to walk down this ramp. They'd cost him lives,

lives of Marines who'd never be able to argue their case against the Luma's methods. *Careless leadership.*

Magnus motioned to the shuttle's steward with a knife-edge hand chop in the air. The steward signaled up the ramp, and a figure emerged in the white mist.

"Splick. That's your asset, LT?" Cheeks said over TACNET. "Wanna trade?"

2

Awen hated atmospheric entry about as much as she hated raw Paglothian sorlakk; both made her vomit. The only difference was that she didn't have to eat sorlakk on a weekly basis. Her hands scrambled for the small bag stowed in the seatback in front of her, but it was missing.

"I got it," Matteo said, reaching for his seat's bag and handing it to her. Just in time too. Awen had purposely skipped lunch for that very reason, and there was still plenty of—whatever breakfast was—to fill the sack.

"Thanks," she said, wiping her mouth with the enclosed napkin. "Have I ever mentioned—"

"How much you appreciate me?"

"How much I hate entry," Awen said.

"Only every time we fly. But you could stand to mention the other a little more often."

Awen pursed her lips and gave him a nod. "Noted." She stowed the sealed bag, sat back, and took a deep breath, grateful the light civilian cruiser was in calm air again. The passenger cabin was smaller than she liked, which made her motion sickness all the worse. She preferred the larger starships since they had better dampeners. Still, the compartment's glossy-white walls and ceiling and comfortable chairs were in pristine condition, which she credited to the Luma's fastidious standards.

Matteo stared out the starboard window, and Awen followed his gaze to the vast expanse of sand below. It reached to the curved horizon, light yellow contrasting with the deep blue of the sky. She'd waited her entire adult life to come to this system, which wasn't that long, considering she was only twenty-four years common. Still, Jujari culture had been her major at the academy—or was it an obsession?—and she'd become more knowledgeable in the history and affairs of the hyena-like species than any Luma before her.

Far below, the capital city of Oosafar rose like a gleaming white obelisk in the late-afternoon light. It stood in stark contrast to the rust-colored dunes and low-slung mountains that surrounded it. While elegant, the city's presence also felt defiant, as if the buildings stood as a bulwark against the seductive power of the Republic. Awen's spirit couldn't help feeling a strange kinship with the Jujari, though their cultures were light-years apart—physically and metaphorically. Still, she admired their ability to resist countless attempts to bring them into the Republic. Awen was drawn to their insistence that joining the Republic would compromise their heritage and that they would rather fend for themselves than eat lavishly from the Republic's table.

That said, she knew that the Jujari people suffered at the hands of their leaders. They were a violent species, prone to devouring their own as quickly as any unwelcome visitors—or even welcome visitors, for that matter.

"Feels like we're coming in pretty fast," Matteo noted.

Awen leaned over his seat arm. She absentmindedly clutched the Luma medallion around her neck—a flame carved inside a golden oblong disk at the end of a leather cord—and squeezed it between her fingers. "New pilot, maybe?"

"Nah. I just think no one wants to spend more time in this system than they have to."

Awen let go of the medallion. "Attitudes like that have delayed meetings like this for centuries. You do understand that, right?"

"Sure, sure, and the universe is all black and white, and everything can be solved if we talk it through. I get it. *I get it.*"

Awen backed away from his seat and crossed her arms. "You know, Matteo, sometimes I wonder why you even joined the Luma."

He feigned a pain in his chest by clutching his heart. "That hurts, Awen."

"I'm just saying, if we keep going into these situations looking for a confrontation, then that's all we're ever going to find."

"Then you don't think it's the least bit strange that suddenly, after hundreds of years, the Jujari want peace talks? Come on."

Awen took in and let out a deep breath. "I admit it's unusual, yes. However, if we don't give them the benefit of the doubt, then who will?"

Matteo shrugged.

"Precisely," she said, poking his arm. "This is our job. We can't expect to find a blaster fight across every peace talk."

"What if that's all these outliers want us to find?"

Awen turned away from him, mumbling that he was an ignorant fool.

Matteo pulled his attention from the window and looked at her. "What was that?"

"Nothing."

"Come on. You know you want to say it."

Awen shot him a wicked glance and raised her chin ever so slightly. Her words were slow and dripping with sarcasm. "I said that you sound just like an ignorant fool, and I have a Repub blaster for you in my overnight kit."

Matteo laughed and rubbed his hands together. "I knew you'd come around to my way of seeing things," he said. He looked out the window again and pointed to something. "Hey, look at that."

"What?"

"You have excellent timing," Matteo said. Awen followed his finger to see a handful of troopers lining the perimeter of the approaching landing pad. "There's my fire team now. Hand me my blaster."

The landing was harder than usual. Awen smoothed her maroon and black robes as the engines cut off, hoping her stomach would settle down just as fast. But she wasn't sure what was airsickness and what was adrenaline. She was finally here. She had dreamed of this moment for the last six years and never really thought she would get the chance to visit Oorajee.

She ordered herself to stay calm. *Savor the experience. Every sight, every sound. Take it all in.*

Through the window, Awen heard muted footfalls and loud orders then the whine of hydraulics as the ramp went down. The flight attendant typed on a wall-mounted keypad then descended out of view in a swirl of white mist. That was when Awen smelled it: her first deep breath of the Jujari home world. It was a strange mixture of curry, sour milk, lavender, and burnt fecal matter. She wrinkled her nose but still savored the fact that she was finally here. She'd made it.

"You've been waiting for this for a while," Matteo said. "Bet it feels surreal."

"It does," Awen replied, unfastening her harness. "Doesn't smell like I thought it would, though."

"Pretty sure no place in the galaxy smells like this."

Awen chuckled then stood up. It felt good to stretch. She turned around to see the rest of the entourage unbuckle and gain their feet. Some of the elders took longer than she would have liked, but this wasn't a day to rush anything. *Slow and steady.*

"Madame Emissary," said the flight attendant in his deep-blue flight uniform. "They're ready for you."

"Thank you," she replied. Awen glanced at Matteo and the others then back at the flight attendant. "We're ready."

The man nodded and gestured down the ramp. Awen took the lead and emerged from the shuttle's shadow into the full force of the sun's glare, a sensation that felt akin to plopping an ice cube on a hot frying pan. Her skin prickled, and the smells intensified as she got her bearings.

"It's even more incredible than I imagined," Awen whispered to Matteo. She felt overwhelmed by the sight of the linens that hung in hundreds of windows. "The *inook* shrouds are stunning. Did you know their thread count correlates with the number of generations in each owner's lineage? Some range into the thousands."

"That's wonderful, Awen. Can we go inside?"

Just then a gruff voice blasted her name from an exterior speaker. The person talking was the trooper closest to her, whose helmet looked like a bat head with a muzzled lion's mouth. His armor was black and gray, and he held a large blaster at the ready.

"Emissary dau Lothlinium," the trooper repeated.

Awen nodded toward whatever eyes lay behind the glossy black visor.

"We need to get you inside. This way."

Awen gestured for the trooper to lead the way but could not bring herself to actually thank the bulky hulk. The trooper turned and walked across the platform toward the building's entrance. He escorted her to a tall archway, stepped through the fabric, and held it aside for her to enter. A moment later, Awen was inside a large receiving room lined floor to ceiling with the white linens that made up the walls. Awen's fellow Luma began to file in while the trooper remained at the entrance.

"That's better." Matteo brushed sand from his robes and wiped the sweat from his forehead.

Awen, too, was immediately grateful for the temperature change. The separation from the outside world was dramatic. She noted just how thick the fabric was. A wide bolt of it streamed down from the center of the room and draped around a bowl of fladaria. She approached the table and felt the heavy fabric between her fingers then looked at the bloodred fruit.

"What is it?" Matteo continued to dab his forehead with his sleeve and puffed out his cheeks.

"It's fruit, and a good sign for us," she said softly, noting how the room swallowed her words. It felt as though she'd been cut off from the exterior world. "It's the ceremonial food of welcome."

"So, what do they put out when they *don't* want you around—bad eggs?"

"No," she whispered, "a severed head from that day's public executions."

Matteo instinctively reached a hand to his throat. "Nice species. Say, where are they?"

"They're finishing prayers." Awen had yet to see her first Jujari in the flesh and could hardly wait. "They won't entertain us beyond this room until they are sure of their god's will for the meeting."

"Heck of a time to figure that out."

Awen rolled her eyes at him then reached for the bowl. She took one of the oblong fruits and bit into it, a small red stream of juice flowing from the corner of her mouth. She knew that "bleeding" when eating was customary among all Jujari tribes, though the fruit was so juicy that she hardly did it on purpose.

"It's okay," she said to the rest of her team as they continued to file in. She motioned toward the bowl. "You'll like it. It's sweet."

Matteo grabbed one of the fruits and tried it, a smile creeping across his wet red lips. Everyone else took a fruit and ate. As the juice was still streaming down the team's faces, all sixteen troopers who'd been outside threw open the fabric doorway and entered with a blast of light and heat.

"Excuse me, what are you doing?" Awen asked. "No military presence is required here."

"We have our orders, Emissary dau Lothlinium," said the trooper who'd addressed her outside.

She noted for the first time how dusty his armor was. It was also devoid of any of the traditional military markings she'd seen, save for a small yellow insignia on the shoulder in the shape of a crescent moon cradling a combat knife. He had a pistol in his chest plate as well as several grenades, and he looked utterly ferocious in the dim light.

"I don't think you understand," Awen insisted, planting her feet, though no one could see them through her thick robes. "The Jujari won't allow this, and quite frankly, neither will I."

"Emissary, our orders are to escort you to and from your ship for the duration of your stay."

"And you've done that marvelously," she conceded with no attempt to hide her condescension. "You may stand down now until we're done."

"Negative."

"Excuse me?" Awen was sure her eyebrows had just hit an all-time high.

"Negative. Our orders are—"

"Listen, trooper," she said, her face mere centimeters from his chest plate. "I don't care what your orders are. You *cannot* be in here right now, and you certainly *will not* follow us in *there*." She pointed to the far wall, which, she expected, opened to a corridor that led up to the mwadim's council tent.

"Our orders," the trooper continued, "are never to let you leave our sight."

"Who has ordered this?"

"A joint task force chaired by Admiral Isaacson and your own Master So-Elku."

Awen could feel the blood rising in her face as she clenched her jaw. So-Elku would never have agreed to such a breach of cultural protocol.

All the troopers started to nudge each other as if laughing about something—probably a joke made over their comms. She'd met her share of soldiers to know the type. Their helmets kept the joke unheard by outsiders.

Fine, she thought. *Let's play.*

"Awen," Matteo pleaded. "Don't. Please."

She cast him a dark look, one he'd learned not to cross. Awen took a calming breath and closed her eyes. She lifted her chin and began to separate her consciousness from the room, from those around her, and then from her mortal self. There, in the Unity of all things, she reached toward the energy that was already racing away from this place. She could see ripples, long strands of color and undulating shapes, flitting off to take their place in the infinite beyond. But she was faster than they were—not as fast as her masters, but quick enough.

She caught up to the first ripples, the trailing edges of laughter. Then she reached the next waves, full-bodied chuckles. She could pick out each man's voice, each nuance. She saw where the laughter began, and then, like a bloodhound on a fresh scent, she zeroed in on the speaker and his careless words. He was making a vulgar conjecture that she would not repeat. But she would toy with him.

Awen left the Unity of all things and opened her eyes. She was back in the present. "Too bad you'll never be man enough to find out, Corporal Chico."

The trooper winced in his armor and took a step back. Helmets pivoted back and forth as the troopers looked between themselves. *Perfect.* Awen guessed they'd be more cautious to say anything inappropriate over their "secure" comms from then on.

"You'll have to forgive them," the lead trooper said. "Most have never met a Luma before."

"And you have?" Awen asked.

"Enough to know not to do anything stupid around you."

"But following me into the inner sanctum of your Republic's longest unconquerable adversary doesn't sound at least a little bit stupid to you?"

"No, ma'am. That's just doing our job. *Stupid* is what the corporal did."

Fair enough. At least this one isn't a total reprobate. She took a deep breath and turned to Matteo. "How come I wasn't informed about this?"

Matteo shrugged.

Then the most senior Luma, Elder Toochu, approached her. "Awen," he said in his frail yet confident voice. He took her hand like a doting grandfather. The elder had a liver-spotted baldpate and white wisps of hair over his ears to match. "Master So-Elku trusts you wholly, as do we all. Know this." He leaned close to her ear. "However, he does not trust the Jujari. Therefore, he perceived that it was in all of our best interests to concede to the Republic's wish to provide you with a security detail. Surely, no harm can come from their protection."

But harm would come. Her mind raced through a hundred history lessons about moments when projected hostility was met with violence and, in the end, death. Worse still, these troopers had to know that they posed little threat to the Jujari. They would be sliced and devoured before a blaster shot even crossed the room. *Okay, maybe that's an exaggeration. But it won't end well.*

"Fine," Awen said, turning to the trooper. "I permit you to escort us. However, you will keep well apart from us, and for the love of all the mystics, keep those blasters down. We don't need a war on our hands, and they won't do you much good anyway."

"We'll keep our weapons in low ready position, Madame Emissary," the trooper said.

"A compromise. Also, I need a name or rank or something."

"I'm SR-2133, Commanding Officer of Charlie Platoon with the Seventy-Ninth Reconnaissance Battalion, Marine Special Units—"

Awen interrupted him with a wave of her hand. "I don't do your numbers and units."

The trooper stared at her. Awen couldn't tell if he was considering how to bite her head off or trying to remember his birth name apart from his indoctrination. *His brainwashing.*

"Lieutenant Adonis Olin Magnus."

"Lieutenant." Moving onto her tiptoes to as close to the trooper's face as she could reach, Awen whispered, "Just so you know, I don't need an escort."

"And just so you know," Magnus replied, the output volume of his helmet lowered to match hers, "I don't need to protect you."

"Then we have an understanding."

"It seems we do."

3

When the first Jujari emerged from behind the linen wall, his voice sounded like the bottom of a Gull-class freighter grinding against a shoal in the Meridian Outskirts. His words seemed to tear a hole in the hull of Awen's soul, and she could sense the troopers bristling at the Jujari.

The hyena-like warrior stood half a meter taller than the troopers and twice as wide. Though they still preferred to run on all fours, the Jujari had evolved to stand on their hind legs and use their forearms as humanoids did, making them a dramatic though terrifying amalgamation of canine and human characteristics. This one wore a crimson sash across his tawny chest and a wide leather belt around his waist; on it hung a holstered blaster and the ceremonial curved *keeltari* long sword. The fur on his shoulders was matted down by a thick red fluid. An uneducated observer would assume it was paint, but Awen knew it was blood from the day's executions.

Awen realized that this was a blood wolf, a member of the mwadim's inner pack. She really wanted to interview him, but she had a job to do. That, and the warrior would most likely slaughter her the moment they were alone, no matter how much of the mother tongue she spoke.

"The mwadim's elect invites that you search your kyat and then to ingest the sharsh should you merit audience," the Jujari said. His words barely seemed to escape his maw of bared teeth as his tongue labored to articulate Republic common. Still, Awen was impressed that this warrior had mastered so much of the galactic tongue.

"Thank you," Awen said in the beast's native language, returning the favor and lowering her head to one side in submission.

The effort clearly surprised him, as evidenced by the way his ears perked up. "One among you speaks the mother tongue," he snarled. "You have been blessed by the Alpha."

Awen bowed again but noticed that the warrior refused to acknowledge her with his eyes. *Apparently, the sexist assumptions were true, even for guests.*

"Uh, Awen, what does any of that mean?" Matteo whispered. The corner of his mouth twitched. She wouldn't be surprised if he'd soiled himself.

"Right," she said, turning to face her group. "The mwadim's sorgil is inviting us to the next chamber, where we are expected to search our souls as to whether our motives are pure."

"How do we do that?" one of the troopers asked over an external speaker.

The rest of the unit turned to glare at him. That was most likely out of line.

Awen took pity on him. "Fair question. But we don't have time for a lesson in the finer points of Jujari etiquette, so you'll just need to follow my lead. The good news is that our *security guards* are exempt, as long as they don't intend to do any talking." She knew the "security guard" jab would land somewhere on the lieutenant's thick head.

MAGNUS HAD NEVER SEEN a Jujari in the flesh before or imagined he'd get this close to one. No wonder the Republic had kept their distance for so many centuries: the beast seemed to embody a level of pent-up violence he would hate to meet without his MAR30. He decided to give this red-shouldered Jujari warrior the name Chief. The dog wasn't the mwadim, but judging by the blood on his shoulders, he wasn't a noob either.

The line of Luma followed Chief into the next room and down a long corridor. Magnus followed as tightly as he could without inviting Awen's scorn. He didn't like how close she was to Chief, but if he got close enough to protect her, she'd just chew him out again. That would look bad on the after-action review. But so would her headless corpse.

It didn't take Magnus long to realize that Awen was going to be much more of a pain in the ass than he'd bargained for. It was one thing to have to babysit the Luma; it was another thing to get assigned Miss Jujari Scholar herself. *Great, just great.*

His private channel chirped. It was the rest of the Fearsome Four.

"What do you got, boys?" he asked.

"Man, LT, I gotta say, she's quite the asset."

"Easy, Deeks," Magnus replied, using Sergeant Michael "Flow" Deeks's real last name to get his point across.

"You afraid she's listening to us right now?" Mouth asked.

"Negative," Flow said. "She's too focused on minding her manners so she won't get eaten. She might be the Luma's dog whisperer, but she's just as tasty as any of the rest of us."

"Wouldn't you like to know," Cheeks added.

"Can it, Cheeks," Magnus ordered.

"Sorry, LT. Just saying she ain't hard to look at, you know? Especially for a Luma."

"Eyes up, and keep the chatter down," Magnus ordered and closed the channel.

His boys weren't wrong. Awen was beautiful, surprisingly so. Her willowy features and pointed ears were unmistakably Elonian—Magnus had known his share of that humanoid species. She wore her black hair in a tight braid, revealing much of her pale skin and mesmerizingly purple eyes. He'd almost stumbled over his first words when she looked at him out on the platform. But Elonian or not, she was a Luma, and he didn't trust them.

Magnus's platoon followed the entourage to a spiral ramp

that accessed the floors above and below. He pinged Wainwright again. "We're at waypoint bravo two, Captain."

"Copy that," Wainwright said. "Ascend to bravo three. No sudden moves, Lieutenant. Orbital is reporting no unnecessary traffic and only a handful of Jujari battleships in stand-down. So we're still green all around. Waiting for you up top."

"Copy that, Captain." The channel closed.

Magnus pulled a little on his MAR30 to feel the pressure of the sling against his shoulder. He knew he could get the weapon up fast enough but didn't like that he couldn't scan the room along the barrel. As any Marine knew, your blaster was your third appendage. It started in basic training and went with you to the grave, so going soft with it was just… *unnatural.*

As the group began ascending the ramp, he felt his nerves start to twitch. *Easy, Magnus. One step at a time.*

This whole setup reminded him way too much of the Caledonian Wars. Good Marines had died because of bone-headed decisions made by people behind desks a million lightyears from the nearest blaster bolts. Magnus had hoped that things would be different in the Recon. But they weren't. Same old splick, just a new planet to dump it on.

In the end, it was all about kowtowing to this culture's needs or that people's wants, and good people got killed because of it. The Repub didn't have a navy and Marines so that they could have tea parties with their adversaries, and he felt they'd forgotten that somewhere along the way.

Just thinking about the changes in the Republic made

Magnus's blood begin to boil. But at the same time, hadn't he made compromises too?

I've got just as much blood on my hands. But he wouldn't if the Republic weren't so corrupt.

A loud bark came from one of two guards stationed at the top of the ramp. Magnus exerted all his will not to level his MAR30 at the beasts. Ahead, Chief conferred with the guards then indicated Awen and her male companion. There was a lot of growling back and forth. And head dipping, like dogs did when meeting alpha males.

"Anybody got ears on that?" Magnus asked over TACNET.

"Negative," all the leads answered as they double-checked with their fire teams. Magnus's own sensors were having trouble establishing the line-of-sight connection to the asset. He'd done a full body scan in the first room while they'd been talking, but without a tracker on the emissary, the dynamic data only flowed when he had a sight line established.

"How's our rear?" he asked.

"Looking fine," Cheeks said. "Mmm."

"Tighten it up," Magnus ordered.

Just then, the two Jujari guards stepped aside, and the Luma began walking again. The group filed past the sentries in single file until it was the platoon's turn.

"It's a choke point," Flow said.

"Man, I don't like this one bit," Cheeks said. "Anyone else feel the sudden urge to MAR these dogs?"

"Shut it down, Recon," Magnus interjected, not wanting anyone to answer Corporal Chico's question. The Luma were halfway through, and Magnus knew he wasn't the only one scanning the space with his entire sensor suite. "I don't want any sudden moves. Eyes forward, and *do not* look them in the eyes. I don't care that they can't see past our visors. They'll feel it." His HUD pinged with everyone's acknowledgment icons.

Magnus was in the lead, following close behind the last Luma. He had to set the tone, or this was going to go sideways in a hurry. While he couldn't smell the guards, he could feel their violent energy. Thick bands of tightly knit muscles wound over their bodies like ropes, each ready to unwind in a flurry of tearing and snapping.

Magnus came even with the guards, knowing they were probably using all their restraint not to end his life. *At least it's mutual.* He saw one of the beasts sneer at him. His MAR30 felt a hundred klicks away. *Don't do it, Magnus.* He willed himself to let out a slow breath, targeting eight breaths per minute. And then, just like that, he was past the guards.

"Clear," Magnus said over TACNET. "Keep it together, Hunters. Own the field."

OTF acknowledgment icons lit up on his HUD. He knew the men were wound tight. But they'd make it through because they were Marines, they were Recon, they were the Midnight Hunters.

Magnus followed the Luma through a low-ceilinged corridor and into a wide anteroom with a basin and pedestal in the middle. Lamps lit each corner.

"Now, what's this splick?" Flow asked.

"Guessing it's another formality," Magnus said.

Sure enough, the asset approached the basin at Chief's insistence and lapped a mouthful of water. She tilted her head back and took a gulp of air to show the water had been swallowed.

"Awww, hell no," Flow said. "We ain't doing that splick. No way, no how."

"I don't think we have to," Magnus said, hoping he was right. "We're not the ones speaking here. We didn't eat the fruit, and they still allowed us in. Checking with command. Stand by."

Magnus pinged the captain.

"Go ahead, Lieutenant," Wainwright said.

"Captain, please tell me we don't need to take off our buckets for this bowl ceremony."

"That's a negative, Lieutenant. They seemed fine with letting us pass without drinking it."

Magnus let out a sigh. "Thanks, Captain. Just checking. Had some nervous boys here."

"Understood. And don't make any sudden moves in the long hallway either."

"Captain?"

"It's another choke point."

"Copy that." Magnus closed the channel.

Each Luma followed the asset as the Jujari led her into a narrow linen-lined passage wide enough for another single-file line. Magnus's HUD lit up with warning indicators, and he switched to thermal imaging.

"You seeing this, LT?" Deeks asked, his voice tight.

"Affirmative." Magnus's pulse quickened. Thermal showed at least two dozen Jujari warriors along the other side of both corridor walls, each holding a long spear. Their heads were bowed. Magnus couldn't be sure, but it almost seemed like their eyes were closed too. Then he noticed the asset: she was at the front of the line with her head back and arms splayed to her sides. His helmet's AI brought up an audio feed: she was humming something, and then she sang something in Jujari.

"LT, what in the—"

"I don't know, Flow," Magnus replied. "Just play along. We're almost there."

"Copy."

But Magnus could tell from Flow's voice that he didn't *copy*. None of them did.

Magnus entered the corridor after the last Luma and kept his head forward. He noticed that the Jujari with the spears were swaying back and forth. *Are they in some sort of trance maybe?* He passed pair after pair, bracing for an attack, waiting for something to happen. But nothing did.

Curtains parted at the end of the hallway, and the asset stepped through. The remaining Luma followed her and then the Marines. Magnus's eyes widened as his platoon emerged into a massive ballroom nearly as tall as it was wide and covered in white linens. Translucent fabric of various colors looped from chandelier to chandelier and was tethered to wooden beams, then it plunged twenty-five meters to the floor where it pooled on lush rugs.

Lampstands dotted the perimeter of the room, as did a host of Jujari sentries—except for the far wall, which appeared to be a solid curtain of gold fabric. More translucent fabric acted as side windows to the massive cityscape beyond. From this height, the group looked down on every other building in the metropolis.

In the center of the room sat at least fifty ornate cushions, more than half of them occupied by Republican delegates and even a few key heads of state. The rest of the pillows remained vacant, presumably for the Luma. Between the pack of cushions and the outer guards stood Wainwright's platoon.

"You made it through the drowsy pack of hyenas, I see," Wainwright said, overriding Magnus's need to accept the incoming audio.

"Yeah. I didn't feel like waking anyone up from their beauty sleep."

"Smart. They obviously need more than they're getting."

Magnus couldn't be certain, but he was pretty sure his CO smiled. Wainwright had become famous during the Caledonian Wars and was someone Magnus admired. The fact that they were able to serve together again—now in the Midnight Hunters—was a career highlight.

"Our assets have been sitting here for over twenty minutes," Wainwright added. "No one's moved. Get your assets seated and see if we can't get this circus going. I haven't eaten since breakfast, and I have a holo date with my wife scheduled for twenty-three hundred."

"Copy that, sir." Magnus sincerely hoped the captain would make that date, but he wouldn't bet on it.

4

PIPER DIDN'T KNOW what was wrong with her parents, but she knew it was bad. Her dad had been coming home late for several weeks, and her mom was spending more time in her room than usual. Piper didn't need any help concluding that something terrible was going to happen.

At first, the little girl thought maybe the marriage was in trouble. Plenty of her friends' parents at school had split up. She knew the essential ingredients of fights and affairs, though the motives still didn't make sense. But this was neither an affair nor a fight because whenever her parents saw each other, they were attentive and affectionate.

Eventually, Piper started to wonder if *she* was the reason for their stress. She'd done plenty of things wrong in her nine years of life. Both parents had yelled at her for messes she'd made, things she'd broken, and attitudes she'd displayed. Again, however, their love hadn't waned toward her. If anything, they'd been more loving in the past few weeks.

She sat balled up on her bed, playing a game on her holo-pad with a stuffed animal wedged against her chest. Her wispy blond hair danced around the edges of her freckled face, illuminated by the holo-pad's glow. Despite their spacious apartment in the capital district of Capriana, Piper had preferred the close confines of her room these last few days. *In here*, she felt safe. The egg-shaped windows looked out on a rain-soaked evening, lights appearing like blotches in one of her watercolor paintings.

Piper heard the front door chime. "I got it!" she yelled, tossing aside the holo-pad but keeping the stuffed animal. Her mom was just stepping out of her own bedroom by the time Piper checked the view screen and swiped open the front door.

"Piper! Wait for me," her mother scolded.

"Oh, hello." A senate courier stood at the door, clearly not expecting a child to answer it. He was dressed in a white uniform and wearing a beret, both trimmed in light blue. "Is your father or—"

"Yes, yes, I'm here," Valerie said, stepping around her daughter. "How can I help you?"

"I have a delivery for"—the man hesitated as he looked at Piper's mother—"your husband."

"A delivery? Couldn't it be sent over—"

"Certified ahead of him. From the senate door. I mean floor, Mrs. Stone," the courier replied while extending a tablet. Piper had seen many men trip over their words because of her mother's beauty. "I assume you're able to accept delivery?"

"Yes, of course." Valerie pushed strands of blond hair behind her ears then hovered her hand over the screen and waited for the confirmation chime. When the screen floated an acceptance icon in midair, Valerie pulled her hand back and took the small orb from the courier.

"It's coded to him," the man informed her, smiling.

"I understand," Valerie said while rolling the data drive around in her hand. "Thank you."

"Have a good night, Mrs. Stone."

"You too."

Valerie stepped away and held the orb in her hands, staring at it. Piper swiped the door closed and looked at the orb too. "Mama?"

"Yes, my love?"

"What do you think it says?"

Valerie's eyes moved from the orb to Piper then back to the orb. "It's important news for our family."

"Is it good news?"

Valerie hesitated again—too long for Piper.

"Mama, is it good news?"

"Yes. It's good news," she said. But for some reason, Piper didn't believe her.

Darin, her dad, missed both dinner and her bedtime. But Piper wasn't asleep when he finally came home. She wanted to get up and hug him but thought better of it. One more reason for him to be upset wasn't what he needed at the moment. Still, she wanted to know what was on the drive, and she knew that her parents would be discussing it at any second.

Piper slipped out of bed, careful not to make a sound, and let a sliver of light stream through her door. She looked across the sunken living room to the kitchen, where a lamp hung over the center island. Her parents sat on either side, holding hands across the counter. They looked so perfect together. They couldn't get divorced; they just couldn't. Her mother was so radiantly beautiful. Piper knew she'd never grow up to be as lovely. And her father was so handsome; she was convinced her mother had found the only prince in all the land.

Piper's father reached out and activated the drive. The orb started to glow a soft orange and then message contents displayed over the counter. Piper's eyes widened as a pale-blue planet spun between her parents. Below it blinked a departure date and three passenger icons with "D. STONE, V. STONE, P. STONE" in bold letters.

Piper closed the door and grabbed the holo-pad from her desk. The motion caused the main menu to light up, and there, floating inches above her hand, were the date and time. Her heart froze. Wherever that planet was, they were leaving for it the next day.

5

Awen sat on a plush poovla in front of the pack. The rest of the Luma were seated on the cushions behind her, except for Matteo, who reclined to her right. The head delegate from the Republic sat to her left, and beyond him sat a cohort of other notables. The seating arrangement was a more "civilized" version of the canine pack gathering, a nod to when the Jujari freely roamed the open deserts. Impromptu rallies around rock escarpments or under locust trees had been replaced with this, the mwadim's *jaree-jah*. Awen sat with her legs crossed, attentively focused on the golden wall of fabric ten meters in front of her.

"To be honest, I'm a little surprised they sent you," said Gerald Bosworth III, the Republic's ambassador to the Jujari and every other outlying world not currently in the fold.

Awen knew not to look at him. Not only would it be a sign to the ever-watchful Jujari that foreign representation was impure, but more importantly, she loathed the man. She'd watched him betray the wishes of more than one civilization upon entering the Galactic Republic's care, hanging their needs out to dry the moment they were committed. As far as she was concerned, Bosworth, with his fat jowls and bushy unibrow, was the incarnation of all that was wrong with the Republic—and the beastly ethos she was called to stand against.

Sensing that Awen wasn't going to reply and that she needed help in interpreting his meaning, he finished his quip. "Since we both know that the Jujari do not tend to talk to women of any outside species, I'm unsure why the Luma are so content to fold their hand this quickly."

"I could say the same about you and the Republic," she said without moving her head.

"How so?"

"The Jujari can smell a traitor by his pheromones."

"Now, now, Awen, there's no need for name-calling." His voice was slick and condescending, like she was a small child to be reprimanded on the playground.

"It's not name-calling when it's your reputation, Ambassador. That, and I felt you should have fair warning."

"Of what?"

"They're going to disembowel you when I tell them to review your history of position changes," she said with a smirk.

The ambassador laughed but with the faintest trace of apprehension. Sensing he was about to object, Awen reached into the fold of her robe and produced a microdrive. "Funny how grievances that get lost in bureaucracy still manage to find their way into the light." She didn't have to see his eyes to know that she'd rattled him. The tone of his next words traded superiority for authority.

"Your efforts—what are they, Awen? They're futile. You and I both know that there is nothing—*nothing*—on that drive that will hold up against the Republic's records."

"That's the interesting thing in all this, Ambassador. It doesn't have to hold up to the Republic."

"I don't follow," the ambassador said.

"It has to hold up to the Jujari. And that's what you always seem to miss."

His fists clenched. "Oh, be serious," Bosworth seethed, spittle flying past the edges of her vision. "These savages are going to get the best deal in the galaxy. Their people will stop being murdered by their government and dying from backwater diseases. And they'll be able to export goods for the first time in three millennia to worlds that have real wealth. Get off your high horse, *Madame Emissary of the Order*. You're not *ready* to play with the big boys."

Awen fought to keep Bosworth's intimidation at bay. *He was a worm—just an arrogant little worm.* But despite the evidence she had, her mastery of Jujari culture, and her power in the Unity, the man made her feel small. And she scorned him for it.

Awen made to say something, but the torches around the room blew out, and a low hum emanated from somewhere behind the golden wall. *It was the desert* shofaree. *Horns of the deep.* Awen had watched the instrument played on many holo-vids smuggled off-system, but never in person. No race had the lung power or physical features to play it save the Jujari, and holo-footage didn't do the instruments justice. *Not by a long shot.*

Originally used to shake their enemies—literally—before battles, the shofaree made the floor tremble. Awen looked down to see her clothing vibrate. Her body was consumed by the sound waves, her soul lifted into a dual state of wonder and fear. When the horns finally went silent, the blood wolf stepped in front of the curtain and turned his back to the gathered audience.

Awen's heart raced. *This was it.*

"I'M PICKING UP MULTIPLE FREQUENCIES," Flow yelled over TACNET. "Ranging from four hundred hertz down to subsonic."

"It's gotta be ceremonial," Magnus replied, unsure if his mic was working. He could hardly make out Flow's voice amidst the noise. Magnus's helmet rattled against his head, and he steadied it with a hand as he surveyed the room. The lamps and chandeliers had gone out, and only a muted version of the early-evening light filtered through the curtains. Then, as quickly as it had come on, the sound stopped.

"And here I was starting to get down to that," Cheeks whispered, betraying the faintest hint of a tremor in his voice.

"It still doesn't make your dance moves any better," Mouth replied. Corporal Allan "Mouth" Franklin got his nickname because of his tendency to spout off whatever popped into his head—which usually just embarrassed the unit but occasionally made everyone laugh.

"Hey, I know we're all hoping to score with Cheeks later tonight, but let's keep it down until then," Magnus reminded them. "We've got a job to do." The Midnight Hunters joked when they were nervous. It was the easiest way to let off steam without literally blowing something up. Regular people wouldn't get that—using humor when killing seemed sadistic, even maniacal. But the Hunters weren't regular people, and for us it was just business. Still, now was not the time.

Magnus watched as Chief took center stage and faced the wide curtain. He barked and whined in a loud voice, chomping through a bunch of words in their native tongue. Magnus watched the time in his HUD, counting the seconds. After nearly a minute of rambling, Chief spread his arms, threw his head back, and cackled. All around Magnus, the rest of the Jujari warriors lifted their voices in a terrifying frenzy of demon laughter.

"Easy, Recon," Wainwright said over general TACNET. "Easy."

Magnus was grateful for the order because, truthfully, he wanted to shoot something. He'd been in a lot of tense situations, but this was one for the history books. His chest was tight in anticipation of a fight.

"It's all for show. All for show," Wainwright assured.

The golden curtains slowly parted to reveal a single Jujari seated in an oversized cushion on a marble dais. Brightly colored fabrics spooled down from a counterpoint above him, spreading to the floor in a half circle.

"That has got to be the *fattest* damn dog I've ever seen," Flow said over the platoon channel. The mwadim wore no sash or belt and lounged unapologetically with his belly up.

All at once, the Jujari lowered their heads and rolled them to one side in an act of deference. Interestingly, so did the Luma. Magnus shook his helmet. *Why don't you just roll over and let them maul you while you're at it?*

The mwadim nodded to the presenter, who then turned to address the pack of visitors. "The Jujari mwadim, blessed be he, welcomes you to his den," Chief said, chewing the words as they escaped from between his fangs. "As he has gifted you with his presence on this day, what gifts do you, pack leaders of the Republic, bring of infinitely lesser worth?"

Several advisors motioned to the Republic ambassador, Bosworth. The fat man labored to lift himself from the cushion, smoothed his uniform, and approached Chief. "If it pleases the mwadim," the ambassador said, offering a rolled parchment, "the Republic wishes to—"

Chief, dwarfing the man by half despite the ambassador's considerable girth, snatched the scroll between two clawed digits and snarled.

Bosworth recoiled. "Uh, yes. Please accept it with… with our sincerest hopes that it procures a long and mutually beneficial relationship with the Galactic Republic."

"He's got to be pissing himself right now," Cheeks said.

"I'm pissing myself for him," Mouth replied. The two shared a nervous laugh.

"I'm moving to the left flank for a better view," Magnus said.

"The emissary's probably up next, and I don't have a clear view of the exchange from back here."

"Copy that," the Fearsome Four answered.

Slowly, very slowly, Magnus began a delicate chassé toward the left side of the room, careful not to stray too far from the platoons. He looked at Awen and then back at the ambassador, who fidgeted with his hands behind his back. If the Jujari were hungry, the man would be more than just a snack—he'd be a whole meal. Magnus smiled to himself.

Chief unrolled the scroll and reviewed its contents. Then, moving up the dais, he knelt beside the mwadim and whispered in his ear. The mwadim sat expressionlessly. If Magnus hadn't known any better, he'd have said the Jujari leader was dead and stuffed like nothing more than a ceremonial trophy. Finally, the mwadim huffed. That was all it took. Chief turned, descended, and held the scroll aloft.

"To the Republic's initial gesture of ten common cycles of no taxation, one trillion credits of trade stimulus, and an outfitted Pride-class battleship"—Chief paused for effect—"the mwadim accepts."

Whatever good cheer had spread among the Republic representatives was quickly overshadowed by the bloodcurdling cackles of the Jujari around the room. Faces blanched, and shoulders hunched. Magnus chuckled as he completed his quarter-circle route to the edge. Once there, he had a perfect side view of the platform, just in time for Chief to speak again.

"And you, Luma pack leaders—what gifts do you bring of infinitely lesser worth?"

Magnus looked to Awen. She held something small in her left hand and had begun to stand when the ambassador caught her arm. Magnus took a step forward and instantly felt movement from the Jujari around him. This was unexpected. The ambassador jerked her toward him, brushing her ear with his bloated lips.

"Looks like he's making out with her ear," Cheeks remarked.

"Pig," Mouth added. "What's going on?"

"Can't tell," Magnus replied, trying to decide whether to intervene. *This isn't good*. But rushing the ambassador wouldn't be a better alternative. Finally, after what seemed an interminably long time, the fat man let go. Magnus could tell Awen was spooked, frozen in a half-standing position. She swallowed, refusing to look at the ambassador.

"The Luma will not keep the mwadim waiting!" Chief barked. The room answered him with cackles that made the hair on Magnus's neck stand up.

Finally, Awen straightened and moved toward the Jujari. *Good. Keep going, little lady*. Magnus didn't care for any of the Luma's politics, but he had to admire this woman's bravery. Magnus wouldn't have been caught dead in her position without his MAR30 and armor. He laughed to himself. *Well, I probably would be "caught dead."*

Chief stood like a statue with his chin turned up and away, apparently unwilling to look at Awen. Still, she stood before him with something clenched in her fist. Neither party moved.

"*Somebody* pissed in his gravy," Flow said over comms.

"Or maybe he just doesn't play nice with females," Magnus said.

Awen and Chief remained frozen. Suddenly, Awen's companion stood up. *Matteo*, Magnus thought she'd called him. Again, Magnus felt the Jujari warriors shift on their feet, eager for a melee. *These beasties are wound tight.*

Matteo moved forward with his head bowed and stood slightly behind and to the side of Awen. Then he reached for whatever was in her hand. To Magnus's surprise—and to Matteo's, judging by his reaction—Awen kept her fingers clenched. Whatever *it* was, she was not letting it go.

The situation grew tenser as Magnus saw the mwadim lean forward. His eyes narrowed as he glared at the two Luma. A new round of cackles rose, and Chief still couldn't bring himself to look down at either Awen or Matteo.

Matteo was urgently pleading with Awen now, and the room was growing frenetic.

"Magnus," Wainwright called over TACNET. "What's wrong with your asset?"

Magnus never had time to respond. A bloodcurdling howl emanated from the dais as the mwadim lurched forward and lifted his snout to the air. Magnus's helmet's audio sensors clamped down on the signal, but still, the sound pained his ears. Everyone in the room ducked—from Marine to Jujari, from Republican to Luma. Magnus winced and closed his eyes, hoping the display of bravado was almost over.

When the howl finally stopped, the mwadim was on all fours, facing the audience. Like the rest of his men, Magnus had just assumed the Jujari pack leader was rotund. Instead, the beast was nearly twice as large as any of the other Jujari, massive in every way.

"Let her come to Rawmut," he growled. Matteo backed away, as did Chief.

Magnus couldn't believe the scene in front of him. There was Awen, slender and unarmed, standing alone before the giant mwadim of the Jujari. The fragile peacekeeper of the galaxy was going toe to toe with the leader of the most violent species the galaxy had ever known.

To her credit, Awen appeared to have conquered whatever she had been wrestling with internally—whatever the ambassador had said to her. She brought the item forward and held it in the cup of her open palms. Then she ascended the dais and stopped a meter from the massive Jujari, whose fangs were as tall as her head.

"This," she said, "is for you."

Just then, Magnus noticed that the ambassador was seething on his cushion and pounding his thighs with his fists. Magnus pinged Wainwright. "We might have a situation here."

"SITREP," Wainwright demanded.

"It's the ambassador. He's agitated."

"Can you get to him?"

"Doubtful," Magnus said.

"We abide by your wisdom," Awen continued, "as your will is perfect. However, I cannot in good conscience remain silent. I speak for your sake, Great Mwadim, no matter the cost to me."

The ambassador was repeating something to himself, his face turning red.

"I want options, Lieutenant," Wainwright ordered.

Magnus glanced over to see the captain step out of formation. "I'm not sure I have any, Captain. The ambassador's going manic. Talking to himself." Magnus looked back at Awen. Amazingly, she was still talking to the mwadim, despite the fat man's misbehavior. But what she said next pulled the pin from the ambassador's emotional grenade.

"Oh, Great Mwadim, this drive contains all the reasons you should be wary of the Republic's proposed alliance."

"Sabotage!" spat the ambassador, struggling to his feet. "Sabotage, I say! Stop her!"

Chief stepped in front of the disgruntled man. It was probably the only thing that saved Awen's life in the end, for the ambassador had barely stood up when the first explosion detonated, and everything went sideways.

6

Awen hurtled into the mwadim's chest then cartwheeled into a cluster of decorative urns. Her body felt like it was on fire, and she couldn't catch her breath due to the pain. Blinking, she tried to focus on the ceiling. Her ears rang. Blood pooled in one side in her mouth, and the sharp smell of thermite bit her nose.

She heard blaster fire and screaming—*so much screaming*. The floor shook underneath her. From an explosion.

Explosions. We're under attack. She had to tell the lieutenant. She tried to prop herself up, but the pain was overwhelming.

Another wave of sound and heat shoved her farther back. Small objects peppered her skin, and more pain racked her body. She was crying—she was sure of it—and she felt embarrassed. She felt exposed.

Something clutched her hand. Something big. A deep voice

and hot breath rushed against her head, then the scent of burning hair.

"Guard it," the voice said in Jujari. A warm paw pressed a cylindrical item into her hand, and another jab of pain pierced her palm. Awen heard a short confirmation trill from the item. "Never let them find it. *Never let him.*"

Awen smashed her eyes closed again and willed them back open. *Focus. Come on, Awen!* On the ground beside her lay the large face of the mwadim. A portion of his muzzle was missing, and his eyes and ears leaked blood. She could make out wet, labored breathing over the sounds of the assault.

"Swear it," he hissed then coughed a spray of red over her. "Swear!"

"I swear it." She wasn't sure if it was her voice talking. Her throat burned, and it felt like someone was standing on her chest. "I swear it," she said more confidently, but the mwadim had stopped listening.

MAGNUS's first thought as he shook off the blast and moved to one knee was not for his platoon or even himself—it was for Awen. She was, after all, his mission; failing to execute his objective was not an option. What surprised him, however, was that he felt some measure of genuine concern for her despite his disdain for the Luma. Though, by the looks of his environment, there wouldn't be many Luma left to aggravate him.

Focus, he commanded himself. *OTF.*

He brought his MAR30 to ready-up position as his instincts went through the OODA loop.

Observe. TACNET was a frenzy of activity, and his helmet's AI did its best to arrange the communications according to chain of command. Distinguishing between orders and the screams of the dying was nearly impossible. Yellow icons for *wounded* and red icons for *killed in action* lined the side of his HUD. But there was no indicator for Awen.

Men and women twirled about in the death dance, their arms flapping in a desperate effort to extinguish the fire on their skin. Even Jujari raced around, clawing, mauling, and biting, their coats alight with flames. Magnus thought to open fire on several Jujari who attacked the Luma—one of the victims had to be Awen—but he realized it was a waste of firepower since both groups of combatants were doomed. The only people he could logically defend were those who had a chance of survival: his men. Recon armor was a decent defense for this kind of incendiary assault, though it still seemed like the platoon had suffered more casualties than he could count. Awen, of course, wore only robes.

Orient. The once-ornate ballroom had become a hellhole in the blink of an eye. Fire licked every strand of fabric, which made Magnus feel as though he were standing inside the sun. Wind from outside fed the inferno until everything that could burn did burn. To his right, primary exfil looked accessible, but he didn't have the best view. To his left was the stage and, most likely, Awen.

Decide. The warrior ethos taught that the last order was always the standing order until the objective was completed. For Magnus, that order was, *Escort Emissary Awen dau Lothlinium to and from her meeting with the mwadim and protect her with prejudice.* So he would find her and stay with her until she was safe or until he could no longer protect her.

Action. It was time to move, time to look for—

A second explosion tore a hole in the floor not ten meters from his position. He flew backward and slammed into a sandstone pylon, narrowly missing the open window. Several Marines weren't as fortunate, however, and sailed past him. Their bodies ripped the translucent fabric from its moorings and shot over the city like comets trailing atmospheric entry flames. The Hunters' screams spiked the team channels as they fell to their deaths, their armor's thrusters failing to engage.

Magnus's power level flashed. One of his cells had been crushed in the impact, leaving him with just over half power. Several other icons blinked at him, indicating damage assessments. The only two indicators that really mattered at present were his oxygen level and his weapons system: both nominal.

"Get up, Adonis," he said to himself. He climbed to his feet and saw a flame-covered Jujari thundering toward him. The fated creature swung its keeltari at his head, but Magnus ducked. He raised his MAR30 and drilled the beast with a blaster bolt to its skull. The Jujari toppled, and Magnus stepped over it. A second canine warrior lunged at his flank, but his armor's proximity sensors registered the motion in time for him to dodge the attack. The Jujari swung a clawed paw with such effort that it spun itself over in midair. The warrior's back elbow hammered Magnus between the shoulder blades, but his armor absorbed the impact. Magnus pivoted and landed a blaster bolt in the beast's burning midsection and another to the side of its head. It was dead before it hit the floor.

A man in Republican attire, or what was left of it, threw himself at Magnus. Bloodied arms slid down his armor, which was bathed in flickering orange light. Magnus begrudgingly pushed the man away, torn about whether to end his misery, and moved toward the dais.

Burning bodies littered the platform; several still moved. Magnus's AI raced to identify non-Jujari life-forms, but the brutality of the ordnance was so indiscriminate that it made the computer's job next to impossible. Against the back wall lay the mwadim with most of his backside blown out. Magnus's helmet's AI suddenly tagged a body between the mwadim and the wall with "high probability."

"Awen!" he yelled through his speakers and bounded over the Jujari carcass. Her robes were burned, and she was bloody, but she was alive. A quick bio scan showed high concentrations of adrenaline, high heart rate, low blood pressure, the onset of shock, and maybe a few broken ribs, but—amazingly—nothing fatal.

She clutched her hands to her chest, mumbling something over and over. "I won't let them have it. Won't let them."

"Awen, can you hear me?" Magnus said.

"I won't."

"Awen! It's me, Adonis—it's the lieutenant. We're getting you out of here. Hold on."

She screamed as Magnus picked her up in one arm. His servo-assisted armor made the task effortless even though Awen hardly weighed a thing. However, Magnus was more concerned about not causing her any more pain than with the amount of energy he had to expend to carry her.

"Asset secure," he said over TACNET to no one in particular. He wasn't even sure who had comms left. When no response came, he decided to ping the shuttle. "*Falcon One*, do you copy?" He waited a beat then repeated himself.

Nothing. More yellow icons switched to red as the seconds ticked by.

Finally, a static-riddled voice came over TACNET. "This… right. All hands… exfil… Zulu Niner." It was Wainwright. Magnus's HUD couldn't pinpoint his signal, but the captain was alive, and now he knew the revised exfil location.

Most of the humanoids had succumbed to the smoke and flames in the ballroom. Meanwhile, a small battle raged between the Jujari and the Marines, most of it in CQB—close-quarters battle. Even though the canines were on fire, they did not go down easily. It seemed like the only sure way to take them down without a blaster was a blade to the carotid or femoral artery or a skull penetration—all while avoiding their razor-sharp teeth and claws.

Magnus took out three of the stronger enemies from his place on the dais while his AI simultaneously laid a course to the exfil coordinates. His HUD projected an illuminated path that ran through the center of the ballroom and back to the main entrance. Magnus jumped off the dais and moved to the right, retracing his earlier steps along the room's perimeter but careful to shield Awen from any burning fabric. As he shifted right, new cackles filled the air.

Magnus saw movement at the entrance, and dozens of Jujari reinforcements stepped into the room. "Perfect." Over general TACNET, he asked, "Anyone got eyes on a secondary egress?" But the channel was still flooded with screams and shouts as men fought for their lives.

Blaster fire streaked at him from across the room, and Magnus ducked behind a pedestal. One shot glanced off his shoulder, deflected by his armor's resonant defense generator. He cursed, knowing Awen's head was there, but when he looked down, he saw that she'd repositioned to his center mass. He had to get her out of there.

The thought had no sooner passed through his brain when a third explosion detonated. The force threw him and Awen backward, only this time, there was no sandstone pylon. Magnus felt the lurch of free fall. He still clung to Awen as she screamed and grabbed at the air. The pair rolled away from the building and plunged toward the city street, but not before Magnus saw a fire spout erupt from the window, the space above their heads filling with debris.

Stabilization measures deployed, his HUD flashed.

A series of powerful rocket bursts jerked Magnus upright and worked against their descent. But the effort was short-lived as the *low power* warning sent the jump system into fail-safe. Gravity stole them back, and Magnus's stomach lurched. He detached his sling's quick-release clip and threw his MAR30 over his head.

The mag lock pulled it between his shoulder blades. Then he selected his grappling hook and aimed his forearm at the building opposite him.

Shoulder and elbow servos whined as the tip launched from his wrist in a concussive burst. Microfiber filament trailed the projectile as it buried itself in concrete and then snapped taut. Razor-sharp hooks deployed in a puff of dust, and Magnus saw the instantaneous *secure* indicator in his HUD.

"Hold on," he yelled to Awen over externals. He wasn't even sure if she was conscious. He hoped she wasn't, for her sake.

His armor's servos had strained to absorb their fall's kinetic energy when the filament snapped taut, more precious power draining from his remaining fuel cell. Their fall suddenly redirected to a lateral pendulum swing, and Magnus extended his legs toward the oncoming building. Both feet crashed into a concrete pylon, the fabric on either side blowing away from the concussion.

Magnus initiated the *rappel* command. He backpedaled the building face like a spaceball player in spring training, the soles of his boots thumping rhythmically down the side. He cast a quick look over his shoulder to see a street filled with curious Jujari. Fortunately, they seemed distracted by the ball of fire atop the building and not the figures coming down in the debris—at least, not the living ones.

Magnus armed the variable-output detonator on his hip, selected *smoke* and *ring pattern*, and let the grenade self-deploy from his torso. The VOD fell the remaining twenty meters to street level and deployed a ring of thick white smoke wide enough for them to land in. His filament reserves had more than enough to get them there, but he wouldn't need it. At ten meters, Magnus severed the line and sailed the rest of the way down. He used both arms to cradle Awen and slammed into the ground.

They'd made it but with little time to celebrate. The words *proximity warning* flashed brightly in his HUD. Magnus did a quick visual scan, but no collision was imminent. Then he looked up. A burning chunk of debris the size of a speeder had broken free of the mwadim's building and was hurtling toward them. Magnus's brain was faster than his helmet's AI as he concluded, *You're not getting clear*.

7

Awen knew they were falling. Her stomach lurched just like it did during shuttle entry. She felt the urge to reach for the small bag in the seat back as the image of a bowl of sorlakk spun in front of her. All she really wanted, however, was a soft bed. *Vomit and sleep*, she told herself, feeling like a small child with the flu. *Just throw up, and then you can go to bed.*

A loud pop startled her. Then the feeling of a thousand knives stabbing her rib cage replaced the nausea and fatigue. She tried screaming, but a jarring change of direction took her breath away. Her head slammed against... a trooper's chest plate. And then she was swinging sideways toward a building. No, *they* were swinging sideways, she and the cranky lieutenant in the black-and-gray armor.

The trooper's feet extended and crashed into a vertical support. Awen noticed the shrouds ripple away from her as if someone had dropped a large stone in a pond. Then she felt herself descending again, a fast-paced *thunk-thunk-thunk* churning beneath her. More stabbing in her sides. And then free fall.

When is this going to stop?

Awen was wide awake when the trooper hit the ground. Somehow, by a miracle, they'd made it out of the building. *The explosion. The mwadim.* She couldn't think straight, but she knew they were safely on street level. The trooper had saved her.

As that thought registered, she felt something deep—deeper than nausea, deeper than the stabbing pain in her ribs, deeper than the headache that threatened to crush her temples together. In the fabric of all things, a disturbance cried to her. It was the tremor of something important. No, something dangerous. And it was racing toward her like a comet.

Awen saw it then, a wave pushed by another wave pushed by another wave. From behind the waves, a force full of dark energy hurtled at her and at the trooper. It threatened to silence them. To silence her. It had the power to shatter her life into a thousand shards, to end all the breaths that were so painful to take.

So she stopped it from coming.

MAGNUS COVERED Awen with his body and braced for impact. He was reasonably sure that this was the end, and he was only sorry that he couldn't preserve her life any longer. In fact, the thought of protecting her filled him with a strange emotion, a sense of purpose beyond his duty—perhaps even a sense of a calling.

And then he grieved. For the briefest of moments, he mourned not being able to see this last mission through to a successful end. He thanked his warrior ethos, which had seen him through so much. It could not see him past this. It wasn't strong enough. *He* wasn't strong enough.

But more, he grieved for Awen. He believed she had more to see. More to do. Despite her insufferable love for this degenerate species, she was worth something. Worth more than him. It was just ironic that she'd die while trying to save a species that wouldn't think twice about killing her.

Then Magnus got tired of grieving. It was exhausting. And he was pissed off. Couldn't death get on with the business of killing him already? Apparently, "hurry up and wait" was not only the unspoken motto of the Galactic Marines but of death too. It was infuriating.

He opened his eyes. *Proximity alert* still flashed in his HUD. The whole "life flashing before your eyes" thing felt overrated.

Proximity alert.

He looked at the clock and watched two interminably long seconds tick by. He chanced a glance at the falling debris.

Like a shooting star suspended in flight, the concrete slab hovered a meter above them.

Proximity alert.

"What in all the cosmos?" he said aloud. He didn't know whether to laugh or cry or shout. He'd gone mad. Or maybe he was dead, and this was the afterlife: one continuous image of your last moment. But he felt himself breathing. He felt Awen in his arms.

Awen. The Order of the Luma. But they couldn't achieve this sort of manipulation... could they?

Suddenly, the mammoth block started shaking. *Time to move*, thought Magnus. He pulled Awen in and rolled out from under the concrete. Whatever power had held it aloft vanished, and the thing crashed into the street, not as if it had only fallen a meter or two but as if it had dropped from the top of the skyscraper with all that kinetic energy stored up inside like a capacitor set to discharge. The force threw him forward. He rolled again, careful to keep Awen close. Bits of debris peppered his armor, scattering around them.

Then Magnus heard her raspy voice. "I'm not completely helpless, trooper."

"No," Magnus replied, suddenly fearful of the woman he held. "No, you're not."

Low-power mode initiated, read his HUD. That meant environmental systems, servo assist, comms, armor defense resonance, navigation, targeting, and weapons systems had all gone offline. The AI would also hibernate. He'd have basic visuals, audio, air filtration, and whatever natural structural resistance his plating could provide. *Not awesome. Definitely not awesome.*

They needed to get off the street, and judging from the cackles rising throughout the city, they didn't have much time.

"We need to find cover," Magnus said. His voice sounded softer than before, but that could have been from the ringing in her ears. "Can you stand?"

Awen hadn't thought of standing. But thinking about it made her tired. *So tired.* And she was hot. The air seemed to burn her skin in a thousand places. She touched her forehead and brushed aside rivulets of sweat, noticing then that she was clutching something in her other hand. She looked down at her blood- and dust-caked fist. She wanted to open her fingers to see what was inside, but they ached too much to move. *The mwadim.* He'd given her something just before…

Before what? What happened to him—and to the meeting? An image flashed in her mind: a misshapen maw and bloodshot eyes.

The mwadim is dead.

No. He can't be. If the mwadim is dead, then that means…

The word—the one that terrified her more than any other—filled her mind. She had committed her life to reversing, to preventing, to eliminating it. *War.*

"I can stand," she said, suddenly finding renewed strength.

"Good." Magnus pointed through the wall of white smoke surrounding them. "That direction, there's an alley. I'll be right behind you."

She nodded and felt him prop her up. Her legs ached, her back ached—everything ached. She was pretty sure something in her left leg was broken. Despite the agony, however, it felt right to stand. The pain meant that she was alive, which meant she was a survivor. War hadn't won, at least not yet.

Awen took one step then another. She found her stride and

then stumbled into a disjointed run. Her one slippered foot took the lead while the other bare foot crunched painfully through the rubble. As she ran, pieces of the falling sky bit into her flesh, the blackened remains still aflame. The smell of smoke seemed to smother her like a blanket, as did the horrific odor of burning bodies. She wondered if some of the ash was from… *from whom?*

Awen passed through the white wall, blinked several times, and saw the gap between buildings. She also saw Jujari, but they were all looking skyward. She ducked into the alley and found stacks of small freight containers, each marked with shipping script and connected by brightly colored graffiti. The stacks funneled her in a zigzag pattern and spat her out in an intersection. She stayed in the shadows and turned around to see the trooper running toward her, blaster extended, head on a swivel.

"We haven't been seen," Magnus said. "That's the good news."

"I assume there's bad news, then?"

"Yeah. The mwadim's building is swarming with Jujari, so our primary exfil is compromised."

"So we can't get back to the shuttle, then."

"The fact is," Magnus said, his black visor centered on her face, "I doubt the shuttle is intact anymore."

Awen swallowed. "Okay, so what's the plan?"

"The plan is to head to Zulu Niner, our secondary exfil. It's three klicks north of the city. But without navigation, it's going to be slow going, and without comms, I have no way of knowing where the rest of the platoon is. The mwadim's building is too hot for us to go searching for anyone, so it looks like we're on our own for the moment."

"That all sounds bad."

"Yeah, well, it's not great," Magnus said, poking his head into the intersection. He looked right and left then seemed to check the fading sun before reviewing the layout of the buildings.

"So, which way's north?" Awen asked. Breaths were getting harder to take, and the heat was stifling.

"Best I can tell, that way." He signaled straight through the intersection with the flat of his hand. "But we've gotta move fast."

Curious, Awen looked at him then stole a glance down the right-hand alley. Packs of Jujari running on all fours raced across the far end, headed straight for the mwadim's building. The left-hand alley was the same.

"Ready?" Magnus asked, and she nodded. "Let's go."

The two of them slipped from the shadows and through the intersection, Magnus keeping a hand on her back while he swept the area with his weapon.

"We're clear," he said.

The next alley had more of the same freight containers interspersed with what Awen could only imagine was food waste and excrement. She moved carefully, taking care not to knock anything over for fear of discovery. The pair of them moved to the next intersection where, again, the left- and right-hand passages opened to streets filled with Jujari. They paused long enough to catch their breath and then crossed to the third block.

Once safely across, Awen stopped in front of another freight box, this one highly reflective despite some scattered graffiti. She stopped when she noticed her reflection: torn robes, much of the fabric charred or missing, and her skin bruised, bloodied, and blackened. It dawned on her, however, that much of the blood came from cuts not her own. *From other people*, she realized. *From the Luma and the Republicans. And Matteo.*

The full weight of the incident in the ballroom hit her then, knocking her to the ground like a rogue wave at the beach. "They're dead." She convulsed, knuckles and knees trembling in the dirt. Then her stomach heaved, and she threw up. "Oh God," she said, wiping her mouth. "They're all dead, then, aren't they?"

"I don't know," Magnus said, crouching beside her. She felt his hand on her back again. "But a lot of people died, yes."

Awen felt hot tears running down her cheeks. *What happened?* The ambassador had threatened her, then the mwadim ordered her to the dais, and then... something had hit her, and she was lying beside the mwadim.

She felt the cylinder in her hand. He'd given it to her. He'd told her to... *what?* She couldn't remember. *Something important.*

Awen suddenly felt sad. Her mission had failed—after six years of training, her first representation for the Luma had ended in ruins. Maybe her father had been right after all when he said, "Stop chasing the stars, Awen."

So, this is what the void feels like. She pushed the tears from her eyes with her palms. Maybe... maybe this had been a mistake. Her thoughts moved back to Elonia, to the comfort of her house and her own bed. She wanted to slide into the dust and take a nap. Just a little sleep; that was all. Then she'd be able to run some more.

"SPLICK!" Magnus shouted. Awen looked up and saw him turn to face three Jujari stalking down the alley on all fours.

MAGNUS WATCHED as the three warriors stood up on their hind legs and drew their swords. *The good news* was that *there weren't four*. The bad news was that he highly doubted he'd be able to beat three at once without his primary weapon—he didn't want his MAR30's report attracting any more contact. He lowered its output, deployed the spring-loaded bayonet below the muzzle, and pulled his serrated combat blade from behind his chest plate.

"Awen," Magnus yelled, "I want you to run."

"Run? Put your gun down, Lieutenant. Let me try talking to them—"

"You're in no shape to negotiate," Magnus said. "And they're in no mood to talk."

"Lieutenant, I really think—"

"I said *run!*"

The Jujari charged. The narrow alley kept them grouped together, which Magnus used to his advantage. He fired three low-energy rounds, each bolt slamming a target in the chest. The charge wasn't enough to kill them, but it went a long way in disorienting the targets and giving him enough time to strike first.

He ran forward and jabbed the first confused Jujari under the chin with his bayonet. The blade plunged through the jaw's soft flesh and into the roof of the mouth. The warrior gave out a muffled howl, the air from his lungs forcing spurts of blood between clenched teeth. The Jujari batted at the weapon, snapping off the blade, and sent Magnus to the ground with his MAR30 still in hand.

The second Jujari blinked at the first, his hackles rising at the sight of his brother's spilt blood. He looked at Magnus and raised his sword, sidestepping the first warrior. Magnus rolled away from the blade's sweep and then used his knife to cut at the warrior's rear tendon above the hock. He heard a faint *snap* as the sinew gave way, and the Jujari toppled over, cackling.

Magnus didn't have time to terminate either of the first two assailants as the third bounded over them and dove at him. The Marine brought his MAR30 up and swung it like a club, the butt meeting the Jujari on the side of the head. The action, however, did little to faze the warrior. He snapped at Magnus, jaws clamping down on his shoulder like a vise. Pressed into the dirt, Magnus felt teeth pierce his armor and slide into his flesh. He yelled and thrust his knife between the creature's ribs.

The other two Jujari joined in, despite their injuries, and fought to grab ahold of Magnus. He was going to have to use his rifle, but he knew the sound would mean summoning more warriors than he could handle. Frankly, he was surprised that more hadn't found them already. A claw scratched at his thigh and punctured one of his reclamation bladders. Another mouth full of teeth snapped at his boot, paws threatening to shred his armor from his leg.

At that moment, each assailant's head snapped back with a

small burst of blood, and before Magnus realized what had happened, the fight was over. He crab walked out from under the carcasses and scrambled to his feet, MAR30 and duradex knife still in hand. He spun around to see Awen, bound and unconscious, held between two men clad in a patchwork of armor. A third and fourth man stood closer to Magnus and leveled blasters at him.

"Don't do it," one man said to him from under an old Repub helmet that was missing the visor.

Magnus only needed to raise his MAR30's muzzle half a meter to draw a bead on him. But based on the assailant's posture, he suspected he wouldn't win the standoff. Still, he had to try. They had Awen, after all. And Midnight Hunters never went down without a fight. Never.

Here goes nothing.

8

Piper held her mother's and father's hands as they were escorted to the front of a security checkpoint. She felt people watching from the long lines, casting menacing looks at her. *But I've done nothing to hurt them.* Still, their hard faces made her feel embarrassed. Even the air felt angry at her, filled with murmuring.

"Right this way, Senator." An armed security liaison led Darin into a narrow black-glassed corridor.

Piper looked between the panes of glass, wondering who watched from behind them. But she had nothing to hide. She stepped into the hall and walked with her chest out, Valerie two steps behind her. Piper wore her extra-puffy coat, a sweater, leggings, and oversized winter boots. Jammed inside her coat was Talisman, her stuffed corgachirp, and in her backpack were her holo-pad, an overnight kit her mother had prepared, and some snacks. "Everything else," her parents had said, "is packed and will be waiting for us on Avolo Four."

Which means what? she wondered as she exited the hall. *It means we're moving.*

Her mind had been racing all morning, thinking of all the things a normal nine-year-old *should* be doing in this situation: hugging her friends, writing goodbye cards, having one more sleepover, saying thank you to teachers. But none of it was going to happen. The kids of other families who'd moved away got to do those things—military families, defense contractors, star system representatives. But Piper had barely been given the time to brush her teeth before leaving for the spaceport!

"Watch your step, sir," the lead liaison said. "Watch your step, miss." The uniformed man took her hand and helped her on board a hover skiff. Piper looked around. No one else in the terminal had one of these. Even the transport shuttle that had picked them up from their apartment had been fancy. *That was because her daddy was important. And he was on an important mission.* But what, exactly, she had no idea.

People stepped back as the driver pulsed the klaxon button. Piper wanted to try pushing it, but she knew someone would yell at her. She reached for the button anyway. Her long press startled the driver. He glanced down and followed Piper's hand to her face, and she smiled at him.

"Piper!" Valerie yelled, pulling her back into her seat, but Piper caught the faintest hint of a smile on her mother's face.

The skiff turned from the main terminal and diverted into a

smaller corridor. Piper looked behind them to see the tiers of the big blast doors contract like an iris. "Where are we going?"

"A starship," Valerie said through a tight smile, having fielded this question a hundred times already. "We're heading to a starship."

"Is it a big one?"

Valerie puffed her cheeks and looked at Darin, who just grinned. "You'll see."

"*Dad*," she said, drawing out the word. "Why do you keep saying that?"

"You'll see!"

The skiff passed by a series of long rectangular windows that looked out on a massive launchpad. *It was the size of a small city.* There, in the distance, serviced by what must have been *thousands* of busy ant vehicles and even smaller ant people, sat at least ten, *maybe twenty*, dark-gray starships. Their slender shapes and sweeping blue accent lines terminated in V-tailed fins and big engine cones. Each ship seemed like it was on a hospital bed connected to pipes and metal arms and bundles of string.

"Is it one of those, Daddy?"

"*You'll see!*" Darin said, laughing.

By the time the skiff stopped, Piper had pulled Talisman from her coat and was showing him everything she saw, especially *the big ships*. The liaisons escorted the family into a private waiting room with a large window that looked down on a single vessel. Piper ran to the window and read the name printed in white letters near the ship's cockpit windows. "*Destiny's Carriage*," she said softly. Her mind went to one of the many old stories she loved, back when speeders had wheels and were pulled by animals. "Is that ours, Daddy?"

"That's the one we're taking, yes, sweetheart," Darin replied. Piper felt him stroke the top of her head. His hands were big and warm.

"It's smaller than the others," she said.

"And faster," he added.

"But why smaller?"

"Because we'll be the only ones on it."

"*The only ones?*"

"That's right." Darin squatted beside her, looking out the window. "Just you, your mom, me, and the flight crew."

Piper wrinkled her brow. "But what about all those other people we saw?"

"They'll get on their own ships."

"Any of them going to where we're going?"

"Not that I know of, Pinky," he said, using her favorite color as a pet name. "They'll still find their way to wherever it is they're going." But for some reason, Piper didn't think her dad was convinced of that.

THE BRIDGE of the *Black Labyrinth* was spacious, spartan, and dimly lit. Officers sat at their terminals and performed systems checks, incoming data dumps, and resource-allocation movement. The hum of the ship's drive core became like a security blanket for the crew: were it ever to go silent, they would know the end was near. Barely audible above it were the incessant finger taps and hushed whispers of techs and the subtle *whoosh* of air venting.

The room looked out upon the remainder of the ship, an impossibly wide and imposing Goliath-class super dreadnought. The admiral stood alone at the observation window, hands pressed against the floor-to-ceiling glass. The crew noted that he hadn't moved in almost thirty minutes; some even took bets on whether he was sleeping. It wasn't until the executive officer summoned him that the lone figure twitched.

"Admiral Kane, I think we have something," the XO said.

"Actionable?"

"Yes, sir. I believe so. It's video captured from the negotiation meeting."

The figure at the window lowered his arms and turned. His bald head was dimpled with scar tissue, and he had one pale pink eye, the other a shade of brown so deep it appeared black. He wore an officer's dress uniform, black from neck to toe but devoid of rank and insignias. Aside from his pale eye, the man's only other outstanding feature was a gold ring, capped with a red stone, on his right pinky.

"Let's have it," he said, stopping in the middle of the bridge.

"Sir," acknowledged the XO.

A holo-projection hovered in front of the admiral, displaying a camera feed from inside the mwadim's pack tent. The view moved subtly from right to left, positioned about ten meters above and to the rear of the room. A woman approached the mwadim, then a Jujari alpha moved to intercept a portly

Republic official, presumably the ambassador. Right then, bright light oversaturated the camera, returning a second later to the developing aftermath of an explosion. The admiral's eyes darted around the image. He raised his hands and started to manipulate the recorded view, shifting it to see better. A second explosion lit the room.

"Sir, if you'll look—"

"I see it," the admiral interrupted, using his hands to zoom all the way to the dais. Amongst several other bodies, the mwadim lay at the back of the alcove along with a woman. The admiral rotated his hand, and the camera spun in to look down on the pair of bodies, the giant hyena dwarfing the woman at least five to one. He noticed an exchange between them, their hands meeting in the chaos.

"I want to know who she is and where she is," the admiral said. "Nothing else matters."

"But, sir, what about the fleet?"

The admiral froze the image and centered on the woman's face. "The fleet," he spat, "will do what the fleet has been ordered to do. *She* is all that matters now. *Find her.*"

9

When Awen came to, her eyelids felt like they weighed a hundred kilos each. Her sheer force of will finally got them to open wide enough for her to see blurry shapes moving in the distance. She felt like a thick blanket had been stuffed inside her head, slowing her ability to remember... *to remember what?*

She blinked. The shapes turned into lines, and the lines turned into bars, and the bars turned into trees. *Where am I?* She tried to raise her head, but the attempt brought on a wave of vertigo. *What's happening to me?*

She tried reaching out to the world around her, feeling with her hands, stretching with her legs. But her limbs weren't responding to her instructions. So she leaned toward the Unity of all things, willing her soul to move beyond the bounds of her... *of my what?* She was having trouble seeing herself—or seeing anything. It was as if her entire existence was wrapped in a shroud… like the fabric walls of Oosafar.

Oosafar. The mwadim!

Awen's heartbeat quickened. There'd been an explosion. Then falling. She pictured running through alleyways and dodging heads. *No, not heads.* She laughed to herself. *Containers. There was more running, and then… the Jujari found us. No.* She tried to shake her head. *That's not right. Jujari* attacked *us; someone else found us. They had weapons and candy and then…*

And then what? But she felt too giddy to keep trying to sort things out, as if all of those jumbled-up memories were funny and she could start laughing at any moment. Maybe she was laughing already.

Her body felt light as if she were floating on a cloud. *Clouds.* Clouds made her happy, and happiness made her want to fall back asleep.

She heard her name being whispered by a chipmunk. *Not a chipmunk. A monkey face. A naked monkey face, or maybe a naked monkey butt. Like baboons have. So disgusting.* And that made her laugh even more because the disembodied thing was talking to her.

"Hi, naked monkey butt," she replied. "What's your name?"

MAGNUS SWUNG from a metal beam with his hands bound above his head, his feet half a meter from a concrete floor. He blinked himself fully awake to see his helmet on the ground. While his armor had taken the brunt of being strung up, his body still ached. His shoulder was on fire, and he noticed bite marks in his armor, claw marks on his thigh, and more punctures on his foot. Dried blood caked the plating. His lips tingled… *from being stunned*. He suddenly remembered the alley and the four men. He looked up and searched the room to find Awen hanging two meters away on the same beam. She was mumbling something, her head drooped.

"Awen!" Magnus said.

She didn't reply.

"Awen, can you hear me?"

Her head swayed a little, and then her eyes met his—sort of. She blinked a lot then said, "Hi, naked monkey butt."

"Uh, what?" Magnus replied, eyebrows raised.

"You're attractive for a monkey butt."

"Awen. Awen, listen, I think you've been drugged."

They must have known she was a Luma. They were suppressing her, and that meant the enemy was informed. Her last feat of magic, saving them from the falling concrete block, must have been draining, and that was what let the enemy get the drop on her. The upside was that she probably wasn't in any pain. He knew she had to have plenty of injuries.

"Okay, NMB," Awen replied.

"NMB?"

"I'm making acronyms," she said with a giggle. "You know, for your name. All you military guys *love* your acronyms."

Magnus couldn't help but chuckle, despite the circumstances. She did have a point.

"Listen, Awen. We need to get you out of here." Magnus

searched the rest of the room. They were in an unfurnished cell with a single barred gate, no windows. Sheet metal made up the walls, and the air smelled like grease. The only light came from work lights in what looked to be a big warehouse on the other side of the bars. There he saw his MAR30, his MZ25, his duradex knife, and his two remaining grenades sitting on a table.

"I don't understand, though," Awen said with a slur.

"Understand what?" Magnus worked at the chains around his wrists.

"How's an NMB going to get us out of here, anyway? You're just a butt."

Magnus rolled his eyes. "Remind me never to take you out drinking with the boys."

"You got it."

Just then, a male voice spoke in a whiny soprano from somewhere in the warehouse. "Look who's awake."

"Yum-yum," another voice said, this one low.

"Somebody get the boss," the first one said.

Magnus saw silhouettes move in front of the work lights as a few figures approached the cell. They unlocked the door and swung it open on squeaky hinges.

Four figures entered the room, each wearing leather, fabric, and mismatched armor plates from any number of star systems —just like the men from the alley. Only these weren't warriors.

"Careful, now," the squeaky-voiced male said. "Don't get too close to that one. He's gonna be a fighter." Magnus decided to call him Weasel, thinking that two could play Awen's nonsensical game. "But this one here"—Weasel turned to Awen—"is going to fight in *different* ways." He removed a knife and scraped the edge along his stubble.

"Look!" Awen gasped in delight. "More butts!"

"What'd she call us?" the low-voiced captor said, his armor unable to cover his bulbous midsection. Magnus pictured a talking turtle head poking out of a geometric shell. *And I'll name you Turtle*. He chuckled to himself.

"How should I know what she called us?" Weasel replied. "She's piped up on drip, idiot." He pointed the knife at Awen. "Now, let's see if she wants to play."

"I really wouldn't do that if I were you," Magnus said.

Weasel turned, noticeably uneasy with the way Magnus stared at him.

"Or what?" Weasel said, stepping toward Magnus.

That's right, Magnus coaxed him, *stay focused on me*. Any movement away from Awen was all he wanted until he had time to formulate more effective goals.

"Or I'm going to adjust the composition of your face forcefully. Most will think it's an improvement."

Weasel let out a long whistle, but Magnus detected the faintest waver in it. This warehouse rat was no trained warrior, just someone's hired scum ball picked off the street and handed a blaster and a regular plate of scrap.

"With what?" Weasel said. "How you gettin' down from your tree, monkey man?"

Awen laughed. "Monkey man!"

Weasel turned toward her. Magnus had to keep his attention away from Awen. "Hey, *Weasel*, can you help me out here?"

Weasel's head whipped around. "What'd you call me, buckethead?"

Struck a nerve, Magnus thought. "Weasel. Wait, that's not your name? 'Cause your boys have been calling you that behind your back ever since I woke up."

Weasel shot the big one a glance. "Uh-uh," Turtle said, waving him off. "I swears I didn't call you nothing. Swears!"

Weasel looked back at Magnus and took a step toward him. "Nice try, buckethead. I see what you're trying to do."

"And what's that, Weasel?"

"Stop calling me that!"

One more step.

"Weird," Magnus noted as if talking to himself. "Maybe his mother's name is Weasel."

That was all it took. Weasel raised a blaster and took another step. Magnus swung his legs out, twisted the blaster out of the man's fingers with his boots, and scissor clamped the man between his knees. His body's weight reversed directions and pulled Weasel off his feet. The man expelled a gasp of air as Magnus's thighs squeezed his body like a vise. Magnus heard his armor's servos kick in, and more pressure was added, snapping a rib. Weasel yelped.

"I'm going to crush you now," Magnus said.

"No, you are not," came a booming voice from outside the cell. The man's presence was so commanding that Weasel stopped fighting for his life and strained to look at the imposing figure at the door and the dozen or more armed men who accompanied him.

"And you would be...?" Magnus asked, still squeezing Weasel.

"The name is Abimbola," the man said, taking a stride into the cell, followed by a few of his entourage. "And I own this establishment. Which means no one crushes anyone here unless I approve of it."

Magnus was instantly impressed with Abimbola's presence. Unlike the prison rats, this man was an impressive hulk of muscle and bone. Magnus guessed he was Miblimbian, since he was almost as big as a Jujari. Bright-blue eyes contrasted with his black-skinned head, and a cliché scar ran the length of the right side of his face from neck to temple. He wore a similar patchwork of discarded plate armor as the other men but chose to keep his tattooed arms bare to the shoulder. A bandolier of frag grenades wrapped his chest, and an old bowie knife in its worn-out sheath was strapped to his thigh.

He was a warrior—one with a code. That was something Magnus always respected, even if the person was on the other side of the battlefield. He despised people who fought merely for fighting's sake. Theirs was a desperate need for validation and identity manifested in a power trip—usually a reckless one. War never told people who they were, only what they were capable of. In contrast, Marines who understood the warrior ethos, regardless of their creed, knew what it meant to fight sacrificially. They took lives so others could go on living their own. That was who true warriors were.

"And do you approve?" Magnus asked, nodding at Weasel.

"Normally, yes," said Abimbola. "But today is the twenty-first day in the cycle, and that is a lucky number for me. So if you crush him, I will have to crush you." Abimbola clucked his tongue and shrugged his shoulders. "Shame."

"Hmm. Getting crushed wasn't on my to-do list this morning. Fair enough." Magnus let Weasel fall to the ground, and the little man gasped for breath as he scrambled along the concrete.

Abimbola nodded. "Thank you. Now, to what do we owe the honor of finding a Repub Marine and a Luma in our fair city?"

"*Your* city?"

"I have adopted it," Abimbola replied, snapping his fingers.

Turtle leaned outside, grabbed a chair, and placed it behind his leader.

Abimbola sat, elbows on his knees, fingers interlaced, the chair audibly straining under his weight. "My own city was… *dismantled*. I have relocated for a time."

So Abimbola is either a refugee or *a convict*. Sensing he shouldn't press the matter, Magnus decided to offer some information, since Abimbola had revealed a sliver of his own. "Well, I was going to say that the Republic wanted to purchase some large plots of real estate to turn into resorts, but we both know that would sound slightly suspicious," he said, eliciting a half smile from Abimbola. "Instead, this lady here got herself on the wrong side of a negotiation, and the Corps asked if I'd look in on her." Magnus looked at Awen, but she'd passed out.

"I see," Abimbola said. "And that has nothing to do with the mwadim's doghouse going up in flames, does it?"

"I *told them* not to play with fire."

"Yes." Abimbola nodded. "One's tendency is to get burned." He pursed his large lips and sat back. "And her? What was she doing all the way out here on Oorajee? I didn't realize the Luma were in the market for vacation properties."

Before Magnus could reply, Weasel pulled something from his pocket. "She had this on her, boss." He handed him a silver metal cylinder marred with soot and dried blood.

"A Jujari stardrive?" Abimbola said, flipping the object in the air and catching it. "Expensive little thing. And"—he glanced at the indicators—"locked up tight too."

"It's not going to be your shade of lipstick, I'm afraid," Magnus said.

"Open it, sir! Let's see what's on it," Weasel said gleefully.

Abimbola looked at Weasel and shook his head. "It is a stardrive. The only person who's opening this," he said, tipping his chin at Awen, "is her."

Despite their aggressive nature and often backward culture, the Jujari still managed to give the galaxy several technological achievements, the stardrive being one of the most significant. The cylindrical devices were not only imprinted with the owner's DNA, but a small neural program in them required a brainwave match. This meant that in order to unlock the device, the owner had to recall the memory of when he or she had been imprinted. The neural software could also detect coercion, so there was no forcing anyone to open one. It was one of the few things in the galaxy that was truly tamperproof, which made it the preferred choice of smugglers, traders, and elitists for high-end data storage.

"You do not happen to know how she got this or what's on it, do you?" asked Abimbola.

"It might be unsightly holo-vids of Weasel here," Magnus replied, trying to be helpful, "but I heard those were banned in most parts of the sector." That produced a small smile from Abimbola and a loud expletive from Weasel.

"Well, judging by the look of her, she is not going to remember how she got this anytime soon." Abimbola sighed and placed the stardrive in his pocket. Then he locked eyes with Magnus.

Magnus couldn't tell if the man was waiting for him to offer more information, deciding whether to let them go, or choosing how to kill them.

"Well," the giant of a man finally said, clapping his hands together and rising, "if that is all, I will let the boys kill you now."

Kill us? Perfect.

Abimbola must have seen Magnus look over at Awen, because he added, "Oh, not *you* as in both of you—just *you*." He pointed at Magnus. "*She* is coming with me."

"The last one run out on you?" Magnus quipped.

Abimbola smiled. "This one is going to be worth a lot of credits to somebody. Stardrives do not just hitch rides on nobodies."

"Monkeys!" Awen suddenly yelled out, startling herself awake.

Abimbola's eyes went wide. "I thought you said she was brain-dead?" Abimbola said to Weasel. "What is this? *This* is not brain-dead."

"We drugged her, boss," Weasel said. "Just like you told us to do with Luma. Got her necklace for you too. She's Luma all right." He handed Abimbola the leather cord and gold medallion.

"You're all so *cute!*" Awen exclaimed. "I want to take you home."

"See," Weasel continued. "I meant she's brain-dead, like, her brain is broken. You know, *crazy*. She's talking all crazy and stuff."

Abimbola looked from Weasel back to Awen. "How much did you give her?"

"Twice what you said. Figured this one was probably dangerous, with a soldier like that protecting her and being way out—"

"Got it," Abimbola said, raising a hand. He walked over to Awen.

"You're not going to want to touch her," Magnus said. "She's highly allergic to people touching her."

Abimbola paused. "So protective for a Marine. If only you all were." The man turned to Awen. "What is your name?"

"That's not a hard question," she slurred. "My name's Awen. Next question."

"Where did you get this?" He held up the stardrive.

"I didn't know monkeys wore lipstick!"

"Told you it wasn't your shade," Magnus said.

Abimbola shook his head. "This is going nowhere." He produced a small syringe from a compartment in his pants, removed the cap, and stuck Awen in the side of the neck.

"You just made a big mistake, buddy," Magnus said, jerking the chains around his wrists.

"Easy, Marine. Stand down. This is just something to bring her back."

Awen winced then took several deep breaths. "Wait… where am I?"

AWEN'S HEAD HURT. Come to think of it, her entire body hurt. And it was getting worse by the second. She blinked several times and noticed an enormous warrior standing in front of her, holding a syringe. She panicked and tried to move away, realizing immediately that her hands were bound overhead. Her attempt at movement brought on a new wave of pain in her wrists and shoulders.

"Where am I?" she said for the second or third time—she couldn't be sure. Awen glanced over and saw the lieutenant hanging about two meters away. "Lieutenant! What—"

"Welcome back," the large man in front of her said. "You have been out for some time."

Awen blinked at him, faint memories of trees and monkeys swirling in her aching head. "Who are you? Why are you doing this?"

"It is temporary, I can assure you, miss…?"

"Temporary because you're planning on killing us or temporary because you're ready to let us go now?" She reached out to the Unity. *It was time to get out of here.* "Because I can assure you that by the time you—" Awen broke the sentence off as a wave of pain severed her concentration from the cosmos.

The warrior wiggled the syringe. "Interesting stuff, isn't it? Brings you back from oblivion but makes it very hard to stay focused. Which, for a woman of your talents, means it is harder for you to do all those marvelous things you do."

"So," Awen said, squinting, "what's next? Torture? Isolation? Interrogation?"

"A woman who likes to get straight to the point. I like that. First, allow me to introduce myself. My name is Abimbola."

"His city got blown up," Magnus added. "That and a bad hair day make him a special brand of *pissed off*."

Abimbola tilted his head, raised an eyebrow, and nodded. "That is not too far from the truth. As for you"—he stepped closer to Awen—"I plan on collecting the ransom on your head."

"There's a ransom for me?"

"Not yet, but once I let the proper channels know you are alive and have escaped that *ugly* scene at the mwadim's tent, I suspect more than a few parties will pay a lot of credits for you."

"And him?" Awen asked, indicating Magnus.

"Him?" Abimbola looked to the Marine. "Why do you even care about him? Isn't he just the Republic's hired gun who is supposed to watch your back while you are… what was it again?"

"Browsing for a vacation home," Magnus offered.

Abimbola smiled. "How charming." He looked back at Awen. "Trouble is, I really do not have the fondest feelings for Republic gunslingers. Something about them just makes me feel—oh, I don't know… like I was stabbed in the back. No, no. That metaphor is too subtle. Perhaps stabbed in the face." Abimbola indicated his facial scar, making a grand gesture of tracing the entire length with a fingertip. "So when I say I *really* do not have the fondest feelings, I do mean *really*."

"Then, you're going to kill him."

Abimbola clucked, nodding as if remorseful. "That is about the measure of it, yes."

"I see." Awen tried again to reach to the Unity but gasped as a fresh wave of pain crashed against her head.

"I suppose you do have at least a little power in this situation, however," he added, "though it probably does not seem very enabling."

"How's that?"

"I am going to let you decide how this buckethead dies. Blaster bolt to the head," he said, making a pistol out of his fingers and placing it beside his own temple, "or something slower. And before you answer, I feel obligated to tell you that bucketheads killed a lot of the people I loved, so when I say that I can kill him slowly, I do mean that I have perfected ways to draw out suffering over several *years*."

"Ooo, he has! He has!" Turtle boomed. "Show her the room."

"Perhaps later," Abimbola said. "Let us give her a choice first."

"And what if I don't want to play your game?" Awen asked.

"Then I will play one of my own." The giant discarded the syringe and produced a poker chip from his pocket. "We will flip for it. Credit symbol, I kill him quickly. But house side up? Your friend will wish you had chosen for him."

Awen swallowed. She considered the man's poker chip and the possibility that maybe, if he was a gambling man, he was bluffing. He might want something else. "So, what do you want from me?" She dreaded the answer that awaited her. She knew what happened to women who got lost on these off-world hellholes.

"Clever girl." Abimbola pulled a small cylinder from behind his back. Awen's head hurt, but she recognized it from the *mwadim*. "You see, I *really* want to know what is on this stardrive. And I mean *really*. Unfortunately for me, however, you are the only person who can access it. So—"

"So I open it for you, and you kill him quickly."

"That is correct."

"Here's my counter," Awen said. "I open it for you, and you let him go, then you collect the bounty on me."

"Awen, no!" Magnus yelled.

"Strange," Abimbola said. "And unnecessarily reckless, nearsighted, and stupid. Though I am not sure that—"

"You're not sure which you want more: to quench your insatiable curiosity about *just what's on that stardrive* or to extract a little more blood from *one more buckethead* because you have a deep-seated vengeance complex, probably from when you were a boy. Am I right?"

Abimbola stared at her. Awen noticed the faintest tic in the corner of his mouth. *Gotcha*, she thought.

"And what if I refuse your counter? I feel you are a little short on leverage."

"You can refuse, of course," Awen said. "And in that case, I'll have no other option than to use my remaining power to kill both the buckethead and myself. No amount of your little medication can prevent me from suicide."

"Suicide that also kills him?" Abimbola laughed.

Awen looked at him deadpan. "You've never seen a Luma go nova, have you."

"Ha! No. And I do not believe it. You are bluffing."

Awen took a deep breath and then forced all her energy into her next few words, knowing they could very well be her last. "Abimbola, I swear on the graves of my descendants that I, Awen dau Lothlinium of the Order of the Luma, will sever my connection with this realm of the cosmos and take every one of you with me. You messed with the wrong woman today."

Abimbola blanched and took a step back, the poker chip clattering to the floor. He looked as if he'd just seen a ghost. "What did… what did you say your name is?"

10

MAGNUS AND AWEN sat in a dune skiff behind Abimbola and Berouth—Abimbola's driver and second in charge—as the vehicle raced away from the outskirts of Oosafar. The skiff's headlights rose and fell along rippling ridges of sand like searchlights sweeping ocean waves for wreckage. Cold desert air whipped at Awen's hair as she sat wrapped in a traditional cooshra, while Magnus enjoyed the peace of his helmet and MAR30 again—they were the only sure bets he had at the moment.

The way Magnus saw it, he was a lone Repub Marine on a hostile planet, cut off from his unit and any chance of being rescued, and surrounded by Jujari intent on killing him for the assassination of their mwadim. That, and he still had a mission to complete.

Great. Just great.

"We are almost there," Abimbola yelled over his shoulder. He tapped the nav screen that glowed on the dash. "Another four klicks."

Magnus could hardly believe the turn of events that had led to this moment. One minute they were strung up, Awen bargaining for their lives, and the next, they were being escorted to a rendezvous point by the warlord himself. *She saved us*, Magnus thought with a growing sense of irony and... *What?* his gut asked him. *Admiration?*

He remained on high alert as they careened over the dunes, but the undulating movement combined with the skiff's low hum lulled him into a reflective state. Not for the first time, he wondered who'd planted the explosives in the mwadim's tent. The Jujari could have had a hand in it; factions within the dogs' political structure were just as likely as with any other species. Maybe more, given their ruthless pack mentality. Still, something this calculated didn't fit their MO, or what little he knew of it. The attack was brazen, yes. But it was also pristine. *Maniacal* was a better word, a study in controlled slaughter.

The first explosion was disruptive, shocking the room into chaos, killing as many stationary targets as possible. It sent the message that security had been breached and put everyone in a panic. The second explosion, caused by ordnance that wasn't set off by the first blast, was meant to insult—if you weren't dead yet, that was your chance to die. But the third was pure evil. For anyone left who was stumbling or crawling their way to an escape—and Magnus had seen more than a few nonmilitary victims crawling toward the windows—the third blast was meant to maim, shatter, and humiliate. It said, *We've been expecting you; we've been watching you. You're not safe, and no one is getting out alive.* Magnus wondered if the Republic was behind it, then scolded himself for even considering that.

But you're nothing if not thorough, right, Magnus? Always have to go digging.

Again, his mind tried to bring up images from the Caledonian Wars, but this was still not the time to wrestle those demons to the ground.

And when will that time come?

The Republic had had its eye on Oorajee long before his time. It was the unconquerable prize, and the Republic loved a challenge. But to forfeit such a gain on the eve of acquisition seemed downright stupid. There was no way they'd risk so much after so long. The Republic had nothing to gain from such a move—unless they *wanted* the conflict. Magnus remembered Awen's words from when they met: "We don't need a war on our hands." But by the looks of it, that was precisely what they were about to get.

Magnus wasn't so naive as to ignore the benefits of the military-industrial complex. He knew that expansion fueled more than just egos—it really did create peace in the galaxy, at least to a point. *Splick, I have a career because of it.* He was one of the few who could do evil things to evil people and still sleep at night. He'd also be the last to spit on his family's sacrifices and their tradition of military service. However, the Republic seemed to be taking an unnecessary risk on Oorajee. It was one thing to contend for peace where it was probable—even sustainable. But war with the Jujari was… his mind searched for the right word. *Suicidal.*

The Luma weren't without their motives either. He'd seen what they were capable of, seen their dark arts wielded in Caledonia. And he knew they hated the Republic. Awen was no doubt the embodiment of that bias. *Okay, maybe not the full embodiment*—she'd clearly stood up for him. She genuinely seemed to want to make the negotiations work, though she was probably more concerned with the Jujari side of things—the Luma were all about preserving the cultures they represented, even if those cultures' ethics were at odds with the Republic's. Still, those bombs were not Awen's work.

So that left a fourth party, one he couldn't draw a bead on. It had the brutality of the Jujari, the precision of the Republic, and the stealth of the Luma. *For what?* The only logical conclusion was, *For all of it.* Magnus figured this party wanted to take down the Jujari, the Republic, and the Luma in one move. But such an idea was crazy, and he felt embarrassed for daydreaming about it. Someone would yell at him any second—like his father. Maybe his CO. Definitely his brother. Thinking outside the box—daring to overstep convention—was what got him in trouble.

Isn't that what they called it? Conventional?

They'd said it was what everybody had "always" done—those horrible things he'd seen on Caledonia.

So why'd you try to stop them? Why not join them?

Because he'd wanted nothing to do with those *things* they did—nothing to do with *them*. With *him*. The images came back now, forcing themselves in like a cold winter wind through the cracks of an old windowsill. Magnus stretched out his arms and braced himself against the cold, willing it back.

Stay away! Stay away from her!

"Stop!"

WHEN ABIMBOLA HAD HEARD Awen's name, something in the man froze. He leaned in and asked her to repeat herself then asked for her parents' and grandparent's names. It seemed a strange thing to ask a captive for, and Awen seemed reluctant to give the names up, but the situation wasn't exactly normal. When Awen finally shared their names, Abimbola had knelt.

He knelt, Magnus recalled in astonishment. There, on the concrete floor, the warlord had laid a fist to his chest and bowed in reverence, and Magnus realized the petite Luma emissary had held her own before two violent leaders in less than a day.

When Abimbola ordered that Awen be taken down, she refused to move until Magnus had been freed and his safety guaranteed. Magnus protested, but Abimbola's security detail let Magnus down faster than he could form an argument. *A little too fast*, he thought as he recalled how hard he'd hit the floor.

"And his weapons," Awen insisted. Abimbola nodded, and the guards returned Magnus's armaments without hesitation.

They fear their leader more than an armed Repub Marine, Magnus noted. *Copy that.*

He stowed his kit and placed his helmet back on his head, firing up the AI and checking systems. *That's strange.* Comms were down. He expertly double-checked the relay connection by bashing the side of his bucket with the heel of his hand. Still nothing.

The two of them were escorted across the warehouse and given brief access to private bathrooms. Awen was given the cooshra to cover her maimed robes and given bandages for the worst of her cuts, though Magnus knew she still needed proper medical attention. When they reconvened in what looked to be Abimbola's war room—an upper-level apartment with holoscreens perched around a large central table—the warlord ordered tea and inclined his head to the open seats.

"Please," he said. "Be seated." The idea of tea hung in sardonic contrast to the rear wall made entirely of Republic trooper helmets. No less than a hundred, Magnus calculated, each charred, dented, broken, or cleaved. Stranger still, Abimbola offered Magnus a universal power cable to recharge his suit and his helmet.

"May I ask why you're doing this?" Awen asked as she sat.

Abimbola settled into his oversized chair and played with a poker chip as he considered her question. "Your presence is fortuitous, a sign from the gods. And if time were not of the essence, I would give you the history that the question deserves. However"—his eyes darted to one of the monitors, which displayed the orbital positions of a growing number of ships—"it seems I will not have the opportunity. Suffice to say, I owe your family a great debt, one I will never be able to repay."

"Well, I… I don't know what to say," Awen replied, blinking several times. "I'm afraid that without more backstory, I really can't comment other than to offer thanks for your sudden kindness to us."

"One day, we will speak of my home—the home of all Miblimbians," Abimbola said.

Which explains his size, Magnus noted, confirming his earlier assumption.

"And I will tell you of Limbia Centralla and those who died, those who survived, and those who betrayed us." Abimbola's eyes shifted to Magnus and held his face in an overly long stare. The trills and chirps of incoming status updates filled the background, punctuated by the sudden tapping of a poker chip on the table.

"Yes. Well, then," Awen said, obviously trying to relieve Magnus of the intense eye lock. "I look forward to the next time we meet."

Just then, two women in silk robes and head coverings entered the room, placing trays in front of Abimbola. They poured three cups of tea then served them.

"Clearly, the gods are at work above us too," Abimbola added, sipping his drink. The teacup in his large hand looked more like a miniature child's toy than an adult cup. "They are about to rain down fire as quickly as they have given me the blessing of your company." Abimbola gestured to the orbital display, which showed both Republic and Jujari designations appearing over the planet.

That's not good, Magnus thought.

"So, it appears that as quickly as you have come into my life, you must depart. Oorajee is not a place I would recommend staying."

"Can you help us get back to the fleet?" Magnus asked.

Abimbola's eyes hung on Awen's face before snapping to Magnus, clearly put off by the sudden intrusion. "I could no sooner get you back to the fleet than betray all of my men. And were I to send you on your own, I fear you would not survive more than a few minutes, so I would fail to honor the blood of Awen's ancestors. Also, I saw you bang on your bucket back there. I am guessing you tried to reach your unit? It is no use, as you no doubt discovered. All comms will be down indefinitely."

"Yeah…" Magnus said slowly. "Jamming tech?"

Abimbola nodded. "Nothing is getting on or off planet unless the Jujari want it to. That, and you happen to be in the middle of the biggest scum hole this side of the Saffron system. The Jujari might not like outsiders, but at least they tolerate non-Repub types, so long as we stay out of their way. 'Round here, you have yourself a bona fide collection of every species imaginable, especially those who have threatened, avoided, or plotted against the Repub. That means that every signal junkie in the Dregs sniffed your boot-up signature before you even blinked at your AI."

"The Dregs?" Awen asked.

"What we call our fair city. Or the inhabitants. Either one. Were you not safe inside Abimbola's care, I would say the Jujari would be the least of your problems."

"So we're stuck," Awen offered.

"You are never stuck," Abimbola said. "Not when I have an Ezo."

"An Ezo?"

Ruins of the Galaxy

"He will get you off planet and wherever you wish to go. He owes me... several favors."

"But we can't leave yet," Awen protested. "We need to look for my team."

Abimbola's eyes dropped to his hands and then back up. "Miss dau Lothlinium," he said somberly, "I suspect you are the only survivor, no small thanks to your man here."

Magnus watched Awen's face. *She knows she's the only survivor by now... right?*

"No, there must be others," Awen said, panic creeping into her voice.

Nope, guess not. Magnus felt genuine pity for her. He'd felt the same thing before but under very different circumstances.

"Listen," Abimbola said, "my marauders have been scouting the area since the first blast. That is why they found you. But based on what they are reporting, there is not much left—of anything. And even if there were survivors, getting close enough to secure them will be impossible. Chances are the Jujari have already—"

Magnus waved the warlord off without Awen seeing. Abimbola registered the movement and, surprisingly, took it to heart.

"They have already tried to rescue those they can. It is best for you to leave, go back to your order, and regroup. In truth," Abimbola said, leaning across the table, "I would take you myself. However, by the looks of things, I am going to be busy here for a long time. As you can see"—he turned to regard his trophy wall—"I never give up a chance to collect buckets."

"But as you yourself said," Awen interjected, "my *man* is the one helping me survive today, so I'd appreciate you exercising self-restraint in your habits."

Abimbola regarded Awen then Magnus. "Then this little encounter of ours may be the first exception to my rule."

"Your rule?" Magnus asked.

"Keep the can, kick the head."

"Can't say I'm not grateful," Magnus said, raising his cup of tea. "Here's to never meeting again."

"Magnus!" Awen called.

He looked over to see her staring at him. He'd been daydreaming again. *Dammit.*

"Are you okay?" she asked.

"I'm fine," he said through his external speaker, hoping the system hid the emotion in his voice.

"You weren't responding," Awen added. "I just... anyway, we're here." She pointed ahead as the dune skiff slid to a halt and powered down beside a small tent village. Only a few lamps burned, indicating the main entrance to the compound. Magnus scanned for life-forms but, to his surprise, found none.

"He should be along any moment," Abimbola said.

"Seems rather quiet." Magnus squeezed his MAR30. Had they just driven into an ambush? *Because now is the perfect time.* "You sure we're at the right place?"

"Abimbola never gets the wrong place, buckethead," Berouth said from the driver's seat.

Ruins of the Galaxy

Magnus's AI picked up motion to the right. "Awen, I'm getting non-bio movement over there." He trained his MAR30 on a gap in some of the tent fabric.

"That is going to be his bot," Abimbola said, vaulting out of the skiff and stretching his back. "Funny bugger, that one."

Magnus slid out of the skiff, MAR30 still pointed at the incoming object. It finally materialized in his HUD, his AI comparing the image against its database of known entries. The list of *possible matches* began with late-model navigator bots, but scans remained inconclusive. "What in the world?"

"Told you," Abimbola said.

The bot shuffled toward the skiff while its round head and two bulbous eyes surveyed each member of the party. It seemed as if someone had taken an old nav bot—generally known for being well articulated so it could squeeze into the copilot seats of most starships—and welded on a wild variety of very lethal, very out-of-place armaments. One forearm boasted a cluster of microrockets while the other housed the upper receiver of an XM31 Type-R blaster. Twin gauss cannons were inconspicuously housed on both shoulders, served with what Magnus imagined was ferromagnetic ammunition provided by feed belts that disappeared into the bot's backplate. Much of the torso was covered with matte-gray-weave duradex plate armor, and a custom-molded translucent blast shield acted as a visor over its face. Magnus had no doubt that, given what they *could* see, there was even more under the armor that they *couldn't* see.

"Hello," the bot said in a chipper tone. "I am TO-96.

Welcome"—his head turned toward the warlord—"Abimbola and guests. My master owes you precisely—"

"He owes me a vacation to the Meridian Palladium and his left testicle," Abimbola said. "And if he does not get his sorry ass out here in—"

"Well, hello there, my finely tanned friend!" an overly benevolent voice said. A man emerged from a tent—stepping out from behind some sophisticated shielding—and walked as if floating toward them. He was dressed in a long gray leather coat, the tails of which nearly touched the sand. Beneath it, he wore a white knit turtleneck, black pants, and glossy black boots. A holstered SUPRA 945 pistol clung to his thigh, and a small data pad was stowed in his belt. His dark hair was swept meticulously to one side, like an ocean wave curling at midnight, and he stared at them with thin eyes and a wide smile.

Magnus didn't like the guy. He was too pretty. But Ezo was also their only ride off this rock, and getting Awen to wherever she wanted to go meant he would be one step closer to rejoining his unit—or what was left of it. There was something else about Ezo, though—something familiar. Magnus couldn't place it, but he had the strange feeling that he'd met the man before. And he hated that he couldn't remember. It made him uneasy.

"I am here to cash in a fraction of your debt to me," Abimbola said, squaring up with Ezo.

"What, no hello? No time for tea? Ezo's hurt, Bimbo."

Abimbola bristled at the nickname and had his own reply—the bowie knife sprang from his thigh as if drawn by the darkness itself and was laid across Ezo's fluffy collar in the space of a single step. Berouth also had a blaster drawn on the bot, and the bot had its XM31 trained on Abimbola.

"Okay, okay. No time for tea," Ezo said, palms up in surrender. "Next time, *next time*."

Abimbola withdrew the blade and motioned to Berouth to stand down. "You are going to escort these two wherever they want to go."

Ezo looked to Awen. "Well, well, well. Who do we have here?" He strode toward her and reached for her hand, but not before Magnus had leveled his MAR30 at the interloper.

"Watch it," Magnus warned.

"Easy, easy, big bucket man! Ezo's not going to hurt her; he just wants to become acquainted. Sheesh."

Magnus flicked off his MAR30's safety. "There won't be any—"

"It's all right, Lieutenant," Awen said, offering her hand to Ezo. "He's just being courteous. Plus, he owes our patron his left testicle, which means if he does anything stupid, you can have his right one."

Ezo froze with his lips a few centimeters from Awen's hand. Magnus noted for at least the second time that day how much he was beginning to like her.

11

G%%ERONIMO% %%NINE%%, as Ezo dubbed her, was the most substantial portion of Ezo's makeshift village in the desert. Disguised to look like a city block's worth of tents, the ship was only hibernating under rags, waiting for someone to summon her drive core to life. Once alive, the Katana-class freighter's thrusters blew apart the pseudo town and launched skyward in a crimson streak.

The red hull's inverted crescent shape drove its way through the atmosphere and then into the silence of the void. From the cockpit, located in the center of the concave sweep, the pilot and copilot could see only the tips of the primary NR220 blaster cannons that jutted forward. The rest of the hull swept aft and terminated in a wide bank of ion-propulsion ports that glowed a brilliant blue.

The Katanas were powerful ships to begin with, each one manufactured with more thrust than it needed even with its modular cargo bay filled. Ezo had taken advantage of this power-to-mass ratio and added military-grade armament, which included not only the twin cannons but also upgraded shield generators, plate armor, and three banks of quantum warhead-tipped K91 torpedoes. Just one could take out a heavy armored transport or even a small destroyer. Ezo assured his two new guests that *Geronimo* was not only one of the fastest private starships in the quadrant but one of the deadliest as well, thanks to his modifications. She was, by all accounts, a prized ship, and Ezo treated her as the gem that she was.

Awen, since boarding *Geronimo Nine*, had disposed of her tattered clothes in the ship's incinerator and then let TO-96 tend her wounds in sick bay. The bot had wanted to talk, apparently eager for company, but she was not in the mood and asked him to go silent. When TO-96 had finally cleared her, Awen traded the sick-bay gown for one of Ezo's knit turtlenecks, a pair of leggings, and some leather boots Ezo had picked from a stash in the unusually spotless cargo bay. Then she gave the captain a course to lay and made her way to the main lounge to get comfortable.

For a smuggler or bounty hunter or whatever he was, Ezo had done remarkably well with keeping the ship in top condition, which included interior cleanliness—something Awen was all too grateful for. While her work with the Luma often took her to worlds with much different standards from her own, Awen always appreciated returning to the order and predictability of Plumeria. Similarly, Ezo's ship was tidy and surprisingly comfortable, much different from what she'd imagined a bounty hunter's vessel to be. It even smelled fresh. Glowing white floors rounded up to polished metal walls and handrails, while the ceiling was regularly spaced with clusters of pin lights. Awen looked around, concluding that *this is what illegal money and contraband can buy.*

She sat with her knees to her chest, back resting against the wall of a recessed couch. The nano-meds were doing their work, easing the pain and mending the frayed ends of whatever had come undone inside. The steady hum of the ship made Awen feel safe even though she knew the void was only a meter behind her.

The void. She heard her father saying, "All you're going to find is the void," warning her not to join the Luma, to stay on Elonia. But she hadn't listened.

She pinched the bridge of her nose as her mind wandered back, replaying the explosions in the mwadim's tent—or at least what she could remember of the incident. She'd sensed the blast soon enough to cover herself and the mwadim with a partial shield but not fast enough to help anyone else. It had all happened so quickly. And now Matteo, Elder Toochu, and the rest were…

Awen swallowed. Her mouth was dry. They were dead, and she hadn't done enough to try to save them.

It wasn't supposed to be like this. She had worked so hard, and for what? For some idiots to rig the meeting and blow the prospect of peace into a thousand pieces? It felt so futile. The galaxy's last great divide was about to be mended, the Jujari and the Republic finally at some sort of agreement. It had been in her grasp. *My father would have understood me. He would have seen what was possible. He would have understood that I was right to leave.*

Awen wanted to cry, and she wanted to sleep. But her exhaustion was more than fatigue. It was a sudden urge to stop being a Luma, to go back home and do something other than whatever all *this* was—to try to forget everything that had just happened. And at the same time, she knew she couldn't forget. She sensed that the faces of the dead would be with her for a lifetime.

Awen was lost in her thoughts, head on her knees, when Magnus appeared with a steaming cup of something to drink. "Made you this," he said, handing the metal cup to her. He had stowed his helmet and gloves and removed several of the bulkier elements of his armor, making him almost normal sized. *He's still too tall.* She guessed it had something to do with his boots.

"Thanks." She savored the small warmth the cup provided.

"I see the bot got you squared away." He sat in an acceleration couch across from her. "Nothing too serious?"

"Nothing too serious," she confirmed. "Nanos doing their work. Just need to rest."

Magnus nodded. "Looks like you were able to salvage your necklace."

Awen instinctively reached for it. "Yeah, it's the only thing I didn't have to throw out."

"Not that you had a whole lot on to begin with." Magnus's face froze. "I mean, it's just that you—"

"Lieutenant." Awen laughed then winced from the pain it caused her.

At Awen's interruption, the trooper sat back and rubbed his forehead, looking relieved. She noted that he wasn't the hardest man to look at… for a buckethead.

"Listen, about back there," she started. "I wanted to thank you for saving my life."

"It's nothing." Magnus waved. "Just doing my job."

"Well, it may have been nothing to you, but it was something to me." She dipped her head, trying to catch his eye. "So thank you."

Magnus looked up. "You're welcome." He glanced into his cup. "You know, I can say the same about you too. That concrete block and the way you threatened Abimbola." He paused. "Can you really blow yourself up?"

Awen laughed again. "Yeah. But it's not the sort of thing you want to do more than once a day."

Magnus looked up, surprised for a split second. "Oh, splick, you're kidding," he said, suddenly smiling. "Sorry. Language."

"I don't expect soldiers to be saints."

"Good, 'cause we're not soldiers—we're Recon," Magnus said. "Anyway, *thank you*."

"You're welcome." Awen took a sip of her drink, trying to think of something else to say. "Good tea."

"Yeah, it's all Ezo seems to have. That and Svoltin single malt whiskey." Magnus paused. "I mean, I could get you—"

"No," she said with a smile and waved him off. "The tea is just fine."

"Good. No one should ever see you drunk."

Awen raised her eyebrows and then realized he must have been talking about her being drugged. She didn't remember much, but she guessed it was bad. "Abimbola's?"

Magnus nodded. "Abimbola's."

"Mind if we keep whatever I said between us?"

"You said something?" He winked.

He was kind of cute; his baby face and deep-green eyes saw to that. She took another sip of tea and noticed the damage to his armor. "I'm so sorry. How are *you*?"

Magnus glanced at his body. "Looks way worse than it is," he replied. "This suit can take a beating."

"Even though you were leaking back there."

"*Leaking?*"

"When we were tied up at Abimbola's, I noticed the ground beneath you. Did you—did you wet yourself?"

"Did I *wet* myself? No, I"—a look of surprise dawned on his face, then he pointed to his thigh—"the Jujari punctured one of my reclamation bladders."

"Reclamation bladders?"

"Yeah, it's how we—"

"Don't worry, I won't tell," she said.

"What? No, I don't think you understand."

"I get it, Lieutenant. Even the big boys get scared." She winked. "How about the blood on you?"

Magnus paused then appeared to give up on trying to justify his leak. "Jujari. Maybe some of my own. But the armor's good at clotting. I'll get treatment when I get back to my unit."

"TO-96 can check you out."

"I'm sure he can, but I'd rather wait."

"Suit yourself, Lieutenant." *Good-looking but still a naked monkey butt. Wait, where did that come from?*

"You can just call me Magnus," he said.

"I think we really should stick with—"

"After what you and I just saw, I'd rather *not* stick with the protocol. *Magnus*, please."

"Magnus," she replied. She found his assertiveness appealing even though it had to do with bending the rules. Maybe he wasn't a dimwitted drone after all. "And you can call me Awen."

"Awen," he replied.

Hearing him say her name had more of an effect on her than she cared to admit. Did it show? She was suddenly extremely self-conscious and hid her face in the cup. *You're an idiot, Awen, and you have no time for this.*

"So, any ideas on who'd want to blow up a room of Jujari, Luma, and Republic officials?"

"That *is* the big question, isn't it?" Magnus sipped his tea. "Someone who didn't want the alliance to happen. Or…"

"Or what?"

"Someone who didn't want the mwadim giving you that," he said, indicating the stardrive on the table. Its slender form and elegant lines looked otherworldly, a soft blue light emanating from slits in its cylindrical housing.

"That would imply that someone knew he had it and that he wanted to give it up," she said.

"Didn't he, though?"

"I don't see how I could—"

"Listen, Awen. I have my own opinions about the Luma. You have yours about the Republic. But if there's ever been a Luma who truly believes in her work—I mean, who embodies the ethos of what the Luma stand for—it's got to be you. The Jujari may be a bunch of—"

"Easy," Awen interrupted.

"A bunch of dangerous galactic pack hunters."

"That works."

"But they're not stupid. And the mwadim was their alpha. Which means he knew who you were—he knew who was coming to help his planet. I'd wager a thousand credits on the fact that he was going to hand you that stardrive with or without a bomb blast. Because he trusted you."

"But why give it to me at all?" she asked.

"And that's the other big question. I don't know. But I'm guessing you're going to make sure his death isn't in vain."

Awen felt her face flush. *Why his sudden confidence in me? Did he—*

"Hey, mind if I ask you what the ambassador said to you?"

"The ambassador?" Awen's mind raced. "Oh, when he grabbed my arm, you mean? Sure. He threatened me."

"*Threatened* you?"

"He was upset that I was about to hand the mwadim a microdrive of the broken promises he'd made with other civilizations."

"I don't follow. You're saying the ambassador—"

"Is a two-timing lowlife who only cares about his comfy credit account and where his next fatty mondollon steak is coming from. He only closes so many negotiations because he tells the incorporating worlds that they'll get whatever they ask for. By the time leaders realize they've gotten the short end of the deal, it's too late. And who's going to stand up to the Republic when they send guys like *you* in as muscle?"

"Listen, we just—"

"I know," she said. "You're just the hired help. You don't do any of the dirty work."

"That's not what I was going to say. Our hands are plenty dirty. I was going to say that we don't support evil when it's exposed."

Awen believed him—not that she thought every trooper resisted evil, but she was sure that at least Magnus did. "You might be the exception, then," she replied, chin raised.

"There are way more good Marines than bad."

She didn't know how to reply to that, so she didn't.

"We're called in to do evil things to evil people. Not everyone gets that, and I don't expect them to. But it's my job, and I do it well." Magnus looked down at his tea for a second then back at her. "Your records on the ambassador's betrayal… they are legit?"

"Yes," she replied.

"Then I could see how he might be pretty upset. And I see how you'd mistrust the Republic."

Awen looked at him, genuinely surprised. "Thank you."

"Plus, the upside to this is you'll never have to worry about Ambassador Bosworth again." Magnus made the sound of a small explosion and spread his hands apart. "So, where are we headed?"

"I told Ezo I need to get to Worru."

"Headed back to the Order," Magnus concluded correctly.

The Order of the Luma had its origin in the ancient city of Plumeria, now the capital of Worru and the galactic center for cultural learning.

"I still wished we could have searched for survivors," Awen said, looking into her tea.

"I get that. But you have to remember the big picture in moments like this."

"And what's that?"

"There's a reason you survived."

"And a reason they died?" she asked.

Magnus pursed his lips. "I didn't mean it like that."

"I know. I'm sorry."

"Listen, the big picture is that you're still alive and you have something important in your possession."

"I'm alive because I had a split second to do something about it, and it still wasn't enough to save them too."

"You… you did something back there? When the first explosion happened?"

Awen nodded.

"More magic?"

"Not magic. It's just that some of us… are *different*. We're able to sense things before they happen."

"The concrete," Magnus said.

"Yeah, like the concrete. We can't see everything before it happens. It can be… *fuzzy*. But I felt something in time enough to get a partial field around me and most of the mwadim."

"Yeah, but not his head," Magnus said with a sniff, remembering the giant dog's mutilated muzzle.

"Like I said, a partial field. It was all I could do."

"Well, it probably saved your life."

"And it didn't save theirs," she said, feeling a sudden wave of bitterness.

"Awen, listen. Blaming yourself isn't—"

"Isn't going to solve anything?" She shook her head, agitated. "For all the mystics! I've heard that speech so many times. When will we learn that it doesn't make people feel any less guilty?"

Magnus swirled his tea then took another sip. "I think we say it because we don't know what else to say. And it's what I keep telling myself."

Awen searched his face. She suddenly realized, to her shame, that Magnus had lost people too. Sure, they were troopers, and they'd expected to die. They were paid to go into those kinds of situations. But that didn't make it any less painful.

"Magnus… I'm sorry," she said, shaking her head. "I didn't even—"

"Bottom line is, you're alive, and now you need to make it count."

Make it count. Awen considered the wisps of steam that appeared above her cup and then vanished. "And what if I don't?"

"What do you mean?"

Awen fought back a sudden urge to cry. She bit her lower lip and closed her eyes. This work might be about as meaningless as a wisp of steam—here one second and gone the next. The years of mounting tension with her parents, her tireless work for the

Luma, the Jujari, and then it had all been snuffed out in a matter of minutes. *Lives* had been snuffed out.

"What if I just want to go back home and be done with all of this?" she asked then cleared her throat. "You know, I was just seventeen when I was asked to attend observances."

Magnus looked at her with a raised eyebrow.

"Sorry. It's six years of monastic training in the Luma's academy. Anyway, I was seventeen. I had top scores in school, was civic minded, and wanted to make a difference. So, when I got the letter, I was beside myself. I thought, you know, this is it. This is my chance to change the galaxy. I loved what the Luma stood for, preserving galactic cultures and keeping them from—"

"From getting swallowed up by the Republic. Yeah, I get it."

"It's just a different way of making progress, that's all."

Magnus didn't look convinced, but it didn't matter. This was her story, not his. "Anyway, my parents fought me on it for months. Said it was a mistake." She wiped a tear from her eye. "But I knew it wasn't. After my first year, my tests revealed that I was a true blood."

"A what?" he asked.

"A true blood. It's believed that everyone can learn to move in the Unity of all things, but true bloods can move through it more powerfully."

"That's what you meant by 'some of us' earlier? About sensing things before they happen?"

"Yes." She nodded and pushed a strand of hair over her ear. "So I thought, that was it. It would prove to my parents that I was destined to be a Luma—that I'd chosen well for myself."

"But they didn't take it that way, I'm guessing."

"No. No, they didn't." She sipped her tea. "The gap widened, and I threw myself into my studies."

"The Jujari?"

"And quantum mechanics," she added with a smile.

"Huh. Overachieve much?"

Awen smiled. "Yeah, well… I excelled in school. No surprise there, I guess. And by the time I graduated and became an elder, I knew more about the Jujari than even my masters. So when the Order received word from the mwadim that they wanted us to serve as council for negotiations with the Republic, I was asked to lead the diplomatic mission."

"That's quite the honor for someone so young," Magnus said then hesitated. "I don't mean any disrespect."

"None taken. And I agree. At twenty-four years common, I'm the youngest emissary to lead a mission in the Luma's multimillennial history."

"Whoa, I had no idea. That's impressive."

"You'd assume my parents would think so too. But now that everything's fallen apart, maybe this was all just a big mistake. Maybe my parents were right."

"Maybe they were," Magnus agreed, "and maybe they weren't. But as far as I can tell, they're not the ones writing your destiny, Awen. You are." He set his tea down on the mess table beside him. "Back on Caledonia, during my first deployment, our platoon had been pinned down on a beachhead, and our CO was trying to come up with options. I noticed a stand of palms to one side and offered to take my fire team to flank the enemy. It was risky. There was no cover between our position and those trees. But I felt that if we had a shot at catching our enemy off guard, this was it. My CO said I was an idiot, called me a bunch of names not worth repeating here. But in the end, he let me go. Said it was my call."

"What happened?"

"I ran my fire team across the beach, took up firing positions in the palms, and surprised the enemy emplacement. My idea worked. CO said it saved the platoon. Bottom line is, my CO wasn't writing my destiny, and neither was my enemy. I was."

Awen caught herself staring into his green eyes longer than she'd intended. She looked down and sipped her tea some more.

"Listen, Awen. I get feeling like you're not in control. Like, other people think you're crazy for doing what you do. And I get wanting to give up. I do. And you know what? You can. No one is stopping you. But I'm not sure you realize what's about to happen—what *has* happened."

"And what's that?"

"We're at war. I don't mean a clash with some small-sector rebels; I mean all-out war. A war that I'm not sure we're going to be able to win. You and I both know that the Jujari lead the largest non-Repub alliance in the galaxy. So, whatever's on that stardrive, and whatever the mwadim saw in you, you'd better make it count, because that may be the only play you have left. You're in charge of your own destiny, so live it before someone else kills it."

12

Abimbola knew something was wrong as soon as he saw the orange glow hanging over the Dregs. Berouth slowed the skiff as it crested a bluff so they could survey the scene below. Flames and billowing smoke rose from the center of the city and stretched into the night sky like the torrent of some violent funeral pyre. Abimbola lifted himself out of his seat to hear klaxons blaring and the cries of a city in upheaval.

"What happened?" Berouth asked.

"They are after her," Abimbola replied, more to himself than to his second-in-command. "Come on, let us go."

The skiff entered the city limits and fought against a rush of pedestrians and vehicles flowing in the opposite direction.

Berouth did his best to point the skiff to the city center, as Abimbola was increasingly confident that the fire had begun in his warehouse.

The streets became less crowded with the living and more populated with the dead as Abimbola and Berouth neared the epicenter. Abimbola saw badly burned bodies, some missing limbs, others torn in two. This hadn't been a fire; this had been a detonation, and the flames were just the aftermath. *More explosives*, he thought, his mind connecting this violence to that in the mwadim's tent.

Whoever had terrorized the mwadim's meeting had done this too—Abimbola was sure of it. But was the girl worth so much devastation? *Perhaps.* He thought of all the women whose lovers had decimated entire worlds for their sake. But maybe they weren't after the girl. Maybe they were after the stardrive and believed that whatever was on it was worth killing innocent lives for.

Abimbola thought of his men, most of whom, he feared, were now lost. And if any of them had survived, they wouldn't be alive for much longer. Still, he wouldn't be the one to abandon them. He wouldn't be the one to go back on his pledge to protect them.

"Let us go on foot from here." Abimbola leaped from the skiff as it slowed. He drew his bowie knife and headed down a side street to avoid the worst of the heat. The roar of the flames moving through the tops of the buildings sounded like a stampede of Limbian granthers on their way to a new watering hole.

Despite the likelihood that the bombers were long gone,

Abimbola kept his head on a swivel, eyes searching for prey. The last thing he wanted was to be picked off by some low-rate sniper, all because he had been too hasty to return to his men. *He'd seen too many good warriors lost that way*. He hadn't survived this long by luck alone.

Abimbola and Berouth made two more turns before they approached the remains of the hideout. The building now resembled the charred skeleton of a defeated behemoth, its metal spine and ribs twisted from the force of a blast, the corrugated flesh chewed away by flames. Abimbola felt the ruins' pulsing heat against his skin, the blackened metal glowing a dark red near the worst of the tears.

"Look for survivors," he said. "But do not expect to find any. Meet back here once you have done what you can. And be careful."

"Yes, my lord," Berouth said.

They moved into the derelict building, picking their way through the wreckage. Abimbola used his knife to move debris aside and pry apart sheet metal. Fortunately, the worst of the fire had already consumed most of what was available to burn, but the heat and burnt rubble made searching difficult.

Twice, his boots stepped on humanoid corpses. At first, he thought they were merely the contents of a supply room or blown-up refrigeration unit. He cursed, kneeling to identify the remains he'd desecrated, but it was no use. The bodies were so damaged that as far as he could tell, they could have been one of the game carcasses from the hunting grounds of his youth. He closed his eyes, made the sign of blessing, and moved on.

It wasn't until he neared the former holding cell where Awen and Magnus had been kept that he heard the first scratching sound of a survivor. He moved toward the toppled metal wall of the cell and started ripping at it with his knife. Abimbola pried away a corrugated plate to reveal the ash-covered face of his prison guard, the one Magnus had called Weasel.

"Hey, boss," the man said in a daze, squinting in the orange glow. "Is that... really you?"

"Yes, yes," Abimbola replied. "Hold on, let me—"

"I don't want to die, boss." The man started crying. Tears created fresh pink lines on his blackened face. "*Splick*, I don't want to die."

"I know you don't," Abimbola said, trying his best to comfort the man but not wanting to lie to him either. He'd seen too many well-meaning people tell those doomed to death that they were going to be all right. He never understood how lying to someone in their last moments of life was honorable. "Did you see who did this to you?" Abimbola hoped to help the man get his mind off the inevitable and provide something useful.

"They were... were..." Weasel coughed globular clumps of red from his mouth, then his eyes went wide in terror as if looking as some demonic apparition.

"Were what? What were they?"

"Ruthless. I was so afraid."

"Who were?"

"Blasters. Anyone they didn't kill, they..." The guard coughed again, wincing in pain. "Interrogated. Wanted to know where the Luma was. Stardrive."

"What did they look like?"

"Said if we didn't tell them, they'd torch the city."

"What did they look like?" Abimbola asked again. "What can you tell me?"

"But I didn't tell them, boss. I didn't crack. So they cracked my ribs. Spine."

Abimbola lowered his head, knowing the guard was moments from death. In truth, he couldn't believe the man had survived at all. "Well done," Abimbola said. "I am proud of you. Any idea who sent them?"

"Darkness. They were darkness."

"Darkness?"

"And black armor," the guard said, his voice fading. "White lines." He started choking, head tossing, eyelids flitting in a spasm. "Please! I don't want to die."

Then the man's face froze in place, suspended in a state of fear. Abimbola reached out and closed the corpse's eyes and made the sign of blessing for the departing soul.

Black armor with three white stripes on the shoulder—Abimbola knew that look. He had seen it before, as if in a dream. He'd been a boy then, hoisted into an air ventilation shaft and told to stay put and not come out until two sunrises after he heard the last blaster shot ring out. The caring people, the ones who resembled Awen, spoke to him and tried to reassure him that everything was going to be okay, that nothing was going to happen to him. But he sensed their fear. He knew they were all going to die. *They're coming*, he heard them whisper to each other. *Try not to make any sound.*

"I believe they left the system on a highly modified light freighter." The trooper in the holo-projection wore a sleek helmet that looked more like the nose of a racing sled than a Marine bucket. The black full-face shield reflected a spotlight from the hoverbot that transmitted the video link.

Admiral Wendell Kane inclined his chin, insisting the report go on.

"Katana class," added the trooper. "Most likely headed to Worru."

Kane nodded. "Plumeria."

"That would be my guess, sir."

"Good work."

"Thank you, Admiral."

"Any witnesses?" Kane asked.

"All loose ends have been taken care of."

"Good. Level the warehouse, and then get back to the ship. Your work there is complete."

"Right away, sir."

Kane swiped the channel closed and looked to his XO. "Ready the *Peregrine* and her crew, then prepare a course for Worru. I'll depart the moment Captain Nos Kil and his platoon return and are aboard the *Peregrine*."

"Aye, sir," the XO said, but then he hesitated.

"What is it?" Kane asked.

"You plan to go after them without any assets on Worru, sir?"

Kane smiled at the man but without any genuine mirth. "Who said I didn't have assets on Worru?"

The XO stared for a moment then nodded and walked away.

Kane turned to face the observation windows, his gloves squeaking as he made fists behind his back. "We'll have the coordinates soon enough. Soon enough. And then the long slumber will be over."

13

The Stones had been aboard *Destiny's Carriage* for exactly two days when Piper started to have the visions. The ship sailed through subspace, bound for an obscure water-covered moon in the outskirts of the Theophanies system, and without a playmate, Piper soon found she was terribly bored. She was curled up in the crash couch in her quarters, drawing on her holo-pad, with Talisman acting as half companion, half pillow.

The picture Piper drew consisted of three people standing on a mountain, looking over a picturesque valley. To one side of the green expanse lay a vast ocean, and to the opposite was a forest. Her mind had begun to wander when suddenly, the drawing came to life. It was not that the lines were animated, as all art programs could do, but that the lines became *real*. Piper was no longer looking at a little girl who held the hands of her parents; she *was* the little girl. Immersed in the image, she was aware of the wind playing with her hair, the warm sunlight dancing across her skin, and her mother and father holding her hands in theirs. She couldn't see their faces, but she knew they were there, were real, and that they loved her.

Far below them, stretching to the horizon, lay the valley. Wild horses raced through it while sea creatures splashed in the ocean and birds flocked in twisting swirls over the forest. The moment felt as real as any she'd ever had—perhaps more real.

Then the sunlight dimmed, and a cold breeze pricked Piper's skin. She shivered, drawing herself close to her parents. She watched as the sea creatures disappeared, the birds dove into the trees, and the horses made for cover. Something evil was coming.

She felt her parents pulling her, their hands yanking on hers—only they weren't pulling her forward or backward. They were tearing her apart. Piper yelled to them, wondering if in their panic they didn't realize what they were doing to her. Quickly, however, the forces working at her hands became painful, so painful that she screamed. It was as if the darkness grew fangs and bit at the middle of her heart. Her parents were literally tearing her apart.

She screamed again, the pain filling her with fear, until she realized that she could no longer hear her own voice. It was as if her mouth were covered with a muzzle: no matter how hard she thrashed her head about, she couldn't shake it free.

She felt powerless, at the mercy of the two people she loved and trusted more than any in the cosmos, at the mercy of their warring hands and lack of concern for her torment.

Stop! Stop! she cried over and over. *You're hurting me! You're* killing *me!* But they could not hear her any more than she could hear herself.

It was then that fear swallowed her like a gaping maw that formed in the ground beneath her feet as if the mountain wanted to swallow her whole. No, it *was* swallowing her whole, pulling her through its gullet, into a stomach devoid of light and beauty. She grasped at the stones around her, fingers digging into the throat of rock that gave way to the shadowy depths below. There was only darkness and fear—the fear of being alone and never being discovered again.

Lost. I'm really, truly lost and alone.

"Piper? What's wrong, sweetie? Baby, you have to wake up. Piper!"

Piper jolted awake. She sat on her acceleration couch, Talisman under her head, holo-pad clenched in her hands. She looked up at her mother. "Mama?"

"Piper, baby! You were dreaming."

"It was… it was horrible."

"A nightmare, love," Valerie said, smoothing back Piper's hair with the warm flat of her hand. "But you're okay now. I got you."

"It was real."

"No, baby. Those dreams aren't real."

Piper became indignant and sat up a little. "No, Mama. It *was* real. I felt it." She shook her head. "I was *there*."

"Baby, you just—"

"Mama!" Piper sat upright. "You don't understand! I was there."

Valerie looked at her daughter and took a deep breath. "Okay, my love. You were there, but now you're here, see? Wherever it was you were, that place is gone, and now you're here with me. With Talisman. Look," she said, grabbing the stuffed animal and placing it in Piper's arms. "He's with you. And everything's okay, my heart. I've got you." Valerie wrapped her arms around Piper and squeezed.

Piper could feel her heart pounding in her chest, sweat beading on her forehead. No matter how much her mother insisted otherwise, she *had* been there, wherever *there* had been. On that mountain, looking over *that* valley and sinking into *that* mountain. She envisioned herself falling down, down, down within the throat of that terrible mountain beast, hands grasping at the stone walls, hoping for something to hold on to. But it all broke away, and she fell into the darkness.

Then she felt something in her hands beneath the holo-pad. Something loose and wet. She wasn't *there* anymore. She was definitely *here* with her mother, with Talisman between her arms. Piper pulled the holo-pad away and looked in her palms, letting Talisman drop to the side. There were bits of rock and dust mixed with blood from her fingertips.

14

"THE CAPTAIN WOULD LIKE to inform you that we are nearly there," TO-96 said from the lounge doorway.

"Thank you, Ninety-Six," Awen replied, looking up from her conversation with Magnus. The bot hesitated and started to turn back. She wondered if she had been too hard on him in sick bay. "Hey, listen. Do you want to come sit with us?"

"Why, Madame Luma dau Lothlinium, I would be delighted." He shuffled toward them, and Magnus gestured toward the open bench seat beside him.

"I don't suppose you want any tea?" Magnus asked with a smirk.

"Ha, ha, ha," came TO-96's mechanical laugh. "That's a good one, Lieutenant Magnus." The bot looked back at Awen. "I must say, it is truly a joy to have you both on board. It's not often we get guests. In fact, the last time we had guests was precisely one hundred four days, sixteen hours, twenty-three minutes, and forty-eight point six two nine seven seven—"

"We get it," Awen and Magnus said at the same time. They looked at each other in surprise.

"My apologies," TO-96 said. "Ezo often grows weary of my accuracy as well. Anyway, I'm afraid the trip did not end well for those clients."

"And why's that?" Magnus asked.

"It turns out our clients were wanted in three systems."

"Sounds like your boss didn't do his homework, then."

"No, no, he did. Our clients had done a masterful job at recoding their records. In truth, I had missed it myself until I discovered a modular algorithm variation in the compression codec."

"A what?" Magnus asked.

"A pattern," Awen explained.

"That's correct!" TO-96 exclaimed, pointing at her. "Well done, Madame Luma dau Lothlinium."

"That's such a mouthful, Ninety-Six. Do you mind calling me Awen?"

"Very well, Awen it is."

"So, what happened to these clients of yours?" Magnus asked. "You turned them in?"

"Turned them in? Why, no, Lieutenant. That would break the third universal rule of bounty hunting."

Magnus jerked back, eyeing the bot with something between skepticism and incredulity. "There are rules for bounty hunting?" He looked to Awen. "You know about this?"

Awen laughed. "Nope. Now I'm curious."

"The third rule states that under no circumstances shall a bounty hunter ever go back on his, her, or its word for the initially stated intent of the contract, regardless of any provisos that may otherwise place the contractor in financial, corporal, or mortal peril."

Magnus laughed out loud. "So you're telling me that bounty hunters have a code?" He shook his head. "And here I thought they were just out for themselves."

"Oh, some are, Lieutenant. That is quite true. But they are untrustworthy."

"This is fantastic," Magnus said, clearly entertained.

"I'm not sure I understand your conclusion, sir. These types of bounty hunters have the lowest earning potential and are, more often than not, wanted by governing agencies, former clients, and other bounty hunters. Moreover, their life expectancy is minimal. Therefore, *fantastic* is not an accurate descriptor."

Awen laughed at the exchange, delighted by the unexpected levity. She liked this bot if for nothing more than making Magnus laugh. Seeing a battle-hardened Marine interact with a high-functioning android unit was pure poetry—awkward poetry, but poetry nonetheless.

"We're going to have to agree to disagree, bot," Magnus replied. "I'm sticking with *fantastic*."

"Very well," TO-96 said. "The *fantastic* clients were deposited on their planet of choice, which ended rather poorly for them."

"But not for you," Magnus concluded.

"That's correct, sir. We were paid before delivering them, and we escaped without taking too much damage to our ship."

"*Too much* damage?"

"*Geronimo Nine* is equipped with an impressive array of armaments. You've also no doubt noticed that my master has modified me with state-of-the-art weaponry."

"I see that, yes," Magnus said.

TO-96 lifted his forearm in front of Magnus. "Would you like to touch my missiles?"

"Would I like to touch your—what? No!"

Awen burst out laughing, tears welling in the corners of her eyes. "Don't worry," she said between fits. "He asked me the same thing."

"Keep your missiles to yourself, bot." Magnus shoved TO-96's arm away.

"Very well, sir."

Awen was still doubled over, laughing so hard that her injuries pained her. "I have not laughed this hard in a long time." She wiped her eyes with the back of her hand. "It hurts."

"I'm glad you're enjoying yourself."

When Awen finally caught her breath and composed herself, Magnus looked back at TO-96. "So, aside from your armaments, what else has your master done to you?"

TO-96 hesitated. Awen realized he was filtering his answer.

"The armaments are all, sir," TO-96 said.

"He's lying," Ezo said from the doorway. "Just following orders, though." Heads turned to watch the captain stroll over and take a seat next to Awen. "His AI has expandable architecture. Clients almost never notice. Which is a shame, as TO-96 is Ezo's crowning achievement."

"Expandable architecture?" Magnus asked. "As in, his AI is giving itself new directives besides the ones you programmed it to have?"

"That's pretty much the sum of it, yes. Not bad."

"*You* did this?" Awen asked.

Ezo nodded. "It's taken nearly ten common years and every extra credit Ezo could siphon. But yeah, Ezo did this. Well, *we* did this," he amended, indicating TO-96.

"Thank you, sir."

"A true unrestricted AI," Magnus mumbled. "In a single bot. That's—"

"Illegal?" Ezo asked. "Quite so. The only thing scarier to the Republic than an autonomous android is a bot with an infinitely learning AI."

"Then how's it not considered sentient?" Magnus asked. "I mean, it's not—*he's* not—sentient, right?" He glanced at TO-96.

"You'd have to ask him that," Ezo replied with a smirk.

"That means he's banned throughout the galaxy," Awen remarked.

Magnus nodded. "Which makes him—"

"One of a kind, sir," TO-96 said. "As are you both, I might add."

"He's even self-deprecating," Awen said with a smile. She studied the bot for a moment. "Do you feel lonely, then?"

TO-96 tilted his head. "I'm not sure I understand the question."

"Does being the only one of your kind in the galaxy, maybe even in the universe, make you feel lonely?"

"I suppose I've never thought of that, Awen. I find Ezo's companionship quite acceptable."

"Thank you, Ninety-Six." Ezo gave the bot a pat on its shoulder.

"Though, now that you mention it, meeting others of my kind could be rather… stimulating."

"Hey," Ezo said with mock outrage.

"I do apologize, Captain," TO-96 said. "I meant no ill will. Protecting your *ass*, as you call it, is certainly thrilling. But if there were others like me, I would surely enjoy meeting them."

"Remind me to build you a girlfriend," Ezo replied.

"Duly noted, sir."

Ezo addressed Awen and Magnus. "Ninety-Six here is Ezo's insurance and guardian angel. Been through plenty of hell together. You can't be too careful in this line of business. In any case, you're both very perceptive. You work together a lot?"

Magnus laughed and looked at Awen. "Yeah… no."

"You should consider it," Ezo said. "You make a good team, it seems. Anyway, Ezo would appreciate it if you kept your observations to yourself. Best not to let the Repub know, as none of their engineers would be able to sleep at night."

"Copy that," Magnus said. "I'm not sure I'll be able to either."

"Thank you for your discretion, sir," TO-96 added.

"No problem."

"And in exchange," Ezo said to Awen, "Ezo won't tell anyone that you're carrying a stardrive."

Awen didn't even flinch. "What stardrive?"

Ezo winked at her.

"Sir," the bot said, "I believe that—"

"Yeah, yeah—we're about to jump out of subspace." Ezo turned to Awen and Magnus. "Did I mention that hyperintelligent companions with advanced powers can also be—"

"A royal pain in the ass?" Magnus said, eyeing Awen. "I know the feeling."

"WE KNOW EACH OTHER, don't we?" Magnus said to Ezo. He rarely played a card in his hand without being assured that he knew what he was doing. Seeing as how he would most likely never see the bounty hunter again, however, he had to ask. They stood alone on *Geronimo Nine*'s bridge. They would be orbiting Worru for several more minutes.

"Know each other? Ezo and the lieutenant?"

Magnus waited for the captain to finish his own question. It was an awkward tactic but effective.

Ezo shook his head, seeing that Magnus wasn't going to jump in. "I think Ezo would remember a trigger-happy trooper."

"Trigger-happy?"

"You did almost blow Ezo away over a simple handshake."

"You wanted to do a little more than shake it, as I recall."

"So you remember *that* but not if you've met Ezo?"

"Never mind," Magnus said, waving a hand. "Listen, I'm leaving, but I want you to do me a favor."

"A favor? More than take you halfway across the galaxy on Ezo's own credits? Ezo doesn't—"

"They were Abimbola's credits. And I can always tell him that you did a lousy job."

"No, no." Ezo waved his hands. "That's fine. What's the favor?"

"Hang out in Plumeria for one more day."

"Come again?"

"Check in on old friends, rustle up a new job, you know—bounty-hunter stuff. Whatever."

"Bounty-hunter stuff? That's not a thing."

"It is now. Just hang out for one more day in case she needs you. Got it?"

Ezo placed a hand on his chest, a smile growing on his face. "*Needs* me? You think she might *need* me?"

"Careful. I'm trigger happy, remember?"

Ezo's smile disappeared. "What's in it for Ezo?"

Magnus had been afraid he might ask that. Ezo was a glorified fence, after all. *No one gets past this sort without a fee.* "Let's just say I'll owe you one."

"As in, a favor?"

Magnus closed his eyes and shook his head. "Something like that, yes."

"Ezo can hang out one more day. Plus, Plumeria is lovely this time of year."

"That it is," Magnus said, knowing that the weather on

Plumeria never changed. It was beautiful *every* time of year. He eyed the man. "Thank you, Ezo."

"Happy to help."

"You thinking of opening it before you leave?" Magnus asked her. They stood in the cargo bay, preparing to disembark, while Ezo and TO-96 conducted their postflight checklist.

The landing on Worru had been uneventful, aside from Awen's ritual of taking a purloined vomit bag from TO-96 and filling it. She and Magnus had joined Ezo on the bridge as they touched down, admiring the city's blend of ancient and modern architecture. The result, Awen always noted, was a city birthed from antiquity but formed by the future. Hand-cut sandstone ribbed high-density pyraglass towers like sail battens, while granite arches supported iridescent plastigon domes that filled the city with color. Whenever Awen left Worru, she felt homesick, and whenever she returned, the world was right again. Worru felt like home.

Like Elonia? she asked herself. *No. Elonia never felt like home.*

She waited a beat, giving the voice in her head a chance to argue. But it didn't. And why should it? Worru had been her home for the last six years—the best six years of her life, when she'd learned so much and had been permitted to dive into her research and form her own worldview on justice and the preservation of galactic cultures. Not only that, but she had thrived and become… *What? An asset to the Order?* Awen could only hope as much. But more than that, she wanted to be an asset to the cultures she was called to serve. But had she really served the Jujari? Or had she just been part of beginning their genocide?

That wasn't my fault. That's not how the pursuit of galactic peace is supposed to work out.

"Awen?"

Her eyes snapped up to Magnus's. He stood beside her, holding his helmet and blaster.

"You all right?" he asked.

"Yeah, I was just…" She shook her head.

"So, are you going to open it?"

"No, the Order's rules don't permit me to." She finished securing the stardrive in a small leather satchel that Ezo had given her. "It was entrusted to me by way of my occupation as a Luma. That is sacred and eclipses whatever individual interests I may have."

"I can respect that. Although, it *is* a stardrive. When will you ever see one again?"

"All the more reason to get this back to the Order. It's well above my pay grade"—she tapped a finger on his armor—"and yours, trooper, if I'm not mistaken."

Magnus sighed. "Fair enough."

Awen put the strap over her head and patted the satchel on her hip. "So, you headed back, then?"

"To Oorajee? Probably. I'll report to the sector chief here, then they'll contact my battalion commander. He'll decide what to do with me from there. But I'm guessing I'll rejoin my unit over Oorajee—or what's left of it, anyway."

"What's left of your unit or what's left of Oorajee?"

"Both," Magnus said. A look of anger and sorrow washed over his face.

"I'm sorry for those you've lost," she said, lowering her voice.

"And I for yours," Magnus replied, looking into her eyes with something like…

What? Genuine care? Or is it desire? she thought then scolded herself. *Don't be foolish. Why would you want that, anyway?*

"Chances are, we'll be seeing action around that system for years to come," Magnus added.

"Years?" Awen snapped out of her thoughts. "Really?"

"Really."

The two of them looked at each other for a moment, then Awen turned her head. *Why does he keep looking at me?* "They're expecting me. So I guess this is goodbye."

"Yup."

"Yup. And I just wanted to say thanks again for, you know, all of the protecting. You can tell your commanding officers that you did well."

"We don't really self-report that kind of thing, but I still appreciate it," Magnus said.

"Yeah, well, maybe I'll put in a good word for you with… whoever it is I have to put in a good word with."

"You do that, Awen. And thank you for saving me too."

"You're welcome. Just be careful telling your troopers that a Luma kept you alive. That might not go over too well."

"I think I'll keep that to myself."

Awen extended her hand. "Take care of yourself," she said, chin raised.

Magnus looked at her hand and paused.

Why isn't he shaking it? Her mind raced through a myriad of cultural protocols. Wasn't shaking hands still an accepted form of professional interaction in humanoid relationships? *Yes, yes. Of course it is.*

Finally, Magnus removed his glove and took her hand. His eyes lit up as she placed a small piece of paper between their palms. Awen liked that she had surprised him by using the Marines' military tradition of exchanging challenge coins in a handshake.

"Take care," she repeated.

"Take care," he replied as the ramp door cracked open and let in the Worruvian sun's warm light. He palmed the paper and replaced his glove. Awen watched as he walked out of the ship and passed two Luma escorts who waited on the landing pad. He tipped his head to both, replaced his helmet, and disappeared around the side of the ship.

15

The two Luma escorts bowed to Awen and informed her that Master So-Elku requested an audience with her at once. She thanked them and asked them to wait. "I need to settle things with the captain." They nodded and walked back to the transport skiff. Awen returned up the loading ramp and found TO-96 stowing crates in the cargo bay. "Have you seen Ezo?"

"He will be down shortly, Awen. It's time for you to leave, I take it."

"That it is."

"I see." He stood upright and walked toward her, extending his hand. "Please accept my warmest regards. It has been inspirational making your acquaintance."

"Inspirational," she repeated with a chuckle, reaching to shake his hand. "I need to meet more people like you."

"More *people*, Awen? I think you have me confused with a sentient."

"The way I see it, Ninety-Six, if we could all learn to be a little more thoughtful like you, the galaxy would be a better place. And for your sake, I hope you find others like you out there in the cosmos."

The bot recoiled, head turning side to side, then looked back at Awen. "Why, I don't even know what to say, Awen. Thank you."

"You're welcome," she said, smiling. She could have sworn she saw the bot blush.

"Leaving so soon?" came Ezo's voice from up a side stairwell. He let his hands slide down the rails and took the steps three at a time. "What a shame to bid farewell to our prettiest client in—what would you say, Ninety-Six? A year common?"

"Based on your promiscuous activity with that Dellophinian last week, I'd say it was more like—"

"And that's enough of that." Out of the corner of his mouth, Ezo whispered, "It was a rhetorical question, you wire brain."

"In any case," Awen said, stifling a laugh, "I wanted to thank you for your hospitality and the use of your ship." She looked down at her clothes. "Should I get these back to you?"

"Please keep them. And think of Ezo fondly," he said with a wink.

"Charming." Awen suddenly savored the thought of getting into new robes and burning Ezo's clothes. "Will business keep you on Worru for any length of time?"

"Just long enough to refuel and take on some minor supplies.

Maybe secure a job worth paying for this jaunt, you know. Just the usual bounty-hunting stuff." Ezo seemed oddly anxious.

"Bounty-hunting stuff? That's a thing?"

"It is now."

"Well, I hope you find compensation. And please be sure to relay my thanks to Abimbola the next time you see him."

"Ezo most certainly will."

"But, sir," TO-96 interrupted, "I thought you said you never wanted to see the warlord again."

"Rhetorical," Ezo seethed between clenched teeth.

"Safe travels, then," Awen replied. "May you find the desires of your heart in the unity of all things." She waved her hand over them in the sign of the Luma and bowed.

Ezo tried to mimic the gesture, but the effort was clumsy. As Awen walked away, he said, "And may you find your unity in unifying your desires by—"

"You don't need to say anything back, sir," TO-96 whispered.

"Splick. Thank you. That was awkward."

Sunlight flashed between sandstone colonnades as the skiff moved quickly through the interconnected plazas. Luma crisscrossed the open squares en route to any number of destinations, from lecture halls to practice chambers. Others walked along cloisters and moved in and out of their cells.

Awen drew in a deep breath of the flower-scented air and savored the sweet smell. It felt good to be home. It was almost as if she'd never even left, such was the pleasant pace of life here. *Only now Plumeria is missing some of her most beautiful souls.* Awen saw the second-story windows of the classroom where Elder Toochu taught first years the fundamentals of meditation. That was where she'd first met Matteo. She imagined him sitting beside the fountain where they spent evenings discussing particle physics—one of her favorite pastimes when not immersed in all things Jujari. He was one of the few people who never laughed at her for geeking out over string theory or advanced quantum dynamics. *I'll never have that again.* Her heart ached.

The skiff turned into a wide circular thoroughfare that led up to the Grand Arielina, the structure that the Luma had esteemed as their core sanctuary since antiquity. Bordered by colorful gardens and flowing streams, the building seemed as though it were hewn from a single block of sandstone stretching several hundred meters into the azure sky. Moreover, unlike other buildings, which betrayed the angular manipulations of cutting torch and diamond blade, the Arielina looked as though it had grown up from the ground itself.

The foundation undulated like the base of massive trees, rising to gentle archways and porticos. The structure continued skyward, providing cover for increasingly smaller verandas before morphing into spires made of twisted stone branches. Brilliant iridescent orbs punctuated the spires and could be seen from almost any point in the city, while a single waterfall cascaded down from among the orbs, redirected at various landings, and finally splashed into a massive pool below the building's main steps.

The two escorts climbed out of the skiff and helped Awen stand. They walked beside her, moving up the grand steps to the sounds of splashing water. How Awen wished she could jump in and rinse herself of the memories of the last days.

At the top of the steps, the escorts bowed and left her in the care of Elder Willowood. The old woman wore Luma robes, but that was where her similarity to other elders ended. She donned a dozen bangles on each wrist and just as many necklaces, each abounding with gold and colorful stones. As attractive as the baubles were, her aging blue eyes radiated even more brilliantly. And capping it all was a mass of wiry gray hair that made her look as if she'd been unwittingly charged by an energy pack.

"Awen," Willowood said, moving to embrace her. "What a joy it is to see—"

Awen cut her off, fell into the elderly woman's arms, and began to weep. She hadn't expected to break down here in the open, but when she saw Willowood, it was like a dam that had grown too fatigued from having to hold back a body of water had finally given way. One minute, the structure looked sound; the next it had broken apart and let through a flood of tears.

Willowood was safe. Not that any of the other elders weren't, but the two of them had formed a special bond the first day they'd met. And in a place as overwhelmingly cerebral and intellectually diverse as Plumeria, connecting meaningfully with others was important. It kept the soul grounded to the beauty of personal relationship when it could easily be lost in the chaos of galactic cosmology. In fact, given the rift that had developed between Awen and her mother, Willowood had become like a surrogate mother. Awen had often wondered if the elder didn't *get* her more than anyone else in the galaxy—maybe even more than she got herself. All the emotions Awen had kept bottled up poured out onto Willowood, tears turning the elder's robes deeper shades of maroon and black.

"There, there," Willowood said, rubbing her old hands along Awen's back. "You're safe now."

"But Matteo," Awen whimpered. She wanted to crawl into a hole and die. The pain stood on her chest like a pillar of granite. "He's gone."

"Yet he lives in the Unity of all things," Willowood replied. "From one form to another, and you will see him again. But what's done is done, and Matteo's part is over." She pushed Awen's shoulders up, held her biceps with aged hands, and looked her in the eye. "Your part, however, is just beginning."

"But I don't want to do this anymore," Awen confessed. "It's too much. It wasn't supposed to go like that, and I don't want the chance for anything like that to happen again. It's got to be over for me. It's over."

"That is a choice you can make, dear, yes. And no one would blame you for it." Willowood let go of Awen. "The time has come for you to stand on your own two feet and make your mark on the galaxy, Awen. You cannot control what is done to you, just like you could not stop those people from dying."

"But—"

Willowood silenced her with a raised finger. "The only thing you get to control is your today. You choose, and the universe responds. The Unity can no more control you than you can control it. In the end, all you can control is yourself, and that is enough business for several lifetimes."

"But those poor people didn't even get to live out one lifetime." Awen wiped the knit turtleneck's sleeve across her face. "It was terrible. It wasn't supposed to go like that."

Willowood sighed, holding Awen's arms again. "No, it wasn't supposed to go like that at all. We saw the holo-feed the Republic forwarded." The old woman grimaced. "I'm so sorry, dear."

"All their bodies, and the fire, it… did the report say if anyone—"

"There will be time for grieving the dead, Awen. But not now."

"Wait. You're saying no one survived?" She felt torn apart by the look of immense sadness in Willowood's graying eyes. Awen searched them for some sort of reprieve, some sort of reassurance, but found none.

"I'm so very sorry," her mentor said.

Awen swallowed the lump in her throat. "So am I."

"Listen," Willowood said, brushing Awen's sleeves with her hands. "You need to compose yourself. You need to finish your mission and make a final statement. Meet with Master So-Elku. Then we can mourn together and figure out the future."

"I would like that," Awen said, trying her best to rein in her emotions. Her eyes felt puffy, and her ribs ached. "I would like that very much."

"Good. Now, then, let's get you to Elder's Hall. So-Elku arranged a private audience."

"Alone?"

"He figured it would be too much for you to address everyone. I agreed. Although, So-Elku…"

But Willowood never finished her thought.

"So-Elku what?" Awen asked.

"It's nothing." The old woman waved her hand. "He's been under a lot of stress lately, that's all."

"Well, it's kind of him to grant me an audience without all the other elders," Awen said. "I don't think I could handle that many people right now."

"And so it is. Come, let's walk."

Awen was grateful for Willowood's arm. Still, Awen couldn't shake the feeling that something was bothering her mentor. The two of them strode through the central hall as birds chirped in the upper arches. The calls tried to lift Awen's soul away from the shadows that plagued her. But she was pulled back down, the sound of her boots clumping along the marble floor—boots in the mwadim's palace—reminding her of death. It was as if clinging to Willowood's arm somehow kept her from falling back to Oorajee.

"Do you think I can change my clothes first?"

"Change? You do look rather fetching in street clothes, you know." Willowood cast her a wry smile. Awen laughed and felt her mood lift ever so slightly. "Never mind me. To answer your question, yes, we'll get you to the hospital as soon as So-Elku is finished with you, and I'll prepare new robes and slippers for you."

"*After* So-Elku, though? Must it wait?"

"I'm afraid so, dear."

"Very well," Awen replied.

"Thank you, Elder Willowood." So-Elku bowed to the woman, his green-and-black robes brushing the floor. He offered Awen his arm as Willowood backed away. The massive wooden doors started to move. Awen felt them close behind her with a deep *whoomph*.

Awen found herself in the vaulted room of Elder's Hall, a spartan circular space whose perimeter was lined with hundreds of seat cushions and whose domed ceiling was a holo-projection of the entire galaxy. Each cushion on the floor was reserved for an elder who had achieved Seventh Level and served a star system. Awen hoped she would be permitted such an honor one day. Until then, she only had access to this hall when she was being assessed or in certain cases, such as when she'd been commissioned to lead the Jujari mission.

It felt very strange to be back. The last time she'd been here, the hall had been alive with anticipation and… something else. Her mind raced. *Hope*. Being selected from amongst the Order's very best candidates for what was surely the most important mission in hundreds of years had been the highlight of her life. Now, however, the hall was eerily still with only So-Elku's and her footfalls echoing throughout the cavernous space.

So-Elku walked her to the far side of the room, a curved wall lined with large windowed cutouts. The portals opened to a vibrant garden lined with paths and streams and covered by the broad bows of seratathia trees. Several dozen butterflies danced across the foliage, flitting from one perfect flower to the next. Awen took a deep breath of the moist air and let her shoulders relax. The scene offered to wipe away everything that had happened if she could only stay here, surrounded by the beauty of this place. But she knew such a reprieve was not meant to be.

"That's it," So-Elku said. "You're safe now." He released her arm and turned to look down at her. He had a bald pate but still wore some dark hair tight to the sides and back of his head. The wraparound connected to a thin line of facial hair that rose over his top lip in sharp angles and then ran along his jaw, missing his chin completely. He had dark, penetrating eyes and wrinkles that reinforced the years of intellectual and mystical mastery of the Luma traditions. As the grand master of the Luma, he was the embodiment of their legacy and the director of their future.

"So, you have returned from the other side of the galaxy, young Awen dau Lothlinium. Dare I ask how you are?"

"Right now, I'm tired, Master So-Elku. But I'm happy to be home."

"I'll have you on your way in moments, I promise."

"Thank you." Awen took a deep breath. "I'm sure you have many questions for me, and I still have plenty of my own. While I can only thank you for selecting me for such an important mission, I fear that I've failed you and the Order in ways I can only begin to count."

"My child, please. You have no need to thank us. It is *we* who need to honor *you*."

"But the mission was—"

"Attempted. Sometimes, that is all we can do—*attempt* the improbable and hope for the impossible. You, I would argue, have succeeded at both."

"*Success* is not exactly the word I was thinking of, master. If you had sent someone else, maybe things would have turned out differently."

"If we had sent someone else?" So-Elku let out a small laugh. "I fear the team would have lost their heads long before gaining access to the mwadim's palace. No, Awen," he said, taking her hands, "it is because of you that we got as far as we did. No one, and I mean *no one*, could have done it more skillfully. That is why we sent you, child. Do not think for an instant that we were doing you a favor. We are not so foolish as you may believe."

"I don't believe you're foolish."

"Then trust me when I say that we were doing what was best for the mission."

"Thank you, master." She took another deep breath and rolled her neck, trying to release the tension she felt. "Don't you think someone with more sensitivity than me would have sensed the explosion?"

"A worthy question. But do you so soon forget that you were not alone? I can think of fewer more sensitive elders than Toochu. It was hard to make everything out in the holo-feed that we received, but I didn't see any of your team react as you did. It seems you placed a shield around you and the mwadim? The helmet holo-cam cut out after the detonation."

"Yes," she said, "but it wasn't strong enough to save him. It barely saved me."

"It's a wonder you survived at all, then."

"I wouldn't have, had it not been for a certain Marine." Her thoughts flitted back to Magnus like a butterfly seeing a flower it liked. She had trouble remembering the details of how he'd done it, but she knew he'd saved her and made sure she got out alive when all the others hadn't. "I couldn't save them," she added. "I couldn't even save myself."

"That may be the case, but you were the right emissary, and you had the right team. Nothing more, Awen. Some things are just out of our control."

"Like the war forming over Oorajee," she said, shaking her head in frustration. She could feel the fatigue betraying her emotions, which were coming to the surface more quickly now.

"Yes," So-Elku said, lowering his head. "That is unfortunate. I fear that we may never…" The master lost himself in thought. Awen wasn't sure if she should interrupt him. Suddenly, his eyes snapped back to her face. "Forgive me, child. Sometimes I lose myself in the Unity."

"You don't need to apologize," she said, putting her hands on a smooth sandstone ledge. The two of them stood, observing the flowers and butterflies under the shade of the seratathia trees. Awen soaked it all in, looking forward to a long night's sleep after her medical review. She was so tired.

"I did notice Ambassador Bosworth speaking with you before the mwadim called you to his dais."

"That's correct, yes."

"May I ask what he said?"

"You may ask anything you wish, master, of course. He threatened me."

"Threatened you?"

"Yes. He said he would hunt me down if I gave the mwadim the microdrive with my research."

"No one likes their secrets used against them," So-Elku said. "Best never to keep any."

"As you've said." Awen yawned, excused herself, and covered her mouth with her sleeve. *Am I really this tired, or is there something in the air?* Her body yearned for a bed. Any bed. "Master So-Elku, is there anything further you need from me? I don't mean to be rude, but I would like to get checked out, and then I just want to sleep for a while. May we reconvene tomorrow? Perhaps even later today?"

"Of course, my child." He turned, took her other arm, and began walking with her back toward the entrance.

"Thank you, master," Awen said, hoping she didn't sound too enthusiastic about the reprieve.

"Awen, I nearly forgot." So-Elku paused to face her in the middle of the hall. "Would you mind telling me what happened to the stardrive?"

Awen looked at him, curious. "The stardrive?" She had nearly forgotten herself. *Of course! How could I have been so inept?* But the fatigue was dulling her senses, and she could hardly blame herself because of how sleepy she felt.

"Yes, the stardrive from Oorajee," So-Elku clarified. "Where is it?"

Awen was about to reach into the satchel when something

odd occurred to her. "I never mentioned any stardrive, master." She looked into his eyes and noticed the smallest tic in the corner of his mouth.

"Of course, you didn't, child. We saw the mwadim hand it to you."

"Ah, forgive me, master." She reached down to the satchel, opened the flap, and removed the cylinder. So-Elku's eyes darted to the device as Awen offered it to him.

"We both know it's no good to me," he said, palms raised.

Despite his words, Awen felt that he desperately wanted to take it. But it was hard to think, and she yawned a second time. "Should I open it now or wait for the others?"

"You may open it now," he replied.

"Very well." Awen closed her hand around the cylinder and prepared to press the activation button. It contained a small needle that would extract a droplet of blood from under her skin. The device would become inert if it determined a mismatch between her brainwaves and its record of encoding, so she let her thoughts drift back to Oorajee, to Oosafar, and then to the mwadim's palace.

Awen winced as the memory of the explosion sent her sprawling into the mwadim. Her ears rang, and she tasted blood in her mouth. Fire lit up the room like the inside of the sun. She saw the mwadim's face, or what was left of it, and felt the prick in her hand. Then Awen placed her thumb on the stardrive's button, and—

Something was wrong. Not wrong with her memories, but wrong with this *moment, here with So-Elku.*

"What is it, my child?" the master said.

"I'm… I'm having trouble remembering." Awen opened her eyes and saw a trail of sweat on So-Elku's temple.

"Keep going," he replied. "You'll find it. I know it's difficult."

Awen closed her eyes again as she fought against the mounting fatigue. It was impairing her ability to think. Suddenly, she realized her mind wasn't drawing her attention to the events in the mwadim's palace but to something far more recent. *Think, Awen. Think!*

She remembered what the master had said—that it was "hard to make everything out in the holo-feed."

No, that wasn't it. Something else. Why is it so hard to think? She was getting tired of feeling like this. "I feel strange," she said, placing a hand to her head.

"You're just tired, my child. You can rest in a moment once you've opened the drive."

"No," she said. "I'm not tired. I'm… I'm…" She looked at him in surprise. "You're manipulating me!"

"Awen, I think you just need some rest. Finish accessing the—"

"You said that the holo-feed cut out when the bomb detonated. But the mwadim didn't give me the stardrive until *after* the explosion."

"What I meant was—"

"No. You said what you meant to say." Awen was furious, and she let the emotion rise from within her. She withdrew to her center and used the fury to push against the walls that seemed to be constricting her soul. Someone had put them there without her permission.

Awen summoned her strength and felt the Unity swirl within her like a waterspout. Then she pressed her inner world away, causing a blast of energy to surge from her spirit, through her body, and into the room. Her eyes flew open. The wave of power blew against So-Elku's robes and made him step back.

Now Awen was alert—still tired, but alert. She could *see* again, and she knew that So-Elku was not safe.

16

"Why?" Awen asked, her face twisted in disbelief.

So-Elku straightened his arms with a quick snap then stiffened his neck. "These are things beyond your control, Awen. That stardrive is the property of the Luma. Do you think you really could keep it a secret from me?"

"A secret? I wasn't keeping a secret from you. You were dimming my senses! I could feel your mind at work."

"I was *assisting* you."

"Assisting me?" A wave of self-doubt washed over her. This was, after all, Master So-Elku. And she was standing face to face with him, in private, accusing him of lying to her and actively manipulating her mind. Maybe she *was* out of line.

"No." She shook her head, deciding on her course. "If you came to know about the stardrive through honest means, and it was that important to you, all you would have needed to do was ask."

"My child, I wanted to make sure you were all right first," he pleaded.

Awen locked eyes with him. "Who told you about it?"

So-Elku took a step toward her and held out his hand. "Give it to me."

"Who told you about it?"

"Awen, I need you to hand me the stardrive *now*."

"That's not going to happen."

"Then I hold you in contempt of the Order."

"You do that," she said, turning away from him. She'd only taken a step toward the doors when her movement was arrested. She couldn't move her legs or arms. It was as if someone had placed her in a pool of water and flash frozen it around her limbs.

Awen watched So-Elku out of the corner of her eye as he walked around her. "I'm sorry your career has to end with imprisonment," he said with a sudden air of superiority that seemed unlike what she knew of him. "You always were our most promising and inquisitive student, Awen. There's no doubt that you would have become a great elder in your time, perhaps even our greatest."

Was it really ending like this? Did she really just brave all the hostilities of Oorajee only to be imprisoned back on Worru at the hands of a traitor to the Order? *No, this can't be the end.* But she was no match for the master—she knew that. She tried to break his grip on her, but So-Elku's powers were too strong.

"You still have one problem," Awen said.

"Do I?"

"You and I both know you can't coerce me to open the stardrive."

So-Elku coughed out a laugh, shaking his head. "My child, my child. When I'm done with you, neither you nor the drive will have any idea that you didn't open it on your own account." He walked over and removed the device from her satchel.

"No! Don't you touch that!" Awen struggled against his invisible grip but still couldn't move. "That's not yours!"

"It became Luma property the moment the mwadim passed it to you."

How does he know the mwadim handed it to me? The whole thing didn't make sense. No one knew of the drive except a handful of off-world vagabonds. And the only person who knew that the mwadim passed it to her personally was Magnus. Even though she disdained Magnus's choice of occupation, she couldn't picture him being a snitch. Plus, he lacked motive, nor did he have access to the order's grand master. None of it made any sense to her.

"You're no Luma," Awen spat.

"Easy, my child."

"Stop calling me that!"

"Now, now. You need to rest." So-Elku lowered his head. "After all, you've had a long trip." Awen suddenly felt dizzy, a wave of vertigo disorienting her senses.

"No," she mumbled, squinting against a sudden urge to vomit. "Stop this." She felt something press against her hand—*the stardrive*—and her thumb moving atop the button. *This can't be happening.* Awen wished Willowood would rush through the door and rescue her. She tried to center herself, to gather her strength to reach the elder. But it was no use. She was too tired.

"There you are," So-Elku said, "lying beside the mwadim at the back of the dais. The second explosion detonates, and his body slides closer to you. You're barely conscious. Then he places something in your hand…"

The images flashed in front of Awen's eyes as if she were experiencing the episode all over again, only this time, she wasn't lying on the ground but hovering a few meters above the scene. A true out-of-body experience. She didn't want to relive this, yet the images were being forced upon her. Then she noticed that something about the memories didn't feel right. This wasn't *her* spirit watching her body. It was too sterile. Too clinical. Too…

Too robotic, like a hover-bot with a holo-cam. Awen realized she was watching a feed of the events in the mwadim's palace from a drone. These were not *her* memories of the encounter; these were what So-Elku had seen. But who would have been recording her? And why would So-Elku and the Order send a hover-bot? It meant that they *expected* this.

Awen's head ached, and the pain was growing more intense by the second. She wished Willowood was here now more than ever, and her heart began to despair as she realized the master's power was too strong for hers. Awen tried to reassert her will against So-Elku's, but doing so only made her head hurt worse. Still, she had to resist. She would rather *die* than lose like this.

"Don't fight it," So-Elku coaxed her. "You see yourself, don't you? Remember. *Remember.*"

"I… won't… yield."

"Remember!" he yelled at her.

"I won't… yield!"

"*Remember!*"

"I WON'T YIELD!"

From across the room came an elderly woman's voice. "Awen? Master So-Elku, what's going on?"

Awen instantly felt the shackles on her body fall away, and the images vanished. She fell to the ground in a heap, gasping for breath. Willowood had sensed her need after all!

"Leave us!" So-Elku yelled at the woman.

Awen blinked, regaining a sense of her surroundings. The cold marble floor felt good on her palm. Her other hand held the stardrive. She swallowed, suddenly aware of blood dripping from her nose, and looked up to see Elder Willowood standing at the open doors. If Awen was going to have a chance of survival, this was it. "Help me," she mouthed to Willowood.

That was all it took for the elderly woman to spring into action. Defying her aged appearance, Willowood raced forward, dipping her head toward So-Elku in concentration. A wave of power rippled through the air and slammed into the man. It hit him hard enough to make him stumble backward. Willowood kept running and reached a hand toward Awen, who grabbed it and tried to stand, but her legs were too weak.

"Come on, dear. You've got to move."

"I don't—"

Awen and Willowood were sent sprawling, sliding across the smooth floor. Awen felt herself slam into the wooden doors, and a shock of pain wracked her body.

"What do you think you're doing, Willowood?" So-Elku said.

"I'm stopping you from whatever *you're* doing." The woman climbed to her feet. Blood trickled from her forehead.

Willowood looked skyward and tore away a section of the domed ceiling. It fell toward So-Elku, who glanced up, sending the sandstone to one side. That was all the time the old woman needed. Awen watched as So-Elku became constricted as if an invisible vise had pinned his arms to his sides.

"You've got to move," Willowood said to Awen. "That won't hold him for long. Come on."

Willowood helped Awen through the massive doors while So-Elku seethed behind them. The man spewed profanity that stung Awen's ears as if some demon had replaced the spirit of the legendary master's soul. Willowood drew the doors shut and waved her hand to seal them.

"Are you okay?" Willowood asked as she tried to get Awen to run down the main hall.

"I think so. He was, he was—"

"He was hurting you. That's all I need to know."

Awen struggled to keep up with the woman, but each step brought renewed strength. Willowood held her hand as they gained speed, heading back toward the Arielina's entrance. Several passing elders tried to inquire of Willowood, but she ignored them.

"I don't know what you've gotten yourself involved with, dear, but we'd better get you out of here," Willowood said.

"It has to do with—"

"Not now. Listen, whatever So-Elku wants, he's probably not working alone. Do you trust that pilot who brought you here?"

"Captain Ezo? I don't really think—"

"Enough to get you someplace safe?"

"I—suppose." Awen felt Willowood tug her down the steps and into the afternoon sun.

"Good. We're getting you back on that ship."

"So, we have a deal, then?" Ezo asked, his boots crossed atop the cantina table.

"You make a delivery of our shipment to Sorrelle, three days, no questions," confirmed the Faddamo trader, the large gills on his neck rhythmically slurping air. "Two thousand now, three thousand upon completion."

"Sounds like a standard contract. And a pretty good one at that." Ezo stuck his hand out to shake and noticed someone across the cantina looking at him with recognition. Ezo knew he had to wrap things up fast. He also wished he'd not told TO-96 to stay with the ship. "I'll receive your cargo, platform thirty-nine. But can we move the time line up? Ezo just realized that—"

"Idris *splicing* Ezo," came a gruff voice from the bar. "Why, if it isn't the bounty hunter who swindled me out of fifty thousand credits over Fiad Six."

"Gormar, how nice to see you." Ezo kept his right hand extended toward his nearly closed client and placed his other on his blaster for insurance. The gray-skinned gargantuan Diim rose from his seat at the bar—his *two* seats at the bar—and lumbered toward Ezo's table.

"Wait, fifty thousand credits?" the Faddamo asked.

"Thought he was dead," Ezo replied then turned to Gormar. "Thought you were dead."

"I almost was, thanks to you alerting those Republican troopers."

"Don't worry about that," Ezo said to the Faddamo, waving his hand and removing his feet from the table. "It was resolved months ago. This fellow has just had one too many whiskeys."

"I haven't even started drinking," Gormar insisted, getting closer.

Ezo looked back to the Faddamo, desperate for the trader to shake his hand. "So, we have a deal?"

The Faddamo looked between the Diim and Ezo then back again. "I think we'll take our business—"

"Perfect!" Ezo said, slapping the aquatic humanoid's hand. The next instant, Gormar drew his weapon and fired a bolt. Ezo jumped back, knocking his chair over as the blast of energy shredded the table.

Wood fragments peppered Ezo's pants, and the astringent smell of ionized air made his heart race. He always loved a good firefight, and it had been a while since his last one. *Too long*, he mused. Ezo's SUPRA 945 was up and aimed faster than most humanoids could think. He squeezed the trigger, and a white bolt grazed the Diim's shoulder. Ezo didn't want to kill the beastie, after all; there was no need for unnecessary violence. Plus, he never knew when an older client, even a vengefully malicious one hell-bent on tearing his arms off, might be a repeat customer if the circumstances were right. He just wanted to make sure the giant thought twice before interrupting negotiations with a client —should there ever be a next time.

"What'd you do that for?" Gormar shouted, dropping his blaster and grabbing the wound. Patrons screamed as they rushed for the exits, glasses and furniture toppling over. Ezo ignored the Diim and looked to the fish-man.

"Platform thirty-nine! Don't forget!" Ezo yelled.

Gormar grabbed his blaster off the ground and leveled it at him. Another blast tore through Ezo's toppled chair, splinters spraying the floor.

"Thirty-nine!" Ezo exited the cantina and squinted against the sunlight.

"Sir," a voice said in his earpiece, "are you enjoying your jaunt to rustle up some new business?"

"Fire up *Geronimo*, Ninety-Six! I'm coming in hot. Three minutes."

"Marvelous, sir. Hold on, sir." There was some commotion in the background. "I say, we have quite enough fuel already. And don't touch that!"

"Ninety-Six! What's going on?"

"I'm sorry, sir. Bawee technicians are putting their filthy hands all over the ship during refueling. Though I hesitate to classify them as technicians. They're more like—"

"Confirm my last transmission!" A blaster bolt zipped over Ezo's shoulder and smacked into a glass storefront across the street. People shrieked and dove to the ground. While there was no such thing as a seedy part of town in Plumeria, Ezo always managed to find the watering holes where the most disreputable residents congregated. He thought it ironic that the street looked like any upscale thoroughfare in the galaxy even though the cantina was rife with riffraff. *Even the fastest skiff still finds flies*, he mused. "Get the ship ready. We're leaving hot."

"I was just going to suggest the same thing, sir."

Ezo hesitated and fired a shot over his shoulder. "Wait—why?"

"Do you remember the very attractive Luma emissary?"

"Yeah?" Ezo dodged another of Gormar's blaster bolts as more people screamed.

"She's back."

17

"Lieutenant?" the man in the holo-vid said, an urgent tone in his voice.

"Go ahead, Colonel Caldwell," Magnus replied.

Magnus sat in the comm officer's seat of a Sparrow-class LAT —light armored transport—trying to ignore the gawks of the two private first-class Marines. They stood abnormally close to the bridge door, acting as if there was some important business with the keypad or magnetic door sliders. He didn't blame them—not for the gawking part but the being bored part. On such a small craft, there wasn't much to do. These old ships were used as a last resort for moving small units around quickly. The Sparrows— which resembled a slender bird's beak with split-V tail stabilizers —were fast but lacked anything in the way of comfort. It was no wonder that this was one of the only military transports left for the sector chief's disposal.

"Seems someone else needs your help more than the seventy-ninth," Caldwell said.

Magnus's heart sank. "Colonel, sir. You just—"

"Listen," Caldwell said with a raised hand. "We both know you don't want to be headed anywhere else but Oorajee right now, but this is direct from Brigadier General Lovell. Change of plans, son."

This week can't get any stranger. Magnus nodded at the two privates in the entrance.

AFTER SAYING goodbye to Awen and stepping off *Geronimo*, Magnus pulled up Plumeria's map in his HUD and left the starport. It had been a while since he'd wandered any city alone, much less a thoroughfare in a veritable paradise. He wondered if there would ever be a day when he enjoyed a place this beautiful while *not* in Mark VII armor. He realized, then, how truly out of place he felt—a Republic Marine in full kit walking through a city of diplomats, academics, and students with large endowments. If Plumeria had a nice beach, which reports said it did, he might be back. One day. But not as a Marine. He suspected that moment would be a long time from now—if he even survived the next decade.

Magnus finally arrived at the substation headquarters and reported to the sector chief.

"Well, look who we have here!" The gray-haired officer rose to his feet, clenching the stub of a cigar in his teeth.

"Colonel Caldwell, sir?" Magnus could hardly believe his eyes.

"In the flesh, Lieutenant."

The two men strode across the room and clasped forearms, the more personal greeting of Marines who'd seen battle together.

"I'm—I'm surprised to see you here," Magnus said.

"Really, son?"

"Well, it's just that—"

"You never saw me as a desk jockey? Well, neither did I. Which means you probably don't ever see yourself in an office like this either. All I can say is *get ready*."

"Copy that, sir."

"Let me look at you," Caldwell said, stepping back to size up Magnus. "You look like splick, son."

"And you look like the medals got too heavy, sir." Caldwell's Repub uniform was unusually spartan, given all the accolades Magnus knew the man could have displayed on his chest. But the colonel was among an ever-shrinking minority who consistently placed unit above career. Less fanfare, more warrior. Which was why this office didn't fit what Magnus knew of the man.

"Come on, have a seat." Caldwell gestured to one of two leather seats and took the other himself. "And let's dispense with protocol, Magnus. We're both *sirs* here."

"Copy that. When did you take the promotion to sector chief?"

"They promoted me after Caledonia. I knew my time outside the wire was done, and I was offered any sector I wanted."

"As you should have been. But I gotta ask... Worru?"

Caldwell chuckled and blew out a plume of smoke. "I know what you're thinking, Magnus. Repping the Marines for the Luma isn't where any cold-blooded Midnight Hunter sees himself retiring, right? But I'm playing a hunch."

Magnus raised his eyebrows. "A hunch?"

"Even the biggest bull loses its way after dark and needs light to get it home."

"How poetic." Magnus grinned, but for the life of him, he couldn't tell whether the colonel was comparing the Luma or the Republic to the bull. This was not what he would have imagined from the war hero.

"Poetic? I live in Plumeria. What do you expect?"

"Fair enough," Magnus replied.

"Enough about me. When they announced you, I nearly fell over."

"It *has* been a long time."

"There's that, yes. But we all thought you were dead, son."

"So, you've heard about Oorajee?" Magnus asked.

"Heard about Oorajee? *Splick*, son! Someone went and organized themselves a war, and the Fearsome Four was handed the first grenade. The whole *galaxy* has heard about Oorajee!"

"So, it's bad."

Caldwell forced a blast of air out of his nostrils. "*Bad* doesn't even begin to describe it, son. Everyone's scrambling from here to Pellu, when who walks through my door but the lone survivor of the attack!"

"Excuse me," Magnus said, his stomach tightening. "Lone survivor?"

Caldwell's mouth froze agape. Magnus had visited this particular darkness several times before. Too many times. His mind went to Flow, Cheeks, Mouth, and the others, a few of whom he'd only met before the mission brief. The uncertainty he'd felt when talking with Awen now threatened to spawn into a demon that was nearly impossible to tame. He'd become an expert at avoiding it. The beast haunted him at night and stalked him during the day. Its claws hunted with anger, its mouth dripped with guilt, and its feet slogged forward with grief. Keeping it at bay took everything Magnus could throw at it.

"Damn, son. I'm sorry. You must've got comm'd out then."

"Lost contact after the attack," Magnus said with a nod, his eyes distant. "TACNET went down. Guessing the Jujari jammed all comms but their own. We were lucky enough to get out of the city in one piece. Then I found a way to get my asset off planet and back here. You're my first debrief, Colonel."

"You were assigned the Luma contingent, then?"

"Yeah." Magnus nodded, his mind bringing up an image of Awen. "Wainwright had the Repub ambassador, I had the Luma emissary." Then his mind went to Wainwright. "Are you telling me that not even the captain made it out?"

Caldwell took a deep breath. "That's what the intel coming out of the system suggests. I'm sorry, son. Granted, we have only visual and thermal scans at this point, but they're not picking up any non-Jujari movement from the mwadim's tower."

"Any word of a search-and-rescue team going in?"

"I'm afraid not. Orbital bombardment is being considered, but right now, there's a multi-fleet standoff."

Magnus's eyes snapped to Caldwell's. "Did you say a *multi-fleet* standoff?"

"Republic and Jujari-allied ships are jumping into the system. Second Fleet has joined Third, and there's even talk that First will be called up from Capriana Prime if the Jujari continue to amass ships."

"But, sir," Magnus said with squinted eyes, "you're talking over half of the Republic's warships."

"So you understand how big this is."

"But that's… that's…" It was even worse than he'd projected to Awen.

"It means the Republic is looking at a doomsday scenario. It's beyond conceivable, maybe even suicidal. I agree." Then the colonel turned thoughtful again. "Maybe we're finally paying the price for turning the helm over to bureaucrats and not warriors."

"Says the man who's put up shop with the Luma." Magnus suddenly remembered his place. "I'm sorry, Colonel. That was out of line."

"I said *bureaucrats*, not *mystics*," Caldwell replied, waving Magnus off. "The way I see it, the only way back from this is with something we haven't tried."

Magnus wanted to argue that they *had* tried it the Luma's way… and it had cost lives.

"The truth is," Caldwell continued, "we may not get the chance to try anything at all. Granted, no one's fired the first shot yet. But if you ask me, we're sitting on a good old-fashioned powder keg."

Both men stared at the floor, lost in thought. Finally, Caldwell said, "I'm sorry about your platoon, Magnus. It's times like this when I wish I hadn't given you and your boys a shot at RIP." Caldwell took a drag on his cigar. "I know it must bring up memories of Caledonia. I'm sorry, son."

Magnus pursed his lips. He didn't know what to say. Admitting that the colonel was right would give the demon ground, and he didn't want to concede more than he had already. But denying Caldwell meant lying to himself, and he was tired of that. *Either way, I'm screwed and inviting the demon a little closer.*

"Thank you, Colonel. I'll be okay."

"Will you, though? I suppose the pain is what makes us who we are. It's what makes or breaks all of us who've worn that armor. It's what made your grandfather great."

"Copy that." Magnus nodded, meeting the colonel's eye. "What are my orders, then, sir?"

"As much as I wish you could stay, you're heading back to Oorajee. Brigadier General Lovell's orders. But I see that you need medical attention."

"Nothing shipboard sick bay can't attend to."

Caldwell raised an eyebrow as he surveyed Magnus's armor. "I know the Mark VII can take a beating, but you gave it a run for its credits, son. You sure you don't want to visit the infirmary?"

"Let me get back to my unit, sir." Magnus realized his error. His unit was most likely gone. "My *battalion*."

"There's a Sparrow leaving in five."

"I'll be ready in four." *Just have to work out an issue with my bladders.* He looked at his thigh. He could almost hear Awen laughing at him.

"One more thing," Caldwell said as they stood. "With most units on their way to Oorajee already, your shuttle crew is made up of a corporal escorting two PFCs back to the front lines, piloted by a navy chief warrant officer and an NCO. So, play nice."

"Fabulous."

"WE'VE RECEIVED a distress transmission from a light civilian cruiser in the Kar-Kadesh system," Caldwell said in the holo-vid. "Night Wing class."

Magnus let out a short whistle. "Someone's got nice taste, Colonel."

"That's because it belongs to a senator."

"A senator? If you don't mind me asking, what's a senator doing all the way out there?"

"We'd like to know the same thing," the colonel replied. "Seems it was a last-minute flight. But the order, flight log, and manifest all cleared. Our guess is they dropped out of subspace due to a drive-core failure."

"So you want me to check it out," Magnus said with no attempt to veil his lack of enthusiasm.

"That's correct. As much as I want you back with your

company, you're our closest asset. Investigate, lend aid, and if your crew can't get them on their way, transport them to the closest sector station."

Magnus rubbed his face. "I'm not questioning your judgment here, Colonel, but there's got to be—"

"Lieutenant, I don't think you understand what's happening over Oorajee. We can't spare anyone, and this order comes at the personal request of Brigadier General Lovell himself. It has a need-to-know designation, and apparently, the general doesn't trust anyone else. Once he heard you were topside, he contacted me directly. I don't think I need to explain the uniqueness of that to you."

"No, Colonel, you don't."

"Good. It seems this senator"—Caldwell looked off-screen at a data pad—"Senator *Stone* has two family members and a small crew on board as well. Sending you the roster now. Make sure they're okay, get them on their way, and then get to the front."

"Copy that, Colonel." Magnus glanced down at the dashboard, eyes unfocused on the myriad of blinking lights, their colors blending together in a kaleidoscope of shapes. All he really wanted was to be back with the Recon, prepping for whatever ground assault the fleet commander had in mind. Instead, he was going on a mission that he knew was a distraction, and he felt powerless to do anything about it.

"Colonel, if you would just hear me out—"

"Magnus, please don't make this harder for me than it already is."

"They're my men, sir. What would you do in a situation like this?"

Caldwell sighed. "I'd be wondering why my CO was ordering my ass to some no-good senator's busted-up party barge when I should be looking for my brothers in hostile territory."

"Thank you, Colonel."

"However, *Lieutenant*," Caldwell said, emphasizing Magnus's rank as if to remind him of his duty, "your orders stand."

Magnus worked his jaw. If the holo-vid had been steel, his eyes would have burned crimson holes right through it. He turned his head away and swallowed. This was the difference between Recon and civilians. Civilians faced hard choices, but Recon were paid to wrestle hard choices to the ground and slit their throats.

He looked back at the colonel and replied in a smooth, even tone, "Yes, sir."

Magnus closed the connection and rocked back in the comm officer's chair, rubbing his face. He knew the mission was a total waste of time, and if anything embodied Colonel Caldwell's suspicions that the Republic was going soft, this was it. The fact was, the Marines were attending to bureaucrats when they should have been saving those who were saving everyone else. The Republic was eroding. No, it had been eroding for a long time. They should never have been on Oorajee, and Magnus shouldn't be going to—*Where is it again?*—Kar-Kadesh.

"You got all that?" he asked the pilot.

"Laying in a course for the cruiser now, sir."

"Good. I'll ready a boarding party."

"We're ready to go, Lieutenant!" came an excited voice from the bridge's entrance. Two PFCs stood at attention, eyes locked straight ahead.

Magnus raised an eyebrow and took a deep breath. "You most certainly are, Privates. You most certainly are."

18

Piper clutched Talisman in her arms as she fell asleep in her stateroom aboard *Destiny's Carriage*. Her fingers had been treated in sick bay earlier that day and were healed within the hour. She tried to explain the dream to her mother—tried to explain that she had really been falling within the mountain—but Valerie insisted that Piper had scuffed her fingertips on the wall. No matter how hard Piper tried to argue, her mother found one excuse or another to explain it away.

Now Piper dreamed again, only this time, she was in her home on Capriana Prime. She was back in her bedroom, Talisman in one hand, her holo-pad in the other. Warm sunlight tapped on her bedroom window like a next-door neighbor asking her to come out and play. She smiled at the sun and swiped open her door, only to discover that she was alone in the apartment. She didn't remember her parents saying they'd be gone.

Despite explicit instructions to the contrary, Piper decided to venture outside by herself. *Well, I* do *have Talisman. He'll protect me.* She opened the front door and walked onto the veranda, the sunlight playing peekaboo through serpentine arches overhead. The rays of sunlight kissed her face and dispelled any sense that this was a dangerous thing to do. She took in a deep breath of the lavender flowers that grew beside the apartment's front door, then she walked toward the fountain. Beyond it lay the elevator, which invited her down.

Ground floor. I should go to the ground floor. To venture so far away from her family's apartment was wrong, though. She was never allowed to do that without supervision. One of her security guards was always beside her when she went outside. Still, in her dream, it seemed all right. Plus, there weren't any other people around that she could see, and she still had Talisman.

Piper called the elevator to her floor. The translucent blue doors slid apart, and the glass bubble invited her inside. The city's buildings glistened like jewels against the backdrop of the great ocean, which was a shimmering blue carpet that stretched to the horizon. *Everything is so perfect,* she thought. *Just the way it ought to be.*

Piper felt like a storybook fairy floating over the city as the pod descended one hundred flights to ground level. She had never been afraid of heights. If anything, her mother had to keep her from getting too close to edges for fear that her "impetuous daughter might take to the sky like a falcon." Piper didn't know what the word *impetuous* meant, but if it was wanting to jump into the air and fly like a bird, then she agreed.

The elevator chimed, and the doors parted. Piper stepped into the lobby and noticed that everything was in perfect order. The carpets were vacuumed, the wood floors glistened, and fresh flowers blushed from countless planters spread around the room. Water caressed three tiers of marble landings and splashed down into an emerald pool. The only thing missing was any sign of people.

Clusters of chairs sat without bodies in them. The recreation area to the far end was empty. All the other doorways and elevators were closed. *How strange.* Piper wondered where everyone had run off to.

Piper clutched Talisman in her arm and hunkered down inside her coat as a chill tickled the back of her neck. She walked across the lobby to the main doors, where the three sets of glass partitions separated before her with hushed whispers. As Piper walked between panes of glass, the sunlight flickered, casting prismatic flares across her face.

Once on the street, she looked left and right, hoping to finally see where all the people had gone. *Perhaps an important person has come to the city. Maybe there is a parade. Or even a ball!* Her heart thrilled at the thought of a real ball with music and dancing and food. The costumes would be extravagant, and all the attendees would be so handsome.

Piper walked toward the setting sun—a warm orb on the horizon, peeking between buildings and reflecting off the great ocean. Suddenly, she thought the city's inhabitants might be near the shore. Her excitement mounting, Piper began to run, Talisman jostling from under her elbow. She felt her fingers slipping on her holo-pad. But the thought of seeing where all the people had gone excited her. She just *had* to know!

Her boots pounded down the pavement, and Piper felt her lungs burning like they did when she'd exerted herself too hard on the playground. She should probably stop and rest, maybe take a drink from the water fountain. But no, the people waited. She wanted to know where they'd gone off to and what had captured their attention. It had to be marvelous if everyone in the city was there!

Her mother would be there. And her father too, surely. They'd most likely saved her a seat, so she didn't need to wait in line. She didn't want to miss a minute of whatever they were looking at. Piper stared at the setting sun. It was so bright. But unlike every other sunset she'd ever witnessed, it was getting brighter. And brighter. Until finally, she had to shield her eyes.

She tasted something salty in her mouth. Her hair began to dance. The wind whipped, and she covered her face with Talisman. The sun had become so bright that she could hardly look at it, stealing only the smallest glance to see that the horizon had turned white. *As white as the sun.*

Piper became afraid then. The sun was no longer friendly, and the wind no longer smelled of lavender. Talisman hid her eyes as the bright white encroached from every side, gusts nipping at her coat and her boots. A sense of panic rose in her stomach. There was nothing she could do, nowhere she could run. All around her, the white consumed everything. Not even Talisman or her holo-pad was distinguishable anymore. Power surged through her like a lightning bolt splitting a tree. The sound was deafening. She shrieked in pain, feeling as though her soul had been torn from her body at the hands of a merciless giant.

Then all at once, it was over. Piper could hear herself breathing in short panicked breaths but heard nothing else. She was alive, or at least she thought she was. So she chanced a look from between tight eyes and clenched fists.

Piper stood alone in a completely different place than the one she had stood in moments before. The white was gone, replaced by gloomy blackness. The wind was also gone, as were the buildings. In their absence stood ruins, gnarled hands of steel and concrete reaching angry fingers toward a murky sky.

But this isn't a different place. It's the same place, just a different time.

Piper looked behind her and noticed her apartment building surrounded by all the other once-beautiful buildings of the capital district, now shadows of their former selves. Where there had been gleaming spires in a pastel sky, ashen ghosts now stood, torn apart by an evil spirit. Their contents lay on the streets like bodies whose entrails had spilled out on the execution floor.

Piper felt herself crying, tears streaming down her cheeks. She looked at her holo-pad on the ground. It was cracked. Talisman had been burned beyond recognition. And she had the distinct sensation that her parents were nowhere to be found.

I am alone. Truly alone.

She reached down and picked up Talisman's remains, weeping for her dear friend. Then she heard something—heavy footsteps clomping through the rubble. She looked up and mashed the tears from her eyes with a dirty palm.

There! She spotted a mound of debris near the place where

the sun had exploded on the horizon. A figure rose from the heap, walking up the back side and looking toward her. Piper squinted, trying to make out details. This was, after all, the first person she'd seen since arriving here. She was curious, but she was also afraid. Very afraid.

"Hello?" she called out, wiping another tear from her vision. "Who're you?" But the figure kept walking toward her, boots mashing the metal and dust.

Piper could finally make out the outline of a suit of armor, not like in her storybooks. No, like… the Republic troopers. But this armor was darker and scarier. It was as if any remaining light around her was sucked into this warrior, like a black hole on the edge of the cosmos. *Nothing* escaped him, and Piper knew right then that *she* could not escape him either. She would *never* escape him.

"Stay away from me," she said then repeated it with more confidence. "Stay *away* from me!"

But the trooper kept walking toward her, one foot after another. Piper turned around and started running toward her apartment building, hoping she might find a passage back inside. She'd be safe there. But when she looked down, her feet weren't gaining any ground.

"Just let me get home!" she yelled. It was so frustrating. Infuriating! She had to get away!

Piper stole a glance over her shoulder. The trooper was upon her now, able to reach out and snag her if he wanted. His armor was huge, and she knew he could crush her in one hand. She tried to run harder but still failed to make even a meter of progress.

"It's all right," the trooper said, his voice coming through a speaker. "Everything's going to be okay."

Piper froze, shocked at how soft the words felt despite the warrior's evil appearance. She turned around, clutching Talisman's burnt corpse to her chest with both arms. "Who—who are you?"

The trooper reached up, unlocked his terrifying helmet, and pulled it over his head. Piper stared at his face, studying it. Memorizing it. And then woke up to a warning klaxon blaring in the ship.

19

Admiral Kane sat alone in his quarters while his flight crew brought the *Peregrine* into orbit over Worru. The Stiletto-class corvette loomed over the lush green-and-blue planet like a hungry raptor searching for prey. Made to be both visually and functionally aggressive, the *Peregrine*'s fuselage was flat on the bottom and sides. The rounded top, however, swept from bow to stern in an arc. Large twin stabilizers raked forward like the ears of a prowling predator, and small port and starboard wings supported oversized weapon pods.

"What do you mean you let them get away?" Kane hissed over the holo-vid.

"I didn't *let* them get away, Kane," So-Elku retorted. "I only said that they escaped."

"There's a difference?" Kane waited for the Luma to say

something meaningful but realized it was a waste of time. "And I suppose you failed to open the stardrive as well?"

"I did," So-Elku said. "The woman still has it."

Kane was growing impatient. The only thing he despised more than failed plans was an inept leader. "So she's on the run with the stardrive, and we have nothing."

"Oh, I wouldn't say *nothing*." So-Elku lifted a small device and wiggled it between his fingers. Kane's interest was piqued.

"You planted a tracker?"

"A maintenance crew had access to the vessel that brought her. Those Bawee can be bought for next to nothing. Regardless of whether she fled, I wanted to know who'd helped her and tie up any loose ends."

Kane hated that the mystic had left so much to chance. The man was not as reliable as he'd assumed, even though he'd managed to salvage the situation by planting the tracking device. "Forward the identification codes. We'll send you destination coordinates once we know where she's going."

"I want reassurances on our deal," the Luma leader said.

"Reassurances?" Kane was beside himself, but he couldn't let his emotions show. The wolf pack would circle for the kill at the slightest sign of weakness. *This is the reason partnerships fail. Because no partner is ever your equal.*

"This escapade has cost me many students," So-Elku said. "I need to know it was not in vain."

"Then you should have counted the cost *before* you agreed to this *escapade*, Luma Master."

So-Elku cleared his throat. "I want sole access to the temple library."

"As I said, I have no interest in your metaphysical dealings."

"I want the woman too."

Kane's eyes studied the man. He had no use for the Luma, let alone their female "expert" on the Jujari. But further negotiations always meant more opportunities for gain. "Additions to the agreement are not in your best interests, So-Elku."

"Do *you* have any use for her?"

"No. But ensuring her survival will cost me. Discretion in violence is expensive."

"I'm not sure I have anything more to offer," So-Elku said.

It was unfortunate that he was so honest. The admiral laced his fingers together and leaned forward. "You will, Luma Master. You will."

KANE RETURNED to the bridge and lost himself in thought as he stared over Worru, hands behind his back. While things hadn't gone exactly according to plan, So-Elku's placement of the tracking transponder had probably saved the Luma master from an inconvenient assassination.

"Captain, sensors are picking up a Republic distress transmission," the comm officer said. "Looks to be heavily coded."

"Log it, and keep scanning," replied the captain. "Navigation, how much longer before we achieve synchronization with the—"

"Wait," Kane said, raising a hand. "What's that distress signal coming from?" He turned and walked to the comm station.

"Seems to be a civilian transport, sir. A light cruiser. Looks like it's in the Kar-Kadesh system."

"Captain, we have synced with the transponder," the navigation officer said.

"Good. Set course and prepare to jump."

"Belay that order," Kane said. "I'm curious about this transmission."

"Sir, there's no reason that we can't—"

Kane silenced the captain with an upraised hand then leaned closer to the comm officer's station. "Can you decode the message?"

"Working on it, Admiral." The officer's fingers tapped the black dashboard, working with the ship's AI. Kane waited but had a sense it couldn't be cracked. Finally, the officer let out a sigh. "I'm sorry, sir, but they used a variable quantum algorithm that—"

"It's not breakable?" Kane asked.

"I'm sorry, no. All I have is basic intel. The ship's ident, basic data on the flight log—"

"Bring it up."

The officer swiped up on the dashboard's surface and sent the field into the holo-feed. Kane scanned the text and then froze on something. He leaned in even closer. "It can't be," he whispered. Under the flight's log order was a name he had not seen in a very long time. He double-checked the date. It was only three days old. *She's alive.*

"Admiral, sir. Do you want us—"

"She's alive," he whispered.

"Who, sir?"

Kane turned toward the captain and stared at him, aflame with dark fascination, like a Venetian mawslip observing a squirming rabbit pinned under its talons. "What an unexpected turn of events," he said, wringing his hands.

"Sir?"

The admiral paced a few steps, holding up a finger to silence the overeager captain. Kane looked again at the holo-feed, trying to see his way through the ether, but there wasn't enough light to outline the shapes. He needed more of the picture before anything would come into focus. However, he could at least make sure no one stole the parts of the scene he already possessed.

He looked up from his scheming and eyed the captain. "Order a Bull Wraith to that cruiser's position. I want the whole ship, and I want the passengers and crew alive. If anyone kills them, they forfeit their lives as payment."

The captain nodded, confused but agreeable. "Yes, sir. And *Geronimo Nine*?"

"We follow her. Proceed with the jump."

20

"Destiny's Carriage, Destiny's Carriage, this is the pilot in command of Republic light armored transport Sparrow Two Seven One." Silence filled the bridge as Chief Warrant Officer Nolan waited for a reply. Magnus stood over Nolan's shoulder and studied the light cruiser through the cockpit window.

"All scans show the ship's systems nominal," said Petty Officer Rawlson, the sensors officer. "No hull breaches, no exterior damage."

"Understood." Nolan gestured to the comms officer to open the channel again. "Destiny's Carriage, Destiny's Carriage, this is the PIC of Republic light armored transport Sparrow Two Seven One. Do you copy?"

More silence followed Nolan's second hail attempt. He ran a pale hand through his auburn hair. "I don't like this," he said to no one in particular.

Magnus felt that sensation in his gut, the one that prepared him to deal with bad situations—like finding a ship full of lifeless bodies. *But I thought you didn't care about a senator and his family.* Magnus knew he could not win the battle of wits with his inner self. People in distress were people in distress, and he was a Marine who was called to defend the weak.

But are all Marines also traitors, Magnus? Or are you only a traitor if you get caught?

"Hail them again," Magnus ordered.

"*Destiny's Carriage, Destiny's Carriage*, this is—"

"Sparrow Two Seven One, this is *Destiny's Carriage*. We read you, Captain."

Magnus hit Nolan's shoulder with a fist—perhaps a little too hard. Nolan shrank away from the blow.

Don't care too much, Magnus. It's just a senator.

"What's your status, *Destiny*?" Nolan asked, rotating his shoulder.

"Boy, are we glad to see you. Drive-core failure knocked us out of subspace."

"How many souls aboard?"

"Six souls, including myself. All accounted for, no injuries."

"Copy that, Captain. Good to hear. Is there any known reason we should not attempt to dock with you for boarding and situation assessment?"

"Negative. Core is contained, all systems nominal."

"Permission to dock to starboard?"

"Permission granted."

"See you shortly." Nolan closed the channel and turned to Magnus. "We'll have a lock in ninety seconds, Lieutenant."

"Copy," Magnus replied. "We'll take it from here."

Magnus left the bridge and walked into the cargo bay to address the three privates. The flight engineer and medic were each nose down in two rucksacks while the corporal was checking an MX13 subcompact blaster.

"Expecting heavy resistance from the senator, Corporal?" Magnus asked.

The young woman looked at him with a measure of surprise and perhaps a little embarrassment. Her flight uniform name tag read Dutch, followed by her designation number. She was small in stature and wore her dark hair cut just below her ears, parted to one side with a few strands falling over her face. She had intelligent brown eyes and seemed reluctant to give up the weapon.

"You can never be too sure, Lieutenant," Dutch replied.

"No, you can't, Corporal. I like that. Never know what uninvited guests we might encounter." Magnus tapped the receiver of his MAR30 and smiled.

"Uninvited guests, Lieutenant?" Gilder, the flight engineer, asked.

"In this part of the void, you never know what sort of things can find their way into a disabled starship." Magnus could hear Caldwell rebuking him. *Go easy on them, Magnus.* He tossed them each a handheld comm. "Since you're not in armor, we'll use these. Channel's preset. One click up will get you the bridge if needed, but only I should be talking to them. Copy?"

"Yes, Lieutenant," they replied, catching the radios one at a time.

"You ever see anything like that, Lieutenant?" Haney asked. "You know, like really out of the ordinary?"

Magnus tried his hardest not to smile at the medic's question. He knew the holo-vids these boys were raised on. Heck, he'd been raised on them too, and he'd seen enough of the real world since then to know that the movies were fake. *The real stuff was way worse.*

"Yeah," Dutch said. "We heard stories about you on Caledonia."

"Stories? What kind of stories?" Magnus was genuinely intrigued.

Gilder stood up, lifted his chin, and pushed out his rather large chest as if he was about to recite the Republic pledge in front of a review board. "Some said you took on twenty 'kudas at once with your bare hands. Then, after that, their ghosts came after you and tried cooking you inside your armor. But you MAR'd them all, held the position for days until reinforcements arrived."

Magnus raised an eyebrow, trying to figure out what crazy version of reality this boy was talking about. *Top Shelf Pass*. He nodded, connecting the dots—the *real* dots. It was three 'kudas, not twenty. He'd stabbed two of them and shot the third with his sidearm. Then he recovered his MC90—that was long before the MAR30 came into being—and cooked their spawn for about ten minutes before his platoon realized what hellhole he had fallen into. It had been a total accident, one that led to finding a back door into the enemy's main fortification. But no use breaking these Marines' hearts.

"Well," Magnus said, charging his MAR30, "then I guess it's a good thing for you that I'm taking point." The privates spoke their assent and stacked up behind Dutch. "If I duck, just make sure you're not standing."

"Copy that, Lieutenant," Gilder said. "I'll stay hidden underneath you and let you take the fire." He winced. "I mean—"

"Stow it," Magnus said.

"Copy."

"Thirty seconds, Lieutenant," Nolan yelled from the cockpit.

"Roger that," Magnus replied then turned to his makeshift away team. "Lock it up, Marines. There's no reason this should be anything but rudimentary, but you never know. In the Recon, we say OTF—own the field."

"OTF," they replied as one.

For Magnus, the next thirty seconds were a strange mixture of boredom and anxiety. Boredom because… well, he wasn't expecting any action, and this was the last place in the cosmos he wanted to be. And anxiety because he had a sudden urge to find out how Awen had fared with her debriefing. Sure, she was a prude. Altruistic? Check. Naive? Double check. Still, there was something about her that he couldn't put his finger on—something that he hadn't felt toward a woman in a long time. Not since…

He shook the thoughts from his head. This wasn't the time to go there.

So when will it be time, Magnus?

It was then that he remembered the piece of paper that Awen had handed to him when they'd said goodbye.

"Ten seconds!" Nolan yelled.

The proximity alarm began to wail as a red light warned against opening the hatch into vacuum. Magnus held the stock of his MAR30 with his left hand and reached into his small chest compartment with his right. He removed the paper and unfolded it with his gloved fingers.

"Five seconds!"

Magnus looked down. On that scrap of paper were three large letters handwritten in old-fashioned black ink: *NMB*. The ship jostled, and the paper slipped out of his fingers.

"We have a lock!"

"Lieutenant?" the senator asked.

"Adonis Olin Magnus, sir. Seventy-Ninth Recon Battalion, Marine Special Units." The two men shook hands, Magnus holding his helmet under his arm and allowing his MAR30 to hang from its sling.

"Senator Darin Stone. Thank you for coming."

"Our pleasure, Senator. I have orders from Brigadier General Lovell to assess your ship's condition and then make necessary arrangements based on the situation."

"Remind me to recommend a promotion for you when I get back to Capriana."

"Thank you, sir," Magnus replied, but inwardly, he rejected

the comment, recognizing it as snarky political jargon. No Marine worth their boots wanted a promotion just because they *showed up* to a broken-down starship on the side of subspace. But Magnus had to hand it to the senator—the man had come to greet them himself. Most men of his status, at least in Magnus's experience, never spoke to anyone below their station, especially troopers.

Magnus and his team stood on a beige carpet inside *Destiny*'s vestibule. Off-white walls with baby-blue trim emitted a soft glow, exuding all the credits spent on a shipwide mood-lighting package. Polished wood rails ran along the corridors on either side, crystal-clear directional signs with frosted letters pointed toward the ship's many destinations, and the vessel smelled like vanilla and jasmine. *The scent of more credits than you'll ever see,* Magnus noted with some measure of jealousy.

The man in front of him wore an impossibly white smile, manicured blond hair, and a luxuriant tan. Those features, combined with his radiant blue eyes, made Magnus wonder if the man was even real. The senator's appearance was so perfect that he transcended age. Magnus couldn't tell if he was old but spent a fortune to turn back the years or young but spent the same fortune to appear statelier.

Magnus suddenly felt out of place. He still hadn't let the medic look at his injuries. Moreover, he hadn't even wiped his armor down. The senator could probably *smell* the Jujari saliva on his boots.

Just then, a woman emerged in the corridor from around the corner. "Darling, who is it?"

There were times in life when something so unexpected happened that it left an imprint on a person's soul. Magnus had plenty of those—so many, in fact, that he often wondered if there was any substance left to mark. Most of his imprints, however, were of the sort he'd rather forget than remember. They'd come to him in the heat of battle or in the nightmares that followed. What happened when Lady Stone extended her hand to meet him was of another sort entirely.

"My love, this is Lieutenant Magnus of the Galactic Republic Marines," the senator said. "He and his Marines have come to rescue us."

"Rescue us?" she said with a wide smile. "How wonderful." She continued holding her hand out until Magnus finally had enough sense to remove his glove and shake it.

"Ma'am," he said, instantly self-conscious about his voice—and his appearance, noting that if he'd felt out of place in front of the senator, he felt like a Jellataun snout fish on a frying pan in front of Lady Stone.

"Please," she said, "call me Valerie."

Magnus was pretty sure he forgot how to speak at that moment. Poetry replaced prose, and he cursed himself for what he was sure would be a failure to construct a coherent sentence in her presence.

Valerie's hair was the color of sunlight, and her eyes sparkled like the sea at high noon. Her skin was so smooth that Magnus suddenly wanted to know what it felt like. The white gown she wore was draped around a body that Magnus swore was some lost temple covered by a thin blanket of powdery snow.

"I'm—here to take you," Magnus said.

Valerie smirked. The senator held his smile but cocked his head in question. And Magnus was almost sure he could hear the privates' thoughts behind him: *You tell her, Lieutenant! That's how it's done!*

Magnus cringed. "I'm here to take *you all* to the nearest Republic substation if we're unable to get you underway again."

"See there, my love?" the senator said.

"Yes, dear," Valerie replied, withdrawing her hand. "We are most grateful for your assistance, Lieutenant."

"There are six souls on board?" Haney asked, stepping to the side.

"Yes," the senator said. "My wife, our daughter, and myself. Then our ship's captain, our chief engineer, and our steward."

"Do any of them require medical attention?" Haney asked, apparently eager to ply his trade for what Magnus could only assume was the first time in the field.

"All of them seem to be in good health," the senator replied. "I will introduce you to them nonetheless, and you may judge for yourself."

"And the engine room?" Gilder asked.

"Yes, of course," the senator said. "I'll introduce you to our engineer, and he'll take you personally."

"Thank you, Senator," Magnus replied. "And this is Corporal Dutch, our ranking NCO and weapons specialist."

Dutch nodded to the senator and his wife.

"Is this everyone, then?" Valerie asked.

"We have three more crew on the bridge of our ship, but they'll remain in place," Magnus replied.

"Very well," Valerie said. "Let's move to the lounge and get everyone acquainted. I'll have some refreshments brought as well."

Magnus tipped his head and gestured forward with his hand, hoping he wouldn't have to use more words with Lady Stone. Yet for some unknown reason, as he followed behind her, he said, "Acquainting is great," and cursed himself for even opening his mouth.

Senator Stone introduced his crew to Magnus's troops, and the steward offered the troopers beverages and a light snack. Gilder declined and insisted that he head straight for the engine room with the ship's engineer. *He was young and enthusiastic, but that counted for something in moments like this.*

As much as the whole situation had taken a peculiar turn for the best, Magnus still wanted to get off the cruiser as fast as possible. *She's married, for galaxy's sake!*

The senator invited the others to sit, but the troopers waved him off, Magnus insisting that their armor would mar their furniture.

"Don't be ridiculous," the senator replied. "Please make yourselves at home."

"You said you had a daughter on board?" Haney asked, taking a seat.

"Yes, yes. She's sleeping," Valerie replied. "I'll fetch her right away. She will absolutely *love* meeting some real-life Marines."

Magnus watched, perhaps a little too long, as Lady Stone exited the lounge and walked down a hallway that led to the staterooms.

"So, Lieutenant…" the senator said, handing him a cup of tea.

What was it with everyone serving him tea lately? At least this guy didn't have a wall of buckets.

"Where did our distress signal summon you from?" continued the senator.

"We were on Worru, sir, making for Oorajee."

"Oorajee?" The senator's eyes lit up, lips held a few centimeters from the edge of his cup. "I hear that's become quite the hot spot in recent days."

"You could say that," Magnus replied.

"I'm eager to hear how the negotiations went."

Magnus lowered his cup and held the man's eyes, suddenly unsure if he should say anything. *Didn't he know?* "Senator Stone, if you would permit me, when was the last time you were in touch with the Republic?"

"Just before we jumped into subspace three days ago. Whatever disabled our drive core also took out our long-range sensors. It was all we could do to send a subspace distress communiqué." The senator placed his cup on his saucer and set them both down on the table. "Why? I sense you have something to tell me."

"Senator…" Magnus hesitated. "The negotiations were…"

His mind flashed back to the explosion in the mwadim's palace. He saw the bodies flying, heard the screams, saw the flames.

"Say it straight, trooper. You're talking to a Republic senator."

"Someone sabotaged them."

"They *what?*"

"Someone bombed the mwadim's palace just as the meeting got underway."

The senator looked bewildered, blinking as he processed the information. "You're absolutely sure of this?"

"Sir, I was there."

"You were *there?*"

"Yes, sir," Magnus said. "As far as I know, I'm one of two survivors. Right now, my entire platoon is MIA. That's who I was headed back to help find before… before I—"

"Before you were tasked with helping some nobody senator and his family on a broken-down yacht who have enough environment and food to last them months while your men remain unaccounted for on a hostile world."

Magnus froze, staring at the man. He resisted the urge to say, *You're damn right*, yet he honored the senator's attempt at straight talk. *It was refreshing.*

"It's all right, Lieutenant. I said it, so you don't have to. And if it were me, I'd be thinking the same thing."

"Thank you, Senator."

"We're not all power-hungry buffoons on Capriana, you know. Some of us are almost tolerable. You, on the other hand"—the senator reached over and placed a hand on Magnus's shoulder—"are the spearpoint of all our decisions. And if I wasn't aware of that before, I certainly am now. I'm sorry for your losses, Lieutenant."

Magnus knew a player when he met one. But as much as he wanted to hate this man for his perfect face—and even more for marrying the most beautiful woman Magnus had ever met—he simply couldn't bring himself to mistrust this senator's words. Which made Magnus hate himself, of all people. *I've already been hating myself for so long; it can't make much difference if I keep it up a little longer.*

"Thank you, sir," Magnus replied. "But until I personally confirm their status, I haven't lost a soul."

"As you've said." The senator raised his cup to salute Magnus.

Just then, Lady Stone reappeared, holding hands with a small blond girl. Everyone stood and watched as the tiny waif entered the lounge. Her eyes were puffy from being awakened long before it was time, and the girl squeezed a small stuffed animal against her pajamas. Lady Stone brought the girl to stand in the circle of adults and introduced her.

"Everyone, this is Piper." Valerie held the little girl's shoulders. "Piper, this is—"

"Him," Piper said suddenly, pointing a finger at Magnus. "It's *him.*"

21

"Buckle in!" Ezo yelled as he and TO-96 raced through *Geronimo*'s startup sequence. Awen took a seat behind the two command chairs and fumbled with the harness buckles. Her hands shook due to equal parts nerves and fatigue. The cockpit hummed with activity as switches flipped, screens glowed, and systems cycled on.

"*Geronimo Nine, Geronimo Nine*, this is Plumeria Tower. We're reading drive-core initiation on platform thirty-nine. You do not have clearance for startup sequence or takeoff."

TO-96 looked at Ezo. "What would you like to do, sir?"

"Put me through."

The bot touched the dashboard. "You're good to go, sir."

"Tower, this is *Geronimo Nine*. Not sure what you're reading. Systems here are nominal."

"Negative, *Geronimo*. Sensors clearly indicate that—"

"Sorry, come again?" interrupted Ezo.

The tower comms operator let out an exasperated sigh. "*I said*, our sensors—"

"Still can't read you, Tower. This must be really irritating." Ezo glanced at TO-96. "How we doing, Ninety-Six?"

"Thirty-seconds, sir."

The tower operator's voice was hard now. "*Geronimo*, we are sending a control crew to board your vessel and initiate the suspension of your credentials until such time as the—"

"Suspend my credentials?" Ezo said in mock surprise. "But then, how can Ezo fly his ship?" He waited as the tower operator hesitated.

"You... He. *No one* will be able to fly the ship. That is the whole point of suspension!"

"Can *you* explain that to Ezo's wife, then? She is not gonna be happy when she hears this."

"Actually sir," TO-96 said, muting the comm. "My records show that—"

Ezo cast him a mirthless smirk. "Not now, Ninety-Six."

The bot looked away then back at Ezo. "Ah. I see. You are attempting to engage in witty banter with the tower operator through the use of sarcastic falsities in order to delay their confiscation of our ship. However—"

"Sometimes, your brilliance amazes even me."

"Why, thank you, sir," the bot said as Awen chuckled. "But—"

"Don't mention it. Time?" Ezo asked.

"All systems are ready for takeoff, sir," TO-96 said.

"Open the line again."

TO-96 unmuted the link just in time for them to hear the tower operator spitting orders into the microphone, seasoned with enough vulgarities to make him unprofessional but not enough to get him dismissed from his post.

"Tower, your attempts to threaten us are truly appreciated. It's exemplary. However, we are leaving nonetheless and wish you the very best. Oh, and please give our regards to"—Ezo leaned back to Awen—"what was his name again?"

"Master So-Elku," she answered, cringing as she spoke the traitor's name.

"Master Su-Echo," Ezo said. "*Geronimo Nine*, out." He turned to his copilot. "Take her up."

"Aye, sir."

Awen felt the ship lift off and bank sharply to the left. She reached out to steady herself, leaning against the turn.

"You expecting any pursuers, Star Queen?" Ezo asked over his shoulder.

"No, I—wait. *Star Queen?*"

"Sure. You probably still have that stardrive on you, right?"

Awen instinctively placed a hand on the satchel. "Maybe."

"That's a yes. Which means you didn't give it to your big boss man, which means he's pissed at you. That means you're a big somebody now—a big somebody with information about something in the 'verse that people want. Big somebodies with stuff other people want are *royalty*. So you're the Star Queen."

"Sir, sensors show energy-disruption cannons powering up. They're going to fire on us," TO-96 said.

"Power to the rear shields."

"Right away." The bot tapped faster than Awen could see. "Power redirected." Just then, two blasts of energy slammed against the hull, shoving the ship forward. Awen's head hit the back of her seat.

"They're pulling out the big guns for you, Star Queen," Ezo said.

"They're—they're *shooting* at us?" Awen asked, bewildered.

"Like Ezo already said, you pissed somebody off. Fortunately, they want what you have, *and* they want you alive."

"Those were energy-disruption pulses," TO-96 added, his head rotating to look at her. "They are meant to disable us while simultaneously opening our command interface to an extra-local takeover. They are powerful, but they will not kill you, Awen."

"Thank you for the reassurance," she said, eyes wide.

"This also means you haven't opened the stardrive yet," Ezo concluded.

"Maybe," she said less confidently. "Where are we going?"

"Deep space. Ninety-Six, course laid in?"

"Affirmative, sir. However, I might remind you that jumping while in atmosphere not only poses significant risks to the local population but lessens our jump success to seventy-one percent, given Worru's substantial gravity well."

"And what are the chances that those cannons disrupt our shields before we reach a safe distance?"

"I calculate a forty-three percent chance, sir."

As if on cue, another pair of disruption pulses struck the aft shields. This time, the cockpit lights went out.

"And now?" Ezo asked.

"One-hundred percent, sir," the bot replied in a forlorn tone.

"Punch it, 'Six!"

Awen watched as the sky outside the ship stretched away from them as if pulled by elastic bands. Then it snapped the ship forward into a sea of elongated starlight.

AWEN HAD EXCUSED herself from the bridge and gone to her quarters to wash her hands and face. She was on the edge of exhaustion and knew that if she didn't get sleep right away, she was going to cause harm to her body. Yet she wondered if she'd be able to sleep, given all that had happened.

Awen felt as though her life had gone from normal to light speed, just like the ship. Acting as the emissary to the Jujari had been enough excitement for one lifetime. But being captured by a warlord, transported by a bounty hunter, betrayed by her master, and then surviving a desperate escape from Plumeria… she'd hardly had time to take a breath let alone process it all.

The worst of it, however, was that she felt alone. Her parents were light-years away, the Order was no longer safe, and she was on some random trading vessel with a narcissistic bounty hunter and his improvised robot. All at once, she found herself wishing Magnus hadn't gone back to his unit. Maybe there was a way he could have stayed. *But that's just silly.*

Awen's door chimed, and the speaker emitted a thin voice. "It's Ezo."

Awen sighed, reached for the towel, and pressed the open button with her elbow.

"How you feeling?" he asked.

"I'd rather not answer that right now, Ezo. But thank you for asking."

"Fair enough, fair enough. So, where do you want to go, Star Queen?"

Awen massaged her eyelids, wishing someone else would answer the question for her. The truth was, she had no idea. And somehow, she felt Magnus might know where to go next.

"I really just want to go to bed," she said, to which Ezo raised an eyebrow. "*By myself.*" She wasn't sure how much more of this character she could take. *I know where I want to go*: a*s far away from him as possible*. But seeing that Ezo was her only viable means of transportation, ditching him didn't seem like the most prudent option.

Awen took a deep breath and threw the towel into the sink. "You said we're headed to deep space, right? So let's start there."

"The farthest sector of the Omodon quadrant," Ezo said. "There shouldn't be any traffic to speak of, so we'll be able to spot a tail if anyone is following us."

"You think someone is following us?"

"No, but we try to take precautions."

Awen nodded. "Smart. And if someone *is* following us?"

"Well, outer Omodon is home to some fairly unsavory systems that may or may not be easily stirred up if a reputable bounty hunter were to advertise that a certain vessel had a very high price on its hull."

"That's convenient," she replied. "Too bad we don't know any reputable bounty hunters."

"Hey, you don't know Ezo," the man said, pressing a hand to his chest. "You just give him a bad rap because he got mixed in with the likes of Abimbola over a bad poker-chip flip. Ezo's a really nice guy, though."

"I'm sure he is," Awen said. "And let's just keep it at that. Nice Guy Ezo."

"Yeah, Nice Guy Ezo. That's me." He brushed a hand through his hair. "So, you ever going to open that stardrive?"

That was the question that everyone seemed to have in common. And the truth was, Awen wanted to know what was on it, too—now more than ever. Who knew what So-Elku would have done to her if she'd resisted him further. Or what he would have done *after* she opened it. Awen shuddered to think of that. She only hoped that Willowood was all right. The elder had risked her reputation to save Awen without needing any explanation. *Perhaps she even risked her life.*

More questions tugged at Awen's mind, and she knew her fatigue wasn't going to produce cogent answers. There was still the matter of the bombs themselves. Who'd set them, and what did they hope to accomplish with so much destruction? And then there was the hover bot that had recorded the mwadim handing her the stardrive. It seemed as if someone had expected the handoff—and as if an informant had ratted on the mwadim.

More than anything, Awen wanted to know why she had been

the one whom the Jujari leader had entrusted with whatever was on the drive. Was it a matter of mere convenience? If someone else had landed next to him, would he have handed it to them just as easily? Maybe there was something unique about her, perhaps because she was a Luma. *But if that was the case, why not dispense with negotiations and set up a private meeting?* The Luma would have jumped at the chance to entertain a private meeting with the distinguished, though violent, Jujari leader.

The questions were too much for her to handle, at least at the moment. She was tired of thinking, tired of trying to figure out how all the puzzle pieces went together. It felt like playing chess in the dark without hands.

Still, somewhere in the back of her mind, Awen felt like the mwadim had chosen her, intentionally singling her out as the one to inherit the stardrive. "Guard it," he'd charged her with his dying breath. "Never let them find it." There had been something earnest in the way he spoke to her, as if they were old confidants sharing a secret. He'd wanted to speak to *her* and no one else.

But then Awen found herself asking another question. *When the mwadim charged me with guarding the device, did he mean the stardrive or what was on the stardrive?* If it had been about keeping the device hidden, that secret was out. But if it was about what was *on* that drive, then... she couldn't know how to protect it unless she knew what *it* was.

She needed to open the stardrive, and sooner rather than later. If So-Elku and others were coming for her, as they most likely were, then she could only protect the contents of the drive in one of two ways: either she learned about what she was guarding before they could, or she died. Of course, there was always a third alternative—So-Elku could force her to reveal the contents *and then* kill her.

I'll give him neither option. "I'm going to open the stardrive," she said.

Ezo's eyes went wide, and he clapped his hands. "*Yes!* Yes, you are! Let's do this!" He spun around. "Ninety-Six, where are you?"

"Wait, what are you doing?" Awen asked.

"TO-96 is a navigation bot. Did you forget already?"

"No, I—"

"Whatever that thing shows you, whatever intel or coordinates—*Ninety-Six! Get out here!*—whatever reward in the labyrinth awaits you, he'll know how to get you there."

"I suppose that *is* helpful."

"Of course it is! *Ninety-Six!*"

"Coming, sir," the bot said as his footfalls shuffled down the corridor moments before he appeared. "I was simply making sure that—"

"Never mind that. Awen's going to open the stardrive."

"The stardrive? How exciting for her."

"For her?" Ezo asked, shooting the bot a surprised look. "Yes—quite so." The bounty hunter walked over to the table in the middle of the room and cleared it for Awen. "Please, take a seat."

Awen approached the table while reaching for the stardrive in the satchel. She sat to one side while Ezo sat across from her, and TO-96 stood between them.

"Ninety-Six, please lower the lights," Ezo said.

"As you wish, sir." Instantly, the lights dimmed, and only the floors emitted their constant white glow.

Awen held the gray cylinder in her right hand, examining it. Its irregular surface and many indentations held dried blood that was now brown and flaking. It was heavier than it looked, something she hadn't noticed before. Or maybe her hand was just tired; it *was* shaking a little, after all.

In a strange way, she wished the mwadim was here to open this with her, to explain why he'd given it to her and what was so important about it. It would be like a professor leading a student through an assignment or a cherished text. Then she thought of her parents, who would marvel that their daughter would be entrusted with such a prized possession from a world leader. *But they have no use for other worlds.* She thought of Willowood and what her wise guidance might mean in a moment like this. And finally, she thought of Magnus. She missed his… *His what? His strength? His ability to protect me?* But she was able to protect herself even more than he was, and she was stronger than even his Republic armor. Still, she wished Magnus was present for reasons she could not explain.

In the end, however, she was alone. Yes, Ezo and TO-96 were with her, but this was not their burden to carry or their battle to fight. Awen was alone, and no one else had been entrusted with this device but her.

Awen placed her thumb on top of the button. She let her mind move back to the dais once again, the horrible memories flooding her senses. The smell of smoke, of burning flesh. The ringing in her ears, the muted screams of the dying. The taste of blood in her mouth, the excruciating pain in her body. And the mwadim.

"Here goes nothing." Awen pressed down on the button, and the micro-needle punctured her skin.

22

Awen placed the stardrive on the table and sucked the blood from her thumb. The device started to glow and then separated with a metallic *click*, splitting lengthwise. From a bright central core, the drive emitted a blue holo-projection above the table, a scene that swirled about like a flurry of light snow. Eventually, thousands of blue pinpoints of light resolved into a three-segmented symbol.

Awen, Ezo, and TO-96 leaned in. "What is it, Ninety-Six?" Ezo asked.

"Searching," the bot replied, his head tilting back and forth as he scanned the three-dimensional image.

Awen found the symbol fascinating. Two opened-ended arches connected at the apexes like chain links, their four ends tapering to points. Bisecting the horizontal plane was a ring that seemed to lock the arches in place. The collection of three shapes slowly rotated over the table, casting blue light on everyone's faces.

"I've never seen it before," Awen said, wondering at the symbol's meaning.

"Neither has Ezo," the smuggler said.

"And neither have I," TO-96 said. "In fact, this symbol is not listed on any of the Galactic Republic's records and does not match symbology for any known sentient species."

"Seriously?" Ezo asked. "I thought you knew everything about everything."

"*Everything* is a relative word, sir."

"Really? Because the way I use it, it's not."

Awen looked at the bot. "Wait, so you're saying it's *not* from our galaxy, then?"

"Not conclusively, Awen. The galaxy is, after all, a very big place."

"Or maybe it's a secret order or something," Ezo added. TO-96 looked at him. "You know, like a conspiracy group, an off-the-books Repub hit squad, something like that."

TO-96 tilted his head. "I don't think so, sir."

Suddenly indignant, Ezo placed his hands on his hips. "And why not?"

"For one, I already *have* a record of all known galactic conspiracy groups and kill teams, known or supposed."

"Wait—you do?" Ezo asked.

"Secondly, those groups don't go around placing their locations on stardrives. We already know where most of their headquarters are."

"Wait, wait—you know that too? How am I just now discovering this? How is Ezo *just now* discovering this?" Ezo looked at Awen, who shrugged. "Ninety-Six, it's like we don't even know each other anymore."

"What can I say, sir? Like a woman, I'm a mystery you'll never fully unravel."

Awen beamed. "Well said, Ninety-Six."

"Thank you, Awen."

Ezo was incredulous, his mouth hanging open.

Awen returned to the symbol in front of them, studying it carefully.

"What does it do next?" Ezo asked.

"I'm not sure, sir," TO-96 replied. "My sensors are not showing any activation functions beyond what Awen has already initiated."

"So that's it, then? It's just some random symbol?"

"It's not a symbol," Awen offered. "Well, not *just* a symbol. Symbols imply a shared meaning between two parties. But I'm assuming whoever coded this drive didn't expect anyone to receive it who knew them already."

"Why do you say that?" Ezo asked.

"Because not even TO-96 here knows this symbol. Which means this little drive is either a long way from home or—"

"Whoever made it wanted it to get into someone else's hands," Ezo concluded.

"Exactly."

"So, any ideas about what it might be?"

"Maybe," she said, reaching for the three components. "I

wonder if it's a puzzle. A key of some sort." She grasped the circle, her hands closing around the light, and twisted it slightly like someone might loosen a stick caught between rocks. Then she maneuvered the arches individually so that they slid out from one another. As soon as the three elements were separated, the arches rotated and embraced the circle with their apexes to the far left and right sides of the new shape, resembling a planet with a ringed debris field. Then a swirl of small lights emerged in the center of the circle, forming a tiny cluster.

"It's a star system," Ezo said. The three of them watched as the system of little lights grew so large that it overtook the symbol.

"And one there's no record for," TO-96 concluded.

"Wait," Ezo said. "You seriously haven't seen this one before?"

"Sir," the bot said, his eyes scanning the swirl of lights, "I am ninety-nine percent sure that *no one* has a record of this."

Awen studied the cluster of lights, looking closely at each planet. "Someone clearly coded this drive with great care. The detail is incredible." She moved her body left and right, up and down. "You're documenting this, right, Ninety-Six?"

"Every millisecond, yes, Awen."

"Good, because—hold on. There," she said, pointing to the fourth planet. "It looks habitable." Her finger no sooner touched the sphere than it expanded to fill the holo-projection. The planet looked like a perfect terrestrial class-four world, capable of propagating carbon-based life. Continents of green floated in large bodies of blue, and two white caps adorned the poles.

Suddenly, the second symbol appeared on the planet's surface, its diamond and two arches centering on a coast near the equatorial line.

"A capital, perhaps," TO-96 offered.

"That's what I was thinking," Awen said.

"Let's get this straight," Ezo interjected. "You're saying that a star system that no one knows about has a habitable planet with a capital city that just so happens to be marked on this stardrive. And that's because…"

"Because someone wants us to find it," Awen answered.

"Haven't you seen the holo-movies?" Ezo said with his hands in the air. "These types of stories never end well. It's why we pay lots of credits to watch them—because seeing someone else get vaporized is much more rewarding than seeing Ezo get vaporized."

"Well," Awen said, "think of it this way. If the Order wants this stardrive, and we have to assume the Republic wants this star drive, then whatever it leads to must be pretty important."

"Important enough to stay away from," Ezo added.

"Important enough to be *very expensive*," Awen corrected. "Making whoever finds it very, *very* rich."

Ezo's mouth froze open, and the two of them stared at each other. *Gotcha.*

"You know," Ezo said, crossing his arms and stroking his chin, "Ezo's having second thoughts about this planet. It might just be worth visiting. Ninety-Six can help Ezo avoid being vaporized. Plus, who knows? Maybe there's a new race of pretty aliens who think Ezo's exotic."

"Here we go again," TO-96 said.

"There's just one problem," Ezo said. "How do we get to a system no one has charted?"

"That's a good question," Awen answered. "And I fear that's where we may not have enough information."

"May I interject something?"

"Of course, TO-96," Awen said.

The bot pointed to a small cluster of three inward-facing triangles floating beneath the planet. As soon as his finger touched them, the planet disappeared, and the stardrive began to pulse.

"What'd you do, 'Six?" Ezo asked.

"I'm not entirely sure, sir. I was hoping that the shape was a data-entry field." The bot leaned back as the space above the table suddenly filled with text that flowed down in vertical streams. TO-96's servos chattered as his head twitched to keep up with the code.

To Awen, the lines of data looked like a waterfall that cascaded down from a source far above them, one rivulet overlapping with others behind it. Even if the characters had meant something to her individually—which they didn't, as the characters were completely foreign to her—she could no more tell what the message said than read a message on a holo-pad as it was tossed across a room.

"You getting this?" Ezo asked with excitement.

TO-96 did not respond, his head still stuttering in the cascading blue light.

"It's not a rhetorical question, 'Six!"

Ruins of the Galaxy

Still not responding, the bot jiggled, his whole body shaking in the effort. The data stream was flowing more quickly now, the characters running together in long lines.

"Ninety-Six!"

Suddenly, the blue streams of light disappeared. TO-96 froze and fell forward, catching himself on the table, Ezo holding the bot's chest in his arms. The bot looked down at the stardrive as it returned to a steady soft glow.

"What in all the cosmos was that about?" Ezo asked, pushing the bot upright. "Are you okay, Ninety-Six?"

TO-96 looked up. "I know where it is."

Then a new item appeared over the table. It spun slowly, taking the form of a funnel with a coordinate designation hovering beside it, written in Galactic common.

"What'd you do?" Ezo asked. "Wait, was that whole thing some sort of download or something?"

"It seems I have received a sizable amount of data, yes. Including precise coordinates."

"To a system outside our galaxy?" Ezo asked.

"To a system outside our universe," the bot corrected.

Ezo and Awen were stunned, looking from the holo-projection to TO-96 and back. "But… how is that possible?" Ezo asked.

"The multiverse," Awen whispered.

"The *what?*" Ezo threw his hands up in the air. "Just great! Ezo's got a bot who's missing a piece of his head and a mystic who's lost hers entirely."

"Sir," TO-96 said, "assertions about theoretical quantum

states do suggest that multiple universes are not only plausible but probable."

"Yeah, I know, I know," Ezo said, waving the bot off. "But did you hear what you just said? *Theory*. None of it's real enough for us to *see* what this stardrive is proposing."

"But *we've* seen it," Awen added.

Ezo was not entertained. He raised one eyebrow and placed his hands on the table. "*You've* seen it," he said without enthusiasm. "You've got to be kidding me, Star Queen."

"We've seen it," Awen repeated, crossing her arms. "The Luma engage with these dynamics all the time. In the Unity of all things. There are more states of being than any one mind can fathom."

"Superpositions," TO-96 added.

"*Superstitions* is more like it," Ezo said.

"That's the technical term, yes. *Superpositions*, that is." Awen glared at Ezo. "For us, however, it is more like layers of reality rippling outward from a single point of action. Each wave represents an alternative state that extends itself into new ways of being. Think of it like a tree that grows limbs, then branches, then twigs, then leaves and seeds. In autumn, seeds make their way into the ground, some of which become new trees over time. One tree can produce an entire forest if the conditions are right."

"Can someone tell Ezo how we suddenly moved from cosmology to botany?" Ezo asked.

"It *is* a quaint analogy," TO-96 said.

"I don't care about quaint!" Ezo exclaimed. "I care about a

star system hovering over my table that no one's ever mapped *in another universe!*"

"Well, sir—"

"No, 'Six! Don't answer. That was rhetorical."

"Very good, sir."

Awen squinted at the new object in the holo-projection. "So, is that a wormhole?"

"No, though I believe it may behave much the same way as a wormhole."

"I'm confused," Awen replied.

"So is Ezo," the smuggler said.

"Without making it too complicated for you," TO-96 said, taking on the air of a professor, "wormholes are essentially gateways that connect two points in the same space-time. Unlike a black hole, however, they contain no event horizon. A black hole's event horizon is known as a singularity."

"Where all things become one," Awen offered.

"Precisely," TO-96 said, jabbing a finger at her. "The problem with a singularity is that it's fairly problematic for anything that needs to stay atomically stable in order to survive."

"You mean, like people," Awen said.

"Like people, yes. Or planets. Anything as you know it will not retain its present form as it is drawn into the gravity well of a black hole."

"But you're saying it's not like either a wormhole or a black hole?" Awen asked.

"As far as I can tell, yes. This cosmic feature has the singularity of a black hole but the portal properties of a wormhole. It appears to make use of something called quantum tunneling."

"So it's like a black hole and a wormhole, but it's not either of them," Ezo summarized.

"Correct, especially since neither term is used by the Novia Minoosh."

"The Novia who?" Awen moved toward the bot, her eyes alight with wonder.

"The Novia Minoosh. They are the race who formed the gate and whose star system we observed."

"Whoa, whoa, *whoa!*" Ezo exclaimed. "They *formed* that quantum-gate thingy?"

"As I said, the Novia Minoosh don't call it—"

"You actually know their name?" Awen asked, leaning over toward TO-96.

"Why, yes. That is what they listed in the data provided to me in the—"

"It's a new civilization!" Awen yelled, completely abandoning decorum. "In the multiverse! I can't believe this!" She started pacing back and forth, her hands fluttering beside her cheeks. Ezo and TO-96 stared. Ezo was surprised by her sudden outburst. This version of Awen wasn't anything like the well-mannered emissary they'd known up to this point. "The implications are…" Awen paused, searching for the words. "Oh, mystics—this is *groundbreaking!* This is *extraordinary!* I mean, the academy always postulated that quantum displacement would populate latticed anomalies, but this! It's…"

Awen was out of breath, glancing back and forth between

them. Then she suddenly remembered herself. She stopped pacing, straightened her back, and cleared her throat. "Forgive me," she said, having regained her composure. "This is a—an important breakthrough, which—"

"It's okay, Star Queen. You can freak out."

Awen threw her hands in the air. "Right? It's unbelievable!"

"I do share Awen's enthusiasm," TO-96 said, "though in slightly less demonstrative expressions. It would appear that this *quantum tunnel*, as I think we should take to calling it, is positioned in the outer reaches of the Troja quadrant." TO-96, now apparently connected to the stardrive, caused it to zoom out without using his hands until the quantum tunnel appeared as a small blip in a larger collection of star systems. "There."

"I've never been that far," Awen said.

"I don't think *anyone's* been *that* far," Ezo added. "We'd have to, have to…" He trailed off as though lost in calculations.

"We'd have to take on a second drive core," TO-96 said.

"A *second* drive core?" Awen repeated. "You can do that?"

"Quite easily, yes," the bot replied. "Or a drive-core modulator if we want to get there more quickly."

"A modulator for higher levels of subspace travel," Awen said. "They increase speed over time, depending on what levels a ship is outfitted to achieve."

"Precisely, Awen."

"A few Luma ships have them, but I thought they were expensive. As in, *sell-the-ship-to-buy-the-modulator* type of expensive."

"Once again, you are very perceptive," the bot said. "In fact, both a second drive core or a modulator currently exceed the balance of Captain Ezo's credit account, which presently rests at—"

"Hey, hey," Ezo said. "Don't you know it's not polite to share our financial status with guests?"

"I was merely trying—"

"You were trying to lessen the Star Queen's hopes of making it to the quantum tunnel," Ezo said, moving around the bot to place a hand on Awen. "And that is no way to treat such a lovely—and respectable—guest." He looked at TO-96. "Don't you see how badly she wants to meet these Novia Nims, Mini, Moosh—"

"Minoosh, sir."

"Nooshes? Awen, I promise you"—Ezo looked her straight in the eyes—"we are going to get you there, or my name isn't Idris Ezo."

"But, sir, your real name is—"

"Shut it, 'Six!"

23

The little girl let go of her mother's hand and approached Magnus. He wasn't sure what to make of the child's identification of him, as he was quite sure he'd never met her before. He would have remembered her or her parents—well, at least her mother.

"Calm down," she said, motioning him with her little fingers.

"Piper, don't be rude, darling," Valerie said.

"It's not a problem," Magnus replied, though inwardly, he always got a little nervous around kids. He'd only had one sibling—a younger brother—and no cousins.

Magnus knelt and placed his helmet on the floor. "I'm Adonis," he said, guessing they should start on a first-name basis. He didn't want to be "Mr. Magnus" to her—that was his father.

"I know."

"Piper!" Valerie scolded. "Mind your manners."

"I'm Piper," she said, holding out her hand.

"It's nice to meet you, Piper."

"Pleased to meet you," she replied, shaking one of Magnus's fingers. Then, in one quick motion, she let go of his hand, dropped her stuffed animal to the floor, and placed both her palms against Magnus's cheeks. Magnus almost recoiled; the gesture was so intimate, and he was a stranger after all. But her face held curiosity and delight, and he felt that pulling away might disappoint her. She smiled at him, her hands pressing harder against the sides of his face as his lips smushed together. Magnus looked up to see that Valerie was aghast.

"I was right," Piper said. "It *is* you."

"It's me?" Magnus asked, looking back at Piper.

"Yes. Of course. You remember, right?" Piper stepped back.

"Remember? I'm sorry, Piper, I don't—"

"After the explosion. You walked up to me. You looked very scary at first. I thought you were a bad guy. I thought you were going to hurt me. But then you told me everything was going to be okay and took off your helmet."

"I'm so sorry, Piper. I don't think I know what you're talking about." Magnus was disturbed by her use of the word *explosion* and even more disturbed by how utterly convinced she was that whatever she was describing had really happened. She spoke as if she believed it—as if she *knew* it.

"Of course you do," she replied, withdrawing her hands. "You and I were just there together. You're so silly."

"You'll have to forgive her," Valerie said, kneeling next to the girl and holding her shoulders. "She's been having very intense dreams."

"It wasn't a dream, Mama. I keep telling you, but you don't believe me."

"Sure I do, darling."

"No," Piper said wrestling from her mother's grip and moving beside Magnus. "You don't believe me. But Adonis does." She looked into his face, wispy strands of blond hair falling over her blue eyes and freckled nose. "Don't you, Adonis?"

Magnus hesitated. For some reason, he felt himself wishing Awen was with them. *She would know what to say.* He looked from Valerie to Darin and back to Piper. "I, uh—"

"But, Adonis," Piper pleaded, "we were *just there*. You—you *rescued* me."

"I'm sorry, Piper, but I don't—"

"No one believes me." Piper reached down for her stuffed animal, spun away from Magnus, and ran around the couches.

"Piper! Come back!" Her mother moved to follow her, but the senator caught her arm. The girl ran down the corridor, her soft footfalls fading away to nothing.

"I'm very sorry for that, Magnus," the senator said, inviting him to sit back down.

"Yes, she's been having very vivid dreams as of late," Valerie added. "We're not sure why or what they mean. All scans show normal brain activity, but there seems to be…"

Magnus watched as the senator reached for Valerie's forearm. *Not the most loving point of connection when trying to comfort someone. Are they hiding something? Because that sure looks like a reminder not to say too much.*

"Seems to be what?" Magnus asked.

"Nothing," Valerie said, waving him off and placing her hand over her husband's. "It's nothing."

Magnus looked between them. Clearly, she'd been about to share more—*wanted* to share more. But her husband was stopping her. "If there's something else going on, you need to tell us. Maybe we can help."

The senator took a deep breath and looked at his wife then back at Magnus. "Her dreams are… there have been some… *manifestations*."

"Manifestations?" Magnus asked, furrowing his brow. "Can you explain?"

"It seems that when she dreams, things happen," Valerie said. "I woke her up from a dream where she said she was falling into a mountain, reaching for the sides of a bottomless pit. When I woke her up, her fingers were… were…"

"Her fingers were bloody, Lieutenant," the senator finished. "As if she had just run them across rough granite."

"And the dream of the explosion she just told you about…" Valerie's eyes filled with tears. "That was last night."

"You don't think it had something to do with your drive-core failure, do you?" Magnus asked, suddenly concerned that maybe these people had lost their minds. Maybe the air was going stale, or there was a containment leak. He knew crazy things could happen in the void.

"We're not sure, of course," the senator said. "This is far too speculative to be conclusive. However, our engineer hasn't been able to assign a cause for the sudden failure."

Just then, Gilder called over the handheld comm.

"Go ahead, Private," Magnus said.

"She's dead, Lieutenant."

"Excuse me?"

"She's dead, sir. The drive core, I mean. I know I'm new to my job and all, but even I can tell you that this core is down for the count. Sucked dry."

"That's what our engineer said, too, Lieutenant," the senator said. "I can confirm his findings."

Magnus spoke back into the radio. "You absolutely sure about that, Private?"

"Sure that it's never gonna push an electron again, sir," replied Gilder. "Whatever hit this thing, it isn't like anything I've ever seen. I don't think I ever even saw a completely depleted core at school. Yet the life support and systems generators are completely intact."

"Copy that. Come on back." Magnus looked at the senator. "Looks like you've got yourself a floating house without a motor."

"So it seems."

"Listen, Senator. I can't say I know anything about your daughter. That's above my pay grade. But I do know we can get you to the closest substation, and you're on your own from there. Is that acceptable with you?"

"Quite so, Lieutenant." The senator stood and extended his hand. "Thank you."

"Our pleasure, sir," Magnus said, shaking it.

"Lieutenant?" came a voice over the handheld comm's secondary channel. It was the warrant officer.

"Go ahead, Nolan."

"A ship just jumped out of subspace. Bull Wraith. And it's got a lock on our position."

"Republic?" Magnus asked.

"Sir, I—"

"Is it a Republic vessel?"

"I can't tell, sir."

"What do you mean, you can't tell?"

"It's not broadcasting any designation classifiers and won't reply to hails. Closing quickly. AI puts it at ninety-eight seconds."

Splick. This isn't good. No Republic ship was that *hard to get ahold of.* The whole thing felt off to him, which meant it was time to leave. And fast.

"Prepare to depart, Nolan. We'll be there in sixty."

"What's happening?" Valerie asked.

"Grab your daughter, and leave everything else," Magnus ordered. Then he broadcast on the primary channel, "Time to jump, team. Exfil on the double."

"ALL SOULS ACCOUNTED FOR," Dutch yelled to the bridge.

"Detach," Nolan ordered Rawlson.

"Detaching." There was a momentary pause, and the ship shuddered. "Ship away, ship away," Rawlson said.

"Well, would you look at that," the senator said, peeking his head inside the bridge. Out the starboard window loomed one of the most foreboding heavy armored transports in the galaxy. Bull Wraiths, while not destroyers, still packed a serious punch for any ship unlucky enough to tangle with one. The black hulk looked more like a battering ram than a starship and boasted two mega-gauss cannons on either side of its nose-forward bridge. Several Titan missile-defense batteries were clustered above and below the hull, while T300 blaster turrets covered the sides.

Beyond weapons capabilities, the ship also had an advanced cargo and rapid delivery system, or ACARD. It was able to stow and deploy everything from munitions and troops to armament and small cruisers faster than most ships could run a startup sequence. It deployed its cargo from four cavities, including one under the bridge, which Magnus always thought looked like a giant maw ready to chomp down on prey. It was commonly said that if the Bull Wraith didn't scare you, whatever was in it should.

"You gotta give us *something*, Nolan," Magnus said.

"Almost ready, sir."

"That's not good enough." He watched the warrant officer finish the start-up sequence, port the two main engine ventricles, and slide his fingers up the dashboard for full engine burn.

"There she is," Nolan said. "Everyone hold on! Engines ahead, full!"

Magnus and the senator grabbed seat backs as the ship lurched forward. The cockpit rattled, and a loud roar filled the air. While the Sparrow didn't meet anyone's definition of comfortable, it was fast, and that was all that mattered at the moment.

"How soon until we can jump?" Magnus asked, yelling above the engines.

"Coordinates almost calculated!" Rawlson replied.

"Jump core standing by!" Gilder added.

"Lock in those coordinates," Nolan ordered. "We need to be gone yesterday!"

The roar would have been deafening had it lasted any longer. Magnus glanced at Rawlson's displays and saw that they were pulling away from the Bull Wraith. A small wave of relief filled his chest. But he'd seen far too much action to know that nothing was over until you'd had at least one good meal to commemorate your survival.

"Locked!" Rawlson yelled.

"Jumping!" Nolan exclaimed and slid the secondary throttle fields to full. But nothing happened. No space-time bend, no light stretch—nothing. To make things worse, the engines suddenly started to wind down.

"I need to know what's going on here, Nolan," Magnus ordered.

"I don't know, sir."

"That's unacceptable!"

"Jump core off-line," Rawlson yelled. "Propulsion off-line. Navigation off-line!"

Nolan spun around. "How's this happening?"

"It's the other ship, isn't it, Lieutenant?" the senator said.

Magnus was afraid of this. While the Republic placed certain limitations on its weapons capabilities, particularly hostile long-range ship-to-ship interfacing, non-Republic fleets did not feel the need to be so ethical. *No doubt a Luma stipulation or some political jockey who wanted to make everyone* feel better *about having the deadliest navy in the galaxy.* But they weren't the deadliest navy, at least not anymore. That was the irony of it all. To make the public feel like you were less of a monster, you had to reduce your battle readiness, which always made you more of a target. It was a brutal cycle.

"Well, I think it's safe to say she ain't Repub," Magnus said.

"Sir," Rawlson said, "we're being towed in."

"Can't throw it off?" Nolan asked.

"Negative, sir."

"She's got us right where she wants us." Magnus turned to the senator. "Sir, I want you and your family in the captain's quarters. It will be the safest place for you until we have a plan."

"But, Lieutenant—"

"Sir, your safety is my mission objective. End of story."

"I understand."

"Dutch," Magnus said.

"Yes, Lieutenant."

"You seem to like that armory."

"Yes, sir," she replied.

"Outfit everyone with a blaster then help me fortify the cargo bay for optimal cover."

"Copy that."

"All hands," Magnus said in a full voice, "prepare to be boarded."

24

For the first time since the attack on the mwadim's palace, hope had returned to Awen—not enough to dissuade her from leaving the Order but enough to make her see this last thing through. After all, no one in three generations had discovered a new race. And beyond that, she didn't know of anyone discovering life in another universe.

Awen had her doubts, of course. The whole thing could be a scheme, someone's idea of a grand joke. But based on how many people had died for this stardrive and the lengths her master—the traitor—had gone to for its acquisition, she very much doubted this was a joke.

A new world in a new universe. She tried to drift off to sleep for the first time in days. Suddenly, all the pain she'd endured felt worth something. It was not all in vain if it meant making the cultural discovery of the century. *Maybe even the cultural discovery of the* millennium.

She began to wonder what this new planet looked like, what color its star was. Then she wondered if the other universe's model of physics even behaved like her universe's. For all she knew, *Geronimo Nine* would cease to exist the moment it crossed the quantum tunnel's event horizon.

But that didn't seem likely. Why go to so much trouble to contact another universe only to invite visitors to their instant deatomization? She opened her eyes in the darkness. *A hostile species might do that. Plus, no one would ever survive long enough to report back, so it would be effective. Diabolical, but effective.*

"No," she said out loud and readjusted her pillow. "That's not going to happen." At least she hoped it wasn't. A race advanced enough to communicate beyond the limitations of space-time surely wouldn't be hell-bent on annihilating extra-local species without even meeting them. Plus, TO-96 seemed to have the physics worked out in that strange head of his—at least in theory.

Awen suddenly felt a wave of guilt that she was not sharing this news with anyone else. The galaxy should know, after all. But who could she contact? Not the Luma, as all communication channels were probably compromised. She wished she could at least speak to Willowood, ask her for advice, maybe even get her to come along. But Awen had already put the elder's life in grave danger—she wasn't about to jeopardize her further.

Next, she thought about her parents. She wanted to contact them. But any efforts to do so would probably only put their lives in danger, she concluded with a growing sense of remorse. If she survived this—if they all survived this—Awen would tell her father that pursuing peace beyond Elonia was possible. And *necessary*.

Awen also wished she could contact Magnus. He would be good to have along on this expedition. *As a professional—a trooper—of course. One I can trust. One who I…*

She couldn't bring herself to finish that thought, at a loss for words that would express her feelings about him.

And what do you feel, Awen?

"Gratitude," she said out loud. "That's all." But she knew she was lying to herself.

Awen felt herself sinking deeper into the bed, the covers pulled tight around her chin. Just as the last wave of consciousness overtook her, she wondered if Magnus had read her handwritten note yet. She smiled.

GERONIMO NINE ENTERED the Psylon system and made port on Ki Nar Four without incident—Awen's vomiting aside. Being on the far side of the Omodon quadrant in the Khimere sector, the back-world planet was a longtime haven for the galaxy's most notorious criminals. Unlike the Dregs, where setting up shop close to the Jujari offered some semblance of protection, Ki Nar Four was for those who truly wanted to disappear from watchful Republic and non-Republic eyes alike. The downside to this, of course, was that Ki Nar Four had its own set of rules and, therefore, its own sets of eyes.

The planet itself was a constantly rupturing sphere of molten lava and charred tectonic plates. Seismic shifts would have shattered anything built on the crust, so the first pioneers established small floating cities a few kilometers above the surface. What the class-two terrestrial planet lacked in the more obvious natural resources essential to sustaining life—such as water and biofuel, which had to be imported—it made up for in raw power. The constant release of elemental gases and heat made ideal commodities that not only supported the energy needed to keep large cities hovering in atmosphere but also served as revenue streams for whoever exported them to the rest of the quadrant. The person who controlled the elements controlled the credits. And that was just who Ezo was headed to see.

"You should stay with the ship," Ezo said to Awen as he checked his pistol in the cargo bay.

"Nice try," Awen replied, moving past him toward the open ramp.

"Whoa, where do you think you're going? You can't be seen walking out there."

"And why not?"

"You're a Luma. Of all planets in the galaxy, this one hates your kind the most."

"Do I *look* like a Luma to you?" Awen said, sweeping her hand over her outfit.

Ezo placed the barrel of his pistol under her necklace and held up the medallion. Awen snatched it away and stuffed it inside her turtleneck.

"It's still best if you stay here, Awen."

"I have to admit he's right," TO-96 said.

"See?" Ezo raised his palms. "Told you."

"This is no place for a lady," the bot continued. "You'll only draw unnecessary attention to us… well, to Ezo, anyway."

"To the both of us," Ezo corrected, looking at the bot. "Why just me?"

"Sir, no one of her caliber has stayed with you for more than a night. I'm afraid that will only serve to—"

"And that's enough of *that*," Ezo said, glaring at the bot. He holstered his pistol and smoothed his leather jacket.

"You might need me," Awen said.

Ezo laughed. "Need *you?* If you haven't noticed, Ezo has gotten along fine without you until now. You may be overestimating your importance, Star Queen. Remember, it was *you* who needed *us* back on Worru."

"Sir," TO-96 said, "by my calculations, Awen's presence does increase your odds of survivability by thirty-eight percent should you encounter violent resistance here."

"*Our* odds, Ninety-Six. *Our* odds of survival."

"Not true. Mine remain well over ninety percent."

"Since when did I ask you about any of this?"

"You always seem to be in favor of things that increase the likelihood that you will survive any given situation. I simply didn't see a reason for that to change."

"Huh, would you look at that," Awen said, returning to the ramp. "Seems we're a trio."

"Hey!" Ezo said, lifting a dark-brown cloak toward her. "At least put this on!"

Awen followed behind Ezo and TO-96, making sure to keep her face hidden within the cloak's hood. Even the bot donned a cloak to keep wayward eyes from resting on his gleaming metal parts. *At least I won't be the only one kidnapped.*

The concrete labyrinth of Gangil, the largest of Ki Nar Four's floating cities, writhed in dark-green light, busy with all manner of life, both sentient and pest. The sulfur from the planet's surface, mixed with decaying life from the pavement, formed a stench Awen had never experienced before and hoped never to encounter again.

The three guests crisscrossed through the grim city streets, boots splashing through black puddles and sidestepping bodies that were sleeping or dead—Awen couldn't determine which. She wished for a flashlight to help pick her way through the refuse but then thought better of it. Sometimes, it was best not to know.

Awen noticed the population increase as they moved farther from the starport and toward the city's center. Beings of every species jostled against her, many marring her cloak with their wet exterior biology. She was suddenly very thankful that Ezo had insisted she wear it.

They passed by eateries that Awen couldn't believe remained in business and walked under red lights that invited pedestrians to gaze through glass windows at things Awen was embarrassed to admit she'd glimpsed. She wiped the sweat from her forehead, noting just how hot the air was even so far above the surface. Several aliens whistled at Ezo, some even calling him by name.

Awen glanced at the scantily clad humanoids then back at Ezo. *Really?*

Ezo wasn't the easiest person for her to like as it was, but seeing how he confidently moved on what was easily the seediest planet she'd ever seen made her question his moral compass even more. She realized—much to her shame—that she'd placed her trust in Ezo because Abimbola had arranged their meeting. *Abimbola*, a warlord from the Dregs of Oorajee.

All at once, Awen wondered if she wasn't a total idiot for opening the stardrive in front of Ezo and agreeing to let him help her. *But I* convinced *him to help me. I practically bribed him with a payout!*

Oh, how she wanted to gag her inner monologue. *But what else should I expect when moving from the halls of Plumeria to the stalls of Gangil?*

Finding Sootriman's den wasn't difficult. It sat in the very center of the floating city like a massive bronze cooking pot complete with rounded lid and torrents of steam. It took up at least ten city blocks, by Awen's estimate, and was detailed with all manner of suspended walkways, grates, circular tube vents, and hatches. The green residue she'd seen everywhere else in the city bled from its rusted holes and exhaust ports. Tattered rags spanned oddly placed decks, and ladders climbed the twenty-story building like skeletons standing on one another's shoulders, each hoping in vain to make it to the summit and achieve some fabled resurrection.

"Let Ezo do all the talking," Ezo said as they approached two massive metal doors. He used the butt of his pistol to pound on the right door. Awen expected the strikes to produce a resounding echo. Instead, the sound was a dull *thud, thud, thud,* betraying just how thick the doors were.

A metal plate slid open above their heads, and a single reptilian eye appeared. It darted around and then looked down, settling on Ezo, then TO-96, then Awen. She winced and lowered her head under the hood.

"Ezo to see Sootriman."

"You're not expected," a lizard-like voice said.

Awen felt a chill travel up her spine. Maybe staying with the ship would have been a better idea after all. *But I wanted this, and now I have it and will have to deal with it.*

"That's true," Ezo agreed. "But when does anyone ever expect their debt holders to come knocking?"

The lizard hissed, moved the eye to all three figures again, then slid the panel shut.

"We're in," Ezo said. The right door unlatched with a *clank* and began a mechanically driven move inward. Ezo turned to Awen. "Don't look around, and don't let anything touch you."

"Understood." She followed TO-96 into the darkness with Ezo leading the way.

Inside the den, light emitted from small ports on either side of the floor every five meters. It was barely enough for Awen to see her steps by and not nearly enough to make out anything at head level. She wondered where the gatekeeper had gone and almost chanced a look behind her. She thought better of it, however, given Ezo's advice, and reined in her impulses.

Instead of exploring the world around her, Awen moved

inward to her spirit, finding herself centered in the Unity. She took several deep breaths to calm her nerves. Then, slowly, she pressed her senses outward, seeing first her body, then TO-96's energy, then Ezo's body. She moved with the ripples of energy that reverberated off every element in the hallway—the floor, the domed ceiling, and the side corridors. Then she felt bodies that lay slumped in passages, rodents that scurried through refuse drains, and several guards who absentmindedly monitored the progress of three unexpected guests through drug-laden eyes. She also sensed something growing along the walls—something with a soul. Something aggressive. Something reaching for her.

In the Unity, everything could become more vivid if enough concentration was employed, including smells. Alien blood mixed with excrement and bodily fluids that she couldn't place. Rotting flesh signaled someone's fate and someone else's meal. And permeating it all was the horrendous stench of sulfur, which was somehow concentrated in these hallways. But at least in the Unity, she could purposely dim certain elements of her surroundings—smells being her first choice here.

Ezo led them up a wide staircase, across some sort of courtyard, and down another hallway. More and more manner of lifeforms appeared the deeper they moved, and Awen felt content to remain in the Unity as long as she could. It was safer there.

Finally, Ezo stopped at a second set of doors, this set even taller and wider than the first. Several guards stood up as the trio approached. Awen examined them from within the Unity. They were a form of reptilian sentient she'd never encountered, standing on their hind legs head and shoulders above Ezo. Their tails slapped back and forth on the wet concrete, apparently excited for the newcomers. Black metal plates covered any exposed flesh not already protected by the lizards' thick scales, and they clasped long energy rods in their claws.

As she examined them, Awen picked up a rather forbidding detail: bits of rotting flesh between their teeth. *At least I know what happens to guests Sootriman doesn't care to see again.*

The foremost lizard flicked its forked tongue and let out a blast of air from its nostrils. "What's this doing back here?" it hissed to no one in particular. "Idris Ezo."

"Ezo's come to settle a debt with Sootriman," Ezo replied.

"Sootriman owes Ezo no debts," replied the guard.

"Ezo begs to differ," Ezo said with easy confidence. Awen honestly couldn't tell if the man was lying or telling the truth.

"How about we just taste you instead." The other lizards started flicking their tongues too, an action that fluttered the realm of the Unity with small vibrations of energy. The beasts were more powerful than Awen had imagined. She sensed the strength of their long, lean, muscled bodies.

"You could," Ezo said. "Nimprinth is not that bad on the palate. Throw in a little wantim glaze, and you'd each be in lizard ecstasy." Ezo's words produced a dramatic hissing response from the guards, so much so that Awen was worried they'd leap on him that instant.

"However," Ezo added, raising his index finger, "if word gets out that Sootriman didn't make good on a debt, all because *you* ate the claimant, Ezo can't imagine what that might do to the reputation of this house. Imagine how upset Sootriman would be." Ezo shook his head in mock wonderment.

"Silence, human!" the main guard said. "You speak simply to tempt us to our own graves." The flicking of their tongues slowed down. "We are not so easily led astray."

"Ezo can see now that you are both clever and cunning," Ezo said with a sigh, his words dripping with disappointment. "And here Ezo thought he'd get you to bite him."

"We may later, if our master decides your claim is not legitimate."

"Looking forward to that."

"As do we," hissed the guard. Then it turned and snapped an order to its underlings. The doors began an arduous sweep toward them, pushing aside small carcasses. Ezo stepped back, along with TO-96 and Awen.

"That was fairly impressive," Awen whispered to him.

"Eh, fight-or-flight instinct is pretty easy to sideline, *if* you know what you're doing," Ezo whispered back.

"And if you don't know what you're doing?" Awen asked.

"When you're dealing with Reptalons? Well, you never live to tell about it, so it all works out in the end. The bright side is you don't make the same mistake twice."

"Right," Awen said. "That's a great bright side."

"You ready to meet Sootriman?"

"Uh, I guess?"

"Just remember, Ezo told you to stay with the ship."

25

Magnus crouched beneath a freight container with his index finger on his MAR30's safety. He'd taken point, insisting that everyone else find defensive positions farther back. Dutch had armed everyone else with MX13 subcompact blasters, ideal for close-quarters combat and limited-range fire. When the ramp went down, if the boarding party was anything but fawning over them in friendliness, Magnus hoped to unleash enough hell that his crew could exfil and find additional cover. They'd regroup and improvise from there. It wasn't a good plan. In fact, it was a terrible plan. But given their current resources, it was the best he had.

Magnus waited, forcing himself to slow his heart rate. Adrenaline did stupid things to your judgment. Sure, it could help in certain situations, but those were few and far between. It was always best to stay cool and pace oneself.

The crew had gone to ground three minutes before, and the ship had touched down inside the Bull Wraith five minutes before. The supposed enemy force had already passed the standard breach-and-entry time line that Republic Marines trained on. *What are they waiting for?*

"Any movement, Lieutenant?" Nolan asked over comms. Magnus had coded the handheld comms into his helmet's TACNET.

"Negative, Cap. They haven't so much as knocked on the front door."

"I know I'm only the pilot here, but doesn't that seem off to you?"

"Affirmative. Either these are the laziest pirates in the galaxy or—"

Or what? Why would anyone capture a ship but not breach it? "Or they don't care about the ships and they want the hostages alive," Magnus said.

"The senator," Nolan offered.

"That's what I'm thinking." Magnus looked over the container at the ramp. "Splick, these bogies aren't coming in. They're just as happy to keep us—" He felt his stomach lurch and a brief wave of vertigo. "We just jumped into subspace," he said to Nolan.

"I felt it too, sir."

"Dammit." Magnus didn't like this. The more known variables, the better, and one more just got knocked off his list. Now they didn't know *who* had them, *why* they had them, or *where* they were headed. However, Magnus was not completely in the dark.

As he began to shape the mental battlefield to his will, intel started to reveal itself, even if it was incomplete.

Whoever had captured them was more brazen and calculated than he'd given them credit for. Magnus realized that every act had been highly intentional—swift arrival, no communication, no boarding. And that worried him. Someone was following strict orders. Their situation was growing more desperate by the minute, and a single plan—a desperate plan—started to take shape in Magnus's head.

"Have everyone assemble here in the cargo bay," he ordered. "New strategy."

THE SENATOR and Valerie stood beside a small container with Piper sitting on top of it. Their flight crew stood next to them. Nolan and his flight crew took up the middle, flanked by Dutch, Haney, and Gilder to form the rest of a half circle.

"I'm not sure how much time we have," Magnus said from the center, "so I'm going to make this quick. The most important thing is that none of us lose our cool. We stay calm, and we all have a better shot of making it out of this without getting our"—he hesitated, looking at the kid—"without a scratch. Copy?"

Various affirmations went up from among the group. Magnus smiled at Piper. "That means you and Mr. Cuddles there—"

"Talisman," Piper corrected, squeezing the stuffed animal tighter.

Kind of a creepy name for a kid to use. "You and Talisman gotta do your best to help everyone stay calm too. You got it?"

"We got it," Piper replied.

"Now, we could be in subspace for hours or even days," he continued, looking around at everyone. "It means once you get to where I tell you, you stay there. You stay hydrated, but you don't move. I don't care if you have to piss your pants—*no one moves.* Copy?"

The group in front of him nodded and gave their verbal assent.

"Good. Now the hard part. Without eyes and ears on the enemy ship's bridge, we won't know our destination port. There are elements of risk with every plan, and this is probably our biggest. Chances are, however, that we'll be within emergency-pod distance of a Republic relay or habitat planet."

"Emergency-pod distance?" the senator asked. "Wait, do you mean to tell me that your plan is—"

"To jettison every last one of us in the Bull Wraith's escape capsules, yes."

The senator was clearly not excited about the plan. "Excuse me, Lieutenant," he said, taking a step forward. "I don't mean to discount your military experience here, but there has to be another way besides inadvertently flinging us into deep space or an uninhabitable planet. Plus, who's to say that *the enemy* doesn't circle back and pick us up?"

"Senator, they'd more likely use us for target practice than pick us up."

The senator blanched. "Lieutenant, I'm not sure I'm following any of your logic here."

"Okay, first of all, they're *not* going to shoot us down."

"But you just said—"

"Under normal circumstances, yes, I said target practice. But whoever they want, their orders have been to take us alive."

"How can you be so sure?" the senator asked.

"Because otherwise, they would have boarded us already. Someone wants at least one of us alive, and my credits are on you, Senator. But that's beside the point. They won't risk firing on any of the escape capsules for that very reason."

"So we're back to them picking us up."

"Which they might do, but not all of us. They won't have time."

"I don't follow," the senator said.

"Assuming that this Bull Wraith was once a Republic heavy-armored transport, which it has to be since no other space dock in the galaxy that we know of is capable of making them, one of the very last things to get recoded are emergency pods."

"Their homing beacons are on proprietary Republic channels," Dutch offered.

"That's right. And since every last one has to be recoded manually, they're way down on the commander's to-do list. As long as we all depart from the ship in different directions—"

"The cavalry is bound to show up before most of us are recovered," Nolan concluded.

Magnus nodded. "And if we're near a habitat planet, even

better. They won't risk an atmosphere reentry recovery. Far too dangerous."

"There's only one problem, Lieutenant," the senator said. "I'm not leaving my family."

Magnus had been afraid of that. Marines took orders and knew what it meant to sacrifice for the greater good. It was part of their warrior ethos. But the family man, senator or not, was hard to reason with when it came to something he wasn't willing to lose.

That's why you've never kept anything that close, isn't it, Magnus?

"Senator Stone, I understand that you—"

"You understand *nothing*, Lieutenant, if you think for one second that I'm putting my wife and my daughter in two separate pods and placing ourselves at the mercy of the void."

"Sir, I—"

"Darin, my love," Valerie said, approaching him from the side.

"No!" the senator exclaimed, pulling away from her hands. "No, Valerie. This is not the best way. I can reason with whoever is helming this ship."

"You don't know that," Magnus replied.

"I'm a member of the Galactic Senate, Lieutenant. And these people *will* listen to reason when the weight of the entire Republic is leveraged against them."

"Sir—"

"Stop trying to reason with me, Lieutenant. There are other alternatives besides this foolhardy errand of yours. We reason with them, find a compromise, and no one gets hurt."

"Or everyone dies," Magnus replied, "because you severely underestimated an enemy who is able to track down a disabled starship, get to it as fast as the nearest Repub rescue team, and then brazenly abduct the entire ship and its crew without so much as cracking a comm or breaching the ship. Whoever these people are, Mr. Senator, they are not going to reason with anyone, because they are playing by their own rules. They're not afraid of you or me and certainly not afraid of the Republic."

He took a step toward the senator. He did not want to embarrass the man in front of his family or his staff, but he also didn't want anyone to die needlessly, not on his watch. Magnus lowered his voice. "So trust me when I say, Senator, I've thought this through, and *this is* the best chance of survival that you and your family will ever have in a moment like this."

Senator Stone eyed Magnus hard. Magnus had the distinct impression that he was toe to toe with a man who'd stood up to the most pompous, sniveling bureaucrats in the galaxy and won. Stone was not a pushover. But neither was Magnus. Had the roles been reversed and they'd been in some political mess on Capriana Prime, Magnus felt he would back off and let the senator get them out of harm's way. He only hoped the senator was thinking the same thing, because the alternative was knocking the man out cold and jettisoning him into the void against his will and without the ability to input course corrections. But Magnus would do it, if he had to, for the sake of everyone else's lives.

"Very well, Lieutenant."

Magnus felt his muscles relax and resisted the urge to take a deep breath. "Thank you, Senator. I will do my very best to ensure that you and your family are as close together as possible."

"I believe you," he replied.

Magnus looked at the others, knelt, and placed a holo-pad on the floor. "All right, team, here's the plan."

"THAT'S THE LAST OF THEM," Gilder said as he dangled upside down in the vertical shaft. He handed the drill and bolts up to Dutch, who set them aside.

"You good, Gilder?" Magnus asked down the tube.

"Roger that," the engineer said.

"Okay, easy does it," Magnus said as Haney and Nolan eased Gilder's legs lower. They continued to lower the engineer down the tube until his boots were almost below the decking.

"That's good," Gilder whispered. He let go of the hatch, which sat on the Bull Wraith's cargo bay floor, slowly slid it to the side, and motioned to be hauled up. Once he was next to them again, Gilder pushed himself onto all fours, face red as a cherry and sweating profusely. He wiped his brow. "I almost passed out."

"So did we," Haney said, stretching his arms. "If you make it through this, I'm suggesting a diet."

"A diet? If I make it through this, I'm eating everything I want!"

"Have that discussion later." Magnus looked at Dutch. "You ready?"

She double-checked her MX13, modified with a suppressor

and an extended energy mag, then nodded. "Locked and loaded, LT." No one had called him that since… *since Flow*. Magnus felt his heart sink just a little.

You gonna get her killed too, Magnus?

"No, I'm not," Magnus said.

"Come again, LT?" Dutch asked.

"Nothing. It's go time." He put on his helmet and started the countdown. "Sixty seconds. Go, go, go."

Dutch slid down the ladder and landed on the cargo-bay floor without so much as a click. Rawlson followed her, and the two of them disappeared.

Magnus pulled up Dutch's badge cam in his HUD and watched as the two Marines leapfrogged beneath the ship's belly. Then they made a short dash to a control panel against the bay's nearest wall.

"They made it," Magnus said through his external speaker. The room was full of the remaining crew and the senator and his family, all of whom breathed a sigh of relief for this first step of the plan.

After several glances out the bridge windows, Magnus realized that the Bull Wraith's crew had made a critical mistake. In their effort to remain anonymous, they'd exchanged physical patrols for systems monitoring. While their suppression dampers kept a captured ship from powering up and attempting to escape, it did nothing to keep the crew from slipping away unnoticed—at least, to a point. Magnus hoped to exploit that opportunity as far as he could.

Dutch and Rawlson were typing furiously on the access panel

when Magnus heard panels unlock and slide apart in the cargo-bay floor beneath the ship.

"That's it," Gilder said, going back down the tube, this time right side up. He crouched under the ship and then gave Magnus a thumbs-up.

"Grates open," Magnus said. "Everyone down, one at a time." They each lined up and prepared to climb down the ladder. Magnus helped Nolan down first, followed by the comm officer, then Haney. Next, he called the senator and Valerie, followed by Piper. Then came the senator's crew. Magnus double-checked to see Dutch and Rawlson return below the ship—his cue to climb down. Magnus had no sooner grabbed the first ladder rung when he felt a sudden wave of vertigo touch him.

"Nolan, confirm you felt that," Magnus said over comms.

"Affirmative. We've jumped out of subspace."

Splick, Magnus thought. "Accelerating the time line, people. Let's move it."

Once underneath the bird, Magnus saw Gilder helping each person slip between the cargo-bay drainage grates that Dutch and Rawlson had opened. *So far, so good. Keep it nice and smooth.*

Dutch had disappeared into the drain shaft when Magnus heard someone order them to stop. He looked across the immense cargo bay and saw a Marine—*no, just a trooper*—in black Mark VI armor. The only noticeable insignia were three white stripes on his shoulder plate. *Republic armor... on a Republic ship.* The trooper brought an MX21 to bear on Magnus... *with a Republic blaster!*

"Honeymoon's over!" Magnus yelled at Gilder and Rawlson

and flicked off his safety. "Get in!"

The very first blaster bolt caught Rawlson in the throat, gouging a hole straight through the man's neck. His body fell into Gilder and knocked the bigger man sideways.

Magnus selected high-frequency modulation on his MAR30. He aimed—aided by his helmet's AI—squeezed, and sent a deafening staccato burst of blue light across the cargo bay. His weapon recoiled against his shoulder as wisps of stray static dissipated. The bolts riddled the assaulting trooper with a tight grouping to the chest. The enemy trooper didn't have time to register that the ultra-intensity bolts hadn't even slowed as they passed through his armor and emerged from the back of his chest. He simply slumped to his knees and toppled over—a corpse—before his helmet smacked the floor.

"Get in the hole!" Magnus yelled at Gilder as the engineer crawled out from under Rawlson's body. An emergency klaxon filled the air. "Come on, Marine! Move that fat ass!"

Startled, Gilder dove headfirst between the grates and disappeared. Then Magnus lowered himself in and scanned the area. Everyone but Rawlson had made it below the grates and down the chute.

"Dutch, you copy?"

"Loud and clear, LT."

"Blow it."

"With pleasure."

Magnus hugged his MAR30 to his chest and jumped down the chute as the control console across from the Sparrow detonated into a fireball.

26

Kane had paced in his quarters for nearly an hour. He massaged his head, trying to ease the chronic pain that had been with him since… too long. Since the war. The pressure had become more acute, however, the moment he'd seen *her* name. He hadn't seen it spelled out like that in a long, long time. And the letters had more of an effect on him than he cared to admit.

Is she alive? Or is this someone else using her credentials to their advantage? His thoughts were restless, and he was torn between pursuing the ship signed out in her name and pursuing the ship that was headed toward the object of his desire.

She was once the object of your desire, said that strange voice inside him. It always spoke so calmly, so assuredly. He hated it.

"Yes. I admit that. But things have changed," he replied, knowing that he was only going to goad the interrogator. But maybe this time he would win. "And that was a long time ago."

So time *is what changed your love?* the voice asked.

Kane bristled. "No, things changed over time."

What things?

Kane massaged his head more. He was already irritated by the pain, the memories, and the deep sense of loss. None of it ever left him alone.

"We had different desires. We didn't mean for it to happen. It just… happened."

I see, the voice said, but Kane knew it was condescending to him.

He didn't need to justify himself here. After all, it was *he* who'd done all the living—all the *dying*—not this counterfeit voice in his head.

But you both had the same desires once, the voice retorted.

"We did, yes."

So time changed those as well?

"They changed over time too, yes."

You're mincing words, Kane. You're not answering the question.

This was infuriating. He'd retreated to his quarters often on every ship he'd ever been assigned to, but even more after he'd become *an admiral. Their pet project*, he reminded himself. And then he'd gone off the grid. But in all this solitude, he only ever succeeded in getting berated by himself. *No*, he corrected. *By the voice.*

Answer the question.

Kane knew what *it* was getting at—what it was trying to extract from him. But he hated to let it be right. He walked over to the sink and mirror on the far wall. He let the water run hot and then splashed several handfuls on his face, hoping his skin might feel it. He shut the faucet off and gripped the metal sink with both hands. Water dripped from his face as he glared at himself in the mirror—glared at *it*.

You could have left this fool's errand and gone after that ship yourself, the voice said.

"I know I could have."

Then why didn't you?

"That's what I have a fleet for."

But she never wanted your fleet.

Kane pounded a fist on the sink. "That was her problem. She didn't want to serve the galaxy either."

Serve the galaxy? the voice said in bewilderment, as if it had just heard something for the first time. Kane knew it was mocking him, as it always did when they sparred about this subject. He glared at it in the mirror, seeing its eyes flick back and forth. *Yet she went to serve the galaxy with* them.

"She was selfish," Kane spat. "All she wanted were the old things. She wasn't open to the possibilities—to what we could have done together."

Or what you wanted to do.

"She had a choice!" Kane noticed spittle running down the mirror. He wondered where it had come from. His hands ached as he squeezed the metal harder. "She had a choice," he repeated.

So did you.

"Is that what this is about?" Kane seethed. "You just want me to admit that I made a choice? That it wasn't time that did it, or distance?"

Yes. That's exactly what I want.

"Fine!" Kane yelled. "I chose! I chose to pursue the greater good instead of her. Are you happy now?"

I don't know, Kane. Are you happy *now?*

"Damn you!" His arms tried to wrest the sink from the wall, saliva bubbling from the corners of his mouth and a small trickle of blood coming from his nose. "Damn you to hell!"

"Admiral," came a voice over the private channel to his quarters.

"Go ahead, Captain." Kane wiped his face with a towel. He noticed blood on it.

"The target ship has made port on Ki Nar Four."

Kane smirked. He folded the towel and laid it over the edge of the sink. "They're most likely refueling, taking on supplies." He paused, brushing the towel's tiny filaments in the same direction. His hands were getting old, the skin thinning. "We wait. Keep our distance. When they jump again, watch for subspace variations."

"Understood, Admiral."

So, you're going after them, concluded the voice.

"Yes," Kane replied.

"Excuse me, Admiral?"

Kane had forgotten to close out the channel. His men

couldn't hear him talking to the voice—that would be too much for them. "Nothing, Captain. Carry on."

"Very good, sir."

Then Kane slammed his fist down to disconnect. The voice waited. Kane hated the pauses. The pauses were the worst.

You could have seen her again, you know, it finally said.

"Seen who?" Kane asked, genuinely unsure which *her* the voice was referring to.

Why, your daughter, of course.

Kane's heart leaped, a feeling he had not had in longer than he could remember. "She's on that ship?" *How long has it been? Fifteen years?* "How can you be sure?"

I'm always right. You just don't like to trust me. But you will. Soon.

"You're right," Kane agreed, "I don't trust you."

Yet you're becoming more and more like me.

"No, I'm not. Now you're just toying with me. I'm going after the stardrive."

Which is exactly what I would do.

"STOP IT! No, you wouldn't."

You could have seen your daughter.

"You already said that."

You could have met your granddaughter too. But you chose, Kane. You always choose.

27

Awen felt like she had stepped into another world, transported as if by magic from a realm of decay to a kingdom filled with wonder. The juxtaposition so startled her that she left the Unity and glanced over her shoulder just to make sure that the Reptalons weren't apparitions. They hissed at her as they closed the doors.

Yup. They're real.

Sootriman's inner sanctum vibrated with all the color and noise of a fancy town square. The enormous glass-ceilinged room was crisscrossed by red-and-gold fabric stretched between tall pillars. Spread under it were clusters of guests, some reclining on lush pillows, some seated at small tables, and others betting on suckow matches played on patches of bare marble floor.

Unlike the hallway, the air in here was filled with the fragrant smells of perfume and spiced meat grilled over open coals. Awen swallowed her saliva as she suddenly became hungry. The air was also alive with music, though Awen couldn't place the style. She noticed colorfully dressed minstrels playing drums, lyres, and tambourines in the far corner.

Like the musicians, every person in the opulent space was beautifully dressed—so much so that Awen felt out of place in her borrowed knit turtleneck, leggings, mechanic's boots, and cloak. There had to be a hundred or more guests, and all were enjoying themselves immensely. The lifestyle of these people was as far from those she'd witnessed during her walk through the city as she could imagine.

A few of the guests looked up at her as Ezo led the way to the opposite side of the room. Awen instinctively hid her face in her cloak, fearing they might notice she was a Luma and hate her like Ezo said they would. By the time she was halfway across the room, murmurs had replaced the music, and the air had grown still.

Awen looked ahead to see perhaps the most surprising sight yet. Atop a dais not unlike the mwadim's sat a gold throne decorated with red fabric. More than a dozen young women sat or lay across the stairs leading up to it, and in the oversized chair sat a rotund woman. Her almond eyes were set in a tanned olive-colored face, and her dark-brown hair cascaded over her shoulders in waves onto a red-and-gold dress made of exquisitely fine linen. She wore gold rings on her fingers and toes, and gold bracelets on her wrists and ankles. If Awen had to guess, the woman on the throne was almost a meter taller than Awen was.

By the time Ezo had reached the bottom of the dais, the

room had gone silent. The woman on the throne watched them with her dark eyes. She hadn't moved a muscle upon Ezo's approach. As the three of them stood there in total silence for several seconds, Awen glanced around the room, expecting Sootriman to appear. But he never did.

For the love of all the mystics, it's her.

As if on cue, Sootriman blinked and started shaking her head. "What possible reason do you have to come crawling back here knowing I'm just going to kill you, Idris Ezo?"

Maybe I should have stayed with the ship, Awen thought, realizing this might have been a mistake. *A very big mistake.*

"Sootriman, darling, it's good to see you again too," Ezo said. "You look as extravagant as ever."

Sootriman sniffed the air, winced, and flicked her wrists. "Not today, Idris." As if summoned by the sound of the bracelets jingling on her large arms, two dozen armed guards emerged from the shadows behind the pillars and moved toward Awen. Unlike the Reptalons, these were human men, each clothed in a simple white tunic and brandishing a plasma spear, which they activated as they walked. The thrumming sound of free energy sent a tingle up her spine.

Awen looked left and right as the guards moved in—presumably to dispatch her, the bot, and Ezo with a few swipes of the golden spears, the magenta-colored blades ablaze with heat. Awen pushed herself into the Unity and prepared to resist the guards. She had not come this far to get hacked apart on some seedy back world.

"Is this how you expected it to go?" Awen whispered to Ezo.

"Totally. This is normal."

"This is normal?" Awen asked, her incredulity threatening to overcome her hushed tone. "She normally tries to kill you when you show up?"

"Yeah, but she won't."

"How do you figure?"

"She might be my ex-wife, but she still loves Ezo."

"Your ex-wife?" Awen looked between Ezo and Sootriman, her mouth hanging open. "Are you kidding me right now?"

"He's not," Sootriman said, rolling her eyes.

"Actually, sir," TO-96 said, "there is one minor detail regarding that outstanding matter."

"What detail?" Ezo asked, snapping his head toward the bot.

"And what do you mean *outstanding*, Tee-Oh?" Sootriman added.

"Well, sir, if you remember your snarky comments to the tower operator when we left Plumeria—I was attempting to tell you about the status of your divorce filing. And if you remember, *she* asked *you* to file the final notice, sir."

"And I did," Ezo said.

"You *attempted* to—correct, sir. However, as you might recall, you also owed and still owe several months of back shipping taxes to the Republic."

"Oh, Ezo, you didn't," Sootriman said.

"I don't like where this is going, Ninety-Six," Ezo said.

"Civil Code number GR 27-2.4 clause 12—"

"I don't care about the code," Ezo hissed, motioning for TO-96 to get on with it.

The bot paused, tilting his head. "Interesting. That is precisely what you told me the last time, sir. Your petition for divorce cannot be processed until those taxes are paid in full."

"So," Sootriman said as coolly as a Frondothian minx in the shade of an ever-palm, "you're saying we're still married."

"That is correct, Madame."

"Son of a—"

"You're still married?" Awen said, running a hand down her face. "To her?"

"Well, this will be remedied shortly," Sootriman said. "I believe I get to collect some sort of death benefit too—that is, if it's not taken in lieu of taxes. Any last words before you die, Idris? Or maybe that monstrosity of yours has something more to add?"

"I have nothing more to share, your ladyship," TO-96 said. "Thank you for asking, though."

Sootriman rolled her eyes. "Kill them."

"Wait!" Ezo said in protest, raising his hands. "You can have the ship."

Sootriman raised her hand. The guards froze, their spears' plasma heads a meter away.

"*The ship?*" Awen asked.

"The ship?" Sootriman echoed.

"Sure. We both know you always wanted it. And Ezo feels wrong about having kept it from you."

"You feel *wrong* about keeping it from me and you want *me* to have the ship?"

"Is there an echo in here?" Ezo glanced at TO-96. "Is there an echo in here?"

"A small one, yes," the bot said.

"You can't give her the ship, Ezo," Awen stated, suddenly aware that he was about to double-cross her—no, he'd lied, and he *was* double-crossing her. There was no *favor* to call in. If anything, *he* owed Sootriman!

Awen cursed herself for getting involved in some lovers' quarrel. She felt betrayed, and she hadn't even seen it coming. *How could I have been so stupid? I should have stayed home.* She felt as though she was living in her parents' house again, with her father talking down to her or her mother scolding her.

Sootriman was on her feet now, descending the steps one at a time as the younger women moved aside. *Curse those legs. Now she's getting the ship too.*

The woman approached Ezo, and Awen realized for the first time that she was easily a head taller than him. "What's your angle, Idris?" she said, striding to within a few inches of his face. "We both know you have one. You *always* have an angle."

"Let Ezo use it for one last job."

"Ha!" Sootriman blurted. "You can't even come up with enough money to pay for the divorce filing but you're willing to barter your ship away for one last job? How did I *not* see this coming?"

"Ezo was hard up for credits," he replied like a room fan trying to plead its case before a tornado. "You can't even compare this to back then."

"You're right, Ezo. You're far more pitiful *now*. At least back then, you knew when you'd been beaten. But now, well, *now* you're just *groveling*. And it's a really bad look on you." Sootriman held a sultry hand to her forehead and took a deep breath. "Bartering for your ship. That means you want something *else* from me too. It means you can't do your next job without something only *I* can provide, and you can't pay for it without pawning your ship to me. That's it, isn't it?"

Oh, she's good—intelligent and beautiful. Awen was suddenly not *as* jealous of Sootriman's legs as before. "No wonder she tried to leave you," she said in Ezo's ear.

"Ezo left *her!*" Ezo protested over his shoulder.

"Please, Idris. Your *girlfriend*—"

"Not girlfriend," Awen interrupted, and Sootriman raised her eyebrows. "Not girlfriend. Nothing's going on here."

"Nothing?"

"Zero," Awen replied.

"Huh," Sootriman said with a look of genuine surprise on her face. "I'm impressed, Idris. Maybe you're maturing after all."

"Ezo can mature, yes," he said.

"*But*—you're still referring to yourself in the third person." Sootriman sniffed the air again and tilted her head. She started to walk around the trio like a prowling tigress deciding how best to eviscerate her prey. "So, what is it you need from me? It can't be more torpedoes. You can get those elsewhere, and they're not worth the ship. And clearly all your navionics work, or else you wouldn't be in the system." She rounded the other side and tapped her plush lips with a finger. "So it's got to be really, *really* expensive. Like—like a drive core."

281

Awen saw Ezo raise one shoulder. Sootriman saw it too. The tigress was getting closer to feasting.

"There we go. Ezo needs another drive core. But"—she tapped her lips some more—"that's not what you *really* want, is it? Unless you've blown your current one, which means you wouldn't be standing in front of me. No, you need a second one for a long trip, one that would best benefit from… oh, Ezo," Sootriman said with genuine pity, hands going to her hips, her head shaking back and forth. "You want a modulator."

If TO-96's sudden head turn hadn't given it away, Ezo's double-shoulder raise certainly would have.

"You really think I'm going to just hand over a modulator to you in exchange for a ship I'll never see again because I let you skip to the farthest reaches of the galaxy?" Sootriman turned to Awen. "Listen, girl. I'm not sure how you got involved with this Bludervian *dimdish* over here, but my best advice is to *run*. Run as far away as you can. He won't kill you." She glared at Ezo. "He doesn't have the nerve." She looked back to Awen. "But everyone else who's trying to liquidate him will. And you seem too nice to be liquidated."

"You'll get it back," Ezo said.

Sootriman snapped her head at him. "I'll get it back?"

"You have Ezo's word."

Sootriman literally looked as if her eyes—pretty as they were—were going to pop out of her head. "I have your *what?*"

"My word," Ezo replied, squaring his shoulders and pushing out his chest. "You have it."

Sootriman started laughing—deeply. It was a laugh that said,

I may be going insane, and if you were worried about your life before, you should be terrified about it now.

Ezo looked at TO-96 then over his shoulder at Awen. "This is normal."

Fast, like a jungle cat leaping on some unsuspecting quarry, Sootriman withdrew a curved blade from somewhere behind her back and laid it across Ezo's neck. Awen hadn't even felt the warning ripples in the Unity. "I need more than your word, husband," Sootriman said, her lips mere centimeters from the man's ear.

It wasn't until the blade nicked Ezo's flesh and a drop of blood appeared that Awen realized the woman wasn't playing. She was going to kill him—and Awen wasn't sure if she blamed her, as morally wrong as that felt. *Maybe I'm becoming like one of them.* That scared her.

"Here," Ezo said, lifting something in his hand. "Take this."

Sootriman glanced down at the offered object, and Awen did too. It was—

The stardrive?

"Ezo, what are you doing?" *How could he?* Awen was shocked. No, she was *furious*. She patted her clothing but realized she'd intentionally left the drive... *on the ship.*

"What's this?" Sootriman asked, removing the blade, her curiosity clearly piqued.

"You can't!" Awen protested. "How did you... you're a coward."

"She's not wrong, darling." Sootriman took the stardrive and examined it. "It's not every day you come across a find like this.

But," she added, looking at Ezo with a sad face, "Jujari stardrives aren't any good without—"

"It's already unlocked," he said.

Then something came out of Awen's mouth that she never thought she'd say. "I swear to all the mystics, Ezo, I will kill you."

Awen could hardly believe she'd said it. Worse, she meant it. She *wanted* to kill him, and that frightened her. This place, these people—all of it was getting to her, corrupting her from the inside out. But none of that changed the fact that she wanted Ezo to die for his treachery. In fact, if she'd thought she could outmaneuver two dozen armed guards plus Sootriman and TO-96 and then the Reptalons outside, Awen would have ended him right there. She knew how too. She could stop human molecules from vibrating in the Unity. Sure, it was *never ever* taught at the academy, but she'd figured it out. She could easily stop every cell in a person's body from moving the same way she'd stopped a block of concrete from falling. Having the nerve to pull it off in cold blood, though—well, that was something else entirely. And *that* was what scared her: she *had* the nerve.

"This means something to you, does it?" Sootriman asked Awen, snapping the Luma out of her obsessive stare into the back of Ezo's skull. "You'd really kill him, for this." She lightly waved the stardrive in the air.

"I—it's because—"

"You don't have to answer that, dear. Hearing yourself say it will only scare you more. I can see it in your eyes anyway. You're wise to restrain yourself, however, as I would just as quickly kill you, and then where would either of you be?"

"Give Ezo the modulator," Ezo stated as he wiped the blood from his neck. "You get the ship when we're done, and now you know exactly where we're going."

"New deal. I keep the ship, starting now," Sootriman countered. "I lend you another ship that already has a modulator on board, *and* I know where you're going."

Ezo cocked his head. "No, no, you don't understand. Ezo doesn't want to fly *another ship* where we're going. Ezo needs *Geronimo*."

"Well, it seems your options are running out, *husband*," Sootriman said as she started back up the steps.

Just then, one of her entourage stepped toward her and whispered in her ear. The young woman was barefoot and clad in a flowing silk dress that hung off one shoulder. Contrasting this, however, was a comms set in one ear beset with several small lights. She also concealed a holo-pad in the crook of one arm.

"Are you sure?" Sootriman asked.

The messenger nodded and showed her superior the holo-pad.

Sootriman thanked her and turned back to face Ezo. "It seems you've attracted some followers, Ezo."

"Oh?"

"A corvette just entered the system. Stiletto class. No designators, and it's trying very hard not to be seen. That doesn't bother us, of course, but it does say a lot about whomever they're tailing. You must have *really* pissed someone off with this." She shook the stardrive.

"We got away clean." Ezo turned to Awen as if expecting her to weigh in.

"What are you looking at me for?" she asked, still furious with him. "We don't fly gunships."

"*Yeah,*" he whispered, "*but whoever your boss is working with might.*"

"*I got away clean,*" she insisted. "*This one's on you.*"

"She's right, sir," TO-96 said. "The likelihood that an adversary placed a tracking device on *Geronimo* is well above fifty percent. It would have been easy for any number of spies to gain access to the ship while—" The bot suddenly froze. "Oh my."

"What is it, Ninety-Six?" Ezo asked.

"I now recall that some of the Bawee were taking an unusually long time in the cargo hold during refueling."

"You *now* recall?" Ezo said with his arms out. "How are you just *now* recalling this?"

"Given the cultural context and mission parameters of our stop on Worru, I was—"

"It's a rhetorical question, Ninety-Six!"

"Quite sorry, sir."

"Ru-Do," Sootriman said, summoning the foremost guard, "sweep *my new ship* for tracking devices, and dispose of them. I want it clean before anyone comes poking around."

"Yes, Your Majesty," the guard replied with a crisp bow.

"Hold on," Ezo protested, "it's not *your new ship.*"

"Negotiations are over." Sootriman ascended the stairs without bothering to turn around.

"Over? But Ezo—"

"Oh, and Ru-Do, if you see any of these three snooping around, kill them on sight."

"With pleasure, Your Majesty," the guard said.

"*Or*... negotiations are over," Ezo conceded.

"Glad you agree," Sootriman said as she sat back down. "You may *borrow* the ship currently in port at docking bay twenty-one. I believe she's fueled and ready for departure. Plus, the way I see it, the *Indomitable* is ready to go. It would take at least one week to get a modulator on *Geronimo*. Given the Stiletto that's about to make port, I'd say you have less than one hour. So once again, Ezo, my idea is your best idea."

Ezo let out a sigh. "We'll take the deal. Plus, the *Indomitable* sounds like a good name for a strong ship."

Awen got the distinct impression that this was how most negotiations went between Ezo and his wife. If Sootriman hadn't been so bent on thwarting their progress, killing them, or becoming the proud owner of some of the most important information ever to reach the known universe, Awen could see herself liking the woman. But for everyone's sake, Awen hoped this was the only time they'd ever meet.

"Have fun exploring the galaxy, Ezo," Sootriman said. "The mystics know you were never talented at exploring anything else."

28

Magnus slid down the steep metal chute, slowing as the incline leveled out. His feet had contacted the first of a series of chute-wide filters meant to separate debris from fluids when he noticed that the large access panel to his left was propped open. He switched his HUD to infrared imaging and saw the team making their way along the gantry.

"Nolan," Magnus said over comms, "SITREP."

"Ten souls, myself included. Everyone but Rawlson is accounted for, sir," Chief Warrant Officer Nolan replied. "Making our way to subsection bravo."

"Roger that. I'm on your six o'clock."

"Copy."

Magnus looked up just as bits of ash and shrapnel landed on his armor from above. He sidestepped into the hatch and started to run. Letting his sling catch his MAR30, Magnus drew his Z from his chest holster and held it in low-ready position. He toggled the weapon to single-round mode and thumbed off the safety, scanning for targets. He caught up with the slower-moving group, checking his retreat every five paces, expecting their position to be compromised any second.

So far, so good. Magnus didn't like how slowly they were moving. He toggled his HUD back to visual and was struck by how dark the passage was. Other than a few small red emergency lights, the maintenance shaft was black. He went back to IR.

"Any way you can light our progress, Nolan?" Magnus asked over comms.

"Negative," the warrant officer replied. The methodical blare of the ship-wide klaxon sounded in the background over the mic. "It's pretty slow going."

"Copy that," Magnus replied, sweeping his Z from end to end.

"Map says we only have another seventy meters."

Just then, Magnus noticed a new heat signature climbing into the tunnel two positions ahead. "Contact." He pointed his Z, bypassing the two team members in front of him and zeroing in on the enemy combatant.

The hostile jerked in surprise, probably at having so many options to target, and raised his weapon. Magnus squeezed off two bolts that flashed white in his HUD and caught the trooper in the shoulder and bicep. A weapon clattered to the gantry, and Magnus sent a third bolt into the base of the enemy's neck, severing the spine.

Magnus made out Dutch's slender figure as she backed away

from the dead trooper and raised her ML10 to cover the new entry point. A second combatant started to climb through, but Dutch ended the attempt with two point-blank shots to the trooper's helmet. The body was pulled back, and a small ball rolled onto the decking.

"Stun grenade!" Magnus yelled. By this point, however, he had run even with the new entry hatch and batted the grenade back through the hole with his hand. He managed two more steps, hoping his body would block as much of the blowback as possible. But he knew that plenty of the grenade's disruption blast would get past him, affecting those ahead.

The grenade detonated in the hall with a high-pitched whine followed by an air-sucking *whump*. He watched ahead as the line of people stumbled to their knees, some falling on their hands. He couldn't make out the girl's status, but he hoped the adult bodies had shielded her from the worst of it.

"Come on, Gilder!" Magnus shouted through his speaker. "On your feet, Private! Move, move, move!" The line started forward again, and as soon as they'd managed another five meters, Magnus returned the enemy's gesture with a frag grenade of his own.

"Cover your ears," Magnus yelled up the line. He pulled the frag from his hip, pressed the three-second timer with his thumb, and tossed the ordnance through the hatch. "Fire in the hole!" He turned to catch up as the grenade barked in his helmet.

The pace slowed. Within a few seconds, however, the line was underway again, and Magnus covered their retreat. Nothing more emerged from the hatch.

The access tunnel ended in a T, and Magnus watched the group turn left—*a good sign*, as it meant that his schematic was still current—and followed them toward the main access hatch at the end of the corridor. Preparing to exit into a larger corridor ahead, he holstered his Z and brought his MAR30 back up, walking backward to cover their six.

"We're at the end of the tunnel," Nolan called over comms.

"Egress," Magnus ordered, "but stay alert. Stay smooth."

"Copy." Nolan said. Magnus heard the warrant officer muscling the corkscrewed lock mechanism. "Opening." A small squeak accompanied Nolan's words.

There was a moment's silence as Magnus held his breath. If there was anyone on the other side of that hatch, they were most likely—

"Clear," Nolan said.

Magnus let out the breath. "You should see a bank of emergency pods along the left wall. Confirm."

"Affirmative. Everything looks good, Lieutenant."

He gave another sigh of relief, though he knew they still had a long way to go. *Victory is made up of one small gain after another. Even hell can be conquered if you do it a step at a time.* Without that mantra, it was easy to get distracted, and distracted Marines were dead Marines. "Load them up, Warrant Officer."

"Copy that."

Magnus was just about to check how much farther he had to go when he noticed enemy troopers come around a bend back in the tunnel. "Contact," he said and raised his MAR30. His AI presented three targeting reticles, and Magnus waited for them to overlap. The moment they did, he fired another staccato burst. The blaster bolts lit up tunnel walls with a strobe effect. All three combatants fell into one another, their armor clattering together.

Magnus turned and kicked Gilder the last meter through the hatch, then he grabbed the overhead bar and swung himself through, landing outside in a crouch. Dutch closed the hatch behind him and spun the lock shut.

Magnus toggled back to visual and looked down the wide subsection corridor. Red emergency lights flashed in time with the klaxon while banks of standard yellowing work lights illuminated painted lines on the floor indicating foot and equipment paths. A seemingly endless supply of crates, carts, and forklifts was perfectly ordered along one wall. Along the other were the entry hatches for the ship's emergency-escape vehicles.

Nolan had secured Valerie and Piper and was seeing to the senator, who was visibly upset. He helped the man enter the tube feetfirst and guided him down. "Watch your head, sir," Nolan said as the senator turned in the vertical pod and rested his back against the padded backboard. The senator buckled the harness around his chest then followed Nolan's instructions to cross his arms.

The senator's remaining three crew members were secure inside pods while Haney, Gilder, and Dutch got squared away. Nolan sealed the senator's canopy and pressed the button marked "Ready/Away," which closed the glass blast doors. Then he asked Stone for a thumbs-up. When the senator gave him the sign, Nolan jogged with Magnus to the next two available pods.

"Any problems?" Magnus asked.

"The senator's a good man," the warrant officer replied. "Cares for his family. But he should definitely stick with politics."

"Copy that. And the nav link?"

"The family's nav computers are slaved to yours, with mine and their captain's as redundant backups."

"Good work," Magnus replied. "Get yourself situated."

Magnus doubled back to make sure that each member of the team was set. He gave and expected a thumbs-up at every set of glass doors. One by one, each crew member replied until Magnus got to the Stones. The senator looked rattled. Valerie seemed calm, all things considered, and still looked stunning, her face illuminated in the pod's halo of white light. She smiled at Magnus and lifted a thumb.

When Magnus got to Piper's pod, he knelt and removed his helmet—not the best tactical move, but he didn't want to frighten the girl in what might be her last moments of life. After all, the whole plan was a long shot. The fact that they'd gotten as far as they had amazed him.

"You okay?" he mouthed.

Piper nodded, forcing a smile. Her blond wisps of hair barely came up to the bottom of the glass doors.

"Everything's going to—"

A blaster bolt exploded into a thousand sparks as it struck the metal wall over Magnus's shoulder. He ducked and covered his head with his helmet, swearing at himself. He looked down the corridor to see it filling with combatants. Several more shots struck the wall, peppering his armor with molten metal.

Magnus's AI had selected the closest targets, and his MAR30

was aimed. His first three bursts took out three targets, forcing the advancing enemy to cover. The action bought him enough time to do the same as he darted to the opposite side of the corridor and ducked behind a forklift. He looked across at the row of escape pods and saw Piper's blue eyes peeking over the lip of her hatch. Blaster fire streaked beside him, the walls showering him with bright gouts of orange and yellow sparks. He wanted to look at Valerie's face, too, but he couldn't look away from Piper.

At that moment, seeing her eyes filled with fear, time slowed down. Magnus had a sudden overwhelming urge to protect Piper's little life at all costs—to live for her as long as possible. The emotion was visceral, flowing from a formerly unknown part of his soul, one he could not entirely explain. It was different from any other instinct he'd ever felt before, enough that Magnus wondered if he was about to die—or maybe he had already been shot, but his body was in shock. All that mattered was that small face, illuminated by explosions of light. She looked to him for protection. For reassurance. For hope. And he wanted to give it all to her, to see her grow into the woman she was destined to be.

Real time hit Magnus in the chest as he suddenly realized that the next available escape pod was across the corridor and at least twenty meters toward the enemy. Heavy blaster fire had him pinned down. He pointed his MAR30 around the forklift and brought its visual sensor up in his HUD. The other end of the hallway was stacked with troopers.

Magnus selected wide displacement and heard his weapon's barrel aperture expand. He squeezed the trigger. The weapon hesitated, building the desired charge in its capacitors, and then released a broad burst of energy down the corridor. Magnus rocked backward. A blue light swept down the subsection and slammed into the enemy. Bodies not behind cover were flung backward. He heard troopers scream even under their helmets, their bodies slamming into and sliding across the deck.

This was his chance. He stepped into the open. But before he could take a second step, more blaster fire struck the ground and forklift. He reversed momentum and dove for cover again.

Dammit. There were simply too many troopers. They'd filled the end of the corridor faster than he'd anticipated. He looked back at Piper. Whatever strange dreams he had of protecting her into adulthood were now gone, obliterated like the blaster bolts exploding in sparks around him. The truth was that he wouldn't live long enough to see her past *this* moment. But he would save her at least this once. He would make sure she had a chance to go on growing, to become the beautiful, strong woman he somehow knew she'd be.

"*Jettison the pods, Nolan!*" Magnus ordered over the comm.

"But, Lieutenant, we have better odds of survival if—"

"*This is about survival!*"

29

Awen sat in the third seat on the *Indomitable*'s bridge and seriously considered asking Ezo to turn the freighter around. In fact, were it not for the mystery ship that had tracked them to Ki Nar Four and the fact that Sootriman didn't appear to be the most hospitable patron, Awen would have insisted he do so. All things considered, however, she was forced to make do with the circumstances, even though she was quite sure the ship wouldn't hold together for more than a few hours in subspace.

Ezo's grand assumptions about the name *Indomitable* were wrong. Whatever *Geronimo* had been with regard to beauty, aesthetics, cleanliness, and condition, the *Indomitable* was the opposite. Built as a commercial Longo-class light freighter long before Awen's parents or even grandparents were born, the ship's hull seemed like it was cobbled together from pieces of a hundred other failed vessels. The fact that any intelligent manufacturer had intentionally designed such a pockmarked walrus was a sin punishable by a thousand deaths. No one in good conscience should ever have let such a bloated hulk see the light of day.

The *Indomitable*'s disklike shape rattled as it left Ki Nar Four's orbit. TO-96 was careful to stay hidden in the shadow of the planet, opposite the strange ship's position from the coordinates Sootriman had provided. *At least we have* that *going for us*, Awen thought. But by leaving them without weapons and with only the most minimal of shields, Sootriman may have already doomed them all to an early grave anyway.

"Hull integrity is holding, sir," TO-96 said.

"Why, Ninety-Six, you sound surprised." Ezo increased the throttle.

"That's because I am, sir. I very much and truly am surprised. In fact, I think it's a miracle that—"

"I got it, wire brain. You don't have to explain it all to me."

"Understood, sir."

Awen clamped her jaw shut to keep her teeth from rattling. Despite the odds, they were back on a ship and preparing to make for the wormhole. She hated Ezo for it—for everything—but had to admit that it didn't matter much what ship they were aboard. *Geronimo* was certainly far more comfortable and safe. And clean. *And*—there were a thousand other things she liked about it. But at the end of the day, a ship was a ship. To her, the discovery was what mattered the most. That, and being able to get there first, to represent the Luma to a new civilization. She wanted to preserve the Luma's way of life from whatever Republic invasion would inevitably attempt to swallow it whole.

Awen was still a Luma, after all, and would be as long as she was wanted. Suddenly, she wondered about Willowood's fate. Had So-Elku reprimanded her—*or worse*—for interrupting a private meeting? No, Willowood had fought So-Elku in the Unity! Such things—well, they *never* happened. So, would she be disciplined? Or had she gathered other Lumanarias loyal to the Order and confronted the master?

"Willowood will know what to do," Awen said under her breath and suddenly longed to see the old woman again. She wished Willowood was with her, traveling across the galaxy to the wormhole.

Once the *Indomitable* was clear of Ki Nar Four's gravity well, TO-96 confirmed the course calculations and made the jump to subspace. "I still don't understand why your wife would ever waste a perfectly good modulator on a ship such as this, sir."

"That's because you have a good conscience," Ezo replied.

"Pardon me?"

"You think the best about everyone. And while it's a naive thing, it's a good thing in a galaxy that's falling apart like ours."

"So you're saying I'm socially shallow but morally superior."

"Something like that. Can we just see if the blasted thing works?" Ezo asked. "If not, Ezo's going to give Sootriman a piece of his mind."

"If not, we'll all be obliterated, our atoms spread across the quadrant for a billion years."

"Yes, and *then* Ezo will give her a piece of his mind." Ezo turned back to Awen. "You may want to hold on to something."

"Like your neck?" Awen asked, chin up.

Ezo rolled his eyes. "Punch it, Ninety-Six."

"Very good, sir. Modulating to factor two—in three… two… one…"

Awen saw the cockpit stretch out in front of her. She felt like she was going to throw up and realized she hadn't located a vomit bag ahead of time. She'd been too nervous leaving the planet to be sick—a real first for her. Now, however, the sense of vertigo that swirled in her head was overwhelming. The sounds of the cockpit felt as if they were muffled by a pillow. Then she felt like her spirit was trying to separate from her body, as if she'd become careless with the Unity or had attempted a new exercise without proper training.

Awen saw herself sitting in her seat, harness fixed over her shoulders, braid floating in the air. She could see each tiny strand of her hair and marveled at the complexity of such a simple feature—the way each fiber interlaced with others, having chosen a seemingly random course through the interwoven locks. Yet the sum of the individual strands was bound in a larger well-ordered composition. It was poetry. It spoke of space-time, of chaos theory, of superpositions, and of the multiverse. It spoke of many destinies, many choices, but all of them leading to one conclusion that, from a distance, seemed as simple and intentional as a braid of hair.

Suddenly, the cockpit snapped back, and Awen vomited a piece of toast and maribliss jam on Ezo. She felt bad… but then, considering what he'd done to her, she didn't feel bad at all.

"Whoops," she said in a dry tone and wiped her mouth with her sleeve.

"We've successfully arrived in subspace level epsilon," TO-96 noted. "Hull integrity at ninety-four percent, core levels nominal, and modulator reactor well within limits."

"Fabulous," Ezo said, wincing in disgust as something slimy trailed down the back of his neck. "Let's try factor three."

"Very good, sir. Modulating to factor three—in three… two… one…"

Once again, the cockpit moved away from Awen. Her stomach lurched, and her head thrummed. This time, however, the pain in her head was more intense. She felt… like she was *dying*. The sensation was horrible. She wanted to breathe but couldn't, wanted to scream but didn't have the strength. As before, she noticed her body sitting in its chair, but this time, everything shook in a violent blur. It was awful. She winced, or at least she thought she winced, trying to rationalize what was happening. It was as if everything was starting to separate, reality coming undone like the fibers of her braid, frayed at the edges.

Then everything slammed to a halt. When her senses came back, they did so with a loud pop in her ears. Her stomach lurched, and she dry heaved onto Ezo's back. This time, she genuinely felt bad.

"I'm sorry," she said, gasping for air.

"We've successfully arrived in subspace level zeta. Hull integrity at eighty-seven percent, core levels in the yellow, and modulator reactor showing signs of stress, but nothing out of the ordinary, sir."

Ezo had shrugged his shoulders such that his neck had retreated inside his leather jacket. "Let's keep it here. I'm going to my quarters, and I'll be back after I've showered. You have the bridge, Ninety-Six."

"Very good, sir."

Ezo unbuckled and didn't even look at Awen as he walked by. *That was probably for the best.*

AWEN LAY IN A BUNK, taking advantage of yet another peaceful opportunity to catch up on some much-needed sleep. She'd claimed the first open berth she could find and closed the door. Aside from the bed, the room had a sink, mirror, toilet, narrow closet, and a desk with a foldout wall seat. The room was bland, painted a dingy greenish gray, and a yellowing ceiling light did anything but convey hospitality. A blanket lay folded on the bed, and she found a second one stowed in the closet. She fluffed the pillow, smelling it to make sure it was relatively fresh, and settled herself in.

Even at the ship's current rate, she felt like her spirit was still, as calm as a leaf sitting atop a pond in autumn. The Unity always seemed closer here in subspace, as if her very essence was a single breath away from being one with all things. She felt the same way when she was in or near water. Both places gave her the sense that a veil had been drawn between her and the Unity. She could not see it, but she knew it was there. And in certain *thin places*, the veil was so gossamer fine that she was sure she could reach right through it and step across to the other side, body and soul.

Awen wondered what would become of the Luma now—what would become of Willowood, of the other elders, of the students and the school. She worried about them in ways that surprised her, as if she wanted to gather everyone who might have been hurt by her strange departure and explain it all to them. She wanted to tell them that everything was going to be okay, even though she wasn't convinced of that herself. But most of all, she wanted to tell them what So-Elku had tried to do to her.

Awen's thoughts turned to her master—her *former* master. She wondered whether So-Elku's plans had captured any other Luma minds as well or if he was acting alone. Perhaps Willowood was right to suspect that he had accomplices. If not, why were guns firing on *Geronimo Nine*? That couldn't be the protocol for some miscreant ship, could it? The more Awen thought about it, the more she feared the worst.

The questions loomed over her like dark storm clouds rolling in from the sea. For the life of her, Awen couldn't figure out what So-Elku wanted with the stardrive. Did he even know what was on it? And if so, why not celebrate its discovery? Instead, he'd acted like some malevolent traitor, unable to explain himself truthfully and willing to use the Unity against her and against Willowood.

Worse still, there remained the unanswered questions surrounding the bombing in Oosafar and who, exactly, had given the master information about her taking possession of the stardrive. *I have to stop calling him that. He would never be her master again. He would only ever be So-Elku, traitor to the Order and despiser of the Luma.*

Awen saw his face. She was back in Elder's Hall, and So-Elku was demanding that she open the stardrive. He held her eyes, locked in a battle of wills that threatened to tear her mind into a thousand pieces. But she fought him, resisted him. She would not give in. It had been Willowood who'd truly saved her, however. Awen didn't know how long she could have lasted against him.

But in this version of the memory, Willowood *didn't* appear. Awen could see So-Elku's face, eyes boring into her soul. She remained frozen, gripped by fear and by the Luma's power within the Unity. She held the stardrive in her hand, her thumb putting pressure on the button. He was pushing her hard, demanding that she conform, that she obey. Awen kept expecting Willowood to burst through the doors and rescue her. But Awen couldn't look away from So-Elku. He was watching her, searching her very soul.

Her thumb pressed down. The needle punctured her skin. Awen's eyes went wide, and she tried to scream, but there was no air in her lungs. She couldn't breathe, and she'd failed to resist him.

No! It can't be! It's not what happened!

And it *wasn't* what had happened back at Elder's Hall. That was not how the events had occurred. *But it is what's happening now.* The contents spilled out of the stardrive like water from a broken vessel onto a floor of black marble. The shapes, the star map, the name of the Novia Minoosh, and TO-96's data file—all of it was spread out on the floor for So-Elku to see. Awen wanted to try to put the vase together and scoop handfuls of the liquid back inside, but she could not pull herself from So-Elku's gaze. His pupils were on fire, his brow furrowed, his lips snarling. And then she heard him speak.

I see you.

Two common days had passed before TO-96 stepped the *Indomitable* down from three tiers of subspace. It was the farthest any of them had ever traveled. In fact, TO-96 calculated that it was farther than their collective journeys combined—not because he had detailed records of their travels but simply because there was no way any of them could have previously accomplished such distances, given their respective lines of work. These kinds of jumps were for explorers with death wishes, not weekend warriors hoping to visit some interesting sectors on their bucket lists.

"Do we have a visual on the quantum tunnel yet?" Awen asked, and TO-96 looked back at her. "What?"

"Awen," the bot said as tenderly as she'd ever heard him, "I'm sorry to inform you, but you cannot *see* a quantum tunnel. They are, by very definition, *unseeable*—at least in so far as a quantum tunnel resembles a black hole with an event horizon—since not even light can escape its gravitational pull."

Awen *had* learned that in school and now felt rather sheepish. "Right. Thank you for the reminder, Ninety-Six."

"My pleasure."

"Coming up on it," Ezo said. "Looks like five minutes at our current speed before its gravity takes us."

"Affirmative, sir."

"Okay," Ezo said, making a few adjustments on the console. Then he turned to face Awen and the bot. "Now, before we do this, Ezo wants to make sure we're all good here."

"What an interesting concept," Awen said through thin lips. "If you mean *still livid with someone for selling us out*, then, no, we're not *all good here.*"

"Listen, Awen," Ezo said, lifting his palms. "She's not going to come after us. It's not her style. That little charade was just her means of satisfying her curiosity."

"*Charade?*"

"And secondly, she doesn't have a bot capable of doing what Ninety-Six here can do."

"Actually, sir—"

"Can it, 'Six!"

"*Seriously?*" Awen said, looking between the two of them. "For the love of all the mystics, you're *seriously* going to lie to me right now, Ezo?"

"In his defense," TO-96 said, "he might not remember that he gave Sootriman a navigation bot as an engagement present."

Awen closed her eyes and pressed her fingers to her temples.

"Hey, hey, what are you doing?" Ezo asked. "Don't go all *Luma* on Ezo now, okay? You can trust Ezo. Sootriman isn't going to—"

Awen opened her eyes and lowered her hand. "I'm not going

to do anything to you, Ezo. I just need some time to process..." She paused. "All of you."

"Ah, okay. Good to know." He cleared his throat and smoothed his turtleneck. "Well, then, can we get back to the part about possibly getting crushed in a quantum event horizon again?" When Awen and TO-96 nodded, he continued. "So, *as Ezo was saying*, let's just make sure we're all agreed with what we're about to do. Since there doesn't seem to be another quantum tunnel next to this one to spit us back out, we may be looking at a one-way trip if we survive."

"I'm not sure I understand, sir," TO-96 said. "I've already informed you that all systems are—"

"*I* understand," Awen replied. "He's making sure that we're ready to stop existing as we know it."

"Ah," the bot said. "A fine question to posit."

"Because, well," Ezo said, licking his lips, "Ezo's never done this. Splick, *no one* has ever done this that Ezo knows of, and Ezo knows of a lot of shady characters."

"He really does," TO-96 said to Awen.

"So this is it, I guess," Ezo concluded. "Ezo just, you know, wanted to double-check. It's kind of a big deal."

Awen felt she should say something. "The way I see it, there are some despicable people willing to kill innocent people to get to where we are right now. More than we can probably count. I burned my bridge to the Luma, and you've used up your last favor with your ex-wife."

"Still wife," TO-96 corrected.

"Right, still wife." Awen stifled a smile. "There's no way we can fight anyone in this rust bucket, and the mystics know I want to meet this new race. With regard to a return trip, I have to trust that these Novia Minoosh already have that worked out. Call it faith if you need to. So it seems that the only way out of this is to move forward. We get there before anyone else does and hope it's the right call. I vote yes. Let's do it."

"I vote yes as well," TO-96 said. "Let's do it."

Ezo looked between them. "You both know that we're the craziest three beings in the galaxy, don't you?" They nodded. Ezo clicked his tongue. "Let's do this, then." He accelerated the *Indomitable* toward the quantum tunnel's gravity well.

"Oh, Awen?" Ezo turned back toward her with a sudden softness in his eyes as if he might cry.

The look almost overwhelmed her. Here, in their last moments together, Awen would catch a glimpse of the bounty hunter's true self. "Yes, Ezo?"

"There's a vomit bag under your seat."

30

"Dammit, *Nolan!* Jettison the pods!" Magnus yelled over TACNET. He toggled his MAR30 to high frequency and reached around the forklift. He squeezed off several more bursts in a desperate effort to give Nolan time to launch the pods. Magnus pulled his weapon back and pressed himself behind cover. He looked across at Piper.

The little girl, still barely able to look over the lip of the viewing port, stared at him in panic. He could make out tears in those big blue eyes. *Why wasn't Nolan following orders?* He was furious. Now this poor child would watch him be cut down by blaster fire *and* possibly not get away in time. Or worse still, he would watch her be captured or killed while he bled out, helpless to do anything about it.

Magnus would have walked across the corridor himself and

pressed every launch button were it not for the fact that he'd be vaporized before getting halfway across. "*Nolan! Do you copy?*"

"I'm trying, Lieutenant!" Nolan sounded frustrated.

"What do you mean *you're trying?*"

"The system's not responding, sir."

You've got to be kidding me. "They locked you out?" Magnus asked.

"Negative, sir. I've got access, it's just not—I don't know, sir."

Magnus looked down and saw that his MAR30 was ready for another wide-displacement discharge. "Listen, Nolan, I'm going to create a window and then come across. I'll hit as many of the launch buttons as I can, starting with the civilians. Whatever I don't get—well, just keep trying."

"Sir, no. I'll figure this out."

"I sure hope you do, for your sake, Nolan. Because if you don't, I'm going to fill your head with plasma myself."

"Aye, sir."

"Here goes nothing." Magnus toggled his MAR30's fire-modes switch. As his arm brought the weapon around, Magnus caught sight of Piper again. He feared this would be the last glimpse he'd ever get of her. He hated that she looked afraid—that was no way to remember a child. But then again, he wouldn't be living long enough to revisit any memories. Then he noticed her eyes. They were no longer panicked—*they were filled with rage.*

Magnus was so startled by Piper's expression that he yanked his weapon back to his chest. She didn't look like a child who was upset with an unreasonable parent or a school bully. No, she looked like she was a lioness about to maul an invading pack of hyenas who'd just taken her cubs. Her brow was furrowed, eyes bloodshot, and he was sure that if he could see her mouth, she would have been baring her teeth. It was, perhaps, the most arresting face he'd ever seen on a child. And it scared the living splick out of him.

A burst of brilliant-white energy exploded from Piper's capsule as if someone had detonated a quantum warhead on the surface of a planet. The shock wave came at him so fast he didn't even have time to flinch. His body was flung backward, colliding with the wall as searing light filled his helmet. The action was followed by a subsonic blast of energy that compressed his chest and squeezed his temples. Even squinting, all Magnus could see was white.

What in all the cosmos was that?

Everything went silent. Well, except for the ringing in his ears. Magnus's HUD was off-line. In fact, his entire system seemed dead, rendering the helmet inoperable. Given the low light, he couldn't see a thing through his visor besides streaks of blaster fire. He pulled off the helmet and blinked several times.

The very first thing Magnus saw when his vision stabilized was Piper's face, eyes staring across the hallway at him. Her look of anger relaxed the moment she noticed Magnus was moving.

Did she just… did she just do that? Magnus was utterly beside himself. He realized he'd been holding his breath and took in a deep lungful of air. Then he looked at the other capsules and saw most of the people slumped to the sides of their pods, each trying to find their bearings. Valerie seemed the most alert of them all, rubbing one of her temples and looking across at Magnus in surprise. The senator looked the worst. In fact, with the amount of blood coming out of his nose and mouth, Magnus was quite sure he was dead. *What in the hell had happened to him?* Magnus didn't remember him getting shot.

Magnus rolled onto his hands and knees, pulled his MAR30 up from its sling, and carefully leaned around the forklift. To his utter astonishment, every enemy trooper at the opposite end of the corridor was laid out cold. Whether stunned or dead, he did not know.

He heard a fist pounding on glass and looked to where Nolan was slamming his pod's cockpit window. He was mouthing the words "good to go" and raising his thumbs.

Magnus didn't need any more prompting. He scrambled to his feet, bolted to the next open emergency capsule, and slid in. He jammed his MAR30 along his right leg and felt it maglock against his thigh. Then he wedged his helmet over his shoulder, buckled his harness, and punched the ready button. A moment later, all the pods launched from the Bull Wraith on Nolan's command, and Magnus was thrown against the straps.

The scream of the pod's main engine rattled above Magnus's head as he shot away from the Bull Wraith. He was instantly immersed in the void, swallowed by a sea of stars—a sea of stars and a planet below his feet.

We've got a planet! Hope kindled in him. This was the best possible scenario, the one he'd hoped for but just assumed he wouldn't be granted because… well, because *that was just the way the universe acted*. But apparently, not that day. Their luck seemed to continue, Magnus noted, as he strained to look over his shoulder, wondering if the Bull Wraith's turrets would attempt to pick them off. It had been several seconds already, and no shots had been fired.

Magnus took a deep breath and leaned forward to see if he could identify the planet. Beneath the refracted pale blue of the bending horizon lay an endless sea of tan illuminated by the system's star. No notable bodies of water, no polar caps, and very few mountain ranges as far as Magnus could tell. It looked just like…

Oosafar. Ho-ly splick. Magnus started scanning the orbits, his head swiveling wildly. His eyes caught dozens of dots orbiting roughly four hundred meters above the planet's surface. Then another cluster. And another.

"The orbital blockade," he said to no one in particular. *It was Oosafar.*

Magnus was called back to his pod's limited flight controls when red warning lights started flashing at him. He flicked up on the small dashboard to see the atmospheric-entry indicator blinking. His capsule was plummeting toward Oosafar, and he needed to input some commands. He pressed the option to confirm entry —the alternative being a full reverse thrust that would send the pod back into the void—and felt the flight computer adjust the capsule's angle of attack relative to the planet's surface.

If Nolan had slaved the Stones' capsules properly, they should be following the same command sequence. Magnus looked over his shoulder to see if he could spot them. Sure enough, three white pods trailed to his left, maybe three hundred meters of separation between each. He couldn't tell who occupied which pod, but all three were executing a similar course change.

"Good job, Nolan," Magnus said then made a mental note to buy the man a drink if they ever made it through this.

Already, the crimson sheet of fire was wrapping itself around Magnus's pod. The small vehicle shook violently, so much so that Magnus was pretty sure it was going to split apart at any second. That, or it was just going to scramble his body to a pulp. His unsecured helmet smashed into his head several times, making him see stars and drawing blood. He fought to grab it and press it against his shoulder. If he'd had more room, he would have put the helmet back on, but the cramped confines of the pod didn't allow for it. Forgetting to put it on before entering would have been a rookie mistake if it hadn't been dead. It was also the first time he'd ever seen a nine-year-old girl do—whatever it was she'd done. *Go nova,* Awen might say. So he cut himself some slack.

Though the beating lasted for less than two minutes, Magnus felt like he'd endured a one-sided boxing match at the academy for an hour. All at once, the capsule sailed into thin air; only the sound of the wind whistled over the glass. The vehicle's systems looked green, and so far as Magnus could tell, the Bull Wraith had made no attempt to hijack them. He glanced over his shoulder again and saw that the Stones' pods had all survived as well. He searched as much of the rest of the sky as possible but couldn't make out any other pods.

The flight computer's limited sensors presented three different landing sites that fit its optimal profile. Without any reference to where they were on the planet, Magnus selected the first one and hoped the Stones' pods would continue to adopt the same input. The small winglets on Magnus's capsule rotated and sent the vehicle on a trajectory toward a flat expanse bordered by a low-lying mountain range to the west and a shallow canyon to the east.

He sailed through the upper atmosphere for a few more minutes as the wind noise became louder and louder. The computer displayed a definitive altitude, rapidly descending from ten thousand meters. He could also see the temperature rising, owing to the desert planet's blistering daytime conditions—conditions Magnus couldn't believe he was about to be subjected to again so soon after leaving.

Thermals buffeted his pod, knocking his helmet from his grasp. He noticed smears of red blood on the sides and visor. He secured the helmet yet again and touched his forehead, his lip, and his ear. *Damn.* He was going to need laser sutures after this.

Once he reached one thousand meters, the pod gave a single sonic and visual warning before deploying the parachute, which pitched the vehicle's nose toward the sky. Magnus hadn't been ready for the violent toss and, once again, banged his head on his helmet.

Magnus stood vertically now, staring out his pod's cockpit window. He did his best to memorize as much of the geography as possible, knowing this might be his only topographical glimpse of their surroundings. He could see a sizable settlement in the east toward the canyon and another in the foothills of the mountain range to the west. He also noticed scorch marks—dozens of smaller ones and a few big ones. *Orbital strikes. They had to be.* Small black-ringed impact craters dotted the settlements, but two larger ones indicated where towns had once stood—now decimated by Republic LO9D cannon hits. Magnus wondered if maybe there had been a friendlier landing site on the list; he'd just assumed that the *first one* meant it was the *best one*. If this was the best, he didn't want to know what the others looked like.

Suddenly, he realized only the Stones' pods were slaved to his—at least, that was what he assumed from Nolan's description. He wondered if the rest of the team's vehicles had presented them with the same options. Magnus went from not expecting to make it out of the Bull Wraith to feeling wholly responsible for everyone's survival. He had, after all, come up with this crazy plan. But the plan—good or bad—had gotten everyone off a hostile ship regardless of where it placed them on the planet. *Well, almost everyone.* He thought of Rawlson and the senator then looked to his left, wondering if the senator was even alive to see this. While Oosafar was deadly down below, it was lovely from above.

Back on the dashboard, large numbers counted down from ten as the altitude indicator flashed the last two hundred meters. He held his helmet tight and braced for impact.

MAGNUS POPPED the canopy off his pod and pushed himself up. The hull still smoked from extreme heat, hissing and creaking as it settled. He slung his MAR30 and cradled his helmet as he ran toward the first capsule about three hundred meters away. When he got closer, he saw Valerie trying to push up her canopy.

"I gotcha, I gotcha," he said, putting his helmet and weapon down and pulling the glass away.

"Piper."

"I think she's next," he said, offering his hands. Valerie took them, and Magnus pulled her up. It seemed so surreal, lifting a gorgeous woman in a gown from a smoking escape pod in a desert. The woman was so light that Magnus thought he might break her.

No sooner had Valerie's feet touched the ground than she began to run to the next pod. Magnus retrieved his helmet and weapon and caught up to her. To his relief, Piper was sitting upright, eyes focused on them as they ran toward her. Her face was red and smeared with tears. No matter how brave she'd been up until that point, her true age fully emerged as she saw her mother running toward her. As Magnus wrested the canopy from its mounts, he uncovered a child in anguish, sobbing as she reached for the safest place in the galaxy: her mother's arms.

They rocked together, sitting in the sand in a dress and a nightgown. Valerie held Piper's head with one hand and her torso with the other, comforting her with gentle words. Magnus felt out of place, as if he was intruding on some holy moment, desecrating it with his voyeuristic glances and bloodstained armor.

He looked over at the last remaining pod then back at Valerie. He raised a hand to her and mouthed, "Wait here." She nodded and continued to console Piper.

With boots sending up sprays of sand, Magnus double-timed

it to the senator's escape pod. The closer he got, the more certain he became that it was the senator's coffin. Red blood splattered the inside of the canopy. As he glanced inside, Magnus saw the senator's unmoving body, the head twisted to the right at an unnatural angle. He unlocked the glass, pulling the canopy from the pod. The familiar smell of death hit his nostrils.

"Splick," Magnus said, reaching to feel for the man's pulse. But the way the corpse's glazed eyes looked unblinking into another realm told him all he needed to know. What scared Magnus the most was that the man had been alive when he climbed into this pod but had died before he even left the Bull Wraith. Magnus turned back and looked at Piper as a chill went up his spine.

31

Kane stood at the entrance to the den. *A filthy hellhole.*

You should fit in just fine, then. It was the other voice. But he'd stopped calling it that.

Kane waved a trooper forward. The man knocked on the thick doors with the butt of his blaster. When the Reptalon's eye appeared, Kane leaned in and said, "Admiral Kane to see the master of this house."

The guard's green eye widened, presumably from seeing the platoon of troopers that Captain Nos Kil led behind Kane. "I'm sorry," it hissed. "Sootriman's not accepting visitors."

"Sootriman?" *So that's his name.*

"No visitors. Leave."

"That's a shame."

The Reptalon's eye blinked. "What?"

"I said, that's a shame."

In a single fluid motion, Kane raised his sidearm—an old MRG compact railgun pistol—and fired a lead projectile into the lizard's eye. The railgun was a relic from the previous century, made obsolete by the newer gauss cannons. Never, however, had the weapon been refit as a handgun platform—until the MRG. The result was an incredibly loud, incredibly destructive kinetic weapon that discharged enough recoil to snap a wrist. The firearm had never left the prototype phase, however, and those pieces that remained were rare. The explosion of green fluid and gore that erupted from the small slit in the door blew back onto Kane's face and chest. The admiral didn't so much as blink but turned aside, moving past the door's hinges, and looked at Nos Kil.

"Blow it," Kane ordered.

The captain nodded and signaled his men. They stacked up on each side as a two-man team dropped an explosive charge into the ooze-dripping slit. The pair rolled away from the door and took cover, one tapping the other twice on the shoulder. Kane holstered his MRG and covered his ears.

A thunderous blast shook the ground as the doors blew off the building. Bluish-white light bathed the surrounding structures like a high-noon sun, peppering their surfaces with shrapnel and a shower of dust.

When Kane turned back to the opening, he didn't even pause to survey the damage; he simply walked over the flaming debris. His boots sank into several masses of formerly living things that were now smoldering clumps of tissue. *They're happier now.* He looked around the putrid squalor of the den's interior.

This was no way to live. The passage smelled of cat urine and mold.

"Lights," Kane said from the head of the line that snaked its way through the corridor. Two troopers fired flares from lower canister extensions on their MX21s, each projectile sounding a hollow *kuh-thunk* as it was lobbed ahead. The flares exploded in a dazzling splash of red light and illuminated several Reptalons, who were still dazed from the breaching explosion. Kane pointed to each target as if his fingers had the power to release blaster bolts. Nos Kil's troopers fired single shots at the reptilian brains, dropping the guards cold.

Kane noticed a strange growth moving along the walls, something serpentine but still fauna. Its gangrenous surface rippled from floor to ceiling and back again. Kane had the distinct feeling that it was going to lunge at them, a beast lurking under the gelatinous membrane.

He spoke over his shoulder at Nos Kil. "Torch it."

"Yes, sir," came the trooper's amplified voice. Nos Kil pointed at a trooper to his right and flicked two fingers toward the mass slithering along the walls. An MF11 flamethrower burst to life and shot a stream of fire at the side of that corridor and then the other. The trooper swept his weapon back and forth, filling the hallway with more and more destruction. Bright-orange light washed the cavity, and Kane wanted to feel the heat prick his pockmarked skin just as it had so many years before. But he couldn't. Whatever the creature was, however, it was not immune to fire and screeched as the molten liquid devoured its moldy flesh.

Several more Reptalons arrived down the corridor, summoned by the commotion. They took no more than a step into Kane's field of view before their lives ended, blaster bolts searing through their scaly heads.

Kane and his men moved past the fire and up the central stairwell, stepping over bodies, before arriving at a set of inner doors. Most of the guards must have already met their end racing toward Kane, as only one lizard remained vigilant, pointing his spear at the invaders. *Faithful or afraid? Let's find out.*

Why do you keep calling yourself that?

Keep calling myself what?

Kane.

It's my name.

Is it?

The last Reptalon guard hissed, "Stop where you are."

"Why didn't you leave your post and assault with your brothers?" Kane asked, still moving across the landing.

The lizard hesitated. "I said, stop where you are!"

"They raced out to meet us, but you stayed here. Why?" Kane tilted his head, examining the beast. *Faithful or afraid?* He wanted to know before he dispatched the monster.

"I am the sworn protector of Sootriman! Don't take another step."

Kane stopped. *Faithful. That's honorable, deserving of a painless death.* "Open the door," he ordered.

"Never!"

Kane raised his MRG and fired another lead projectile. The Reptalon's head exploded like a green pumpkin, showering the walls with brain and bone. The lizard's body continued to stand, its legs and tail staggering to keep balance without a central nervous system. Kane walked toward it, pushed the spear aside, and shoved the headless body to the ground.

The admiral walked to the doors and pounded on them with a gloved fist. "Sootriman!" The heel of his hand came alive with pain. He banged again, an act that caused microfractures in his bones. "*Sootriman*," he seethed, feeling possessed by the sudden rage he held toward this molten planet's strangely named ruler. He struck the doors a third time, the pain searing up his arm and flaring in his mind.

But you can take it, he—it—said. *The pain makes you come alive, makes you thrive.*

"*Sootriman*, open your gates, or I will."

A moment later, a mechanism shuddered and began to splay the doors apart. Kane rolled his chin as the den's light caught him in the eyes. The place was filled with otherworldly sights and sounds far different from the ones he'd just passed through.

How flagrantly inconsistent. Inconsistency was not to be tolerated. It was the enemy of order. Without law, there was only chaos. Chaos consumed all until there was nothing left to feed upon.

That's what it's done to you, Kane, hasn't it? The inconsistency took everything from you, everything you held dear. It gorged its bottomless stomach on what you loved until there was nothing left to love.

Kane moved into the room, his troopers fanning out behind him. They targeted anything that moved but stayed their trigger fingers, awaiting his command. A woman sat atop a dais at the far side of the room. Kane noted that she was exceedingly beautiful even from this distance. *Sootriman's wife? Or Sootriman herself?*

The woman waved off several guards who seemed eager to approach the intruders. *A wise move.* Their plasma spears were charming and a truly violent weapon—something Kane could appreciate. However, every weapon had optimal engagement scenarios, and plasma spears were no match for advanced blasters. Unless they had some concealed secondary weapons, a confrontation would be no contest, and he was sure the woman *knew* that.

The admiral arrived at the base of the dais as his troopers took up defensive positions throughout the room. He didn't even need to see them to know they had blocked the exits and held the most likely hostile threats at gunpoint. Always keen for an opponent to show their hand, Kane waited for the woman to speak first. So much could be gleaned from the initial tremors of someone's voice in a moment of anxiety. Often, the effect rattled the speaker more than the listener. Likewise, an absence of anxiety could signal that the potential adversary was so hungry with rage or power that they ignored healthy fear. Or alternatively, they could just be as confident as they projected.

Kane stood with his chest out, MRG holstered on his hip, hands folded behind his back. He waited, wringing his hands in his glossy black gloves. The squeak satisfied him. Patiently, he stared up at the woman. *Sootriman.* But she was unflinching.

The admiral tried to decide which type of victim she would be—someone who did not respect how easily he could dispatch her or someone who was truly a worthy adversary, as consistent in the face of death as she'd been while building this floating empire over the least likely of planets. He hoped she was the latter. He would interrogate her, if so, and see how far she could go before breaking.

"I am Admiral Kane of the Paragon," he said in a low voice, finally deciding to go first.

Are you?

Kane hesitated. *You can't be talking to me. Not now. Stop it.* "I am Admiral Kane," he said again. He winced in frustration, face contorting. "Of the Paragon."

The woman watched him with odd fascination. She was studying him like a hunter studies its prey.

But she's in no place to have any advantage, Kane. Take her now.

"I am Sootriman, tamer of Ki Nar Four's tempests. What brings you to my domain, Admiral Kane of the Paragon?"

She's not using your real name. And neither are you. Be consistent, or be nothing at all.

"I've come in search of a ship," Kane answered.

"A ship? Well, you've come to the right place. Though I fear that whatever deal we strike will involve far more than you may be willing to pay, given how many of my *pets* you've slain and the dents you've put in my den."

"A modified Katana-class light freighter. She sought port here. We—"

We? Who do you mean, Kane? You and me? Or is this still about you and your men?

"We've been—"

Which is it? Answer me.

"Yes?" Sootriman prompted.

Kane wrung his hands tighter behind his back. This was *not* the time to be having a conversation with himself. But it was happening more often, and the pain was getting stronger.

Focus. Focus!

But he couldn't focus, not with the voice constantly interrupting him. That, of course, was the trouble with it all—he was tired of the lack of consistency in himself. He was always torn between one thing and another—between abandoning his men or taking them with him, between leaving the Republic in peace or slitting its throat to end its misery, between going after his family or pursuing the fortunes the stardrive offered. For every decision he made, the other presence was there to protest. And he could never appease it, never satisfy its insatiable need to demand from him what *ought* to be done—who he *ought* to become.

But you know what you ought to do; you're just too afraid to do it.

"*Shut up*," Kane said.

"Excuse me?" Sootriman asked, her eyebrows raised.

Shut up? That's no way to talk to yourself.

"I said, *shut up*."

Please, old man. I can no more cease talking to you than you can leave your body. I'm simply waiting for you to come to the same conclusion that I have.

"Now, you listen here…" Sootriman said.

"*STOP TALKING!*" Kane roared. He whipped the MRG from its holster and squeezed the trigger. The weapon barked and blew off the top of Sootriman's throne. Splinters rained down on her hair and shoulders. Her guards made to lunge, but Nos Kil threatened them with his MX21.

"I want to know where the Luma went," Kane said, moving his pistol to the first civilian his eye caught. "She has something I want."

"I believe you have come to the wrong place," Sootriman said, raising her chin.

Do it.

It's a civilian.

I know.

But I… I've never killed civilians in cold blood.

But you were fine with blowing up dignitaries and diplomats?

That was different.

How?

Kane hesitated. Maybe it wasn't any different. Maybe this was all just part of saving the Republic from itself—from saving the galaxy from the darkness that he knew the Republic was summoning. The work was dire, but it had to be done. And he knew in his heart of hearts that he was the one to do it.

Do it. Do it now.

Kane's hand shook.

DO IT!

Kane squeezed the trigger. Several people screamed. Sootriman looked at Kane, horrified.

"I want to know where the Luma went," Kane said again. Only he was no longer Kane. He was someone else entirely, and he pointed his weapon at the next civilian he saw.

32

The mood on the *Indomitable*'s bridge was somber as the ship approached the coordinates for the quantum tunnel. The cockpit lights were dim, which allowed Awen a clear view of the vast array of stars beyond the window. Expanding in the center, however, was a black spot that looked like an oil spill on a canopy. *No, it isn't like something has blotted out the stars; it is more like something has removed them completely—as if* nothing *was there at all.*

Ezo was laser focused on helming the vessel, his eyes constantly checking for increases in speed and changes in attitude relative to the event horizon. TO-96's normally chatty self was surprisingly withdrawn, and he was all business as he monitored the ship's systems. Blips, pings, and chimes went off in steady succession as the sensors fed more data to TO-96.

Awen felt completely useless. She sat, strapped into her chair, fidgeting. If she'd been a mechanic, maybe she'd be in the aft, taking care of the drive core. If she'd been a trooper, she thought maybe she'd be in a gunner's seat, but then she remembered that the *Indomitable* didn't have any weapons systems. *Okay, so no gunner's seat. What can I do?*

You're a Luma, Awen.

Scolding herself for not thinking of it sooner, Awen closed her eyes and settled her center. Here, in the core of who she was, lay the beginning point of her existence as well as its end, the place where her life flowed from and where it would cease when she died. This center was her truest self, the one whose thoughts and feelings she trusted more than any of her personality's many layers. If she listened carefully enough, she could hear the true narrative of her life, not the dozens of false ones she told herself —and certainly not the ones that others spoke over her. But spending too much time in the core was uncomfortable if not dangerous for the uninitiated.

"It is possible to see too much of one's self too soon," Willowood had said during an early lecture at the academy. "Unless you know yourself well, it may seem like you're meeting a stranger at first. Therefore, it is best to make introductions slowly and treat yourself gently."

She didn't know why she was recalling all of this as the ship neared the quantum tunnel. It seemed an inopportune time to wade into the existential dynamics of the Unity of all things and the role of the true self. *Best to keep moving, lest I meet too much of myself.* She ignored the sudden desire to linger and stretched out her senses in the Unity.

Awen saw Ezo and TO-96, both of them faithfully attending

to their various control surfaces. She saw herself and the bridge and then the whole ship. Outside in the void, she could see beautiful ripples expanding away from the *Indomitable* as if the ship was a stone skipping along a lake's still surface at sunset. The stars in the distance hummed, resonating like fireflies on a summer night. And there—directly in front of her—was a light brighter than any sun she'd ever laid eyes on. *The quantum tunnel.*

Had this epicenter been as bright in the natural realm, and her vision optical, Awen was sure she would have covered her face with her hands and still been able to see the brightness in her mind. The tunnel's light in the Unity was *that* all-consuming, that all-embracing. For a brief moment, she thought her flesh and bones would melt at the light's intensity, but then the feeling was gone.

In the Unity of all things, however, Awen could make out not just luminescence but coloration as well. The light was not white but a coalescence of many colors—some she had never even seen before. In fact, the closer to the center she looked, the more densely packed the colors became.

Awen kept looking for the point at which the quantum tunnel began, like the center of a target. She moved forward in the Unity, sure she would make it out at any moment. But the farther her senses stretched into the beyond, the more the beyond invited her in, swallowing her vision. Rather than finding a point on a map, Awen found a direction on a horizon, a continual summons that she could not see the end of. The quantum tunnel's gravity was pulling her presence in the Unity from her physical body. Farther and farther it stretched, going so far that she feared journeying into it might separate her from her body. *Forever.*

The thought startled her, and she recoiled, snapping back into her mortal body. She gasped and noticed that her body was shaking.

"You okay, Star Queen?" Ezo said over his shoulder, his voice rising above a commotion on the bridge.

Awen realized she wasn't shaking from her fear alone but from a very physical quaking of the ship as well. "I'm fine," she said, gripping the arms of her chair.

"Getting rough," Ezo said, stating the obvious.

"The tunnel's gravity also seems to be employing a compression scheme that will most likely have an adverse effect on our physiology," TO-96 stated.

"You mean *our* physiology," Ezo corrected, indicating Awen and himself.

"Quite so, sir. My apologies. Though I do not think I will be without effect either, nor will the ship," the bot said, looking around.

With each passing second, the ship shook more rapidly, as if someone was turning up the oscillation pattern on an audio device. The pitch rose higher and higher, and Awen noticed an acute pain in the middle of her head. "Does anyone else feel that?" she yelled.

"And here Ezo thought it was just his hangover," Ezo replied, squinting through a forced smile.

"I am not clear on what you are referring to," TO-96 said,

"but I am aware of the quantum tunnel's density now beginning to approach terminal levels for matter in our universe."

"*Terminal,* as in *lethal?*" Ezo asked.

"Correct, s-s-sir," the bot stuttered. The lights in his eye sockets flickered.

Awen's vision began to diminish, and it seemed like the entire cabin was shrinking. A wave of vertigo struck her so hard she knew she was nanoseconds away from vomiting. Strangely, she felt guilty that she would not have time to grab the bag that Ezo had placed under her seat.

AT FIRST, the voice sounded like it was underwater. Awen tried to focus her blurry vision, but a combination of searing pain near her temples and a strong urge to pass out kept her from making out anything beyond fuzzy shapes. The voice continued to speak until Awen finally heard her name.

"Awen… hear me?"

She blinked several times and noticed an arm. Then she saw a hand. She moved the fingers. It was her hand. The shapes in her field of view started to clarify.

"Awen? Can you hear me?"

She tried to speak, but no words came out. A face was getting closer to hers. Its eyes were enormous. It was terrifying!

"Awen?"

And then her stomach lurched. She was so tired of throwing

up. Awen wiped spittle from her lips, using the hand. She could smell bile in her nostrils.

"I got you," it said. She knew that voice. It was—a friend. No, it was just…

"Ezo?" she asked.

"Phew! Star Queen, you had us worried there for a moment."

"Worried?" Awen repeated, finally getting her bearings. She was on the bridge of the *Indomitable*. They'd been headed toward something important—toward a hole in space. *The stardrive. The Novia Minoosh. The quantum tunnel.*

"Did we make it?" she asked.

Ezo smiled. "We sure did, Star Queen."

Awen returned his smile and tried to stand up.

"Easy there," he coached, insisting she stay seated. "You've been out for several minutes. The jump hit you hardest of all, it seems."

"Her vitals are stabilizing," TO-96 said.

"But we really did make it, yes?"

"Indeed, Awen," the bot replied. "Just as Ezo said. And the jump seems to have been almost instantaneous. By my calculations, one point eight attoseconds. That is a billionth of a billionth—"

"Don't think she cares right now, 'Six."

"Ah, yes. My apologies." TO-96 knelt on her other side and offered his hand to her. Awen grasped his and Ezo's hands and stood. It took a moment more for her to get her balance. Then she stared out the bridge window, her eyes widening, mouth agape.

TO-96 leaned in and whispered, "Welcome to metaspace, Awen."

Instead of brilliant white, the stars here were various shades of purple set against the same infinitely black background. A fine pink-hued cloud connected the millions of lights like a spiderweb that looked as if it had been blown about at the hands of an ancient wind. Other smaller gems twinkled in the distance, flickers of green and blue and gold. The entire scene seemed to pulse with otherworldly energy the likes of which she'd never encountered before.

"It's... *magnificent*," Awen said, spellbound by the sight. She felt a surge of emotion so strong that tears welled in her eyes. Almost a minute passed before she finally found words again. "I... I can't believe I'm seeing this."

"Nor can we," TO-96 said.

"I'm just glad you made it through," Ezo said. "We were worried about you there."

"Thank you," she said, turning toward them. "I'm fine. Really, I am." She smoothed her turtleneck and noticed the puke stain. It smelled terrible.

"Let's get you some new clothes," Ezo said.

"Thank you. But what about the planet?"

Ezo smiled at TO-96. "Go on," he prompted.

"Ithnor Ithelia is right where they said it would be," TO-96 replied, naming the planet for the first time. Awen mouthed the words back at him in wonder. Then the bot input a few commands, and the ship began a slow turn to starboard. The stars pitched across the window until a brilliant purple star flooded the bridge with light. The ship's sensors adjusted the window's transparency to reduce glare. As the *Indomitable* continued its rolling arc, a new object began to fill the field of view.

Appearing from the lower right was a massive planet whose greens and blues were nearly iridescent in the purple sun's light. Countless flecks of white and gold sparkled on the planet's surface. The world looked like nothing Awen had ever witnessed, nothing she'd ever imagined. She'd felt overwhelmed before, but now she was overcome with emotions so strong that she wept openly. One hand covered her mouth, and the other pushed back tears and loose strands of hair. This was the single most beautiful thing she'd ever seen in all her life.

"Ithnor Ithelia," she whispered. "You are breathtaking."

FOR THE FIRST time in her life, Awen didn't vomit during atmospheric entry. She was too excited to be sick, though she doubted there was anything left in her stomach to throw up. She was also too excited to be mad at Ezo—at least for a little while. She pressed herself up against her harness like a little kid trying to look out the family skiff's front windshield from the back seat. Purple-blue light saturated the landscape—what little of it she could see—and continued to bathe the cockpit in the otherworldly glow.

Once the ship's rate of speed had decreased and the vibrations subsided, TO-96 began conveying sensor data to Ezo and

Awen. "The atmosphere is… surprisingly conducive to biological life as we know it. Trace amounts of other compounds but nothing that should impede your ability to breathe normally."

"So you're saying you're pretty sure we won't die?" Ezo asked.

"I calculate that there is less than a three percent chance that one of the trace elements is lethal, correct, sir."

"That's good enough for me."

"Me too," Awen said. "How long before we can touch down? I don't even know what the protocol is for something exploratory like this."

Ezo looked at her and raised his shoulders. "Me neither, Star Queen. But it is your expedition, technically speaking. Your op."

"Awen," TO-96 said, "might I suggest reviewing data from the preliminary sensor scans to aid in your decision-making?"

"That sounds like a wonderful idea," Awen said. "I'm assuming I can unbuckle now?"

"Aside from thermal sheering or atmospheric anomalies, both of which the ship's dampeners can account for, I would say everything will be smooth from here."

Awen undid her harness and climbed out of her seat. "How soon before the scans are finished?"

"Well, we will need several more hours to complete a full planetary rotation. However, I'm bringing up the preliminary scans now." TO-96's head twitched back and forth as he worked with the *Indomitable*'s AI to present query results. Three holo-projections displayed across the dashboard, indicating…

What? Awen wondered, moving between Ezo and TO-96 for

a better look. All she saw were jungle-covered mountains, none of which looked like good candidates for landing a starship, let alone being hubs for an advanced sentient species to congregate in.

"These represent the three largest cities detected on this hemisphere," TO-96 said, "one of which happens to be the one indicated on the stardrive—here." He pointed to the center image and started it rotating.

"I don't understand," Awen replied. All she saw was a pyramid-like mountain with countless protrusions on its surface, all of which were covered in foliage. The city looked more like a spiny mass in a dense jungle than the shining metropolis she expected. "Are they—are the inhabitants jungle primates or something?" She looked at Ezo and then at TO-96, wondering if they were as confused as she was.

"Ah, I think I understand your assumptions. This is a visual scan only. Here," TO-96 said, looking down at the dashboard. He eliminated the two peripheral projections and expanded the center one of the city until it nearly filled the bridge. "This should help you."

All the green vanished to reveal one of the most stunning cities Awen had ever seen—it even rivaled the architecture and grandeur of Capriana. Delicate spires towered over latticework skyscrapers, serpentine sky bridges wove between monolithic domes, and countless causeways and canals formed a footprint so mathematically perfect that Awen wondered who could have designed and written such a beautiful algorithm.

"It's spectacular," she whispered.

"You can say that again," Ezo said.

"But I still don't understand it," Awen said. "Why the foliage? Are we saying… this city's been reclaimed by the planet? That would mean—"

"It's abandoned," Ezo concluded.

Awen's heart sank. *To come so far, to risk so much, to witness so many people's death's, all for a lost civilization?* She knew the discovery would not be a total loss, of course. Such a find would merit decades of excavation and cultural findings to last centuries of analysis by the Luma. But still—she was hoping to discover the most important find of all: *life.*

"Ninety-Six, what about life signs?" she asked.

"I'm sorry, Awen, but besides basic and complex organisms one might find in any jungle throughout our galaxy, there is nothing notable—nothing that I'm sure you're looking for."

Awen lowered her head. "Keep scanning, Ninety-Six. But let's look for a place to land."

"As you wish, Awen."

33

Magnus dragged Valerie and Piper across the desert in a makeshift sled as the sun baked them raw. They were headed east toward the canyon and the closer of the two settlements he'd seen from the air. With any luck, they'd arrive by nightfall.

Magnus had taken one of the glass canopies, flipped it over, adhered several pads from the downed capsules to it, and covered it with fabric from the parachutes to act as a shade. Then he repurposed a few meters of his grappling-hook line, tied it around his waist, and connected it to the sled.

Valerie and Piper sat quietly under the white shade as Magnus hauled them eastward. The little girl had even managed to hang on to her stuffed animal, which was looking less stuffed and more animal. *A rabid animal.*

He knew the females were grieving the loss of the husband and father now buried in a shallow grave. Magnus had wanted to bury the man properly, but there wasn't time for anything like that. Death by exposure and discovery were both very real possibilities if he didn't get the mother and daughter to safety soon. Magnus had dug a pit for the late senator using his helmet then laid his body to rest. The man deserved a Republic funeral, but if the senator were to speak from beyond the grave, he would insist that Magnus get them to safety. At least, that was what Magnus would have said had the roles been reversed. Valerie and Piper had wept as Magnus finally covered the man's face, forever concealing him in the dust of Oorajee.

After constructing the sled, Magnus cut vents in his helmet using his duradex knife. Both the helmet's main battery and its backup battery were completely depleted. He was sure the AI's processor was destroyed, too, given the charred components that had failed to survive Piper's strange energy explosion. The helmet's only uses now were as a sunshade, as eye protection, and —he'd most recently discovered—as a shovel. It reminded him of when the old Mark IV helmets had crapped out on his unit during the Caledonian Wars. As had been the case back then, he wished the helmet could seal his suit from the sand, but the granules found their way into *everything*. He swore as a handful of the stuff rubbed against his groin.

For once, Magnus wished his armor was *any* color but black. Without the suit's cooling system online, the armor felt like an old convection oven, but he knew he'd need it for its protective abilities should they encounter resistance. *And they would encounter resistance.*

He squeezed his MAR30 between his hands. Fortunately,

Piper's devastating power surge hadn't knocked his primary weapon out of commission. His Z and his remaining frag grenade were still online as well. *At least he had those.*

He wanted to ask Valerie about the girl's powers, but it was a conversation he simply didn't know how to start, at least not in front of Piper. Plus, what would he say? *So, your daughter shoots energy from her mind and kills people. How does that work?* Magnus shook the thoughts away more than once and contented himself in merely being the Marine that would see them to safety. *Leave the other stuff for people smarter than you, Magnus.*

He stopped every half an hour to provide his passengers a small drink from his limited water supply. The truth was, Magnus needed it more than they did, given his exertion, but he preferred to help them to his own detriment. And anyway, he'd pushed himself through worse. *One more meter, one more kilometer. OTF. Just make it to your next meal, Magnus.*

As the sun began its descent behind them, Magnus could make out hints of white on the horizon coming from a series of low buildings. The sight worried him, however, as the white, while it could have been paint or ceramics, was most likely linen. *A Jujari village.* He'd been hoping for another Dregs settlement or something. He placed his index finger on his MAR30's safety as if to make sure it was still there and hadn't melted from the excessive heat.

Magnus's mind flashed back to the mwadim's palace, where he'd terminated several Jujari warriors before finding Awen's helpless body behind the dais. Then he and Awen had escaped down the street as he wrestled three strays in the dusty alley. If he could place a wager, he'd put money on having to kill more Jujari before the night was out. Once again, Magnus was protecting innocent lives from certain death by sheer will and, when the time called for it, violence of action—the kind of violence only the Recon was trained to dispense. He thought of his brothers, the ones he'd lost. *No, the ones you'll find.* The heat was messing with his head.

The faces of his men flashed before him one at a time. He saw them amidst specific memories from the past, each laughing, smiling, or doing something stupid. Just a few days before this last mission, they'd spent the night at one of their favorite watering holes on the outskirts of Capriana. Flow looked up from one too many Klindish ales and let out a belch that would have rivaled an elephant's trunk blast.

Flow could drink, Magnus mused as he shook his head, reminded once again of how the black-skinned warrior had gotten his nickname. *'Cause ale never stopped flowing*—so much so that Flow had been unaware that he wasn't wearing any pants that night. Some of the other Recon guys had removed them hours before, but Flow didn't care. "Doesn't change the taste of the beer," he yelled and called for another round.

Corporal Miguel "Cheeks" Chico, on the other hand, had two arms around two different alien girls at the bar. He was completely unaware that they were "anatomically incompatible" to him, as the doctor had later said. Cheeks told the story with pride the next afternoon in the barracks as he showed off bandages that were wrapped around his abdomen and buttocks. He'd more than lived up to his nickname.

Mouth was the storyteller. Magnus had no idea if anything Corporal Allan Franklin said was true, but he didn't care. Mouth could get guys laughing around a table faster and louder than anyone Magnus had ever met, and it had earned him the strange but appropriate moniker.

The memories, mostly of the Fearsome Four, kept Magnus company as he trudged through the sand. He realized more and more how much he cared for his men—how much he missed them and hoped they were still alive. If any of his brothers were still on this cursed planet, he would find them, dead or alive. Fate had delivered him right back to where he'd started, which couldn't have been an accident. He was here for a reason. No comms, no food, almost no water, and limited weapons—*which was* really *pissing him off*—but he never backed away from a challenge. *The Recon never quit, never gave up, and never gave in to anything but mission success.* If his men needed rescuing, he would get it done, and if their bodies needed burial, he would see to it. *On any other planet but this one.*

Suddenly, an image of Awen hung in his mind. She was sitting on Ezo's ship, her knees tucked up to her chin as Magnus handed her a cup of tea. The herbal smell warmed him somehow, as did her face. Despite being a prude, she was…

What was she, Magnus? He fought with himself as his feet stomped through the sand. *She was beautiful.* Her purple eyes—and something about the way she smiled at him—haunted him. Awen was also feisty, and he liked that. Most people just took orders from Magnus, or else he had them detained or thrown in the brig. Plus, most women he'd ever been around had seemed too easily enamored with his uniform or his commanding presence. But not Awen. From the very start, she'd defied him. It had irritated him, for sure. But it also had an endearing quality. He liked that she wasn't a pushover. She was petite, but she was a fierce one.

Magnus felt empathy for Awen. She'd lost people in her team, and that was never something a person forgot. The nightmares, the guilt, the second-guessing—all of it was very real and very dangerous. Magnus had known good men who, after being subjected to similar scenarios, had lost their minds and were never able to reenter civilian life after being medically discharged from the Marines.

He wondered how Awen was doing and if she'd returned to normal life on Worru. He recognized that *normal* was a relative word given all the things she'd seen. Still, he wondered how her after-action review had gone—if that was even what the Luma called it—and if she'd endured any negative fallout. *Probably not. She survived a nightmare, and her COs surely understood that.* He felt the urge to check in on her, to send an external call over TACNET.

And say what, Magnus? "Hi? How are you doing at being a Luma, Awen? Learn any new spells lately?"

The more he thought about it, the more he realized he sounded like a complete idiot over TACNET in his imagination. *Good thing comms are down, a-hole.*

Night approached as Magnus reached the settlement. He was grateful for the fading light, certain that he'd been spotted earlier in the day. Only a completely inept sentry could have missed his black armor trudging toward them across the desert in the daytime. But war had taught him that the cover of night could often erase many daylight missteps. Magnus expected he would have an easier time of gaining access to shelter in the village's outskirts as the sky darkened; he only wished that his thermal imaging was online to give him a tactical advantage. The Jujari might be a superior biological force, but his night vision would have leveled the playing field. Instead, his helmet now accompanied the ladies, as the visor was too dark for the fading light.

"Are we almost there, Mr. Lieutenant Magnus, sir?" Piper asked from the sled. The steady swoosh of sand under the glass became more noticeable as the night air grew still. Magnus could feel the temperature dropping, too, as the sun's glow faded from the sky.

"Yes, Piper," he replied, licking his cracked lips. "We're almost there."

"And what will we find?"

"Piper," her mother reprimanded. "That's enough."

"But I want to know what we'll find, Mother."

"We're going to look for water, something to eat, and a safe place to sleep," Magnus replied, not minding the little girl's questions nearly as much as he might have. Hearing her speak reminded him who he worked for and who he would fight to protect. Life, *this life*, was precious and worth dying for. *And I will die for you, Piper Stone, if I must.*

The faint glow of fires began to appear throughout the village—some on rooftops in braziers, others from within the linen walls of sandstone buildings and standalone tents. Smaller fires burned atop lamp stands, while dozens of wall-mounted torches illuminated streets and archways.

Magnus pulled the sled behind the skeleton of a blown-out skiff that lay on its side. So far, he had not attracted any attention, at least none that had warranted inspection from the village's inhabitants. For that much, he was grateful. With any luck, this town would be sympathetic to the Republic cause and welcome them with open arms.

Were you born yesterday, Marine? You're so naïve sometimes.

No, I'm optimistic. But he knew his true self was right. He hated when *that guy* was right.

"Pardon me, Mr. Lieutenant Magnus, sir," Piper said, her teeth chattering, "but I don't see any food or water yet. I don't see a bed either."

"Piper, be patient," Valerie chided.

"It's okay," Magnus said, catching the glint of Valerie's eyes in the distant torchlight. Despite the wind- and sunburn, the woman's face still looked like fine porcelain. "She's right to question me." He looked down at Piper. "I haven't found any of those things yet, but I will. For now, I need you to wrap yourself in the parachute and stay close to your mother, okay?"

Piper nodded.

"I'll be back in a few minutes. No sound, no movement, copy?"

"Copy?"

"When I say 'copy,' you say 'copy' back to confirm that you understand me."

"Copy back," Piper said in a tiny voice.

Magnus smiled. "Right."

Suddenly, the little girl reached out to him. Magnus wasn't sure what to do. Seeing her little hand, he realized just how *different* it was from everything else he knew—from war, from violence, from death. *Take it, you idiot.* He slipped off a glove and placed a finger in her palm. Her fingers wrapped around it.

"You always save me, Mr. Magnus. You always do."

Great. No pressure. But the truth was, he *wanted* to save her more than anything else. He would too—at least, he would try his best. Someday, he might fail her. No one was perfect. But not that day. That day, he would be the warrior in her dreams.

GROWLS AND BARKING came from deeper in the village as Magnus left the skiff's cover, eyes scanning for motion. He ran forward to a heap of metal. As he took cover, he realized he was at the bottom of a shallow, blackened bowl. *An orbital strike.* Not from one of the big LO9D cannons, as there wouldn't be a village left standing if that had happened. *No, this was a smaller laser strike* but still nothing to mess with. The metal he hid behind was charred and gnarled, and even in the moonlight, he could make out the telltale blast ring around the impact crater only a few meters away. This village had been assaulted sometime over the past few days.

Along with the distinct scent of laser fire, Magnus could smell campfires and cooking meat on the wind—something pungent and oily. The inhabitants here were the survivors of the strike or squatters who'd taken advantage of the aftermath.

Magnus's MAR30 was in low-ready position, giving him the ability to freely sweep the shadows and still bring the weapon to bear faster than most humanoids could blink. Without his helmet's AI to call out targets, he activated the weapon's holo-sight display, which hovered over the rail and extended down the barrel. The information-rich HSD projection was only visible from the operator's perspective and emanated in relation to ambient light so as not to light blind the operator.

Magnus maneuvered to the opposite edge of some debris, stole another glance downrange, and moved out. He headed for a low-walled well and sank below its sandstone blocks. He noted its position and hoped it had potable water at its bottom.

Again and again, Magnus picked his waypoints, scanned for the enemy, and moved. *Slow is smooth, and smooth is deadly*, he reminded himself, mentally reciting one of the many unofficial mantras of the Recon.

He was ten meters from the village's outermost structures and wished his helmet were functional. With a working helmet, he would have been able to see and tag every living thing without them ever knowing. Instead, he used his senses to try to guess where potential threats might be hiding.

A large broken portion of the village wall was visible to his right. Through it, he could see several tents with no internal lights on. The structures were made of sandstone pillars with linen walls and canopies. Magnus figured that either the inhabitants were asleep or these were unused, maybe even supply tents—*wishful thinking*. Only idiots would keep food, water, or weapons caches along the perimeter of any enclave.

Magnus left his MAR30 to the care of its sling and withdrew his duradex knife while moving to the first tent. He pressed his back against the nearest sandstone pillar and listened for movement. No breathing, no rustling. Odds were, the tent was unoccupied. He squatted and turned, cutting a vertical slit in the linen. The blade made silent work of the task, and Magnus peeked inside.

Once through the slit, he found only the remnants of a former occupant's sleeping quarters. The Jujari equivalent of a cot—a nested litter of straw covered by a blanket—was strewn with windblown sand and refuse. And it stank. He pushed his toe through the shards of a broken clay vessel and flipped open a small box that turned up nothing.

Magnus turned his knife on the inner wall that bordered the next tent and slit his way through. Once again, he found sandblown litters and smashed containers. The third tent yielded more of the same. *These tents are going to be dead ends for resources*, but at least they would serve as cover for the night if he couldn't find anything else.

Magnus chanced a glance out the main entrance, keeping himself within the linen folds. A hard-packed street ran to his right and left, bending in a concave shape around the perimeter of the village. Torches lit the lane every fifty meters, casting orange light between long swaths of shadow. Judging by the lack of tent lights here and the noise beyond, he guessed that most of the settlement's inhabitants had congregated near the village center.

Magnus stepped into the street and crossed to the closest unlit tent. He entered with his knife at the ready only to find another old litter. Feeling more confident, he checked several more tents and found stale bedding, refuse, and the remains of various containers.

Now it was time to see if the tents with lights on were occupied. Magnus maintained strict noise discipline as he rolled his boots into and out of each step. He stalked to the nearest glowing linen tent and double-checked his six, listening for any signs of life. He could hear heavy breathing from within. Ever so gently, Magnus used the tip of his blade to crack the folds of the tent's entrance. Unless the occupant was staring directly at the spot where he placed his knife, they would be none the wiser.

A small oil lantern sat on the floor, wick flickering with the last drops of fuel in the glass bowl. And there, curled up like a massive lapdog, lay a Jujari warrior, fast asleep. A sniper blaster rested against one of the sandstone pillars, as did a pair of binoculars and the warrior's keeltari long sword. The warrior had no other possessions, which meant he was traveling light. A sentry, Magnus concluded, realizing he and the women had just stumbled into the best possible scenario.

While the village had no doubt been a bustling hub of Jujari sectarian life in its former years, it was now being used as a military outpost. *And a poorly run one, at that.* Where barking families and wild commerce had probably once filled its streets, warriors used the town as a safe haven. *But from where?* Magnus figured they'd been displaced from another village or city.

Between the orbital-strike craters that he'd seen from the air and the one he'd stood in on the outskirts of the village, there was plenty of evidence that the Republic had already begun its assault on the planet. But judging from this pack's lack of vigilance, as exemplified by this slumbering mongrel, they weren't expecting enemies on foot. *Which meant the Republic hadn't sent a ground-assault force yet.*

He left the Jujari unharmed, figuring a dead body would raise the alarm sooner rather than later. At the moment, he needed as much time as he could to get the women hydrated and to cover. Still, he needed to know what size force he was up against. Magnus found a gap between tents that served as an alley, and he sidestepped his way down it toward the center of town. The light ahead grew brighter. He was careful not to catch his armor on the linen walls, moving like a shadow. *A shadow that slays. A Midnight Hunter.*

The alley broke to another hard-packed lane lined with torches, only these were closer together than the others. The circumference of the village's circular shape was also constricting. He was nearing the center. He crossed to the opposite side of the street, hidden in darkness, and entered a similar gap between tents.

Up ahead, he could hear the snarling, garbled speech of the Jujari. Then, as he approached the end of the alley, he saw firelight dancing off the side of the remaining meter of tent fabric. He slowed, edging forward.

Magnus peered out from the shadows to see at least three dozen Jujari warriors gathered around a sizable fire pit. An oily carcass rotated on a spit, flames leaping every time black fluid dripped onto the coals. The beasts collectively lapped from metal buckets as the smell of something fermented wafted into Magnus's nostrils. The scene was like that of any of a thousand warrior tribes across the galaxy: the calm after or before a storm when the fighters reveled in the fleeting breaths of their short lives. Brothers drank beside brothers, commiserating in their shared fate as those who would die for the society they prized above all else.

Magnus realized that not only were these warriors not expecting a ground assault, they weren't expecting any kind of assault. *Which means we've not been seen.* It wasn't much, but it was something. And Magnus knew that every advantage, no matter how small, could be capitalized on to bring him one step closer to mission completion.

For the moment, he needed to return to the women, get some fluids in them, and find a place to sleep for the night. With any luck, this troop might vacate at first light—or after their communal hangover wore off. Magnus withdrew into the shadows. As he sidestepped the way he'd come, he heard Piper scream in the distance.

34

Awen descended the *Indomitable*'s ramp with all the wide-eyed wonder of a child who'd just discovered chocolate cake. She could hardly contain her excitement as she took her first step onto the alien planet. Her boots pressed into the thick grass of the clearing TO-96 had landed in. Lush stands of trees lined every side, and just a few hundred meters beyond, Awen saw the city's first foliage-covered structures.

The urban sprawl rose toward the purplish sky like a mountain range covered in a green blanket, and Awen thought it was magnificent. She was most struck, however, by the metropolis's size.

No, it should be classified as a megalopolis, *at least by our standards.* The shipboard holo-projections hadn't conveyed its scale to her.

The air itself was warm and filled with fragrant smells. The scent of blossoming flowers mixed with the full-bodied earthiness of a forest's underbrush, one alive with sprouting flora and decomposing matter. Insects buzzed, and strange calls trilled and blatted from within the trees.

"Are you capturing all of this, TO-96?" Awen asked, unable to pull her eyes from her surroundings.

"I am indeed, Awen."

"Good," Awen responded, still not looking back at them. "Keep logging everything you see. This place is… it's fantastic." She took several more steps forward.

"Star Queen, hold on," Ezo said, pulling yet another blaster sling over his head. He already wore a backpack filled with supplies, two canteens, his holstered SUPRA 945 pistol, and a blaster rifle slung over each shoulder. "We need to proceed carefully. We have no idea what's out there." He grabbed several more energy magazines and tucked them into open battery slots on his belt and inside his coat.

"It's not like we're going to war or something, Ezo," she replied, wincing at just how many weapons he'd been able to drape on his person.

"I feel I must side with Ezo here, Awen. Since this planet is completely uncharted, it would be wise to take extra precautions for personal self-defense."

"I get it," Awen said. "But how many weapons do you really need, Ezo? Doesn't Ninety-Six have enough to defend us from a small Republic invasion force?"

"I admit that my armaments are—"

"Rhetorical question!" Awen and Ezo said in unison. They smiled at one another and gave a laugh. The mood was light, which Awen thought was a good sign. They were, after all, the first people in their galaxy to step foot on this alien world—perhaps even the first in their universe.

"Well, come on, already!" Awen protested. The two bounty hunters walked down the ramp and into the grassy field with her. TO-96 activated the motors, and the giant vertical door whined shut behind them.

"The first main buildings are due north, eight hundred meters," TO-96 reported. "The capital city's name is simply listed as Itheliana."

"Itheliana," Awen repeated, "capital of Ithnor Ithelia."

"That's correct," the bot replied. "We're presently standing in what appears to be the remains of an old plaza surrounded by residential structures just inside the woods. I suggest we stay within the main thoroughfare."

Looking in the direction the bot indicated, Awen saw only a wall of green. "Why don't you lead the way," she replied, gesturing with her hand.

"As you wish, Awen."

TO-96 took the lead as the trio moved across the open area and into the first group of trees. The light didn't diminish so much as it *changed*. Awen looked up. At first, she thought the leaves were translucent, allowing the sun's light to pass through them and kiss the jungle floor. But as she passed some leaves near a low-lying branch, she realized the foliage was not translucent but luminescent.

"The leaves are glowing," she said in amazement. "How is that even possible?"

"They appear to be bioluminescent," TO-96 answered. "Much like some forms of algae in our universe. According to my initial scans, the light is a surplus of what each leaf consumes, perhaps supplying it for layers of flora beneath it."

"Fascinating," Awen said, noting the complex symbiotic relationship the trees had with the low-level species beneath them. She reached out to touch some of the leaves.

"Ezo wouldn't do that if he were you, Star Queen," Ezo said.

TO-96 stopped and turned around. Seeing Awen's extended hand, he added, "I must agree with Ezo on that point. We don't yet know the chemical composition and biological compatibility of the planet's life with your own."

Awen pulled her hand away. "Fair point."

The trio continued through the forest before arriving at a pair of buildings connected by an arch about ten meters over the jungle floor. Awen could make out dozens of glass windows, an elevated portico, and several awnings that extended into the surrounding tree limbs. All of it, however, was smothered by tree limbs, creeping vines, and vegetation, which sprouted from every crevice and crack.

"Maybe it was some sort of gatehouse," Ezo offered.

"Correct, sir," TO-96 said. "Records show this was one of the city's many entrances. The term *gatehouse* would be a misnomer, however, as defensive fortifications appear to be nonexistent."

"So you're saying the city wasn't defended?" Awen asked.

"That appears to be the case, Awen. Both during the period of its initial construction all the way to its last use, it seems that the Novia Minoosh were never preoccupied with the threat of invasion. Here, let me show you."

TO-96 squared up to the buildings and suddenly emitted a wide beam of light. The holo-projection filled the foreground with an overlay of the city. *As it once was.* "This is what it looked like?" she asked in wonder.

"Correct, at least insofar as the data provided to me conveys."

"It's… it's—"

"It's beautiful," Ezo said.

"Yes." Awen nodded, biting her index finger.

The holo-projection seemed to melt away the overgrowth, revealing gleaming surfaces and delicate architecture. Windows spiraled out to meet sweeping walkways suspended over intricate sidewalks. Planters dotted open plazas while arches rose and fell across them like the waves of an ocean swell. In the center stood the largest arch, bearing a script that Awen had never encountered before. Its elegant lines looked like they overlapped one another in three dimensions even though the text was clearly engraved on a two-dimensional surface.

"What does it say?" Awen asked.

"The translation, at least as far as I can manage, says, 'Welcome to all those who wander and wonder. Find direction in darkness, find meaning as one.'"

"Clumsy, but poetic," Ezo replied. "So, you can read their language?"

"I would say I am learning to," TO-96 said. "They provided what they want us to know. I am parsing the rest."

Awen blinked at TO-96's holo-projection. Her imagination

was lost in what it must have been like to wander these city streets when this civilization was at its height. What did the people look like? What clothes did they wear, what songs did they sing, what food did they eat? How were their family units structured, and what form of government did they employ? The reality was, however, that she'd never know. Judging by the amount of growth around the ruins, it had been hundreds if not thousands of years since any living thing had occupied this place.

Awen felt a sudden sadness like she was mourning the loss of an old friend who'd passed away years before. The initial sting of death was long gone. In its place was the festering absence that bred a lifelong sorrow. It was an emotion that held on like a stiff joint or a bruised bone.

Yet... She stood there, looking past the holo-projection into the rest of the city.

Yet it feels like we're not alone. Like they're still here. She couldn't tell Ezo or TO-96 how she knew they were being watched, but she was convinced they were—convinced that this civilization was not completely lost. The notion defied her sense of logic, of course, but so did most of what was to be found in the Unity.

Awen closed her eyes and withdrew to her inner self once more. If there was something to be found, she knew it could be seen in the Unity of all things. She stretched out with her senses, observing herself, Ezo, and TO-96 as mere blips amid a planet fully awake. The impression of vitality was so overwhelming that Awen was nearly pushed from the Unity. She held on, forcing herself to stare at the cascading ripples of life that emanated from each place she focused on with her inner eyes. Each tree, each plant, each flying, swinging, and crawling creature radiated a life force more intense than anything she had seen before. *But how? How could one planet's life be so vibrant, so intense?*

"Are you okay, Awen?" Ezo asked from inside the natural realm. Her inner senses felt the words before her ears heard them.

"Yes," she replied, first from inside the Unity and then with her physical mouth. "This planet is incredible. I've never seen something so... *alive*."

Then Awen shifted her focus toward the urban structures, eager to see what treasures they might hold. Her inner eyes searched the first ones and then froze. Aside from seeing the buildings in wonderful detail—far more than TO-96's holo-projection could have rendered—Awen noticed that a strong life current raced through the walls like bundled conduits of energy. The pipelines glowed green with a corona that faded from pink to white.

"The buildings," Awen said aloud. "They're inhabited."

TO-96 raised his forearm with the XM31 Type-R blaster affixed to it. As if someone had threatened a beehive by swatting it with a stick, the nearest building's colors shifted to an angry red and sent out high-frequency ripples in the Unity.

"Wait." Awen extended her inner hand, placed it over the bot's arm, and gently pushed it down. TO-96 jerked away, as she thought he might since her physical hand was nowhere near his arm. "They're not hostile, at least not as far as I can tell."

"Wait—*they?*" Ezo asked. "As in, the buildings?"

"No, not the buildings, exactly. It's more like something that makes up the buildings. Or is flowing in the buildings."

"And you can tell they're not hostile?"

"They didn't like TO-96 raising his blaster," Awen replied, noting that the red had turned back to the greenish, pink, and white glow from before.

"They didn't like it?" Ezo asked in disbelief. "How can you—"

"Relax, Ezo," Awen said, placing her inner hand on his shoulder for emphasis.

Ezo winced and let out a yell, trying to brush the unseen touch from his body. "Splick! Was that you?"

"Yes, Ezo."

"Don't scare Ezo like that," he said, placing his hands on his knees and trying to catch his breath.

"More exists on the other side of the seen universe than you can imagine," she added. "You'll just have to take my word for it."

Ezo placed a hand on his chest and stood upright again. "Okay. So, you don't think they're hostile." He looked to TO-96. "Any ideas where they want us to go, Ninety-Six?"

"The only destination indicated on the stardrive is Itheliana as a whole."

"The whole city?" Ezo said.

"That's correct, sir. By my estimation, their invitation was simply to arrive and to explore."

"Explore?" Ezo asked, clearly stunned by such an idea. "The whole city? But it would take an entire lifetime!"

"Based on square kilometers, you may not be far from the truth."

"I might have something," Awen interjected. "There's some sort of pulsing, moving inward. It seems to have a definitive direction. Like… it wants us to follow."

"It wants us to follow it?" Ezo asked. "Ezo's not sure—"

"I told you to trust me, didn't I?"

Ezo cleared his throat. "Yes. Yes, you did. Just please don't touch Ezo again like that. It's… it's weird."

"I won't have to if you keep up with my instructions. This is *my* expedition after all, isn't it, Captain?" She could tell he wasn't sure how to respond to her when her eyes were closed. Ezo raised a hand and waved it over her face. "Yes, I see you just fine, Ezo. Relax."

"So weird," Ezo mumbled, lowering his hand. "Okay, lead on, Star Queen."

THE TRIO WALKED for over an hour, every street revealing a breathtaking view, inspiring architecture, and ingenious engineering. TO-96 kept his holo-projection displayed for Ezo's sake while Awen remained inside the Unity. The trio stopped only for Awen and Ezo to rest their legs and take long drinks of water from their canteens.

Not only did the buildings get taller as they moved toward the city's center, but the streets and sidewalks moved upward as well. Some spiraled over themselves, while others leaped skyward with ramps, bridges, or elevated corridors. And while the jungle continued to retake the structures, it did so with less ferocity as the city moved up and away from the planet's surface.

Whatever beings had once lived here, they certainly seemed to have had the stature and preferences of humanoids in Awen's universe—only larger. The doorways leading into buildings allowed her nearly twice as much clearance as she needed. She imagined the streets bustling with shoppers, enterprisers, and families, all flowing past one another on their various errands. Transportation lanes supported elegant vehicles that whisked people from one point in the city to the next. All around her, life swelled, rising and falling like the troughs and peaks of ocean waves.

In the present, however, there was nothing but the sounds and smells of the forest. Awen wondered just how old Itheliana was and how long it had taken for the jungle to retake the land. She also wondered if she was the first to tread here since… since whatever happened to this species happened. Had others discovered it before her, perhaps others in this universe? TO-96 had called it "metaspace." Perhaps these people had been conquered by a superior race in their own galaxy, though the city entirely lacked signs of war. Maybe a plague had wiped them out.

Whatever it was, it had not taken them out completely. Something still lived in the walls and floors and ceilings. Something moved in the pavement and the concrete. As sure as Awen was of her own life force in the Unity of all things, she was convinced that this place contained some remains of sentient life even if it was a shadow of its former glory.

They walked on for another hour, following Awen's direction as she followed the rhythmic pulses that summoned her forward. Even though Ezo couldn't see what she could, he often intuitively chose the correct turn in a street or fork in the sidewalk. She wondered if the life force rippling through the city also summoned him in unseen ways.

As they rose in altitude, the buildings grew increasingly massive and more elaborate. The structural interconnectivity produced an emotion in Awen—a sense of confidence, interdependence, and reliance on every other thing around her. It was as if these people had embedded the ethos of their culture within the walls of their buildings.

By the third hour, the trio had summited the city's uppermost echelon. Here, one building stood out. Its multitiered construction eventually formed a tall spire that seemed to struggle against the creeping vines in a desperate effort to launch itself into the void. Yet the sinuous fibers wrapped around it, forcing the spire to stay grounded, forever bound to the prison of its foundation.

"In there," Awen said, pointing to the structure's large main doors. She could sense they led into a long hallway that proceeded to serve countless rooms, corridors, and plazas. The building was truly immense and felt *all-consuming*, as if it had an appetite for sentient minds to explore its many secrets. Yet the structure wasn't a *hungry* creation that threatened to swallow them. Rather, it was already well-fed—satiated from the nourishment of a thousand generations—and, in fact, offered something to those who wished to partake.

"It's a library of some sort," Awen said.

"A library?" Ezo asked, taking a moment to look around. "A library is fitting." He ran a hand through his hair. "We'd need a mountain of books to uncover everything there is to know about this magical place."

"And that's precisely what I think it wants to share with us."

For the first time in over three hours, she opened her eyes and stepped out of the Unity. The transition was a shock, as she knew it would be. Remaining in the Unity for that long was difficult, dangerous, and—when you finally reemerged—disappointing, for nothing ever looked as vibrant and rich in the seen realm as it did in the unseen. Still, she was, like all other Luma, a mortal being in a corporal body. She was not meant to stay in the Unity—no more than a mammal was meant to stay submerged underwater beyond its capacity to hold its breath.

Awen blinked, stretched her neck and arms, and looked around at the green jungle that covered every surface. Gone were the details of the city streets, buildings, and windows. Gone were the doorways, facades, and meandering hallways. Instead, they were standing in the ruins of some ancient temple square, surrounded by monolithic shrines to cosmic gods.

The three of them had traveled as high as was possible in Itheliana. The far horizon, which she could see between gaps in the buildings, showed alternating patches of blues and greens, signaling vast oceans and wide stretches of lush terrain. All of it was set beneath the now-fading light of a purple sky. She had to admit that even outside of the Unity, this place was spellbinding.

As Awen turned back to examine the grand entrance of the library, she noticed TO-96's holo-projection displaying another inscription across a broad arch. "More text?" Awen asked, pointing toward the Novian script.

"Yes, Awen. It reads, 'The temple of all we've gained, and the cost of all we've left behind.'"

Ezo let out a grunt. "Seems a little ominous if you ask Ezo."

"Anything that involves a cost is ominous-sounding to you, sir."

Ezo snorted. "You cost me a lot, Ninety-Six. Maybe I'll trade you in after this."

The bot pulled back. "I would like to think that I have more than made up for my compositional expenses, sir."

"Some days, I wonder."

Awen almost laughed at the exchange, but the weight of the moment kept her focused. "Shall we go in, gentlemen?" She tried to step toward the front doors, but her feet suddenly held fast to the moss-covered ground. She looked down, thinking a vine had ensnared her, but her boots were clear. It was as if something had welded her feet to the ground. She tried budging them again but to no avail.

Awen glanced at Ezo. To her surprise, he was looking down at his feet too. "Ezo can't move his legs," he said, his voice rising in panic.

"Neither can I," Awen replied.

TO-96 looked between them. "I see nothing which would indicate our immobilization," he offered, pointing to his own legs, "but I am stuck as well."

Awen's stomach caught in her throat. "That's because it's not something physical."

An all-too-familiar male voice boomed from across the plaza behind them. "Well deduced, young Luma."

Awen twisted around. "No!" she blurted.

So-Elku stood with his head bowed and his eyes closed. Beside him were two other senior elders, their hands tucked in the sleeves of their red-and-black robes. So-Elku slowly raised his head and opened his eyes.

"No!" Awen said again as her chest tightened. "How are you here? That's—it's not possible!"

"Nothing's impossible, Awen," the Luma master replied. "Not in the Unity. You of all people should know that."

"I am sorry to interrupt, Awen, but does this man pose an imminent threat to you?" TO-96 asked.

"Yes!" Awen yelled more loudly than she intended. She could see Ezo struggling to bring up one of the blasters draped over his shoulders. "Very much, yes, Ninety-Six!"

"Very well." The bot spun his torso one hundred eighty degrees, and he raised his arm. Before Awen could blink from the blasts, a cluster of microrockets leaped from behind his wrist. The munitions crossed the square and exploded in a sharp burst of red-and-orange fire. Ezo was also able to fire several bursts of blue blaster bolts in the same direction. The concussion blew Awen's braid off her shoulder and peppered her skin with debris. She lowered her arm from over her eyes to see the smoke clear. So-Elku was still standing, unmoved.

"Well, that was highly ineffective," TO-96 said as he examined his forearm.

"It's not your fault," Awen said.

She was incredulous now. *So-Elku* must have been the one tracking *Geronimo* since Plumeria. *But they'd switched ships.*

"How did you find us?" she asked the traitor.

"Yes," a voice said from another corner of the square. "How *did* you find them, So-Elku?"

Awen turned to see an older bald man, dressed in black, stepping into the open. He was flanked on both sides by two dozen troopers in black armor, blasters raised.

"*Kane,*" So-Elku spat. "How nice of you to provide those coordinates you promised."

"Well, it seems you didn't need them after all," the man in black said, motioning for his troopers to fan out.

Wait, so... So-Elku wasn't tracking us, but this *man was? Or, maybe they've been working together.*

Suddenly, Awen felt So-Elku's grip loosen around her feet. She closed her eyes and entered the Unity. Sure enough, the Luma master had diverted his attention to this new man. *This new threat. The man called Kane.*

"I thought we had a deal," So-Elku replied. "But I'm beginning to wonder if that was ever your intent."

"Perhaps if you had been more patient, you—"

"You would have looted the place yourself and left me with nothing," the Luma master spat.

"Conjecture," Kane said with a flick of his hand.

"And in exchange for what?" So-Elku demanded. "My betrayal of the entire order?"

"Come now, I think you did that a long time ago, So-Elku," Kane replied.

Awen opened her eyes and noticed Kane's troopers spreading around the perimeter. She looked at Ezo and then TO-96. "*Hey,*" she whispered. "*Let's make a break for it. Inside the library. You ready?*"

"*Ezo still can't move his feet,*" Ezo said.

"*You will.*" Awen closed her eyes and reached for Ezo's legs. She gently moved So-Elku's power aside. She did the same for TO-96 and then herself. The master was clearly focused on Kane and his men. Awen noticed that the entire plaza's life force had changed from peaceful green, pink, and white to angry red and white hues. Whatever was about to happen wasn't good.

"*Now!*" Awen shouted.

At that moment, the first barrage of blaster fire lit up the square like a fireworks display.

35

Magnus was off and running before he had time to see what the Jujari would do. Hopefully, their drunken stupor would lessen their reaction time, and with any luck, Magnus could get to Piper first. Why the girl had screamed he didn't know, but he feared the obvious: they'd been discovered. Or worse.

With his MAR30 back in his hand, Magnus pumped his legs, brushing past fabric walls and beating a line toward the skiff on the outskirts of town. He could hear the Jujari barking orders and saw several new torchlights flicker to life around the tents. Magnus sprinted across the first street and was about to cross the next when he slammed into a Jujari warrior coming out of a tent. Magnus toppled over the mutt, and both rolled to a stop in the dust.

It was the sleeping sentry from earlier. Magnus noted the sniper blaster in his paw and the binoculars around his neck.

The beast seemed just as surprised as Magnus. His eyes widened in disbelief and then suddenly narrowed to those of a hunter. But before the warrior could even raise his blaster, Magnus fired a short burst of blaster bolts under the Jujari's chin from his MAR30. The point-blank rounds severed the brainstem and produced a shower of gore that sprayed onto the tent fabric nearest them. But it also gave away Magnus's position. If the revelers weren't roused from their campout at that point, they didn't deserve to be among the Jujari's warrior class.

Back on his feet, Magnus bounded out of the settlement's last row of tents and through the gap in the wall. He skirted the well, dashed behind the metal in the orbital-strike crater, and neared the overturned skiff where he'd left Valerie and Piper. He prayed to whatever deity was left in the galaxy, hoping the women were still there—or at least still alive if they'd been captured. He would find them, and he would save Piper.

Magnus slowed to half pace, flicked off his safety, and stalked around the obstruction with his MAR30 pointed on target. His halo-sights were ready to acquire whatever beast stood behind this obstacle and send them back to hell. As he rounded, he saw a pair of upraised hands. Human hands. Then another and another.

"*Don't shoot!*" whispered a familiar voice. "*It's just us.*"

Magnus lowered his weapon to see Dutch, Haney, Gilder, and Nolan hunkered behind the skiff along with Valerie and Piper.

"Is that why you screamed?" Magnus asked Piper, running to join them.

The little girl nodded sheepishly. "I'm so sorry, Mr. Lieutenant Magnus, sir. It was an accident. They startled me."

He wanted to tell her off, tell her she'd just alerted the Jujari, but he knew it was pointless. Anything short of a grasshopper would have made the poor kid scream in these conditions. He could dress down the other Marines instead, but their approach had probably been as careful as they could make it. The most important thing was that more of his people had survived the Bull Wraith, and now they needed to prepare for a fight.

"Do you have weapons, and can you move?" he asked the newly assembled team.

"Affirmative, LT," Dutch said, holding up her MX13. "Thirsty, some heat exhaustion, but otherwise ready to kick some Jujari ass."

"Copy that," Magnus said. "We're looking at a bad stack-up, maybe six to one, and we've lost the element of surprise." As if to reinforce his point, a few bloodcurdling howls went up from the village. The Jujari were mustering. "You're each going to have a field of fire. Dutch, I want you here in the center with the Stones. Nothing gets to these civilians, copy?"

"Copy."

"Gilder and Haney." Magnus pointed to their far left. "I want you behind that boulder to cover any attempts to flank us. Nolan, I want you to the right, behind that half wall, same thing." Each of them assented and prepared to break. "I'm on point behind that obstruction," he added, indicating the metal heap in the shallow crater. "Nobody—and I mean *nobody*—shoot me, copy?"

"We won't let you down, sir," Dutch said.

"What about me, Lieutenant?" Valerie asked.

Magnus eyed her. "Can you shoot, Mrs. Stone?"

"I know my way around that MZ25 in your chest plate well enough."

She seemed confident, and Magnus didn't have time to argue. If they were all going to die, each of them deserved to go out with some measure of dignity. He pulled his Z from its holster, flipped it around, and handed it to her. Valerie grabbed it and pulled her dress off her leg as she assumed a shooting stance. She checked the magazine and charged the weapon. Then she selected the single-shot mode with her thumb, pressed the Z out from her chest with a nearly perfect two-handed grip, and aimed at something in the distance.

Satisfied, she returned the weapon to low-ready position, double-checked that the safety was still on, and looked at Magnus. "I'll make these Jujari work for every meter they want to gain on us."

If Magnus had had the time, he would have left his jaw on the sand. Instead, he closed his mouth and charged his weapon. "Listen up, everyone. This is about to become a danger area. You *wait for me* to fire the first round. Then pick your targets. Squeeze, don't jerk. Stay in your assigned fields of fire. And for the love of the galaxy, don't shoot your point man. OTF."

"OTF," the Marines replied.

The cobbled-together fire team broke for their respective positions, and Magnus raced out to the front of the line. He didn't like the odds, not one bit. *But the fight's not over till you're dead, and you have a lot of blaster bolts to burn before then.*

The Jujari snarls grew louder until Magnus was aware that the warriors had started filing out from the walls and into the open. He selected wide displacement on his MAR30, knowing he'd only get one chance to use it to the greatest effect, and brought the weapon to bear around the edge of his cover. He flicked off the safety. No less than eight Jujari warriors with blasters extended moved toward him, completely unaware of what was about to happen. He'd hoped for more, but eight was what the dealer dealt.

Magnus squeezed the trigger and absorbed the recoil. A wide blast of blue light swept across the sand, lighting up the wall and tents beyond like a bolt of lightning. Jujari bodies flew back, their blasters and swords blown out of their hands. The report was deafening and succeeded in disorienting the rest of the enemy.

All at once, the night air was on fire with blaster bolts, the first volley coming from over Magnus's shoulders as Dutch and Valerie unloaded on three Jujari who were just outside the blast radius of Magnus's first shot. Next came bursts from Nolan on the right, followed by Gilder and Haney on the far left.

Magnus selected the MAR30's high-frequency setting and used his holo-sights to zero in on two Jujari who'd taken cover behind the small well. He squeezed off two bursts and watched as the dogs fell backward, one spinning from a strike to the shoulder. Their hulking bodies were ill covered and exposed, making them easy targets.

Nolan picked off one more Jujari who was ducking for cover. The blaster bolt from the warrant officer's weapon caught the enemy in the soft tissue beneath his chin, snapping the beast's head backward, feet thrown toward the sky. Nolan might have been a sailor, but the man could shoot.

So far, by Magnus's count, they'd taken down no more than sixteen enemy combatants in the first few seconds of the fight. As good as that was, he knew the enemy had walked into this fight blind and would regroup quickly. Magnus's fire team's positions were no longer secret, and the Jujari were natural hunters.

The enemy returned fire as they found cover, some mutts dashing back into the safety of the village. Blaster rounds seared the air above and beside Magnus; he could see his other team members being pinned down behind cover as well. This was a textbook return assault. The next step was for the enemy to flank their positions under suppressive fire. Which was exactly why Magnus wanted to be forward of their line.

He looked right and left to see which side would send scouts first. He spotted two enemies to the left. Gilder and Haney were pinned down and would be easy targets if they didn't spot the enemy. Magnus sighted in the beasts and fired four bursts. The staccato groupings peppered the Jujari, striking legs and arms and catching the far one in the head. The bodies tumbled and sent up a plume of sand and blood. Magnus looked over his shoulder in time to see another warrior advancing along the right flank. He swung his weapon around, sighted in the Jujari headed toward Nolan, and squeezed. The burst formed a tight grouping on the combatant's bicep and drilled sideways out the other shoulder, searing both the lungs and heart.

Magnus pressed his back up against his cover and paused long enough to see the energy indicator on his MAR30 replenish, ready for another big draw. That was when he felt something bump against the other side of the metal heap. *The enemy.* He could hear Jujari cackling to one another. They were going to try to jump him.

He selected Distortion on his weapon and heard the side mag plates spring outward. The helmet's AI made this sort of shot so much easier; without it, Magnus was only using the holo-sights along with his best guess. *Still, a good guess is better than the shot you never take.* He stepped away from the metal heap, turned toward it, and squeezed the trigger.

The distortion field the MAR30 produced was not visible to the naked eye. Instead, it reached through the inanimate metal and found the Jujari's living matter on the other side. In less than a second, the wave was separating molecules, bursting blood vessels, severing nerves, and disrupting tissue. Magnus heard the Jujari howling as their bodies disintegrated in what was arguably the most painful death possible.

When the round was spent, Magnus turned back to cover and toggled the weapon to High Frequency. He noticed that Dutch's skiff had absorbed so much blaster fire that it was glowing orange from the heat. Likewise, Gilder and Haney's boulder was red and getting chewed apart. Nolan's cover wasn't much better.

Magnus realized that if the Jujari couldn't outflank them, they were going to try to flush them into the open by concentrating fire on their protection. It was a brutal strategy and a costly one in terms of munitions but effective nonetheless. If Magnus's team didn't have cover, it didn't matter how destructive his MAR30 was; there was no way he could protect them all.

Magnus chanced two more glances downrange toward the tents, but the blaster fire was growing so steady that he risked being picked off. The angles of attack were also changing, which meant the enemy was taking cover in the town and spreading out. Magnus cursed and cursed again. There were too many, and they were outmaneuvering Magnus's unit.

Someone screamed. Magnus looked over and saw Gilder drop to the ground. Haney was on him instantly. *Nothing like getting shot next to a medic.* Gilder was still in the fight, however, because he was swearing at Haney to get off him and tried to raise his MX13 around the boulder. *That's how we take it. OTF.* Magnus peeked around the corner of his emplacement to pick off an enemy.

Magnus noticed three warriors trying to advance toward Nolan again. The warrant officer was lying on his belly now, trying to stay as low as possible under the withering assault. Magnus suddenly wondered if maybe he should have taken the right flank instead; it had the weakest cover. Consciously putting Marines in harm's way was the worst part of being a commanding officer. It was the part of the job no one ever told you about, recruiters never warned you about, and your family never asked you about. It was also something you tried to forget but couldn't.

Magnus removed his remaining frag, pressed the one-second timer with his thumb, and pitched the ordnance at the advancing Jujaris' heads. As soon as the grenade left his hand, Magnus dropped to the ground. A beat later, the frag exploded, drilling down on the enemies with a barrage of superheated metal and razor-edged ceramics. The beasts were thrown to the ground from the blast as their bones shattered under the impact.

Magnus realized he was out of grenades and sent another burst of blaster fire into some tents. Jujari returned fire, and sand sprayed over Magnus's body. He wiggled back to cover and sat up. His amount of safe area was shrinking. He was getting pinned down. *This is it.* His makeshift fire team had put up a good fight, but the adrenaline was wearing off, and soon they'd all feel the brunt of the day's dehydration. When that happened, there would be no way to stay up with the number of enemies that would rush their flanks.

As he thought about how it might end, Magnus realized how stupid the whole operation had been. Maybe if they'd stayed in the Bull Wraith, they could have reasoned their way out of the situation like the senator had proposed. Maybe if they'd chosen the other settlement toward the mountains, they would have found inhabitants friendly to the Republic cause. And maybe if Magnus had stayed with Piper, she wouldn't have screamed when the latecomers approached. *Maybe, maybe, maybe,* Magnus said to himself, mocking his ego. *But this is what you chose, so time to pay the piper.*

Piper.

Magnus's eyes went wide. *Maybe she could do that explosion-blast thing again.* He looked her way but only saw Dutch taking blind shots over her shoulder. Even if he could reach her, what would he say? *Hey, Piper, you know that thing you did that killed your dad? Yeah, can you do that again?* No, it wasn't something a person could just turn on and off. The girl's freakish abilities were just that—

freakish and, therefore, unreliable. And even if they had been reliable, he couldn't ask her to do it on command. *Congratulations on weaponizing a child, Magnus.* He felt dirty even for thinking it.

Maybe she would ultimately blast them all to hell at least to get herself free. But Magnus knew he wouldn't live to see it. He'd gotten her as far as he could—it was up to her to do the rest.

Magnus changed the MAR30's rate subsetting from burst to full auto, took a deep breath, and looked skyward. *Here goes nothing.* Then he leaned around the corner and squeezed the trigger. He saw the first blaster bolts land on a Jujari's head and then—

The whole scene went nova. Magnus was thrown off his feet. He flipped end over end as an immense blast threatened to pop him from his armor. The concussion was so fierce and the heat so searing that Magnus thought he'd left this life for the next. He sailed backward and lost his grip on his weapon.

When he finally slammed to the ground, sand and stones pelted his head like crowd-control shotgun rounds. The blast of whatever berated him was unrelenting. His MAR30 whipped around at the end of the sling, slapping his legs. He fought to keep his eyes shut, but the wind and the heat were sure to fold back his eyelids and stab his brain.

Then all at once, it was over. The light, the heat, the wind, it was just… *gone.* Magnus coughed. His ears were ringing, pulse racing, and nose sniffing as he inhaled the smell of burnt ozone, burnt hair, and burnt flesh. His eyes were full of sand, and he imagined plunging his head into the sea just to flush the gravel from his face—and to soothe the pain of his melting skin.

His body screamed at him as if someone had tried to cook him alive inside his armor. Even though the flames were out, the oven was still hot. He wanted to peel his suit away like an orange rind, but he lacked the energy. He was simply too spent. It seemed like the blast had flushed all the adrenaline from his veins. Plus, he worried that maybe his armor was the only thing holding him together—that if it was peeled off, it would take his skin with it.

He coughed again and heard himself laughing. Faintly. *It is me, isn't it? Yes*—he was laughing—laughing at the planet, at the Republic, at the galaxy. He'd just *survived*—he just *lived* through an orbital strike from an LO9D cannon at close range. *Close range? It was damn near on top of my head!* Any closer, and there wouldn't have been anything left of him.

Left of us. Magnus suddenly remembered his team—he remembered Piper and Valerie. *Splick, they'd been behind the skiff, no armor, pinned down by blaster fire.*

Magnus tried to raise his face off the sand, but the attempt brought more pain to his neck and back. He tried to blink, but that only made his nerve endings shriek. He couldn't see and could barely hear, and any effort to move was met with the worst agony he'd ever felt.

A tremor traveled through his body, and his stomach convulsed. *Dammit.* He hated throwing up. But this would be worse. Every nerve in his body screamed as he vomited on the sand next to his head. Only a small mouthful of bile came out, but the pain was so intense that it knocked him out.

Another tremor awakened Magnus, which led to another dry heave. He cursed his body for the involuntary reflex function. *There's nothing left to purge!* But he knew reasoning with his soon-to-be corpse was a pointless exercise. He heaved and blacked out again from the pain.

When Magnus came to again, he felt more tremors. He prepared for yet another wave of nausea, another episode of convulsing and passing out. He supposed it was his body's way of coping with the trauma—of helping him pass into the afterlife to join the Recon warriors before him, to join his grandfather and maybe his brother.

No, my brother's in hell. But isn't that the same place you're going, Magnus?

He couldn't bring himself to answer the question.

The tremor was getting stronger, and Magnus braced himself. He urged his body to make this the last time around, as he simply couldn't handle the pain. It was too terrible. He'd heard of people—mostly torture victims—begging for death. Well, he was there. He wanted death. He would even taunt it if he had the energy to.

The tremor came as a low sound in the desert and traveled into his prostrate body. He still couldn't hear and wondered what was left to make noise after that explosion anyway. His ears still rang but not as loudly. Time had passed, and he felt himself nearing death. He couldn't see and couldn't bring himself to move.

The tremor stopped. Then he felt small thumps that were like... footsteps. Someone was walking toward him. Several someones, in fact. He wished he could turn his head, open his eyes, and at least give himself the dignity of defending himself against the death blow.

"There he is! That's him!" a small voice said from far away. It had to be an angel, maybe even one of those chubby cherubs in one of the old paintings. Maybe *it* would decide his fate, blessing him with heaven or damning him to hell.

The footsteps fell closer, and someone touched him. Pain shot down his nerve endings.

"Get him out," another voice said, this one deeper—much deeper.

"Please be careful with him," the little voice said. He knew that voice—knew *her*.

"Piper?" Magnus tried to say but was worried his lips hadn't made the sound he'd wanted them to. He tried again, but the word hadn't sounded any better to his muffled hearing.

"Don't talk, Mr. Lieutenant Magnus, sir. You're hurt really bad, it looks like."

It looks like? What do I look like? He wanted to open his eyes, but it felt impossible. The pain was far too intense. It felt like he'd been raped in the face by a gravel pit. He tried to say something back to her, tried to ask her if she was okay, but his mouth wouldn't cooperate. Nothing in his body would. He wanted to shout—*tried* to shout—but nothing but garbled sounds came from his throat.

"Easy there, buckethead," the other voice said. *Buckethead.* He'd been called that before. The memory was familiar but too far away to catch, like a faded dream or a scene in an old holo-movie that had grown blurry over the years. The man's name was on the tip of his tongue. "You'd better hang on, or else you're gonna have one really disappointed little girl on your hands. Plus, I'd be forced to add your helmet to my collection, and we both know how much that would piss you off."

36

The plaza lit up as Kane's troopers started firing on So-Elku and his two elders. Awen ducked instinctively and closed her eyes, forming a one-way barrier between the assault and her team.

"The enemy of my enemy is my friend," TO-96 said poetically, "but is that still the case here?"

"I don't think so!" Awen screamed.

"Shoot someone!" Ezo yelled at the bot.

"Very well, sir."

Ezo grabbed Awen's arm and darted for the library doors as TO-96 unleashed a barrage of fire at both forces. His micro-rockets targeted multiple troopers as his XM31 directed a constant bead of laser fire onto So-Elku's shields. Awen covered her ears as gauss cannons on the bot's shoulders fired twin projectiles that zipped across the plaza in rippling sonic waves. The crack made her wince, almost knocking her over, as the kinetic missiles vaporized the torsos of two black-armored troopers. Their heads launched ten meters before bouncing across the moss-covered stone.

Kane noticed the bot and redirected some of his men to fire on it. Fortunately, Awen's barrier held up against the first several blaster bolts. The energy slammed into the invisible shield and spread out over it like liquid slapping into a boulder.

"Let's move, Ninety-Six!" Ezo called over his shoulder. "Inside, now!"

TO-96 continued to cover their retreat into the building as Ezo flicked on a flashlight at the end of one of his blasters. Ezo let go of Awen's arm. She ducked behind a large column and released the barrier she'd formed outside.

"Come on!" Ezo yelled as he darted down the hallway.

Awen took a breath and followed him, glancing back to see TO-96 bring up the rear. The hallway was enormous, far larger than Awen had imagined. Dozens of wide columns ran down either side, supporting a ceiling nearly thirty meters above them. She also noticed that there was less foliage in here. Within a few seconds, her boots were clumping along dusty marble floors.

"She sold me out!" Ezo yelled as they ran. "I can't believe she actually sold me out!"

"Sold *you* out?" Awen replied, her anger burning red hot. She'd figured it was best to overlook his treachery, as it hadn't really harmed their mission. *Until now, that is.* "You sold me out, you traitor!"

"Hey, I was just trying to get us here, okay?"

"Which led to everyone getting here!" Awen yelled.

"So it didn't work out like Ezo thought it would. So shoot me."

"Maybe I will!"

"If I may, sir," TO-96 interjected, "do you think that your wife is simply upset that she is still your wife?"

"There is that, yes," Ezo said.

"You're infuriating, Ezo," Awen said, keenly aware of the firefight that grew behind them. "We'll discuss this later. For now, we need to find somewhere to hide and make a plan."

"Can do, Star Queen," Ezo said. "Ninety-Six, what do we have for layout?"

TO-96 brought up the holo-projection again, this time minimizing its luminosity to better conceal their position. But it was enough light for Awen to see by. Suddenly, a doorway ahead of them glowed red.

"There," the bot said. "This door leads deeper into the temple."

"Perfect," Ezo said. "Hold on—did you say *temple?*"

"Yes, sir."

"I thought you said it was a library, Awen."

"I did. That's what it felt like. I don't know their actual names for things yet!"

"Wait," Ezo said, holding up a hand. "Do you hear that?"

"It would appear the firefight has ceased, sir."

"Exactly," Ezo said.

As if on cue, several blaster bolts flew down the hallway and exploded in showers over their heads. Ezo yelped, ducked, and then returned fire with one of his blasters. He squeezed the trigger on full auto, illuminating the expanse with a lightning storm of rapid fire. "Go, go, go!" he yelled.

Awen dashed through the doorway as TO-96 joined Ezo in laying down covering fire. Then Ezo ducked inside, followed by the bot, as more blaster bolts struck the walls around them.

Once inside, TO-96 resumed the projection and indicated several more doors. "All of these provide access to corridors both above and below us with the least likelihood of entrapment."

"Let's go up," Ezo said.

"Up?" Awen asked in surprise. "Why up?"

"Because we can regain access to the exterior faster and scale down. Get back to the ship. Maybe even sabotage their ships if we're lucky."

"We go down," Awen countered. "We have more city to hide ourselves in, less exposure. Plus, we don't have to worry about falling off anything."

"But, Star Queen—"

"My op, Ezo. Mine."

Ezo grunted. As if to emphasize her point, a blaster bolt found its way into their chamber and lit the place up in a shower of sparks. "Fine, we go down."

"For what it's worth, Awen," TO-96 added, "I heartily agree with your logic." Another blaster shot glanced off a pillar and nearly took off the bot's head.

"Come on!" Awen yelled, pulling the bot's arm toward the first door TO-96 indicated that went down.

They stepped onto a wide landing and started descending a spiral ramp. It hugged a wall on one side and had a hexagonal latticed handrailing on the other. The floor was covered in a thick layer of dust, but there was no foliage to speak of. It now seemed that the jungle dared not enter this far inside the temple.

Around and around they went, descending farther into the building. Blaster bolts slapped the railing, spraying Awen's clothing with molten metal. She brushed the slag off as Ezo leaned out and returned fire straight up.

"They are gaining on us," TO-96 noted matter-of-factly.

"Thanks, Captain Obvious," Ezo shouted as he dodged some incoming blaster fire. "Hadn't noticed." Ezo fired several more bursts as they ran. "Can't you do something, 'Six?"

"Like what, sir?"

"You know, something cool. Something to delay them."

"Certainly, sir." TO-96 activated a hatch under his chest to reveal what Awen thought were bombs or grenades or something. Three slid out, and the bot selected each and threw them at intervals up the spiral ramp. The devices clung to the ramp's underside and blinked with a bright red light.

"You should cover your ears, Awen," TO-96 said as they ran.

"What about me?" Ezo protested, putting his hands up.

"Not your op," the bot replied.

The trio had run down another story when TO-96 detonated the uppermost device. Even though the blast was at least three stories above them, Awen could feel the concussive force push her into the sidewall. She almost tripped head over heels. Then large chunks of the ramp sailed by, some colliding with the railing beside Awen, showering her with rubble.

The blaster fire stopped momentarily as the troopers above them hesitated. Awen could hear their footfalls falter even as the debris impacted with the floor somewhere below them with a thunderous noise.

"Don't slow down," Ezo said, pushing Awen gently with his elbows, his hands still over his ears.

"Second detonation," the bot warned.

The next blast was closer than the first and caught Awen off guard. The sound rattled her head and made her ears ring even with her hands covering them. But the explosion caught at least two troopers off guard, too, as they whizzed by in midair. One slammed against the railing next to her, his scream audible when his helmet was ripped from his head and his body was sent cartwheeling. The trooper was silenced a beat later when his skull struck the next level down with a wet *crack*.

Awen wasn't stopping now. More rubble careened off the ramp and exploded on the floor far below. She ran for all she was worth, legs pumping, chest burning. She barely heard TO-96 call for the final detonation, then it filled the space above her with fiery light. She stumbled into the wall, tearing her sleeve and scraping her arm. Another trooper sailed beside her and landed somewhere below.

"Almost there. Keep running." With the bot directing them, the trio descended farther and farther as blaster shots ricocheted off the railing. They finally neared the bottom level, and TO-96 said, "In there," pointing to an archway in the wall.

Ezo and Awen nodded, wiping dust and debris from their faces. Once through the doorway, Ezo swung his flashlight around. TO-96 followed a moment later and lit the remainder of the room with his holo-projection. They were in another cavernous space, this one a rotunda lined with seven doorways. Light filtered down from a panorama of stained glass.

"Which way?" Awen shouted, her ears still ringing. She'd no sooner spoken than the ramp outside began to shake. She, Ezo, and TO-96 turned in time to see the ramp collapse. Massive blocks caved in and spilled through the opening as a plume of dust shot into the rotunda. Awen covered her face and coughed. It sounded like a mountain had cleaved in two as massive blocks sheared against one another and landed in heaps. The mangled bodies of Kane's men were mixed among the wreckage, a few of them moaning as death finally overtook them.

When the cacophony finally dissipated, Awen wiped her eyes and examined the former opening, now sealed shut with broken stone.

"Well, that solves our pursuer problem," Ezo said.

"Unless they have heavier ordnance, I agree," TO-96 said.

"Why do you always have to be such a downer, Ninety-Six?"

"A downer? I am unfamiliar with that term, sir."

"Everybody be quiet," Awen ordered, raising her hand. "I hear someone out there."

"There's no way anyone survived that, Star Queen," Ezo said.

She waved him off and addressed the bot. "TO-96, are you sure there are no other ways into this rotunda from out there?"

"Checking," the bot replied. "Yes, I am sure. The entrance we are looking at is the only way into this rotunda from the upper section."

"Eeezo…" called a muffled voice from the other side of the rubble. The small hairs on the back of Awen's neck stood up. "Eeezo… I have something for you," the singsong voice called.

"Did you hear that?" Ezo asked, suddenly looking pale in TO-96's holo-projection.

"Yes, I heard it," Awen admitted. The voice was so creepy that she hated to acknowledge she'd heard it.

"Who… who is that?" he asked.

"Let me check." Awen closed her eyes and reached out in the Unity. She moved past the rubble and examined the vertical shaft. The walls pulsed an angry red color as if the living energy within them was upset with the destruction. It looked as though a bomb had gone off in the space, ripping the ramp from the walls and bringing down half the structure along with it. Then she reminded herself that a bomb had gone off in it. *Three of them, to be exact.* She looked around in the Unity and noticed a life-form descending a thin string like a spider crawling down a single strand of webbing. Another chill climbed up her neck.

"I see someone." Awen narrowed her focus and looked more carefully, pulse racing. "Wait, no. I see two people."

"Who are they?" Ezo asked.

Awen moved in, trying to clarify the face of the person who spoke to them. "It's—I think it's Kane. The bald man from the plaza." Awen breathed a sigh of relief. Perhaps this meant that So-Elku had been killed. Then Awen scolded herself for feeling relieved at the prospect of another person's death. *But he did just try to kill me.* She'd be justified in hastening his death, wouldn't she?

"Eeezo… come out, come out, wherever you are."

It was Kane, and he was grinning a horrible, murderous, treacherous grin. *Who is he?* She grew more terrified with each passing moment. He dangled from two rappelling lines anchored high above them. Then Awen noticed a second form hanging beside him in another harness.

"There's someone else, but I can't make them out," Awen said.

Ezo coughed.

"Is that *you*, Eeezo?" Kane asked.

"What do you want?" Ezo yelled through the stone.

"What do *I* want?" Kane replied. "Why, nothing at all. I already have everything *I* want. Well, *most* everything I want. *Do you?* Yes, I do, and stop talking. We're not alone yet. *Yes, we are. You ordered the men back to the ship.* That's right, I did."

Ezo looked at TO-96 and then to Awen. "Who's he talking to?" Ezo asked quietly. "Is there someone else out there?"

"Yes," Awen replied. "But the person looks to be unconscious, dangling beside him. They've rappelled down together."

"Is he crazy?" Ezo asked her.

"Maybe," she said, lifting her hands. "How should I know?" But then Awen noticed something about the man's face. His image in the Unity seemed turbulent, like two faces sliding in and out of one another. It startled her so much that she gasped. Fear like she'd never felt before clamped down on her chest. One face looked human, but the other looked... *What?*

Awen stumbled into Ezo.

"You okay?" Ezo asked.

She managed to stay in the Unity and back away from Kane, her spine tingling. "Something's very wrong with that man."

"Ezo's picking that up too." Ezo looked to the blocked entrance and raised his voice again. "We would love to negotiate with you, Captain Crazy, but unfortunately we're late for a dinner reservation at this great new meta-restaurant we found."

"Negotiate?" Kane laughed. "I don't want to negotiate. I just want you to have what rightfully belongs to you."

"*Rightfully belongs*—sorry, what? What do you mean, Kane?" Ezo looked to TO-96. "That's his name, isn't it?"

"Yes, I believe so, sir," replied the bot replied.

"You don't have anything that belongs to Ezo," the smuggler continued.

"Uh, actually," Awen said, "he kind of does."

Kane had awakened the prisoner next to him with a stab of a contact syringe.

"Say hello to your husband," Kane said to the woman coming awake beside him.

"Ezo?" Sootriman said in her unmistakable voice.

"Love Sauce?" Ezo yelled, his voice tense.

"*Love Sauce?*" Awen asked.

"It is a truly irritating pet name, to be sure," TO-96 agreed.

But Ezo wasn't paying attention. He'd raced forward and was moving rocks by hand. "What have you done to her, Kane?"

"Oh, nothing. Not yet, anyway. *But you will.* Yes, of course, I will. *Now?* No, but soon."

"Who is he talking to?" Ezo asked, looking over his shoulder at Awen.

"No one else is out there but her," Awen insisted, but she knew what she'd seen.

"He's crazy," Sootriman cried. "Ezo, he's completely mad!"

"I'm not *completely* mad," replied Kane. "*Well, half of you is sane, at least.* That's true, but the other half? *Not so much.*"

"He's attached a bomb to my line, Ezo!" Sootriman yelled.

"What?" Ezo asked in shock. "What do you mean?"

Awen steered clear of Kane and whatever haunted him then moved up the second rappelling rope. She saw a device with a blinking light much like the ones TO-96 had used to blow up the ramp, only this one was larger—much larger.

"You might recognize this device, Awen." Kane laughed. "*Might she? You think so?*"

Awen noticed the second face conversing with the human face in a disjointed spasm. It was truly terrifying. "I don't recognize it, Kane. Now, let the woman go."

"You don't?" Kane shrieked. "How utterly ironic! You're looking at it right now, aren't you?"

"He's going to kill me, Ezo!" Sootriman yelled.

"Baby, hang on! We'll get you out of there. We'll figure something out." Ezo turned to TO-96. "Can you blow this?" he asked, pointing to the rubble that blocked the entrance.

"Not without placing your wife in significant peril," the bot replied.

"It's the very same kind I used in Oosafar," Kane continued. "In the mwadim's palace. *Yes, just like the palace.*"

"Wait—what?" Awen asked.

Kane hesitated. "Do you mean to tell me…? *She never saw it! You never saw it, Awen? What a pity. Genius is always wasted, as is irony.*"

"You are the one who sabotaged the meeting?" Awen roared, her anger threatening to pull her from the Unity.

Kane laughed, throwing his head back and spinning around at the end of his rope like a drunken spider. Awen felt tugged toward her mortal body, but she wanted to see Kane's face up close, to memorize it, to emblazon it on her mind's eye for all time.

I see you, she thought.

Kane's face bubbled and morphed as the other face tried to emerge again.

And I will never forget you.

"*I see you too*," Kane said. But it wasn't Kane; it was someone else—*something* else. The second face started to emerge, eyes black as pitch, teeth pointed. Its features bunched up in a snarl. Then faster than Awen could react, the apparition leapt at her.

Awen screamed and fell out of the Unity, panting. She grabbed her chest with both hands. A burning sensation moved up her neck and flooded her face. Dread and… something worse. Emotions boiled in her chest that she'd never felt before. Her mind felt co-opted by thoughts she'd never imagined, sudden visions of slaying Kane in ways that made her want to vomit.

Focus, Awen! She shook her head and looked at Ezo. "Kane's got a bomb on her line ten, maybe fifteen meters up. I think it's on a countdown, maybe a remote switch. I can't be sure."

"Sir," TO-96 said, "if the blast itself does not kill her, the fall will."

"I got it, Ninety-Six." Ezo placed a dusty hand on the bot's arm.

"Wait," Awen added. Something about Kane's words bothered her. "I think there are more."

"What do you mean, *more?*" Ezo asked.

"Kane just said that this is 'just like the palace.' There were three explosions in the mwadim's palace, not one. So if I'm right, yes, the first blast will kill her. But the second and third blasts will kill us. We have to get out of this rotunda if we want to survive—as in, *right now.*"

Ezo swallowed and looked at her. "Awen, can you do something?"

Awen returned his gaze, unsure what he meant, at least at first. "Do something? No, I can only…" But then she understood what he meant. *He means, "Can you kill him?"*

"Awen," Ezo pleaded. "Do something." He reached for her hands.

But she pulled away. *Can I kill Kane right now? In cold blood? But it isn't cold blood. He's threatening a woman's life. Plus, he's already killed scores of others on Oorajee and who knows where else.* Was this her true self suddenly arguing in favor of murder? Awen resisted another lunge from Ezo's hands. Then she grabbed her head. *Can I do it? Can I stop the man's body cold?*

You can, yes.

Where was Magnus when she needed him? This was his domain—doing evil things to evil people. She wasn't trained to kill other people, to end someone's life. But that didn't mean she couldn't—that she wouldn't. The visions of slaying Kane seeped into her mind's eye again.

"Yes, Ezo," she said, trembling. "I can."

"Thank you," he whispered, gripping her hands.

"You must let go of me," she said.

Ezo jerked away. "Sorry, yes. Of course. Whatever you need."

Awen closed her eyes. In an instant, she was in the central shaft, searching for Kane, but he was gone. She looked up in the Unity and saw the fleeting ripples of his presence as he left the chamber. Then she spotted two more explosive devices farther up Sootriman's rope, attached at intervals.

"They hoisted him out," she said. "I can't, I—"

"Can't what?" Ezo asked.

"I can't kill him," Awen said in defeat. "He's too far away." She expected Ezo to yell at her, to hit her body and rip her out of the Unity. But no blows came—no scolding, no dark words.

Instead, Ezo asked, "Kill him? I just want you to save her!"

Ezo had never asked her to kill Kane. *That was all you, Awen. Ezo only wants his wife back safe and sound.* She shuddered as the emotions washed over her, wave after wave. She'd almost put another life in danger, all because of an obsession with... *With what?*

"Can you save her?" Ezo shouted, enunciating each word mere centimeters from Awen's face. The sound rippled out through the Unity like a clarion call on a winter's morning.

"Yes," Awen replied with tears streaming down her face.

What had possessed her with this growing obsession to kill, to murder—first Ezo, and then Kane? *Kane*. Images of his *other* face flashed in her mind's eye. That *thing* had pulled on her soul. Perhaps it had tried to corrupt hers, too. She shuddered. How long had it been afflicting her, preying upon her more base instincts? Had it begun in the mwadim's palace?

Awen looked up at the bombs and then down at Sootriman's helpless body. "I can save her, and I will. I will save us all."

Finding Sootriman's body, she focused her attention on the air around the woman then the gravity pulling her downward. Awen had never attempted anything like this before, but without it, Sootriman was as good as dead. They all were.

Awen forced the air molecules to condense, bonding together in a bubble that surrounded the woman. At the same time, Awen tried to ease gravity's pull. Sootriman let out a small scream as she felt herself become weightless; she was levitating inside of a translucent sphere twenty meters above the ground.

"Is anything happening?" Ezo asked.

"Not now," Awen said between clenched teeth. She knew that any sudden move might shift her focus and inadvertently reverse Sootriman's molecular structure. Confident that she could hold the woman, Awen forced the air molecules to condense further, an act that severed the rope.

"Uh, I'm free of the rope," Sootriman said.

"Hold on, what'd you say?" Ezo yelled. He looked at TO-96. "What'd she say?"

"I believe she said she is free of the rope, sir."

Awen began lowering Sootriman as carefully as she might lower a child in a basket from a burning building: swiftly, but not hastily. Inside the Unity, ripples of color emanated from Sootriman's bubble and reverberated up the shaft. Awen glanced at the bombs and wondered how much time she had left.

"I'm descending," Sootriman yelled. "I don't know how, but I'm descending."

"Just hang on," Ezo replied. "We'll get you out of there." He looked at Awen. "We're gonna get her out of there, right?"

"Ezo! Not now!" Awen was starting to lose her grip on Sootriman. The pressure was getting to her. She guessed she had another ten meters to go, but gravity was fighting hard to reclaim its hold. Awen exerted more energy, giving of her own soul to keep Sootriman aloft. But the effort required was more than she could bear, and the woman started to pick up speed. Sootriman yelped.

"Sootriman?" Ezo asked, running toward the rubble at the entrance.

Awen let out a gasp and fell to her hands and knees. She'd been forced from the Unity like a wet bar of soap squeezed from a clenched fist.

"Are you okay, Awen?" TO-96 asked.

"I'm fine, Ninety-Six," she replied, panting. "Thank you."

"Sootriman? Love Sauce?"

"I'm fine, Ezo," she replied through the rubble. "I'm down."

Ezo clapped his hands and gave a shout. "Ha! You did it!" He took Awen by the shoulders and hugged her.

"Not yet," she countered. "Now we have to get her out. Then we make a run for it. Tell Sootriman to stand on the far side of the space and to get behind some cover."

Ezo turned back to the entrance and shouted through the wall of stones. "Make sure you're at the back of the room, baby. Find something to hide behind. Can you do that?"

"Yes, I can do that," Sootriman replied. "There's a lot of debris, but I can get there."

"Good. Just be careful."

"Tell her to do it quickly," Awen added.

"And move quickly!"

Awen began crawling then, headed away from the entrance. "We need to move away."

Ezo bent down to help her stand.

"Thanks," she said. "We don't have a moment to spare."

TO-96 moved to Awen's other side and put an arm under her. They crossed the rotunda's floor and headed to the far side.

"Lay me down right there behind that pillar," she instructed. They did so, easing her head to the dusty marble floor. "Okay, leave me. And get yourselves to cover."

Ezo hesitated, looking like he was about to protest.

"Now!" she ordered.

The bot and Ezo dashed to the next pillar and took cover. Awen closed her eyes and was back in the Unity, moving into the shaft again. She saw Sootriman climbing over the ramp remains and heading to the far side. Then Awen focused on the pile of rubble that blocked the entrance to the rotunda. There was more debris than she'd realized, a fact that reinforced her assumption that she would not have the strength and endurance to move the rubble as a mass or the time to move the components individually. There was only one way—one impossible way—but she had to try.

From deep inside her spirit, Awen summoned the remains of her energy and willed it forward into the blocks. It flowed from her ethereal body and moved into the stonework like a purple fluid as rich as the Ithelianan sky. It meandered between crevices, filling cracks and soaking into rough edges. Awen sensed the grain of the stones, noting temperature, composition, and consistency. It was as if she existed, in that moment, within the form of every block, stone, and pebble.

Awen sorted through the rubble and found the largest blocks, the ones that seemed most likely to prevent someone from passing through. She focused on these, her purple life force penetrating deep into the stone. Then she checked on Sootriman one more time to make sure she was hidden. Awen had never attempted anything like this before, and she didn't want to harm the woman if she could help it. She didn't want to harm *any* of them.

Awen took a long, deep breath and pushed with all of her might. This was not like leaning against a broken-down skiff, trying to get it to move, or even slamming up against a locked door, hoping it would budge. No, this was more like finding herself crouched in the center of a very tight space and attempting to stand—and attempting to expand her entire self-presence into immovable surroundings.

In this tight space, Awen felt as though she was buried in the center of a planet. She fought claustrophobia. She fought fear. She fought the sudden urge to retreat from the endeavor and cocoon herself away from everything—from this place and from Ezo and from TO-96. From Kane and So-Elku. From the Luma and the Republic. From Magnus. From her parents.

Here in the Unity of all things, Awen could go anywhere. She could leave her mortal body and traverse the universe—the *multiverse*, now that she knew it existed. She could be anywhere she wanted, free of the pain, the fatigue, the frustration. Awen wanted to hide and never be found.

She wanted to. So badly, she wanted to. But she chose against it. She chose to stay and finish what she'd started.

Awen felt as if she was resisting the gravity of a planet that bore down on her soul and threatened to pulverize her. But she wouldn't allow it. Resisting it would cost her everything, maybe even kill her. But she would not be dust that day. She would be the incinerator. She would turn everything else to dust.

Awen's body—both ethereal and mortal—shook. A violent sound filled her ears like the roar of a waterfall. She smelled earth and dust and smoke. The purple fluid ebbed and flowed around her, pulsing with light as she expanded within the epicenter of each block and large stone. In their molecular structure, Awen existed as a force, a presence of such power that not even atoms could deny her access to their bonds. There was a sudden silence.

And then Awen exploded. Power let loose from her soul like a clap of lightning. Every lick of purple fluid that was interwoven between molecules and atoms suddenly tore through the material world like incendiary fuel. The violent explosion began at a subatomic level, ripping at bonds, and ended in the rotunda as the blocks blew apart—not as smaller debris but as fine dust.

Awen was free, released from the confines that had threatened to crush her. She felt herself snap back to her corporal body and gasp. The air rushed into her lungs so deeply she thought they might burst. Thunder echoed off the rotunda walls but soon faded like the tinkling of wind chimes.

"Are you all right, Awen?" A firm hand touched her shoulder.

Awen opened her eyes, blinking. Fine purple mist danced all around TO-96's head, glinting as if caught by sunlight through a morning window. At first, she thought she was still in the Unity, seeing the remains of her work rippling through the ether. But then she realized this dust was real, not a construct within the Unity. *From what? Not the rocks I decimated.* That dust would have been the fine gray of stone. Instead, this was… purple, like part of her soul.

Awen shuddered as a chill raced down her spine. She tried to get up, but she was spent. "Ninety-Six," she said softly, "we need to get out of here. But I can't. I don't think I can move."

"I will take care of you, Awen." The bot leaned over and scooped her up in his arms.

She looked into his face and tried to smile. "Thank you, Ninety-Six," Awen said, barely able to hear her own voice. She was as tired as she'd ever been. Then she looked back toward the entrance. Covered in a glowing mist of sparkling purple, Ezo and

Sootriman emerged from the archway, running toward Awen and TO-96.

"We are ready to leave now," TO-96 offered.

"Yes," Awen whispered. "I think we are too." She felt the bot turn toward an exit on the far side of the rotunda. She felt Ezo and Sootriman appear beside her and run alongside TO-96. And just before the deep darkness pulled her into oblivion, she felt the heat of a thousand suns erupt behind them and the presence of a black-eyed monster chase them into the void.

37

"Mr. Lieutenant Magnus, sir?" a small voice said as Magnus neared consciousness. Someone's hot breath filled his ear. He wanted to see who'd spoken but couldn't get his vision to cooperate.

"Piper?" Magnus asked. "Is that you?"

"Yes! Yes, it is, Mr. Lieutenant Magnus, sir!"

Piper, the strange little girl he had rescued from the Bull Wraith, was safe. He couldn't believe it. There had been a firefight. At the village. The Jujari outnumbered them. And then... *what?*

Magnus tried to open his eyes, but the effort was painful. He squinted, which caused even more pain. He heard himself swear then remembered that a child was next to him. His voice was hoarse.

"Mama, he's awake! Come quickly!"

Magnus reached a hand to his face. He felt gauze over his eyes and traced it around his head with his fingertips. He wasn't wearing his helmet or his armor. *Where is my MAR30?* He panicked. Suddenly, he remembered the flash of light and the end of the world. An orbital strike. He'd survived a danger-close orbital strike!

Magnus tried to sit up, but his body constricted in pain. His lungs and throat were tight. He let out a loud moan.

"Don't try to move by yourself, Mr. Lieutenant Magnus, sir. Mother will help."

Footsteps padded across the floor as someone neared. "Lieutenant Magnus?"

Magnus instinctively turned his head toward the new voice even though he couldn't see. Only a dim light flittered through the gauze and his closed eyelids. "Yes," he replied then cleared his throat. He tried to sit up again.

"Easy, Lieutenant." It was a woman's voice, one he knew. "This is Valerie. I'm going to help you sit up. Is that okay?"

"Yes," Magnus said, suddenly feeling vulnerable. Needing help just to sit up was… demeaning. But somehow, her asking him allowed him to retain some level of dignity. "Thank you."

"No problem. Now, let's see here," she said, moving closer. Magnus could feel her warmth and smell her hair. The scent was like sinnowilt blossoms on a warm spring morning. "The good news is that doctor says everything is healing well." She reached behind his head. Her fingers were thin but confident as if this wasn't her first time attending to the sick.

"What's the bad news?" Magnus asked.

"That you have me as a nurse."

He could hear her smile.

"Oh, I'm not so sure that's such a bad thing," Magnus said. The words had no sooner left his mouth than a shooting pain charged up his spine and seared the base of his skull. He winced but managed to keep from letting out a childish yelp.

"Easy, easy," she said, helping him sit up.

"Thank you," he replied as she stuffed some pillows around his tender body.

"The doctor says we can remove the bandage over your eyes, but it will still be a few more days before the nanobots have finished their magic. You want to try to remove it?"

Magnus nodded. "Thanks." He felt Valerie begin to unfasten something and then gently unspool the gauze. He tried to help by moving his head opposite her tugs. With every pass, he noticed more light behind his eyelids.

"It's really a miracle you're even alive, you know."

"The orbital strike?" Magnus asked.

She nodded. "It struck just in front of your position."

Magnus replayed the last moments in his mind. He'd been fighting the Jujari four to one—maybe five to one. He couldn't remember exactly. All he knew was that they were moving in on his fire team's positions, and he was running out of options. His mind stretched to remember their names. Corporal Dutch had taken the rearmost position with Valerie and Piper. Private First Class Gilder and Haney took the left flank while Chief Warrant Officer Nolan, the navy pilot, took the right. Magnus was on point. He'd been leaning out to fire when everything went white.

"You weren't hurt?" Magnus asked as the final gauze strip peeled away from his scabby eyes, yanking against his eyelids.

"No. I had a little angel with me."

Magnus guessed she meant Piper, but he had no clue about what to infer tactically from the remark.

"You can try opening your eyes, Lieutenant, but if it hurts too bad, don't force them."

Magnus's eyelids fluttered as he attempted to open them. They felt glued shut, like he'd slept all night with a bad cold and had them crust over.

"Hold on." She sounded like she was rummaging through a drawer. She moved back to him, and he felt the heel of her hand press against his cheekbone. It was warm. "A few eye drops. This won't hurt."

Fluid filled the inside corner of his eyes and spread along the lashes and against his corneas. It was cool but didn't hurt, just as she'd said.

"Try that."

Magnus's eyes flickered open. He saw only hazy light and generic shapes, but he could make out Valerie's head and long flowing golden hair. He didn't need to remind himself how stunning she was. He wished he could focus on her more clearly.

"Mr. Lieutenant Magnus, sir? Anything?" Piper asked.

"Piper," Valerie said with a chiding tone. "No questions."

"But, Mama!"

"Just shapes," Magnus answered. "Everything's pretty blurry, though."

"That's about what the doctor said to expect. Pretty blurry is totally normal with how badly your eyes were damaged." She paused, and Magnus sensed she wanted to say more but restrained herself.

"How badly were they damaged?"

Valerie lowered her head.

"What's—what's wrong, Mrs. Stone?" he asked.

"Valerie, please," she said, placing a hand on his forearm. It was the first time he'd been touched by a woman like that in… *How long has it been, Magnus?*

"Your face was badly burned. But the skin reconstruction was fairly straightforward. Your eyes, however, were much worse."

"They're totally bioteknia now," Piper said.

"Piper!"

Magnus swallowed. "What?"

"They'll just be blurry until they take," Piper continued.

"Young lady, back to your quarters right this instant!"

"Yes, Mama." Her voice was sullen. "Goodbye, Mr. Lieutenant Magnus, sir."

Magnus tried to speak, but he was too stunned by this news—assuming it was true, of course. No sense getting worked up over a misunderstanding. He listened as Piper's footfalls faded away.

As far as Magnus could tell, he and Valerie were alone in what appeared to be some sort of makeshift recovery room. He heard people talking somewhere else in whatever building they were in, and the strange smells of medical cleaning solution and skiff fuel mixed in his nostrils.

"You'll have to pardon her. She's—"

"Is she right?" He swallowed. "Did they go bioteknia on me? For my eyes, I mean? Is she right?"

"Yes, Lieutenant," Valerie said without hesitating.

Magnus looked down. Blood rushed to his head, his pulse quickening. Adrenaline, something he'd spent years learning to subdue, punched into his system unabated.

"Lieutenant, I understand that—"

"No, you don't understand, Mrs. Stone."

"I understand that you will never be allowed back in the service, Lieutenant."

Magnus looked up at her. She did understand. "I'm sorry," he replied.

"So am I."

Magnus felt his breaths coming in short bursts, like the staccato blaster fire of his MAR30 on high frequency. He was having trouble staying in control. This was the end. Not of his life, of course. He supposed he would eventually be grateful for that. To never serve in the Republic Marines again, however, was just as bad as being dead, at least as far as he was concerned.

It didn't feel real. None of it did. Maybe he was still dreaming, still shaken from the orbital. He'd wake up soon. This was all just a bad dream.

"Lieutenant? You, okay?"

Magnus looked up. Her features were still a mess of fuzzy shapes. "I just need a second."

Her hand moved along his arm, rubbing it gently. It felt good, comforting. Loving.

Get a grip, Magnus. You have to pull yourself together, Hunter. Own the field... but only Recon Marines truly OTF. Now that I'm not Recon, what will I own?

This was all splick. He'd talk to Colonel Caldwell and get a release to go back downrange. He shouldn't be panicking like this. He wasn't some noob—he was a Midnight Hunter with the 79th Reconnaissance Battalion.

But he knew the regs. Human tissue couldn't be hacked, but bioteknia could. No one had ever done it, but it didn't mean that some alien species wouldn't jeopardize an entire battalion of modified Marines and win a major victory all because they had superior code splicers. There were no exceptions to the regulations. Ever.

"Who made the call?" Magnus asked.

"I did," Valerie replied without hesitation.

Magnus blinked several times, tears welling in his eyes. From the pain. She knew what it meant for him, yet she'd still made the call. This woman he'd only just met. She had forever altered the course of his life without even consulting him. That was what the rich did, wasn't it? They controlled whatever they wanted to and made all the decisions, no matter how or whom their decisions affected. He'd seen it play out a thousand times in worlds all over the galaxy. He'd just never thought it would happen to him. *Though it seems fitting payback for your past sins, doesn't it, Magnus?*

"Neural cohesion to the optic nerve was deteriorating in both eyes," Valerie said.

"I don't want to hear about it," he replied, waving her off. He couldn't take her reasoning. There was nothing she could say that would explain it away.

"The cellular tissue was dying, Lieutenant. Faster than we could regenerate it."

"No." Magnus shook his head.

"It was bioteknia or—"

"No!"

"Or you would be blind forever."

"You had no right to choose for me!"

Silence fell in the room like a heavy snowfall. Magnus's heartbeat thumped in his ears. His skin was hot, sweat beading on his forehead. *But you know all about choosing for others, don't you, Magnus?*

"You had no right to choose for me," he repeated, softer now.

"You're right."

"Huh?" Magnus looked up at her. Was she wiping away tears?

"You're right. I didn't have the right to choose for you. But I had a responsibility to fight for you." She pinched her nose then wiped it with the back of her hand. "Fighting is… well, it's—"

"It's ugly."

Valerie huffed. "Yeah. It's ugly. And you're just making the best call you can with the information you have. Either I let a Marine go blind for the rest of his life, or I give him a shot at seeing again. Either way, you were out. I just chose to give you a chance to stay downrange somewhere else in some other way."

Valerie took a deep breath, and Magnus could see her shoulders sag. She moved away from him and sat down on a stool. The woman was shaken up.

Magnus sniffed and shoved his upper lip beneath his nose, fighting back tears. He looked down at his hands folded in his lap, bandages wrapping select fingers, knuckles, and both wrists. He flexed his hands, balled them into fists, then opened them again.

He wanted to be mad at her, whoever she really was. Valerie clearly knew what she was talking about medically. And based on the way she'd handled his MZ25 outside the village, she had military training too. This couldn't be easy for her, and he'd been too hard on her. Were he in the same position, he would have picked the same course of action. And she would probably be just as pissed as he was if she were a career Marine.

The proverbial snowfall in the room continued to swallow all the sound save her soft sniffs.

"Thank you," Magnus finally said.

Valerie looked up. "What?"

"Thank you. For choosing for me to see again."

She stood up and walked over to him, her hands reaching down for his. "You're welcome. And thank *you* for saving our lives."

"You're welcome. I only wish that I could've saved your—"

"There was nothing you could have done," Valerie said.

Magnus's mind flashed back to Piper and the burst of energy that had exploded from her pod on the Bull Wraith. Then he remembered pulling back the blood-splattered canopy on her father's capsule and burying his body in the wastes of Oorajee.

"Your daughter… is she…?"

"Not now," Valerie whispered. "Another time. When it's safer."

Heavy footsteps fell in the corridor outside the recovery room, and Valerie pulled her hands from Magnus's. A large shadow filled the room, and Magnus was aware that a man stood over Valerie.

"The gods smile favorably on you, buckethead," said the deep-bass voice that Magnus remembered from his last stop on the desert planet.

"Abimbola," Magnus said, squinting.

"He has not lost his memory, I see," Abimbola said.

"No, he has not." Valerie pulled a data pad from a countertop. "All vitals look stable, brain activity normal. The bioteknia eyes are taking and should be fully integrated within the next few hours."

"Just in time, then."

"In time for what?" Magnus asked.

Abimbola waved a hand, ignoring the question. "Can you believe how our paths have crossed again, and so soon? First, I save you from the Jujari and bombs, and now, I save you from more Jujari and an orbital strike from your own Republic. The gods either want you dead or want me to protect you."

"Let's hope it's the latter," Magnus said.

"Yet you continue to surround yourself with beautiful women." Abimbola gestured at Valerie. "Where do you find them? What could you possibly possess that makes them fawn after you?"

"There's no *fawning* going on here," Valerie protested.

"First, the Luma princess of Elonia, and now this epiphany from Capriana." The black giant of a man leaned away and regarded Valerie. Then he waved a heavy finger at Magnus and stepped closer to him. Magnus could smell the metal from the grenades in the bandolier Abimbola wore across his chest. He could also make out a long facial scar that ran to the giant black man's collarbone. "You know, I second-guessed my decision not to kill you," he said, flipping something—one of his poker chips—in the air and catching it. "My wall needed one more bucket. But I have never seen a man fail so miserably yet attract so many females as you. I think you are a marvel worth permitting to live, at least for a little while longer until I figure you out. I would do it for the fair dau Lothlinium alone."

The mention of Awen brought a sudden pang to Magnus's heart. Since waking, he hadn't thought of her once, yet only a few short days before, she was all he'd been concerned with. Her delicate face and violet eyes evoked a longing that made him—uncomfortable. She represented everything he was not. He knew she didn't understand why he pulled his trigger, and he certainly couldn't understand why she put so much faith in seeking peace with killers. Still, he felt something for her, perhaps more than he cared to admit.

"What am I in time for?" Magnus asked, hoping to redirect the conversation.

"Sharp, this one," Abimbola said to Valerie. "You were most likely right to save him and let him see again."

"In time for...?" Magnus prompted a third time.

"Your friends are alive," Abimbola said. "Well, at least some of them, we think."

Magnus blinked, hope rising. "Dutch?" His mind raced to remember the others again—things were still a little foggy. He looked at Valerie for confirmation. "Gilder, Haney, and Nolan?"

"Ha!" Abimbola clapped. The sound made Magnus see stars. "No, they are resting already. Seems they will make full recoveries. I do not mean *those* friends."

"I don't understand," Magnus replied, trying to will his new eyes to focus on the warlord.

"Of course you don't. Your friends—your fellow bucketheads. My Marauders think some of them survived the ambush in the mwadim's palace."

"Wait. You're saying my Hunters are alive?"

38

"Where am I?" In a panic, Awen tried to sit up.

"Easy, love. Easy," a woman's voice said.

Awen felt a hand on her shoulder and another behind her head. She looked up and saw Sootriman's tan face and consoling eyes. "Sootriman?"

"Yes, love. It's me."

"You're—you're alive."

"No small thanks to you," Sootriman said, stroking the top of Awen's head.

Awen let out a sigh. "The last thing I remember was…"

They'd been in the rotunda, separated from Sootriman and a man. *Kane… and the other being.* A chill ran down Awen's spine. The memory summoned a sense of fear she'd never known before.

She fought to distance herself from the dark face while trying to piece together the events in the rotunda. Awen had rescued Sootriman and blown apart the rocks blocking the archway. She'd done something in the Unity that she'd never attempted before. It had spent her. And it had scared her. *He'd* scared her.

Then Awen remembered TO-96 picking her up. He carried her away from the light of a thousand suns and from the black-eyed monster.

"The rotunda—it exploded."

"It did, yes," Sootriman said. "But we managed to get clear. Something shielded us from the blast until we could find shelter."

"Shielded us?"

"We thought maybe you had something to do with it."

"No, I..." Awen thought back. She didn't remember putting up a wall. She'd been too exhausted. Maybe the memory was slow in coming, however. Or maybe it was... a reflex. "I don't know."

"No need to worry, love. We're all safe now, including you, and that's what counts."

"Ezo and TO-96 too?"

"Ezo and Tee-Oh too," Sootriman replied. Her smile was warm and her eyes friendly, in stark contrast to the ruthless though beautiful warlord Awen had met on Ki Nar Four.

"I'm so thirsty. Can I sit up?"

"Slowly, yes." Sootriman helped Awen sit up.

She looked around the room. Along two sides of the room, large windows lunged away from the dusty floor and connected with the ceiling at an angle farther out. Purplish early-morning—

or maybe evening—light poured through, giving way to a panoramic view of the jungle-covered city below.

Awen felt like she was in a large corner office in some exotic administrative building. It smelled musty. Spiral floral designs covered the marble-like floors, and the ceiling was a patchwork of recessed honeycombs that had probably once housed lights. Strange-looking furniture was arranged along the walls, faded and dusty from ages of neglect. Awen was lying on some sort of cushions stacked on a desk in a makeshift bed. Her blanket and pillow looked like they were from the Indomitable—the ship that had brought them to the metaverse. She wore an oversized captain's jacket, a tattered T-shirt, and green cargo pants, all surely holdovers from the Indomitable. Suddenly, Awen reached for the necklace around her throat, fearing it was gone.

"It's still there," Sootriman said. "Don't worry."

Awen breathed a sigh of relief. The Luma medallion offered her some sense of assuredness to this otherwise chaotic existence. "Where are we?"

"Tee-Oh eventually found a way out of the rotunda's tunnels and got us situated in this space. Ezo and I thought it would be more comfortable for you as you slept. Here," Sootriman said, offering Awen a canteen of water. "Drink this."

"Thanks." Awen sipped slowly. The canteen looked like it was from the Indomitable too. "How long have I been sleeping, then?"

Sootriman took the canteen and capped it. "About a week."

"A week?"

"Tee-Oh will have the exact duration, of course. The days are about nine hours longer here, so that takes some getting used to. We're still trying to use common time so we don't hurt our bodies."

"A week?" Awen repeated, looking at her surroundings again.

"Seems you expended a lot of energy to do what you did for me."

Awen blinked at Sootriman. *Was the effort to save Sootriman's life really so costly to my body and soul? Did I hurt myself somehow?*

Sootriman reached out and held Awen's hand with her own warm, strong one. "Thank you, Awen. Thank you for saving my life. Thank you for saving *all* of our lives."

Awen looked up at the woman, whose wavy brown hair glistened in the lavender sunlight. "You're welcome." She swallowed. "So, where are they now—Ezo and Ninety-Six? And why didn't you just take me back to the ship if it's been a week?"

Sootriman pulled a tall stool over and sat, finding the appropriate piece of furniture for her generous figure. She'd ditched the red-and-gold dress Awen remembered from Ki Nar Four, but she still opted to keep her legs bare. Now she wore a pair of green shorts cut from military pants, a black shirt that she'd pulled the sleeves from, and a pair of black trek boots—all items that seemed to have been pulled from the Indomitable.

Sootriman brushed strands of hair over her ear and took Awen's hand again. "The Indomitable was disabled."

"Disabled?"

"The boys salvaged what they could, but we couldn't go back."

"Who? Who would have…?" Awen's mind filled in the blanks. "Kane."

"That's what the recovered holo-footage showed."

"You said Ezo and Ninety-Six were able to salvage some things," Awen said. "Why didn't they just blow it up?"

"If it were me?" Sootriman put a hand to her chest. "I would have done it to insult my victims."

Awen stared at her for a beat. "Remind me never to cross you."

Sootriman nodded and winked. "You're beautiful *and* smart. My kind of woman."

She thinks I'm beautiful? Awen thought, astonished. Sootriman wasn't exactly the type of person to dole out compliments haphazardly, so that was high praise coming from the likes of her. That, or Sootriman felt sorry for her.

Either way, I'll take it right now, Awen thought. Then the deeper implications of the Indomitable's condition hit her. "Wait a second. That means we're stranded."

"It does." Sootriman took a deep breath. "That it does."

"Do they—do we—have a plan, then?"

"Not yet. The boys are out exploring the city for that very reason. Hoping to find solutions. They had to wait a little bit at first. Seems that Kane and his troopers were wandering the city, too, looking for who knows what. But after a few days, we watched their dropships leave, and then their starships left the system—most likely went back to our universe."

"So they didn't suspect we survived the explosions in the rotunda?"

"It's doubtful. TO-96 said that madman put enough trinitex in that tunnel to punch a small hole in a Goliath-class destroyer. Even if we survived, they probably figured we wouldn't be leaving anytime soon without the Indomitable and would live out our days here."

"We'll get back," Awen said, clenching her fists. "We have to get back." She thought of Willowood and the rest of the Luma, wondering how many had remained loyal to the order and how many had been seduced by So-Elku. Then she thought of Kane and shivered. There was no telling what that man was capable of. Clearly, he was looking for something here in Itheliana that he needed—that he wanted for some destructive purpose. *He knew about this place, but how?*

Awen's thoughts turned to the Jujari. She wondered if they had not inadvertently provoked the violence in the mwadim's palace. Did Kane approach the mwadim about the stardrive earlier, and did the mwadim see through him and resist? Perhaps the ambush had been Kane's way of forcing the mwadim's hand and getting what he wanted.

All this speculation still didn't help Awen answer the biggest question: why give up the stardrive at all? She didn't understand why the mwadim would do such a thing, given its clear significance to every sentient life-form in the galaxy. The fact that Kane knew the answer to this question and she didn't made her nervous. Who knew what that *madman*, as Sootriman had called him, was capable of.

Awen's thoughts turned to her parents. The prospect of never seeing them again put a lump in her throat. They'd fought for months before she left to attend observances on Worru. They'd never see eye to eye on the Luma and on what the "proper way" to serve the galaxy was—that much they'd made clear. Truthfully, when she left, she didn't care if she ever saw them again. But that had just been the sentiments of impulsive youth. Confirming the reality of never seeing them again forever, she was sad—perhaps even afraid. This wasn't like getting stuck on the other side of a quadrant for a year or two. At least in that scenario, you could send transmissions and share some semblance of life's happenings. The planet of Itheliana was as removed as two people could be this side of death.

Then she thought of the person she was least expecting to think of: Lieutenant Adonis Olin Magnus. Admittedly, she'd been pretty rude to him when they first met. But her experience with the Galactic Republic's Marines in the past hadn't exactly filled her with confidence about their humanity. "Blaster fire and funeral pyres" went the old adage among the Luma, and that about summed it up as far as Awen was concerned. But Magnus had shown more concern than she expected. His kindness had caught her off guard. *As did those green eyes and that bearded baby face,* she thought. He had, she also reminded herself, saved her life. Though that was a mutually shared gift. She recalled the falling concrete slab and Abimbola's jail. *We're probably even,* she concluded.

Despite her speechless delight at being the first Luma to ever journey to Ithnor Ithelia—and discovering the metaverse!—she had a visceral desire to get back to her native universe as soon as she could. She would return to explore this spectacular new world. Hopefully, the quantum tunnel would remain open for several more years. But discovery paled in comparison to survival, and she had to get back to save her people—and to save the galaxy from whatever So-Elku and Kane were planning.

"We just have to get back," Awen whispered.

"It's not looking great for that, love."

"What do you mean?" Awen looked up.

"Well, it's safe to assume that Kane was looking for alien tech, probably starships. He's an admiral, after all."

He's an admiral, of course! Why didn't I think of that sooner?

"No ships, then?" Awen asked.

"Plenty of ships," Sootriman corrected. "Thousands of ships, actually. Quantity is not the problem, however."

"It's quality," Awen concluded.

"Exactly. As far as Tee-Oh can tell, this entire civilization has lain dormant for more than a thousand years. Maybe much more."

"They've been extinct for over a thousand years?" Awen asked, wondering who else knew about this race. *Were we the first to explore the city?* Her mind swam with the implications. "So that means the Jujari have had that stardrive in their possession for… for…"

"For a very long time, unless they got it from another species, of course. Either way, it's safe to say that it was in circulation long before the Galactic Republic, the Sentient Species Alliances, or even the Star Faring Council."

"So we're late to the date." The large room suddenly took on a melancholy air. This place would not yield the discoveries Awen had hoped for—namely, life. There would be no encounters with any sentient species here. No one was coming back to greet them. Awen knew, of course, that there was no price to be put on what they might take away from future archeological expeditions. But in terms of finding sentient life, that hope was gone. "Maybe TO-96 can cobble together something," Awen said, trying to cheer herself up.

"That's the hope, yes. But, Awen, you have to remember, *a thousand years*. The fact that these buildings are still standing is a testament to the Novia Minoosh's ingenuity."

"And maybe it will be that way for the starships they find too."

Sootriman looked out the windows. The white purplish light from the sun was growing stronger, marking the beginning of the alien day. "I hope you're right," she finally said. "I really do. But a thousand years is a long time for anything to sit dormant and deteriorate, love. I think you need to prepare yourself for what we've already accepted."

"And that is…?" But Awen already knew the answer.

"We're going to be here for a very long time."

MAGNUS and AWEN return in GALACTIC BREACH, available now on Amazon.

For more updates on this series, be sure to join the Facebook Group, "J.N. Chaney's Renegade Readers."

Read on for a bonus short story and novella.

LIST OF MAIN CHARACTERS

Abimbola: Miblimbian. Age: 41. Planet of origin: Limbia Centralla. Giant warlord of the Dregs, outskirts of Oosafar, Oorajee. Bright-blue eyes, black skin, tribal tattoos, scar running from neck to temple. Wears a bandolier of frag grenades across his chest and an old bowie knife strapped to his thigh. Never leaves home without a poker chip.

Adonis Olin Magnus: Human. Age: 30. Planet of origin: Capriana Prime. Lieutenant, Charlie Platoon, 79th Reconnaissance Battalion, "Midnight Hunters," Galactic Republic Marines. Baby face, short beard, green eyes. Preferred weapon: MAR30. One of the "Fearsome Four."

Allan "Mouth" Franklin: Human. Age 28. Planet of origin: Juna Major. Corporal, heavy-weapons operator, Charlie Platoon, 79th Reconnaissance Battalion, "Midnight Hunters," Galactic Republic Marines. One of the "Fearsome Four."

Aubrey Dutch: Human. Age: 25. Planet of origin: Deltaurus Three. Corporal, weapons specialist, Galactic Republic Marines. Small in stature. Close-cut dark hair, intelligent brown eyes. Loves her firearms.

Awen dau Lothlinium: Elonian. Age: 26. Planet of origin: Elonia. Order of the Luma, Special Emissary to the Jujari. Pointed ears, purple eyes. Wears red-and-black robes and has a Luma medallion around her neck. Won't back down from anyone.

Darin Stone: Human. Age: 34. Planet of origin: Capriana Prime. Senator in the Galactic Republic. Husband to Valerie Stone, father to Piper. Impossibly white smile, well-groomed blond hair, radiant-blue eyes. Luxuriantly tan.

Gerald Bosworth III: Human. Age: 54. Planet of origin: Capriana Prime. Republic ambassador, special envoy to the Jujari. Fat jowls, bushy monobrow. Massively obese and obscenely repugnant.

Idris Ezo: Nimprith. Age: 27. Planet of origin: Caledonia. Bounty hunter, trader, suspected fence and smuggler. Captain of *Geronimo Nine*. Wears a long gray leather coat, white knit turtle-

List of Main Characters

neck, black pants, glossy black boots. Preferred sidearm: SUPRA 945 blaster pistol.

Josiah Wainwright: Human. Age: 35. Planet of origin: Capriana Prime. Captain, Alpha Platoon, 79th Reconnaissance Battalion, "Midnight Hunters," Galactic Republic Marines. A legend in his own time.

Michael "Flow" Deeks: Human. Age: 27. Planet of origin: Vega. Sergeant, sniper, Charlie Platoon, 79th Reconnaissance Battalion, "Midnight Hunters," Galactic Republic Marines. One of the "Fearsome Four."

Miguel "Cheeks" Chico: Human. Age 26. Planet of origin: Trida Minor. Corporal, breacher, Charlie Platoon, 79th Reconnaissance Battalion, "Midnight Hunters," Galactic Republic Marines. One of the "Fearsome Four."

Shane Nolan: Human. Age 25. Planet of origin: Sol Sella. Chief Warrant Officer, Republic Navy, pilot in command of light armored transport Sparrow 271. Auburn hair, pale skin.

So-Elku: Human. Age: 51. Planet of origin: Worru. Luma Master, Order of the Luma. Baldpate, thin beard, dark penetrating eyes. Wears green-and-black robes.

Sootriman: Caledonian. Age: 29. Planet of origin: Caledonia. Warlord of Ki Nar Four, "Tamer of the Four Tempests," alleged ex-wife of Idris Ezo. Tall, with dark almond eyes, tanned olive skin, dark-brown hair.

TO-96: Robot; navigation class, heavily modified. Manufacturer: Advanced Galactic Solutions (AGS), Capriana Prime. Suspected modifier: Idris Ezo. Round head and oversized eyes, transparent blaster visor, matte dark-gray armor plating, and exposed metallic articulated joints. Forearm microrocket pod, forearm XM31 Type-R blaster, dual shoulder-mounted gauss cannons.

Tony Haney: Human. Age: 24. Planet of origin: Fitfi Isole. Private First Class, medic, Galactic Republic Marines.

Valerie Stone: Human. Age: 29. Planet of origin: Worru. Wife of Senator Darin Stone, mother of Piper. Blond hair, light-blue eyes.

Volf Nos Kil: Human. Age: 32. Planet of origin: Haradia. Captain, the Paragon. Personal guard and chief enforcer for Admiral Kane.

Waldorph Gilder: Human. Age: 23. Planet of origin: Haradia. Private First Class, flight engineer, Galactic Republic Marines. Barrel-chested. Can fix anything.

Wendell Kane: Human. Age: 52. Planet of origin: Capriana Prime. Fleet admiral of the Galactic Republic's Third Fleet, captain of the *Black Labyrinth*. Leader of the Paragon, a blackoperations special Marine unit. Bald, with heavily scarred skin. One eye pale pink, the other dark brown.

William Samuel Caldwell: Human. Age 60. Planet of origin: Capriana Prime. Colonel, 79th Reconnaissance Battalion, Galactic Republic Marines. Cigar eternally wedged in the corner of his mouth. Gray hair cut high and tight.

Willowood: Human. Age: 61. Planet of origin: Kindarah. Luma Elder, Order of the Luma. Wears dozens of bangles and necklaces. Aging but radiant blue eyes and a mass of wiry gray hair. Friend and mentor to Awen.

Piper Stone: Human. Age: 9. Planet of origin: Capriana Prime. Daughter of Senator Darin and Valerie Stone. Wispy blond hair; freckle-faced. Wears a puffy winter coat, tights, and oversized snow boots. Carries a holo-pad and her stuffed corgachirp, Talisman.

Rawmut: Tawnhack, Jujari. Age: Unknown. Planet of origin: Oorajee. Jujari mwadim of Oosafar on Oorajee. Chief of the massive hyena-like warrior species.

JOIN THE RUINS TRIBE

Visit ruinsofthegalaxy.com today and join the tribe.

Once there, you can sign up for our reader group, join our Facebook community, and find us on Twitter and Instagram.

If you'd like to email us with comments or questions, we respond to all emails sent to ruinsofthegalaxy@gmail.com, and love to hear from our readers.

See you in the Ruins!

STAY UP TO DATE

Join the conversation and get updates on new and upcoming releases in the **Facebook group** called "JN Chaney's Renegade Readers." This is a hotspot where readers come together and share their lives and interests, discuss the series, and speak directly to J.N. Chaney and his co-authors.

Join the Facebook Group

He also post updates, official art, and other awesome stuff on his website and you can also follow him on **Instagram**, **Facebook**, and **Twitter**.

For email updates about new releases, as well as exclusive promotions, visit his website and sign up for the VIP mailing list.

Stay Up to Date

https://www.jnchaney.com/ruins-of-the-galaxy-subscribe

Enjoying the series? Help others discover the Ruins of the Galaxy series by leaving a review on **Amazon.**

ACKNOWLEDGMENTS

Special thanks to Jennifer Sell and Sarah Carleton for their editing, and Beth Lynne and Kim Husband for their proofreading.

Christopher wishes to thank: Douglas Gresham, James and Sarah Cammilleri, David Seaman, Kirk Gilchrist, and Mike "Ezo" Kim for your support and encouragement. My primary military consultants, Pat Mooney, Walt Robillard, and Dominique Sumner: your valor inspires me. My primary sci-fi consultant, Mauricio Longo, for your astounding breadth of knowledge which is exceeded only by your kindness. And to Matthew Titus for going to such great lengths to care for these characters.

This book was written with the insightful feedback of my Recon alpha readers. Each of them helped shape the characters and the plot and kept me from wrecking the story on more than one treacherous shoal. I am grateful to all of them. Very special thanks to the fine work of Matthew Sampson, Kevin Zoll, Myrna Pace, Kathy and Roger Saladin-Smith, Jon Bliss, Nathan Jaffrey, Caleb Baker, Joseph Wessner, Chris Mooney, Shane Marolf, Brian Moore, Josh Jensen, and Nathan Reimer.

The RATs include: Shane Marolf, Josh Jensen, Sam Smith, Nathan Reimer, Kevin Zoll, Jonathan Morasse, Tom Graban, David Woodkirk, Christina Chen, Jeremy Cutler, Caleb Baker, Patrick R. Buchanan, Brian Moore, J-M Sandquist, Matthew Sampson, Lana Romanov, Dirk Taylor, Christopher Shaw, Richard Adams, Pieter Lugt, Sean Buckles, Dave Buckles, Elizabeth Bettger, Joseph Wessner, Matt DuMont, Jim Clark, Holli Manzo, Benjamin Daley, Tyler Davis, Meagan Schober, Matthew Dippel, Sarah Abshire, David Seaman, Nathan Jaffrey, Joshua Czyz, Myrna Pace, Rafael Kovacs, Dale Jones, Marc Appel, Aaron Seaman, Elyssa Krivicich, Christopher Perry, Volker Bochen, Shawn Shepard, Derek Jackson, Edward Andocs, Robert Gettler, John Cartin, Stu Perry, Ruben Jauregui, Tom McCullough, Aaron Koreny, Deborah Miller, Justin Ford, Jonathan Bliss, Joseph Gerbino, Vernetta Shipley, Alissa Hiramine, Paul Almond, Kevin Paul Murphy, Maggie Sullivan-Miller, William Kenney, Adam Proulx, Oliver Longchamps, Mike "Ezo" Kim, Nanette Rivera, Scott Storer, Jack Reeves, Jeff Pitcher, Tim Phipps, Daniel Kimm, Eric Pastorek, Matthew Titus, William Ingram, Geoff Brisco, Byl Kravetz, Joe Smith, Mauricio Longo, David Gilbane, Gerhard Kraider, Adam

Hazen, Michael Bergmann, Alexzandyr Biernat, Ken Moser, Greg Cueto, John Clark, Jason McMarrow, Rodney Bonner, Jake Marzano, Ben Espen, James Connolly, Chris Mooney, Walt Robillard, Andrew Wang, Randall Beem, Pat Mooney, Billy Jepma, Tabitha Rodgers, Brian Lieberman, Damon Suiter, Anthony "Haney" Hayner, Jaymin Sullivan, Steve Forrester, Josh Ostrander, Allison Christiansen, Danny Gatlin, and Steve Clover.

ABOUT THE AUTHORS

J. N. Chaney is a USA Today Bestselling author and has a Master's of Fine Arts in Creative Writing. He fancies himself quite the Super Mario Bros. fan. When he isn't writing or gaming, you can find him online at **www.jnchaney.com**.

He migrates often, but was last seen in Las Vegas, NV. Any sightings should be reported, as they are rare.

Christopher Hopper's novels include the Resonant Son series, The Sky Riders, The Berinfell Prophecies, and the White Lion Chronicles. He blogs at **christopherhopper.com** and loves flying RC planes. He resides in the 1000 Islands of northern New York with his musical wife, and four ridiculously good-looking clones.

AUTHOR'S NOTE

Hey, I'm Christopher Hopper, creator and co-author of Ruins of the Galaxy.

Basically, everything you just heard is the result of my midlife crisis.

You're welcome.

This is the Author's Note section of the audiobook where I get to follow R.C. Bray and act like it's no big deal. Except, it's a huge deal, and I'm still freaking out about it.

Let me explain.

2017 and 2018 were pretty difficult years for me. There were several things in my personal and professional life that reached a tipping point. I had hit the proverbial glass ceiling—and dang, did it hurt. The first part was, I had no idea what to do about it.

During these two years, I fell in love with audiobooks. They kept me company during my daily commute, long trips, and even

Author's Note

quick runs to the grocery store. And every time I started a new book, I'd just got excited, because I heard those magic words:

"Podium Audio presents Expeditionary Force, written by Craig Alanson."

"Podium Audio presents Galaxy's Edge, written by Jason Anspach and Nick Cole."

You're probably familiar with this sensation of anticipation - because as a fan of science fiction there's a very slim chance this is your first audiobook performed by R.C. Bray - and if it is your first then I'm so jealous of all you have to discover. Hold on tight.

These stories became my friends during a hard season of life. They were an escape when I needed relief, and I looked forward to visiting them whenever time allowed.

It wasn't until the fall of 2018 that some light started to break through the clouds of my life. I was fortunate to be able to take a two-month sabbatical and start seeing two different counselors. By the way, I highly recommend finding a good counselor and meeting with them consistently. Even if you think your life is just fine, mental health is no joke, and problems can arise faster than we think. They certainly did for me.

With all the free time at my disposal, I decided to start to research a lot of the authors whose books I'd enjoyed over the last two years. In particular, I found a fascinating podcast featuring the aforementioned Jason Anspach and Nick Cole—two of my favorite living science fiction authors. In it, they spoke about the joy they got from writing, and the necessity of being true to yourself—not doing what you're "supposed to do" or what "someone

Author's Note

else wants you to do," but doing those things that bring you true joy.

I heard them talk about being grownups who were paid to play with action figures in their backyard sandbox, and I thought, "Oh my gosh, I want to write stories like that."

So I started writing.

At first, I had no idea what I was doing. While I'd written and published several novels in the past, each to varying degrees of success, writing futuristic science fiction was totally new to me. And it made me really nervous. Star Wars, Dune, The Last Starfighter, Flight of the Navigator—these were my childhood. And if I messed them up by doing a disservice to the genre, the cosmos would surely smite me. But at the same time, I felt I owed it to myself to try. After all, I was on sabbatical—what else was I gonna to do?

I began asking people online if they would like to read my chapters as I wrote them. Many said yes, and before long, I had a group of about 100 beta readers. As if that wasn't cool enough, I was shocked to find that they actually enjoyed the stories and the characters. In fact, many of those people are still with me today, reading my chapters every week. I'm honored to call them friends.

Likewise, Magnus, Awen, Abimbola, Ezo, TO 96, Sootriman, and Piper also became dear friends. They helped me work through many dark days. They also turned out to be very important to my healing process. Each one of them reflects elements of my heart, and watching them interact helped me reconcile some of the inner conflicts I was wrestling through at the time—some

Author's Note

innocent and childlike, like Piper holding onto her corgachirp, Talisman, trying to come to grips with her powers, others jaded and harsh, like Abimbola doing his best not to kill Magnus simply because of the bucket on his head, and still others carefree and genuine, like the beloved TO-96 who just can't seem to figure out how to use idioms like everyone else. These charters were as much a part of my therapy as going to see counselors.

As I learned more about the business of writing and selling books, I also began to develop friendships with several authors who I esteemed. One of those was J.N. Chaney. In fact, Jeff was the first best-selling author who, when I asked him, actually volunteered to read the first page of book one. That floored me, as did what happened next—he invited me to partner with him in publishing what you know today as Ruins of the Galaxy.

The series became such a hit that midway through 2019, I was able to start writing full time. In less than 1 year, I went from glass ceiling to dream job, and I haven't looked back.

Not only have I worked hard to gain the trust of listeners and readers, including yours, but I've also had the incredible privilege to meet many of the authors who inspired me. But perhaps the most poignant touchstone in all of this is going back to where it began, and now hearing the great R.C. Bray say:

"Podium Audio presents: Ruins of the Galaxy. Written by J.N. Chaney and Christopher Hopper. Performed by R.C. Bray."

Dang, I just peed my pants a little. Again.

If you're in one of those dark seasons, and this book has provided an oasis for you, I want to remind you that you're not alone. I might not know the details of your path, but I know the

Author's Note

pain, frustration, and loneliness it comes with. Whether you're in your car, on a bus, talking a walk, or just sitting down somewhere, the fact that you've allowed this story into your life as a companion is one of my life's great privileges. Thank you. I also want to remind you to seek help beyond the book. Whether that's through a wise family member, counselor, place of worship, or crisis center, your life is worth contending for, and I believe there's someone out there willing to help you find health.

To connect with Jeff and me online, you can search for the Renegade Readers Facebook Group, as well as the Ruins of the Galaxy Facebook Group. I'd also recommend visiting ruinsofthegalaxy.com, where you can email me, pick up apparel, and maybe even score one of Abimbola's poker chips. (Yes, they do exits, and they're pretty sweet).

So here's to many more adventures of playing together with our action figures in the backyard sandbox.

Thanks for listening.

This is Christopher, over and out.

Clayton, New York
January 2020

THE NIGHT OF FIRE
A RUINS OF THE GALAXY SHORT

Magnus should have been more concerned with the blaster bolts flying over his head than he was with what his drill sergeant had called "the weaknesses of the flesh." But he wasn't.

Incoming blaster fire was still a problem. A big one. The enemy was holed up in a small mountain in the center of the island. Routing them out was going to take all night. But right then, Magnus's body was complaining more about an entirely different enemy. No, it wasn't the sand and salt that had managed to find their way into every crevice in his armor; parts of him that he didn't know could go raw were chafing. He was tired, sore, hungry, and done with being shot at. But none of those were as bad as the enemy currently wreaking havoc in his gut. No amount of discipline, armor, or team readiness had prepared him —or any of them—for the squirts.

When the waterborne virus first started hitting the Marines,

The Night of Fire

Magnus had been concerned with manners. They all had. His unit had dug small latrines and tried giving one another some privacy. But as the days turned into weeks and the infection spread, they'd abandoned all sense of decorum. Now the Marines went whenever they had to, most going right in their armor if they were in a firefight. Like they were right now.

"Splick! There I go again," Chico yelled over their TACNET fire team channel. "Dammit!"

Private Miguel Chico was stacked up behind Magnus, along with two other members of his newly formed fire team: Private Michael Deeks and Private Allan Franklin. The four of them had taken cover behind the remains of a bamboo hut on the south side of the island.

Magnus had been given command of the fire team after Sergeant Cartin took a high-energy blaster round clean through the helmet the night before. Magnus could still see the wisps of smoke around the hole floating up through his memory. Cartin had been one hell of a Marine, taking out his share of 'kuda before meeting his end, even saving several lives in the process. As a corporal, it was Magnus's job not to get blasted in the head—and to try to keep his guys safe while staying on the mission objectives.

"Wash it out when the sun comes up, Private," Magnus replied.

"Yeah, but just don't do it upwind of me again, would ya?" Deeks asked. "You nasty, boy."

Chico punched Deeks in the shoulder. "Not as nasty as what your mom said to me last night."

The Night of Fire

"I swear to all the mystics, if you talk about my momma one more time, Chico…"

"You're gonna do what?"

Magnus had to break it up; he knew where it would go. That was part of why he was growing to love these guys so much. They were fast becoming like brothers to him. And he didn't need to lose any more of those in this war.

"Who's ready to make a run with me, boys?" Magnus asked.

That got their attention. Almost.

"Chico doesn't need to," Franklin replied. "He's already got plenty of runs of his own."

Chico stiffened. "I swear to all the mystics, Franklin…"

"Tighten it up, boys," Magnus said, muting their respective TACNET channels. If these three guys weren't the most aggressive fighters he'd seen in Bravo Company yet, he would have asked to be reassigned. As it was, they were crass smack-talkers who had terrible comms discipline, which verged on being belligerent. But they could fight; that was for damn sure. Magnus had already watched them put down more 'kudas individually than most fire teams were doing collectively. And that was just the kind of fire team he wanted to lead.

"We have orders to get this island cleared by sunup, and I don't want to disappoint First Lieutenant Vanderbilt when he comes walking down the northside beach head."

Magnus saw a comms request icon in his HUD coming from Deeks. He opened the channel.

"With all due respect, Corporal, but ain't no way I'm interested in impressing the LT," Deeks replied.

Magnus had a mischievous tone in his voice. "I know that, Deeks. And you know that. But Chico and Franklin are still hoping he'll ask their mommas out on a date."

"Corporal Magnus for the win!" Deeks said, punching Chico in the side of the arm.

"Punch me one more time, Deeks. Go ahead."

"Let's stay focused," Magnus said, smiling through the sand, salt, sweat, and splick filling his helmet. "We have a job to do."

The jabs at Lieutenant Vanderbilt weren't completely misguided, though they certainly would have been met with severe consequences had anyone been listening over comms. Vanderbilt had made some seriously boneheaded decisions over the past several weeks, at least as far as Magnus was concerned. The officer had ordered Marines into some downright asinine scenarios that could have easily been avoided. The one they were in right now was a great example.

The small island of Mo'a Ot'a had a small mountain summit in the center, leftover from some ancient volcano. All approaches to the summit consisted of a gentle rise through a lush jungle. That was, of course, except for a ravine carved by a mountain stream that ran down the south side. As was to be expected from the lieutenant, he had ordered Magnus's team to move up that very ravine. Magnus had tried to protest—respectfully—but Vanderbilt had "no time for the backassward opinions of grunts."

Magnus swore that if he was ever promoted to the position of an officer, he would treat the Marines under his command differently. He wouldn't play with their lives over some vain attempt to impress his commanding officers.

The worst part, at least as far as Magnus and the others were concerned, was that none of the islands could be strafed by fighters until *after* they'd been cleared. *A lot of good that does us*, he'd thought when he heard the news.

Apparently, islanders were reported to be dug into the hills in an attempt to wait out the fighting. And since sensors were having a hard time distinguishing between friend and foe, the Marines had to sort the good from the bad. This meant liberating survivors *and* dominating the enemy. But so far, in over six weeks of intense fighting, Magnus hadn't found a single islander—at least none who were alive.

"Three 'kudas moving along our left flank!" Deeks yelled.

"And I got two more converging on our right," Chico said.

The battle was getting hot. They'd made plenty of progress, bounding from boulder to boulder, fighting a true uphill battle with every step. But the ravine's steep walls gave the enemy a clear tactical advantage. The best Magnus and his fire team could do was to catch the 'kudas before they flanked his team from above.

Magnus's helmet AI identified the targets with compass-heading indicators and distances. He used his eyes to select the next nearest one behind Deeks's target and sighted in along the barrel of his MC90 blaster. The Repub had promised that a new neural interface was coming down the pipeline for their helmets.

The tech claimed to rid operators of the optic command protocols that they'd mastered in basic training.

Wouldn't that be nice, Magnus thought. The Marines on the ground had yet to see anything in the field, but he looked forward to the day that the new interface was a mainstay in the Corps.

Thirty-eight degrees up and to his left, Magnus zeroed in on a 'kuda taking cover behind a palm tree. His helmet's red-hued thermal-imaging system was working like a charm, showing the enemy combatant as a white blotch resting its back against the trunk. The 'kuda seemed to be fiddling with the battery pack for its main weapon. Magnus put the reticle in the dead center of the tree trunk and squeeze his trigger.

A single blaster round flashed in his HUD as the bolt streaked up the ravine. It split the trunk in two, shooting splinters in all directions. Magnus ducked under return fire from other elements but managed to watch the combatant he'd hit slump on the far side of the tree. It collapsed in a heap with its weapon and battery falling from two scaly hands.

"Scratch another one for me," Magnus said, recharging his MC90 and sighting in the next target. The MC90 wasn't the latest or greatest in the Repub arsenal, but it was standard Marine issue for a reason. Magnus had grown to appreciate its ruggedness and subsequent reliability. Other blasters promised to offer better fire superiority and more features, like the prototype MAR30 that the spec ops Marines were said to be getting in a few years, but that was a long way off. And as far as Magnus was concerned, the MC90 did just fine at killing 'kudas.

The Akuda were a native species of Caledonia—just not the

ones that lived on land. While the planet's islands' inhabitants consisted mostly of humans and other humanoid species, its underwater citizens were what the Marines called "fish with an attitude problem."

The attitude-ridden aquaticans preferred to live underwater, but they were able to extract needed respiratory gases from both water and air. This, combined with powerful hind legs that had evolved over the millennia, allowed them to move on land when the need arose. And, apparently, the need had arisen when the Akuda decided they wanted to be the *only* species to inhabit Caledonia.

Because it was a member of the Galactic Republic, the planet's civil war required the Repub military to be called in. At first, every Marine had relished the idea of deploying on the paradisiacal planet. The elite came to Caledonia to bask in endless sunsets and get drunk on fifty-credit cocktails. But any dreams of sunbathing and frolicking in the surf had disappeared when the Marines realized just how badly the 'kuda wanted their genocide.

Magnus squeezed his trigger again, taking out the third fish Deeks had spotted. Chico and Franklin cleared the right side, then Magnus gave the order to leapfrog farther up the stream. Each Marine took a turn advancing, dodging incoming enemy fire, then hanging back to cover the others.

Their boots—standard issue for Mark IV armor—did little to help them along the wet rocks. They slipped constantly, bashing their knees and wrists on the rounded rocks. The 'kuda, on the other hand, moved at a dizzying pace, gliding across the rocks with the ease of Tanglothian banshee lizards.

"Incoming!" Franklin was on point and leveled his MC90 on a pair of 'kudas that leaped off a short waterfall at him. Despite their speed, the fish lacked fire discipline, and their blaster bolts went wide. But what Franklin lacked in agility, he more than made up for in blaster superiority. Magnus watched him aim, squeeze, and follow through. The Marine turned to the next target—still in midair—and repeated the pattern. In less than a second, two scaly bodies crashed in the shallows beside Franklin and rolled to a stop.

"No time to take pictures, boys," Magnus said over TACNET. "Let's get over that waterfall."

The four Marines helped one another over the rock ledge and onto the next landing. More boulders provided cover while the sides of the ravine grew taller and steeper.

"Gettin' pretty tight through here, Corporal," Deeks said. "Did brass give you exfil coordinates yet?"

Magnus shook his head. "Not yet. Trust me, you'll be the first to know when I do."

Chico spoke up next. "It's just we're getting pretty deep up here. Grid shows…" Magnus could tell the private was checking the TACNET map. He knew it didn't look good. "Splick, it shows us pretty much out here on our own. The other fire teams are well to the west and east of our position."

"Copy that," Magnus replied. "I see it too."

"No backup then," Franklin concluded.

Aren't you just Captain Obvious today, Magnus thought, holding his tongue. Best to save insulting these noobs for after they survived this. "No backup," Magnus repeated. "Which n gotta own the field, Privates. You copy?"

"OTF!" they repeated as one.

Magnus tapped the side of his helmet. Five more targets flickered to life on sensors, way too close for comfort. Apparently, his rig needed a tune-up.

"Contact!" Magnus barked. "Five, coming right down the stream!"

His Marines took cover, leaning around boulders with their MC90s charged and at high ready position. Approaching like blue wisps of water vapor, the 'kuda materialized ten meters ahead, weapons blasting water and rocks on full auto. Magnus pulled back, narrowly avoiding a blaster bolt to the head. Then he leaned out again and targeted the nearest fish. His blaster bucked against his shoulder as the bolt sizzled through the damp air and struck the enemy in the throat, flipping it backward. The 'kuda corpse splashed into the stream and flopped around in death throes.

Deeks took out two 'kuda that tried running up the side of the near-vertical ravine. They made it high enough to turn and point their weapons at Deeks. But that was all they got to do. The Marine fired a short burst of full auto, stitching the side of the rock wall and tearing both fish in two.

Chico and Franklin, meanwhile, took out the remaining two fish, firing from a cluster of boulders along the bank. They poked their MC90 between gaps in the rocks, striking the enemy before they even had a chance to spot the Marines.

With the wave of enemies put down, Magnus walked up to

The Night of Fire

the fish he'd hit. It was still thrashing. He fired a second round into its head, and the churning water went still. "Clear."

Magnus examined its bulbous eyes and long teeth glistening in the moonlight. Scaly blue skin covered its blaster-riddled flesh. "Ugly as hell," he whispered.

"What was that, Corporal?"

Magnus waved Deeks off. "Next level, boys. Up and over."

The four of them scampered up another small waterfall, but Magnus could tell the incline was getting steeper. The topo map confirmed it, showing that the tallest waterfalls were just ahead. There was no way they were climbing those in the dark. He cursed Vanderbilt under his breath. *This was a stupid line to take.*

Chico started waving an arm. "Corporal," he said, tension rising in his voice.

"What is it?"

"We've got…"

But Magnus saw it too. Apparently, the fish knew the Marines were climbing into a dead end.

"We've got six coming down the ravine, eight to the west, another eight to the east—no, wait… Make that ten to the east—"

"And we got five more on our six!" Deeks yelled. "I don't know how they crept up on us, but they did!"

This is bad, Magnus realized. *This is real bad.*

"TACNET's reading contact in forty-five seconds. Let's take cover against that waterfall." Magnus pointed twenty meters ahead to the next feature in the stream. The Marines followed

Magnus as he slid across the boulders and stumbled over the round stones.

"I count six more to the south," Chico said over comms.

Dammit. The Akuda smelled blood in the water; that was for damn sure.

Magnus jumped around the last boulder and found himself wading into a pool up to his knees. The waterfall above him was easily ten meters high—the tallest yet. It would at least provide cover from the 'kuda approaching from above. His fire team would also get a clear line of sight on the ones approaching from the south. The only combatants that really worried Magnus were those flanking them from the ravine edges.

"Corporal Magnus, you sure this is a good—"

"There's no good position for this one, Franklin. The Corps doesn't pay you to be sure; they pay you to fire."

"Copy that."

Magnus double-checked the TACNET map. "Contact in ten seconds. Rack a charge, boys."

Magnus heard the energy whine of the MC90s and watched as his men took a knee in the shallows, water splashing hard at their backs. If it was to be their last stand, Magnus was proud of them. They had looked fear in the eyes and stared it down, shoving their blaster barrels in its mouth and pulling the trigger all the way to the grave. He doubted history would remember their names—hell, he doubted the Corps would even find their bodies after the 'kuda had feasted—but he would at least die knowing they'd done their best to follow orders and own the field.

"OTF, boys."

"OTF!" they replied as one.

Magnus watched in his HUD as the red dots converged in their location, forming a solid ring around his team. Magnus's thermal sensors showed the first 'kuda as it leaped high into the air, vaulting over the lower falls and into the rock bed twenty meters downstream. It fired wildly. Blaster bolts splattered into the waterfall behind Magnus. He squeezed two rounds and struck it center mass.

A second 'kuda jumped over the ledge and took the first's place. This fish's aim was far better, and Magnus narrowly missed being shot in the helmet. He returned fire with another two-round salvo and dropped it. But in that time, five more fish had climbed up and moved toward the waterfall.

Deeks, Chico, and Franklin were busy covering the flanks, firing on anything that moved. And plenty of things moved. The sides of the ravine seemed alive with otherworldly objects. Fins, sinewy arms and legs, glimmering teeth, iridescent eyes—it all scrambled down the steep sides in a slide of mud and rocks. Blaster fire lit up the narrow ravine, flashing off shiny scales and plate armor. Bodies careened through the air and splashed into the pool at the Marines' feet. Some of the bodies still moved, the claws on their webbed hands grasping for the Marines' legs. Magnus fired several shots into the growing piles of bodies, keeping the groping limbs at bay.

Despite their best efforts, however, Magnus knew they wouldn't walk away from this fight. His HUD showed more reinforcements filling in from all corners. Even if his fire team had enough energy magazines and accuracy to take down the current wave, there was no way they would have enough to fight off the second.

"Don't let up!" It was all Magnus could think to say. That and: "OTF!"

Deeks and Chico mumbled a response between shots, but Franklin didn't answer at all. Bodies were falling down on top of them, and their MC90 barrels glowed white in his HUD.

This is it, Magnus realized. *This is our last stand. Damn 'kudas.*

Magnus fired on several more that crept up the center stream. His energy mag went flat. He reached for a new one on his hip and slammed it home, then he unloaded on two 'kudas crossing the pool. He drilled both of them. But it was the third and fourth that he didn't have time to shoot. They flew through the air, claws and teeth bared in the moonlight.

A blast of water erupted behind Magnus and pushed him forward. He would have slammed into the oncoming 'kudas were it not for the fact that they, too, had been thrown away from the waterfall. His HUD went bright white as several trails of light and smoke propelled enemy bodies a dozen meters over the stream before consuming them in a massive explosion.

Magnus pushed himself off the pile of corpses and strained to look behind him. He was blinded again, however, when a sputtering strobe of blaster fire spewed from the waterfall and raked no fewer than eight 'kudas. Magnus watched in awe as limbs flailed, heads snapped, and teeth shattered. Finally, a projectile so massive it could only have been fired from a Gauss cannon blew out from behind the waterfall and struck the streambed. The sound spiked his audio sensors; even with them temporarily

The Night of Fire

muted, the thunderclap still made Magnus's ears ring. The concussion decimated 'kuda bodies, flinging dozens of them skyward while Magnus and his Marines were thrown into the waterfall.

Magnus felt a hand grab his shoulder and wrench him down. His body hit something hard—the ground, he was pretty sure. His HUD flickered from the impact, and he could feel his armor's servos dim.

What in the hell was going on?

Whatever hand had grabbed him let him go. Magnus rolled over and looked up. There, standing over him, was a... *Is it a teenage boy?* Magnus blinked then activated his external speakers.

"Kid, what are you... what are you doing here?" Even asking such a thing felt surreal. To be talking to a teen. In a cave. Behind a waterfall. Holding a...

What the hell are those?

In his hands, the teen was holding what looked to be arms. Robot arms. With weapons on them. Magnus saw micro rockets, along with the guts and barrel of what looked to be a prototype XM31 blaster.

Magnus blinked several more times. *How bad was I hit?* He couldn't be sure. Maybe this was just some weird version of the afterlife.

"You've got to get up," the young man said. He looked maybe seventeen or eighteen. Small. An islander with narrow eyes. *Maybe a Nimprinth?* He was wearing a backpack overflowing with odd metal parts. "That won't keep them away for long. You've got to move, soldiers."

Magnus grabbed his MC90 and gained his feet. His helmet bumped into the low ceiling. Deeks, Chico, and Franklin had been blown into the cave entrance too, but each of them was standing.

"What the hell is going on, Corporal?" Deeks asked, his voice sounding as bewildered as Magnus's had. "What's this splick about?"

"Seems we found our first survivor, Deeks."

The other men looked at the teen; Magnus could practically guess the expressions on their faces as they took in the thin young man and his assortment of robot parts and black-market weapons.

"What the—"

"Come on!" the kid said, motioning them toward a small tunnel. "This way!"

"Fine by me," Chico said. He darted after the kid, followed by Franklin and a still-dazed Deeks.

"Keep on him," Magnus said over TACNET. "Seems to know his way around here."

"And around an XM31," Chico added. "I like this kid."

Magnus switched to optical sensors and turned on his armor's exterior shoulder lights. The rounded tunnel looked as though it had been carved by hand. Magnus followed Deeks's rear end, hunched over, boots plodding through ten centimeters of water. The tunnel meandered deeper into the mountainside until it opened into a vaulted room. As soon as Magnus had stepped in and straightened his back, a door slammed shut behind him.

"This way," the young man said, continuing to motion Magnus's fire team forward.

Magnus marveled at what he saw. Aside from a small bed mat and cooking area that doubled as the young man's heat source, the rest of the room was littered with racks and work benches. Every square centimeter of space seemed overtaken with wires, cables, tools, and parts. How the young man had acquired so much stuff Magnus had no idea. That he'd gathered it in this peculiar place was astounding. The kid must have been a genius—a savant. That is, of course, assuming he'd built something notable. But if the display of firepower at the waterfall was any indicator—he had.

"Hurry! You have to keep moving!" The kid stood at the far end of his hovel, pointing toward an exit tunnel.

"What about you, kid?" Magnus asked.

"I'll be right behind you."

"I'd really feel better if you lead the way."

"No, no. I have to do something here. This tunnel is easy to follow. I'll be right behind you."

"You promise?"

"I promise. Now, go!"

Magnus nodded at Chico, who then ducked into the tunnel, followed by Franklin and Deeks. Their shoulder lights waved back as they ran in a crouch. The ground was dry, and Magnus felt the cave begin to head downhill. Whoever had carved it—presumably the kid—had done a masterful job. And it had probably taken a very long time, even with the right equipment.

The tunnel snaked through what Magnus figured was the

The Night of Fire

north side of the mountain. His TACNET link had gone offline when he entered the cave, and nothing but local sensors were feeding data to his helmet's AI. Audio sensors continued to feed the *clip-clop* of their boots and the scuffing of their armor against the tight walls and low ceiling.

After several minutes of back-breaking running, Chico finally said, "I think I see something up ahead. Looks like… like ferns or something."

The tunnel expanded little by little as the path leveled out. Finally, the tunnel opened up into a dense jungle covered in ferns and palm fronds. A TACNET link was established, and with it came several incoming messages from command.

"Looks like Vanderbilt's been worried about us after all," Chico said.

"Nah." Deeks shook his head. "He was worried about the scourge he'd take for sending four Marines on the dumbest mission of his short career."

"Copy that," Franklin said.

"Listen, we're not going anywhere until that kid comes back."

"Copy that, Corporal," Deeks replied. "He saved our asses back there."

"And we're gonna make sure we save his by getting him off this pile of splick."

As if summoned by their talk, the young man was yelling something from down the tunnel. Magnus boosted his audio sensors and leaned his head back into the cave. He looked and saw the boy swinging a flashlight wildly.

"What's he saying, Corporal?"

"He's saying 'run.'"

"You think those 'kudas broke through?"

"Dunno, Deeks. But I'm guessing we're in for another firefight. OTF, boys."

"OTF!" they replied, racking charges in their MC90s.

Magnus watched as the kid closed the distance, still carrying the robot arms and a backpack full of parts. "He's coming in hot. Stand back."

The young man blew from the cave like a blaster bolt, tearing into the ferns without breaking his stride. He was placing some sort of device in his mouth… *maybe a rebreather?* Magnus and the others knelt to point their weapons down the tunnel, their high shoulder lights cranked to high intensity, piercing the darkness.

They waited for the 'kudas to round the far corner. And waited. And still waited. But nothing came.

"I told you—run, Marines!" came the kid's voice from farther in the jungle.

Magnus turned to see him waving his rebreather in the air.

"Run! Get to the water!"

"Anybody else get the feeling this isn't about no 'kudas?" Deeks asked.

Then an idea struck Magnus. If this kid was some sort of tech savant, why else would he hang back in his mountain fortress then make a run for the ocean?

The kid shouted something that snapped Magnus from his thoughts.

"Binary bomb!"

"What'd he just say?" Deeks asked.

"Ah, splick! It's the ocean!" Magnus exclaimed. "He's heading for cover! Let's get out of here!" Without another word, Magnus was on his feet and chasing after the boy. His fire team followed. They charged through the ferns like a pack of Boresian taursars, high-kicking all the way down the hill. They gained so much momentum that Magnus feared his legs wouldn't be able to keep up. But whether by adrenaline or sheer force of will, he managed to keep his feet beneath him.

Magnus opened an emergency channel to Lieutenant Vanderbilt over TACNET. "This is Corporal Adonis Magnus"—he double-checked the topo grid in his HUD—"on the island's north side, with a credible ABSB threat."

He could hardly breathe. He double-checked the IFF markers —identify friend or foe—to see just how many Marines might be in whatever blast radius the kid's ordnance might envelop.

"Corporal Magnus, I need threat confirmation. Are you actually seeing…"

Magnus heard the disbelief in the LT's voice. Not that he blamed him. *But for all the mystics, there isn't time to explain!*

"An antimatter binary sini-trex bomb?" Also affectionately known as "a big splickin' bomb" off the record. The weapon's modulated antimatter was one half of the explosion, and the sini-trex was the other. When combined, the two created one hell of an explosion. And as simple as it seemed, the safest place to avoid the initial blast and the subsequent fallout was under water.

How this kid had gotten his hands on such a device, Magnus had no clue. But he also didn't have a clue as to how he'd survived for what must've been a year or more, on his own, in a hole under a mountain.

"Yes, Lieutenant. Found a survivor, and we have reason to believe—" He couldn't gulp air fast enough, even with his suit working overtime to hyperoxygenate his blood. His feet pounded ferns into the soft soil, his leg armor breaking small branches in two. "We have reason to believe he's booby trapped the mountain."

"Booby trapped?"

"Affirmative."

"Ah, splick."

Magnus hoped the LT was taking him seriously. Seriously enough to expedite his intel. Lives depended on it. There wasn't time to argue. He prayed to the mystics that his superior would do the right thing.

What was taking so long?

Up ahead, Magnus could see the glimmer of moonlight on countless waves stretching to the horizon.

Finally, an all-comm channel opened, filled with Vanderbilt's voice. "Attention, all units in the AO of Lima Kilo Niner. Exfil to the closest-point ocean entry. Credible ABSB threat confirmed. I repeat: Get off the island and submerge for cover. ABSB detonation imminent."

Maybe the LT's not that bad, after all, Magnus thought.

If the kid had planted an explosive, it was going to be big—at least if his display back at the waterfall was any harbinger. Magnus looked at the grid again and started to notice Marine

The Night of Fire

icons moving toward the island's perimeter. *There you go! Come on! Keep going!*

Magnus and his fire team had made it to the sand. The surf was another twenty-five meters ahead. The kid had already disappeared into the black water. They were going to make it.

For whatever reason, Magnus looked over his shoulder. Maybe to make a visual inspection of their retreat, or maybe out of habit to not leave anyone behind. He didn't know. But in that moment, a light as bright as the sun flashed in his HUD. For a split second, there was no sound. Just pure white energy. But when that split second was up, a sound as loud as a starship colliding with a planet blew into Magnus and sent him flying.

A fissure ran across Magnus's HUD as the concussion of the binary explosion sent him hurtling a hundred meters out to sea. It felt as if his head, arms, legs had been ripped from his body. He slammed against the water like a child's toy skipping across concrete.

When the energy finally decided to let him go, Magnus felt his limp body melt into the waves, swaying gently into the cool embrace of the ocean. He blinked as water trickled through the crack in his visor. It tasted salty, like the sweat covering his face. But it was cool, cool enough that all Magnus wished for was to take a long bath in it.

Farther and farther he sank, wishing to shed his armor and just swim. He stared up at a strange light that shimmered over him, far above the water's surface. It reminded him of the military parades back home on Capriana Prime. Of fireworks. Of weapons displays.

Of fighter flyovers. He could smell the festival foods, the late-night campfires, and the scent of perfume and alcohol. He heard music and people laughing. It was as if he could simply step into that world. If he could only climb up to it… But it was just too far away to reach.

"Emergency flotation devices deployed," said a voice in his head. No, not in his head. It was *around* his head. Someone was talking to him very close.

Magnus blinked. Something popped then jerked him upright. His legs swung down beneath him, and his head tipped forward. He was ascending. He was floating. Toward the surface of…

Magnus blinked again, trying to put the pieces back together. Trying to suppress the sharp pain in his head and the ringing in his ears. Suddenly, his head burst through the water's surface, and his eyes filled with the sight of a small mushroom cloud climbing into the sky.

"Great mystics…" Magnus said softly. Everything came back to him. The firefight in the stream, their rescue at the waterfall, the kid and his cave—and him telling them to run.

He torched the island. He actually torched the entire island. Son of a bitch…

Magnus's HUD began its reboot sequence. As soon as it was active, more warning indicators than he could count started racing down the left side of his display. "Yeah, yeah, yeah," Magnus said aloud. "You don't like a binary bomb blast. I get it." But thanks to the Repub engineers, and some hefty fund reallocations by old Marines who had decided to take up politics after they'd retired, Mark IV armor was made to withstand such blasts —at least to a certain degree proportional to distance from

The Night of Fire

ground zero. Unlike a blaster bolt, whose force was concentrated, broadly dispersed energy was easier for the suit to handle. Well, at least that was what the manual claimed. Until a few minutes ago, Magnus had doubted that claim. But not anymore.

Amazingly, no bones felt broken. And other than a massive headache, he couldn't sense anything else the matter with him. He would need a few days in a gene-therapy tank, no doubt. But that was a paid vacation as far as he was concerned. With any luck, he might even get a cute nurse. *Who knows?*

"Corporal Magnus," a voice said over the comms. *At least those are still working.* "You copy?"

"That you, Deeks? Tag idents aren't registering."

"Ha, sure as hell is."

"You in one piece?"

"I think so. My testicles seem a little farther up than usual. That normal?"

Magnus chuckled. "Listen, you got eyes on Chico or Franklin?"

"Chico looks like he's doing laps on a rooftop pool, and I'm pretty sure Franklin's taking a piss."

"I've been holding it for hours, Deeks. And we're Marines, aren't we? After so much time in the void, we finally get to play in the water again. So sue me."

"I'm not judging you, Franklin. Just telling the NCO how it is."

Magnus laughed. He'd just survived a binary explosion and being blasted a hundred meters out to sea, and his fire team was busting each other's balls.

This is the life, Magnus. This is where you belong.

He loved his job. Loved the service. And for the first time since joining, Magnus had been thinking about doing more with his career, like moving out of the enlisted ranks altogether. But not for the reasons of evading scenarios like this. In fact, it was just the opposite.

Colonel Caldwell, who was like an uncle to him, had told him to attend the academy from the beginning. But Magnus had refused. For one thing, he wanted to know what it was like to fight on the ground with a blaster in his hands. He just couldn't see himself as an administrator who killed the enemy from a distance.

But for another thing, Magnus wanted to forge his own way through the service. His brother, Argus, had felt the same way. They had both picked similar paths, ones that put them on Caledonia in this gritty war instead of behind a holo-desk somewhere. If either of them went to the academy, like their grandfather had, they would just be dogged every day by their grandfather's broad shadow. Magnus knew things would be handed to him. Any promotions he received wouldn't be *his* promotions—they would be his grandfather's.

But with two months of heavy combat under his belt, Magnus was beginning to see a potential bright side to becoming an officer. He'd endured several missions with terrible orders from officers who had never seen 'kuda offal dry on their armor. But he had. Perhaps he would lead differently because he knew what it meant to lead from the front. And while Magnus hadn't seen his younger brother in several weeks, he wondered if Argus might have had similar thoughts about the COs and the need for better leadership. *Or would he?* His brother always had insisted on doing things his own way. But those memories were still so painful to think about. *Time would heal it, though, wouldn't it?*

Caldwell had extended the invitation to attend officer training school once again, not three months ago. Magnus did have enough education under his belt to make the move if he wanted. And having the last name Magnus had its upsides too: he could do just about anything he wanted.

The more he thought about the colonel's offer, and the more time he spent sloshing up mountain ravines in the middle of the night, the more he wondered if it wasn't the right call to make. Maybe up there at the top, he could effect some change and keep dumbass officers from doing stupid splick to good men. *Like these guys. Hell, I'd take these guys with me to the end of the galaxy and back.*

There, floating in the ocean, armor cracked and his cells mutating with antimatter fallout, Magnus decided what kind of officer he wanted to be. A fighting one. A sacrificing one. One who never gave up on his man because he knew he would always have men who never gave up on him.

"Corporal Magnus, this is Falcon Nine-Nine-One-Zero-Four. Do you copy?"

The audio was cutting in and out, but Magnus made it out clearly the second time the pilot hailed him. His eyes lit up. "Falcon Nine-Nine-One-Zero-Four, this is Corporal Magnus. I read you loud and clear."

"Roger that, Corporal. We have your IFF marker on grid. Hang tight, inbound in thirty seconds."

The Night of Fire

"Copy that, Falcon. We'll be…" Magnus smiled. "We'll just be sitting here, pissin' in our armor."

The four Marines laughed. It even sounded like the pilots were in on it too.

Deeks's voice broke Magnus's revelry. "Hey, anyone see that kid?"

"Negative," Chico and Franklin said.

Magnus looked around, but neither his eyes nor TACNET sensors had any reading on an extra body nearby. "Think he's gone, fellas. Damn shame too. I would've liked to get his name. Buy him a beer."

"Buy him two," Deeks said. "Next time."

T'ai Hau survived alone at sea for five days. But he wasn't really alone, of course. He had his robot.

The bot had been his sole companion as war and disease wiped out the only life he'd ever known. Somehow, though, T'ai had survived. He'd built a life for himself with his robot, biding his time and preparing for the day that he would be rescued.

The evacuation had gone pretty much how he'd expected it to. Though, now that he'd thought about it, he *had* underestimated the bomb's mass. The explosion had been much larger than he had intended. In the end, however, it got the job done. He just hoped the Marines had survived in their armored suits.

Eventually, T'ai floated toward a large luxury ship. A true pleasure yacht. He'd seen them pass by his island plenty of times in his childhood. They never stopped to talk. They just circled once or twice, taking pictures with their long-range cameras.

This vessel had several decks and looked like it could sleep thirty or forty people very comfortably. He hauled himself onboard, pulling his backpack behind him, and rested on the aft deck for at least an hour while the sun dried his clothes and warmed his skin. When he was rested, T'ai stood and began looking around the ship.

Everything he saw was opulent. The dark-stained wooden decks, the white leather furniture, and the dark windows—all of it said that whoever owned this boat was wealthy beyond reason. The owner was also hanging off the bowsprit, along with the remains of several other people who'd been onboard. Apparently, the Akuda weren't fond of this captain or his friends. But the fish had no use for ships, and so they'd left it adrift.

By the looks of it, that had been several weeks ago, maybe more. That meant no one was coming for this ship. So T'ai had it all to himself, and that suited him just fine.

After propping up his half-built robot in a comfy couch, T'ai went about taking stock of supplies on the ship, beginning with food and potable water. Survival was one part luck and another part proper planning. In order to build a life beyond the ruins of his home, he would need both fortune and strategy.

Next, T'ai began by repairing the dead ship. It was a lot of work, but it wasn't difficult work. All the tools he needed were onboard, and he had plenty of time. In fact, he quite enjoyed the new environment. It was a nice change of pace from his cave.

Within a few days, T'ai had the drive cores operational again.

The Night of Fire

The ship hummed beneath his feet, surging forward under his command like the massive bull whales in the southern hemisphere.

He labored with every light fixture, pipe, strip of carpet, and wooden panel. He willed the giant boat back to life one day at a time, just as he'd willed his robot to life. Weeks turned into months before T'ai realized he wanted to leave. Not leave the boat. Leave Caledonia. This place… was no longer his home. It had been once. And he loved it. Rather, he loved what it had been. But he did not love it anymore. He thought, perhaps, that the yacht might have changed his heart and given him something more to love. Some reason to stay. But in the end, it was empty, like his cave. Like his island.

He looked at his robot, which was nearing completion, and wondered if they should try to journey into the void together. He wanted to get away from here, away from the cursed planet. But he couldn't do that, not yet anyway. Not without at least talking to *her*. And to do that, T'ai knew he would need more than just a robot and a boat. He needed a new identity. There was no way her parents would ever allow him to speak to her, unless… he wasn't himself. He had to become someone different.

T'ai moved below decks into the captain's quarters. It was where he kept all of the personal belongings of the former crew. Their watches, jewelry, wallets, and purses. He pulled out identification cards of two men he found the most handsome, then he laid them out on the captain's dining table side by side.

The men's faces smiled pleasantly, as if the pictures had been taken when they were in the middle of a long vacation to some exotic destination. Their skin was deeply tanned, like his, and their eyes were almost the same shape. *Aren't they? Or perhaps not.* Perhaps T'ai would also need to change that about himself to be accepted by her parents.

He returned to their wallets and pulled out small card drives, each displaying softly glowing numeric values followed by the republic C icon for *credits*. The numbers were in hundreds of thousands, some in the millions. Hacking the accounts would take less than a day of code slicing. T'ai suddenly realized he was rich. He would have enough money to buy himself a new identity, one that would let him speak with her. To ask her if she wanted to go with him to the stars.

T'ai returned to the two pictures of the handsome men on the table. They smiled at him. So he smiled back. Then he did what seemed like the most logical thing to do. He decided to give himself a new name. It would be the first step of many in his new life. The first name of the man's card on the left was unique. T'ai had never heard it before. While the last name of the man on the right was an island name from another chain far to the north. Combined, the two made a new name with a nice ring to it.

Yes, T'ai thought. *That will work well.* He could see her liking it too. Maybe even her parents would like it.

T'ai found an old writing utensil and a pad of the beautiful white paper that he'd seen tourists use. There, at the captain's table, he wrote his name for the very first time.

Idris Ezo.

DEMONS AT WAR

A RUINS OF THE GALAXY NOVELLA

1

"Argus, stand down!" Magnus ordered. His MC90 was trained directly on the man's sweat-covered forehead.

"You're gonna shoot me?" Argus replied. "Over this?"

"I wouldn't have my weapon up if I didn't mean to use it. Now *stand down*."

"So… this is what it comes down to then." Argus looked to the side with a disgusted chuckle. "Figures. You never could stay out of my business."

In as calm a voice as he could summon, Magnus said, "Argus, I won't ask you again. Put your weapon down and step away from the woman. This is your last warning." He moved his finger from the trigger guard and placed it on his trigger.

Since joining the Corps, Sergeant Adonis Olin Magnus hadn't imagined that he'd be aiming his weapon at another Marine—let alone his younger brother.

Two Hours Earlier...

"Please tell me this ain't happening, sergeant," Flow said over TACNET. He lay prone across the peak of a thatched roof, along with Magnus and two other fireteam members. Their overwatch position looked down the main dirt road leading out of the tropical village turned luxury resort. They'd retaken the island of T'io Mi'on a few days prior, turning the Caledonian bungalows and a five-story hotel grounds into a makeshift COP—combat outpost.

"It sure as hell is," Magnus replied, using his helmet's AI to zoom in on the individuals walking down the road. A man in long crimson and black robes, hands extended palms up, led four weaponless Marines in a steady march to what Magnus was pretty sure would be a catastrophic end. "And I don't like it any more than you do."

"Son of a bitch," Flow replied, repositioning his sniper rifle on the dense straw.

With over two years under their belts together, Magnus could tell when Flow and the others were pissed or tense—this was one of those unique times where they were both.

"You think if we take the Luma out anyone will notice?" Mouth asked.

"It's a risk I'm willing to take," Flow replied. "But you're gonna get Magnus in trouble for even talking about a stunt like that."

"It'd be awfully easy to do," Mouth added. "Just a little slip and—"

"Shut up," Flow said, hitting the other lance corporal with an elbow.

Flow and Mouth, along with the third man on the rooftop, Lance Corporal Miguel "Cheeks" Chico, had been with Magnus since their first deployment on Caledonia. The fact that they'd survived as long as they had was nothing short of a miracle. And, being the only Marines who'd survived the infamous binary bomb detonation on the island of Mo'a Ot'a eighteen months prior, Magnus and his boys had become known as the Fearsome Four, at least among enlisted Marines. But title or not, nothing could make Magnus feel any better about the scenario unfolding below them.

"So who was the brass monkey who okay'd this?" Cheeks asked.

"Wasn't a general," Magnus replied. "It was Dorman." Magnus registered their collective hesitation as shock.

"Mystics... what a splickhead," Mouth replied.

"You know... he could be listening right now, don't you?" Flow asked.

"You think I care what that son of a bitch hears me say? Right now, I *hope* he's listening. Cause with what I did to his wife last night, he's gonna need—"

"Shut up, Mouth," Flow said. Magnus looked over to see Flow elbow Mouth in the helmet.

"Forget his wife," added Cheeks. "Now, his daughter..."

"Bring it back, bitches," Magnus said. "They're almost to the end of the road." Magnus watched as the Luma approached the designated meeting point—a bamboo bridge over a wide mountain stream. The water cascaded down several sets of short falls before splitting a beach and disappearing into the ocean.

Until the Caledonian Wars—as the back-and-forth conflict was being termed—Magnus would have given his left nut to vacation here. The quadrant's elite used these islands as their playground, and it was easy to see why. The grass huts, ultra-modern luxury estates, aqua green waters, and lush volcano-draped forests were the backdrop for any number of holo movies. All he needed was a girlfriend. And, given how cute the native women were, he'd bet a month's credits he could find a date before the end of the conflict if he wanted to.

But between the 'kudas, the heat, and the damned squirts that plagued every Marine on the planet—save the desk jockeys—Magnus had had enough sand, sun, and surf to last him a lifetime.

"I still can't believe Dorman let the Luma talk him into this," Flow said between sips of water from his Mark IV armor's hydration straw.

"The major's just trying to wrap this thing up," Magnus said.

"No qualms with me, sergeant," Cheeks replied. "A version of life that doesn't include having sand up your ass every damn day? Bring it."

"I can solve that." Mouth laid a hand on Cheeks' armored butt. "Just stop sleeping naked at night and we won't be tempted to keep pouring sand down your crack."

"You just like the view," Cheeks replied.

Demons at War

Magnus ignored the comment. "But the big thing is that Capriana is tiring of war."

"Because they've fought so hard and so long," Mouth said as if speaking to a toddler who'd just fallen down.

Magnus chuckled. "The Senate and the Corps want an endgame timeline, so they're trying everything they can."

"But this?" Flow asked with the flat of his hand pointing toward the unfolding scene below them. "Dorman really wants to trust a Luma emissary with the fate of our mission?"

"It's not the mission I'm worried about." Magnus replied. "The village is secure and we've gained the foothold on the island that the brass wanted."

"And I think I still have that foot up my ass that you lent me," Cheeks said. "You want it back yet?"

"Keep it," Magnus replied. "I have another."

"Copy that, sergeant."

"If you're not worried about the mission," Flow said, aiming along the barrel of his MC90, "then what are you worried about?"

Magnus pointed downrange. "Those four right there. I'm pretty sure this wasn't in the sales pitch they got when they signed up."

The Luma emissary and the four Marines were on the bridge. While the mystic looked tranquil, the Marines looked wired. Magnus felt bad for the noobs who'd been roped into this. It was like leading lambs to the slaughter. But the Luma had insisted that he be given four unarmed representatives of the Galactic

Republic's fighting force in order to show that their desire to talk peacefully was legitimate.

"If Dorman wanted to talk so badly, why didn't he go out there himself?" Mouth asked.

"Listening…" Flow said, reminding Mouth with a with a tap on the side of his helmet that the brass was most likely monitoring the TACNET channels. Mouth grunted, rolled his head side to side, and re-centered down his weapon's site.

"So…" Flow said, turning toward Magnus. "This Luma prick… is he supposed to be a 'kuda whisperer or something?"

"That's what I've heard. Believes the Akuda tribal leaders are willing to negotiate."

"And you think they are?"

Magnus jerked his head back. "Hells no. They're in this to win it, just like we are."

"Copy that."

"Alright, that's enough chatter," Magnus said in the tone that made everyone go comms silent. "Focus on the op, scan your sectors, and let's give those boys some covering fire if this splick goes sideways."

Flow, Mouth, and Cheeks replied with green icons that chirped in Magnus's HUD. The next voice heard over TACNET was Second Lieutenant Wainwright.

"All fireteams, report in," Wainwright said. When all the units had confirmed their positions around the village, indicated with Ready icons on the topo map in Magnus's HUD, the platoon commander continued. "We're five minutes out still, but I want eyes tracking everything that moves. You see something, tag it. If it even smells like 'kuda, call it out. And *if* the time comes," Wainwright said, stressing the conditional word, "and I give the order, I want everything that's not a Marine to eat sand. I don't want our boys having anything but a nice leisurely walk back to the village."

The second lieutenant was ever the professional, but he also lived up to the Corps' mantra of "leave no Marine behind," which was why the platoon loved him so much. He was one of the rare COs that the enlisted Marines liked… maybe even revered given how often he fought alongside them. And Magnus had a feeling Wainwright would leave the Luma to his mystical powers until the commander was absolutely certain that the four privates were safe.

"Own the field," Wainwright said before closing the channel. Each fire team lead replied with a simple text in the sidebar: "OTF."

"Movement, east side," Flow called out. "One hundred twenty meters, between the uprights. Tagging it now."

Magnus relayed the intel to the platoon commander via his helmet's neural interface. Wainwright replied in the chat with an "acknowledged" prompt and instructed Magnus to keep tracking.

"I count three 'kuda," Flow added as he tagged them in everyone's HUD. Sure enough, three of the mutant humanoid fish emerged from around a bend just beyond the wooden gate that marked the entrance to the vacation village. Their shimmering scales and iridescent eyes were easy markers to pick out. They padded along the sandy path using their overdeveloped hind legs, fins flapping as they moved. And while they appeared to comply with the "no weapons" clause of the absurd meeting, Magnus knew their razor-sharp teeth and lethal claws were an even match for an armored Marine wielding a combat knife.

"Steady, boys," Magnus said. This was the first time he could remember where any Marine had gone so long without firing on one of the fish. "Steady."

"You really think they want to talk this through?" Cheeks asked with an amazed tone.

"Would you?" Magnus replied.

"Hell no!" Then Cheeks cleared his throat, apparently checking himself. "I mean, no, sergeant. I wouldn't. I'd want to go in weapons-hot and take out every last one of these bastards, then cook their fillets over a bed of coals on the beach."

"My sentiments exactly," Magnus replied.

The three hostiles continued to make their way toward the bridge. Magnus looked back at the Luma emissary. The robed man continued to offer his hands out, palms up. *Mystics, this guy has a death wish*, Magnus thought. According to what little he knew of the Order of the Luma, emissaries spent years—often their whole lives—learning about one species or another. And when the time came for the Republic to enter peace talks, the Luma were there to make sure the Senate didn't walk all over them. But from what Magnus had heard, the dialogues were always one-sided, and it was the Republic who got the barrel end of the blaster.

Magnus had never met a Luma before, but given their reputation, he had no desire to. And if this fin sucker was going to do anything but make sure the four Marines with him made it back to the village alive, he'd be damned if he didn't shoot the emissary himself.

"Fifty meters to POC," Flow said, referring to the plan's primary point of contact.

"Hold," Magnus said, reminding his unit not to fire prematurely... *because mystics know they want to.* Hell, Magus wanted to more than anyone. But he hadn't been promoted to sergeant just because of his last name, even though he was sure that had been a contributing factor. The same went for his baby brother, Argus. But there was no way either of them could escape their grandfather's legend. *Best just to try and honor it instead.*

"Thirty meters," Flow reported. The lance corporal spoke just above a whisper. Magnus hated how quiet things got over comms just before his unit saw action. It never ceased to amaze him how much his Marines talked before and during a conflict... but that intense window of silence just before things got real? That was the worst. Secretly, he was hoping one of those fish would make a move so the platoon could get this dumbass distraction over with.

The fish continued to waddle toward the bridge, eyes bulging above their long-snouted slits of teeth. They moved awkwardly, but it was deceptive—at full speed, these demons could overtake any human. Why the damned freaks of nature couldn't remain content in their oceanic habitat, Magnus had no idea. Little was known about the species and their culture... that was, unless the Luma there was willing to share his notes. *Not likely*, Magnus thought.

Somewhere along the line, the fish wanted to be the only

native inhabitants of Caledonia, and that didn't sit well with either the island dwellers or the Galactic Republic. The senators, it was said, rather liked this planet. And for more than just the stunning views. Suffice to say, they rarely brought their wives on government trips here. Magnus didn't exactly blame them in their lust—the Nimprinthian women were a sight to behold—but he did question their fidelity.

"Ten meters," Flow said.

Magnus tracked the three fish to the bridge and then opened a channel to Wainwright. "Lieutenant, do we have ears on the Luma?"

"Negative," Wainwright replied. "The emissary insisted they go weaponless, and—according to him—the Akuda can detect TACNET transmissions and consider all non-biological forms of communication a threat."

Magnus ground his teeth. "Copy that." He closed the channel and reported Wainwright's intel to the rest of the fire team leads. All they could do was watch.

Suddenly, the center 'kuda started to grow animated, throwing its sinewy forearms in circles.

"Whoa, whoa," said Flow. "Wha'da we got here?"

"Easy," Magnus said, though he tightened his grip on his MC90. The fish continued to gesture emphatically, snapping its jaws in quick bites. "He doesn't look happy." Magnus noted that the two other 'kudas were starting to grow restless too.

"I don't like this, Magnus," Cheeks said, dispensing with protocol and calling the sergeant by his last name.

"Hey, is anyone else detecting an energy reading?" Mouth asked.

"Splick," Magnus said. He switched his view from optical to radio spectrometer. A faint yellow glow emanated around the center 'kuda. "I got it." He reopened the channel to Wainwright. "Are you seeing an energy spike?"

Wainwright didn't reply at first, then said, "Affirmative."

Magnus used his eye-tracking command to expand his HUD's view of the bridge and center on the fish. But the damn Luma emissary was blocking the reading, making it harder to discern.

"Could be residual," Flow offered up. "It's faint enough."

"Is that what your gut says?" Magnus added.

"Nope."

"Mine neither." Magnus placed the center of his targeting reticle on the 'kuda's head but kept having to sweep over the Luma to get a clean shot. "Dammit. I'm assigning these bastards to you guys. Tagging now. Get ready to take out the two side 'kudas if they do anything stupid."

"Copy," said all three men.

Back in optical view, the Luma emissary appeared as though he was trying to calm the main 'kuda using slow downward motions with his hands. He also gestured several times to the four Marines with him. For their part, the Marines remained where they were, arms at their sides. But Magnus knew they had to be pissing in their armor. Still, the 'kuda "spokesfish" grew more agitated.

"Probably not my place to say, Lieutenant," Magnus said over comms, "but I don't like it."

"Neither do I, sergeant," said Wainwright.

Suddenly, the four Marines started to back away. The three fish snapped at the air with their teeth. The emissary also took a step back—the man lowered his head as some sort of energy field began to glow around his body. "What the hell?" Magnus said.

"I'm detecting a second energy reading around the Luma," Mouth added.

"I don't like this…" Flow said.

Suddenly, the 'kuda on the right reached toward the center fish's back and pulled something. It looked like a long string…

With a pin at the end.

"It's an ambush!" Magnus yelled over comms.

He'd barely finished the sentence when the foremost 'kuda detonated, swallowing the other two in a shockwave that rippled all the way back into the village. Magnus hardly flinched, however, watching as the four Marine privates were vaporized along with the fish. As for the worthless Luma, the emissary in his glowing energy field was flung backward and went flipping down the dirt road.

The Luma had enough of the *dark arts* to know when to protect himself, but not enough to protect the four Marines he had slaughtered? "Son of a bitch," Magnus yelled.

A dozen 'kuda sprang up from the wide stream, bringing weapons to bear on the Luma who was attempting to retreat toward the village. The emissary took a blaster bolt in the back of the leg, sending him to the dirt in a sprawl. Another bolt drove into his anus, while several more kicked up dirt around his arms. He tried to cover his head, but a final blaster bolt punched through the base of his neck. The Luma's head twitched once, cocked at an odd angle, and his thrashing stopped.

Flow, Mouth, and Cheeks were already returning fire when Wainwright yelled over comms. "Contact, north and south sides!"

New enemy icons popped up on Magnus's topo, indicating Akuda infantry emerging from the ocean to their south—his right —and the volcano hillside to the north—his left. Normally, Repub scanners picked up most enemies, but the 'kudas were beginning to learn how to outsmart some of the hardware. How, Magnus had no idea, but he guessed it had something to do with the marine physiology.

"Fire teams four, five, and six," Wainwright said, "right flank, clear that beach. Fire teams two and three, left flank. I want that jungle purged. Fire team one, clear that stream. Be advised, second and third platoons are en route from the west, ETA five minutes."

The stream was Magnus's. He relayed the order to his boys then joined them in laying down steady blaster fire. He sighted in on a fish taking cover near the smoldering remains of the bridge, ranged at seventy-five meters. The fish was popping in and out of a concrete support's shadow, taking potshots at Marines on the roof adjacent to Magnus. But the 'kuda had developed a pattern that made predicting his next appearance only too easy. Magnus squeezed one round, sending a blaster bolt into the fish's head. The creature flipped backward and splashed in the water.

The next enemy he saw had positioned itself between some

large boulders and a cluster of palm trees—an ideal place for an afternoon cocktail or an evening tryst. At the moment, however, it was the sight of a bloodstain as Magnus drilled the 'kuda in the throat and upper chest, pummeling it with a three-round burst from his MC90.

Magnus's third kill came when he spotted a 'kuda making a dash for a small outbuilding closer to the village's edge. While the enemy was fast on land—dangerously so—a well-trained Marine could pick off a 'kuda as long each shot was well-timed. In this case, since the fish was running at an oblique angle to Magnus, it was only too easy to lead the target. He squeezed. The blaster spat a magenta-colored round that struck the fish in the sternum. It tumbled and buried its head in the sand, legs folding over its back. The rest of his unit had made quick work of the Akuda in the stream, so Magnus confirm-cleared the map of hostile icons.

"Fire team one, shift left," Wainwright ordered. "We need overwatch to the north!"

Magnus tapped Flow on the head and pointed north. "Here we go, boys," he added. They backed off the thatched roof, slid over the side, and landed on the dirt path that connected several of the private bungalows. In the center of the village rose a five-story hotel. It's glass exterior, wooden beams, and fabric awnings made it look more like a beach-bound sailing yacht than a luxury resort.

"Let's make for the hotel roof," Magnus said. Fire teams two and three were already on the ground, moving into the jungle. Taking the roof meant Flow could unleash even more destruction

Demons at War

from his sniper rifle, while the rest of his fire team called out targets and aided the boots on the sand.

Magnus hauled ass around the hotel pool, pushed into an interior lobby, and headed toward a stairwell sign. He charged up all five flights, feeling his armor's servos assist him as he climbed. But the Mark IV needed some serious upgrades in the future—at least if he had anything to say about it—and more powerful servos would be critical if the Corps was going to remain a formidable fighting force in the galaxy.

Magnus was out of breath when he punched through the rooftop door and stepped back into broad daylight. "This way!" he ordered, pointing to the northern edge. They bypassed several mortar emplacements that had been ranged in to cover the beach —Magnus had no doubt the weapons would be fired up soon in order to cover the COP's southern border.

As soon as he looked down, Magnus's AI began overlaying friendly and enemy positions on his HUD. Fire teams two and three were advancing methodically, but more 'kuda kept appearing from the trees. Magnus wondered if they'd found a cave with some sort of ocean access inside the mountain.

"Flow," Magnus said, "see how far back you can start taking them out."

"Copy that," Flow replied. The Marine had already removed the MS900 sniper blaster from his back and was opening the bipod under the barrel.

"Mouth, Cheeks, I want you leading the fire teams, but no friendly fire."

"Roger," the two men replied as they began shooting targets marked by the fire team below.

Magnus leaned against a cooling unit and steadied his breathing. "In position, lieutenant," he said to Wainwright.

"I see you," replied the CO. "Happy hunting."

Magnus shouldered his MC90, activated the sights, and double-checked that his helmet was paired with the weapon's firing system. His weapon wasn't like the fancy new prototypes the Corps was developing. But the MC90 was reliable and—despite only having two firing modes—was fairly versatile. Plus, in a firefight, the best weapon was the one you were shooting

Magnus called out three targets for Flow before taking aim at a 'kuda snaking down a trail to the far right. The fish had clearly chosen its path well, avoiding the central blaster fire from teams two and three. Magnus guessed it had plans to flank the Marines. The 'kuda's plan probably would have worked too, were it not for the two rounds that Magnus placed center mass. The fish fell down an embankment and stopped dead against a palm tree trunk. In comic relief only a Marine could appreciate, a coconut fell from its lofty height and landed on the 'kuda's head. *No way anyone's believing that one*, Magnus thought to himself as he filed the occurrence under *"Stories I'll Never Tell."*

The Akuda continued to charge from the jungle, racing down the volcano's southern face. By mid-afternoon, the Fearsome Four were running low on ammo as their superior position had afforded them a continuous supply of targets. Fortunately, fire teams from second platoon came to resupply them.

"The platoon commander says we can relieve you if you

want," said the team lead, her accent heavy, and one Magnus couldn't quite place.

"Thanks, Sergeant Meenaz, but if it's all the same to you, we'll stay on until the flow stops."

Apparently unable to resist the opportunity, Lance Corporal Michael "Flow" Deeks replied, "Oh, the Flow never stops, baby."

Meenaz looked at Flow and then back to Magnus. "Whatever works for you guys, we're good."

"Welcome to the party," Cheeks added over comms, giving Meenaz a super cheesy tip of his helmet.

"Dumbass," Mouth said over a private channel. "You know she can't see your face."

"Exactly," Cheeks replied. "Right now, I'm her wildest fantasy."

"Hey, Mr. Wild Fantasies," Magnus said. "Why don't you turn your attention to the three 'kudas coming down your left flank."

"Dammit!" Cheeks yelled. He spun around and brought his MC90 to high ready position then fired on the trio.

2

THE AFTERNOON TURNED out to be a steady defense of the village as 'kuda poured down the volcano's side face and assaulted the hotel. TACNET data and comms updates revealed that the rest of the hastily created COP was experiencing similar assaults with equal success. The enemy wasn't throwing everything they had at the village. "Just enough to wear us down," Magnus said to himself.

"What was that, sergeant?" Flow asked.

Magnus sighted in on a fish who was slinking through a cluster of boulders. "Just talking to myself, Flow." He squeezed his MC90's trigger, sending a blaster bolt through the woods and into the 'kuda's chest. A second shot landed centimeters from the first, boring a small hole in the fish. It slumped forward into a rock, the last of his breath escaping through the new outlet.

"About how the 'kuda are wearing us down?" Flow asked.

"Something like that." Magnus fired on another fish that was making a run for a large fern. The trio of blaster rounds caught it mid-stride, causing it to tumble head over heels. It collapsed, shooting up forest debris in its wake. The whole afternoon had been like this—taking out one fish after another. "Just feels like they want to keep us occupied, draining our resources."

"Copy that," Flow replied. Magnus watched the lance corporal send a single blaster bolt from his MS900 into a fish's head, obliterating its skull.

The Akuda weren't exactly the smartest aggressors in the quadrant. In fact, they'd been known to send countless fish to their deaths for reasons Magnus never understood. But when the planet's oceans seemed to offer an endless supply of the gill-headed bastards, what did it matter? Sure, the morality of willfully sending thousands upon thousands of soldiers to certain death seemed insane to Magnus… but he wasn't a fish. For all he knew, that was completely logical—and ethical—to the Akuda.

But Magnus also had a strange feeling that maybe the Akuda weren't as dumb as everyone thought. The fish had demonstrated a level of groupthink that was startling, organizing mass movement without the use of conventional communication systems. And they certainly fought like mad hellions in close quarters combat, schooled in some sort of primal fighting techniques that the Corps had been trying to reverse engineer for over a year. It was only the Repub's superior weaponry that had given the Marine's a temporary advantage along the way, but all energy weapons need ammunition and maintenance.

Which meant maybe this war wasn't going to be about firepower...

It was going to be about attrition.

And that's why Magnus was worried. It didn't matter how good your weapons were or how well your troops fought. If you couldn't resupply your warriors, no amount of battlefield superiority would help you win a war of overwhelming numbers. The Marines might kill a hundred of the fish for every ten Marines, but the fish would just keep coming until there were no more Marines to resupply.

Cheeks had just finished downing a pair of 'kuda making their way down a wee-worn path near the volcano face's middle when Magnus heard voices on the roof behind him.

"Need any help, sergeant?" someone asked.

Magnus noted that the person wasn't speaking over TACNET, just open air. So he expected to see a civilian when he turned around. Instead, he was met by four Marines in black and gray Mark VI armor, carrying their helmets under their arms. They were also wielding... *the prototype MAR30*. Neither the armor nor the blaster were in production yet. *Supposedly*. He'd fired that weapons platform once during a battalion demo day, but it was rumored to be years away from production. And the Mark VI suit? He'd guessed it wouldn't see the light of day anytime soon either. But, damn if it didn't look good.

"If you're in the mood to fish for your dinner, be my guest," Magnus said, removing his helmet in order to talk with them face to face. He extended his hand toward the foremost Marine. "Sergeant Adonis Olin Magnus."

"Sergeant Adam Musgrave," the man replied. "We're with the—"

"The 79th Recon," Magnus interjected.

"What gave it away?"

"Actually?" Magnus eyed the man from head to toe. "It was the beards. Nothing sticks out like non-reg."

Musgrave and the other three operators chuckled. "Ain't that the truth."

"First thing I did when I got out of indoctrination school," a second Marine said, feeling his orange-colored beard, "was grow it out."

"It only took you twelve months," said another man in the squad.

When the heckling died down, Magnus said, "Well, nice to have you boys here. But only for a few minutes, I'm assuming?"

Musgrave nodded. "We had intel that 'kuda were massing in this direction and we were asked to check it out, but it looks like you've got it under control. So we're being tasked with an op further downrange."

"I'd hardly call this massing," Magnus said, throwing a thumb over his shoulder, "but it's keeping us out of trouble."

"I hear that," Musgrave said. "If we ain't shooting something, we're pissing on something else."

"And pissing only gets Marines in trouble," Magnus replied.

"Oorah," said the red-headed Marine behind Musgrave.

"Say," Musgrave said, wiping a finger over Magnus's name placard on his chest, "I've heard of you, sergeant. Well, maybe not you, but—"

"He was my grandfather."

Musgrave gave Magnus an impressed look with a raised eyebrow. "You don't say. Not every day you meet the grandson of an esteemed war hero. You have a brother too?"

"Argus. He's with our company, fourth platoon." Magnus could practically feel the Fearsome Four ease their fire rate—he'd never talked about his family with them.

"Damn. Two Magnuses in one conflict. 'Kuda bitches better run."

Magnus cleared his throat. "Well, like I said you're welcome to pull up a chair and score some kills if you guys want."

But Musgrave waved him off. "No way we're squatting on someone else's perch, Magnus. We'd better get a move on anyway. Daylight's slipping, and recon does their best work in the dark."

Magnus extended his hand again, saying, "Pleasure to meet you gents."

"Hold up," Musgrave said, reaching to his chest plate. He de-magged a black sheath from his armor and flipped it over in his hand. Then, pointing the handle toward Magnus, he said, "This is for you."

Magnus looked down at the offered gift, taken aback by Musgrave's generosity. The spec ops boys always got all the fun toys, so even without seeing the knife, he knew it was high-end kit. Exchanging small tokens of appreciation, recognition, or even friendship was fairly normal in the Corps. But when something like this was extended… well, Magnus knew it was no small thing.

He took the sheath and pulled out a prototype duradex combat blade, then he whistled. "What's this for?"

"For being stone cold," Musgrave said. "Those three sluggers behind you haven't stopped firing since we got here, which means they respect your orders, and you turned to meet us instead of telling one of them to, which means you were willing to deal with what was most likely an inspection from a butt-scrunched CO instead of making them do it."

Not willing to negate his points, Magnus replied, "Thank you, sergeant."

"My pleasure. And do yourself a favor when this is all done."

"What's that?"

"Consider the recon. We could use some heat like you. All four of you."

Magnus looked at the knife and then back to Musgrave. "Maybe we will."

"I'll put in a good word for you with Caldwell," Musgrave added with a wink. "We don't hand those knives out to just anyone, ya know. Own the field, bitches."

"OTF," Magnus replied.

"No fair," Cheeks said, looking over at Magnus. "I want a knife."

"You don't get a knife," Mouth said. "The mystics already gave you a cock the size of a Madras donkey's. Knives are for everyone else."

"Hey, speak for yourself," Flow said, throwing Mouth an elbow a second after he dispatched a 'kuda with his MS900.

"I'm just saying, Cheeks here's got—"

"We've all seen," Flow said. "No need to revisit my nightmares."

Magnus sighted in on a cluster of 'kuda taking cover behind a copse of palms. While he could eventually pick them all off himself, it'd be more efficient if he had some help. "Hey, big dick and friends, shift right. Marking the targets on your HUD."

The boys laughed as Magnus felt them turn to the right. They locked onto the icons he'd illuminated and opened fire. Their blaster rounds met plenty of targets that poked around the trees, but even more ripped their way through the trunks and hit the fish where they hunched. With so much overwhelming fire, the enemy toppled out from behind the palm grove like wheat cleaved from a field.

"You thinking of putting in for recon school?" Flow asked.

Mouth answer first. "After that invite, he'd better be."

"Damn straight," added Cheeks. "You get a bead to the major like that, you take it."

The truth was, Magnus didn't need the favor. He already knew Caldwell—no small thanks to his grandfather. But this was the very thing he was trying to avoid. Favors. He didn't want handouts, he wanted justice. *You get what you earn, and you miss what you weren't good enough to target yourself.* So he had a hard time knowing what Musgrave saw in him—a Marine worth his plate armor or just another Magnus.

"Maybe when all this is over, I'll look into it," Magnus said. "You never know. But I'll only do it on one condition."

"Dick enlargement therapy?" Mouth asked.

"Shut up, Mouth," Flow said, this time striking him with the butt of his weapon.

"Watch it!"

"I'm taking you with me," Magnus said.

"Right." Flow chuckled. "Cause that's how it works."

Magnus knew what Flow meant. You didn't pick who went with you to one side of the Corps or another. That was like shouting at the ocean and telling it not to send waves to a certain part of the beach. No, the Repub told you where you were going, and that was that.

But if Magnus was going to leverage his connection to Major Caldwell, it wasn't going to be for himself. It'd be for these three mag draggers. Flow, Mouth, and Cheeks had been with him… to hell and back, and then back to hell a few more times. They'd weathered splick no one had seen before, at least as far as Magnus imagined. So if there was some way into an elite fighting unit that got to do things for the Repub that made a difference, he wanted to see them going. They deserved it. More than anyone else, and certainly more than him.

"I'm serious, boys." Magnus tracked and fired on another fish, dropping it in a flopping heap of gills and fins. "If the Corps wants me in recon indoctrination school, then they get all of us. If not, no deal."

Flow ceased fire and looked over at Magnus. "Mystics, you're serious right now, aren't you."

Flow couldn't see his face, of course, but Magnus was giving him the most serious look he could. "And if they don't want us, I'll buy you your damn knives. That goes double for you, Cheeks —dick or no dick."

"Definitely dick," Cheeks said.

3

First, second, and third platoons held the village on T'io Mi'on well into the evening, resisting the Akuda's steady assault with unrelenting streams of fire on both northern and southern advances. Unlike some of the other firefights Magnus had endured, this one was relatively benign, though he and the others still lamented the unnecessary loss of three of the four Marines who'd accompanied the Luma emissary to the bridge. Magnus knew the event would remain with him long into the future, standing out as a sore spot in the conflict. He'd already distrusted the Order and their methods, but now—seeing everything firsthand—he swore he'd never trust a Luma again. *Mystic bastards*, he thought.

As Magnus finished debriefing with Wainwright in the company's makeshift HQ—a deluxe bungalow in the hotel's shadow—he walked out to find the rest of the Four lounging in some broken lawn chairs by a fire pit.

"Damn, this martini is good," Flow said with his helmet off. He sipped from the water line protruding from his collar, making a show of how amazing it tasted.

"You wish," Magnus said. The truth was, they were all ready for some much-needed leave. It had been ten months since their last evac to Capriana, and they'd seen their fair share of action since then. In fact, the last two months had provided the most intense engagements of the entire conflict. Their platoon had cycled out more than half its numbers, and Magnus knew Mouth and Cheeks were both showing signs of PTSD, though neither man would admit it, and Magnus was reticent to bring it up.

Rumors of Marines having psychotic breakdowns during the lulls in between firefights were becoming more common too. Several arrests had been made in barracks where things had gotten out of hand. Fortunately, none of Magnus's direct reports needed to be subdued… at least not yet. He cursed the day that he'd need to order one of the Four to stand down.

Magnus pulled up the splintered remains of a wooden cabana chair and sat by the fire. "Pour me one, would you, Flow?"

"No problem, sergeant," he said, then leaned into Magnus's face with his neck.

"Mystics, Flow, this isn't a make-out session!" Magnus shoved the man off him. "Plus, you smell like splick."

"You don't smell much better."

All four of them laughed as Magnus set his helmet on the

grass. He leaned back and looked up at the stars. "Mystics, if this were any other season of my life."

"Copy that, big daddy," Cheeks said. Then he put his arms up as if leaning them over the shoulders of some imaginary people on his lap. "I have a blonde on this leg and a brunette on this one."

"Just two?" Mouth asked, looking at Cheeks in amazement.

"Nah…" Cheeks placed both hands a half a meter from his groin as if he were holding a space ball. "Third one's right here."

"Yeah, you wish," Flow said, kicking Cheek's hands away from his crotch.

"What about you, Magnus?" Cheeks asked. "You never talk about having girls back home."

"For one thing," Magnus said, studying the stars, "it'd just be one girl."

"Come on now, sergeant," Mouth said. "We all know you're man enough to—"

"Not saying it wouldn't be fun, boys. But I leave that to you. I can barely handle one as it is. I'm just saying, all I need is the love of one woman, and that's enough."

"Now there's an old-school romantic for you," Mouth said.

"So who is she?" Flow asked, leaning in.

"Nobody right now," he replied, nodding up to the stars. It was a half-truth, of course. He was seeing someone if it could be called that. But in his gut, he wasn't convinced the relationship would last. "But she's out there, somewhere."

There was a momentary pause. For a second, Magnus wondered if he'd gotten through to his philandering fire team.

Then Cheeks asked, "You know what this means, boys? Sergeant's just been banging Nimprinthian babes when we're all asleep."

Laughter filled the firelight. Magnus let the three of them carry on for a minute, before saying, "Alright, alright. Ease up on the natives, boys."

The crackle of the fire and the distant murmurs of other teams enjoying the peace and quiet retook the plaza. The humid smell of the salty air and flowers had replaced the odors of burnt ozone and charred flesh. Magnus could stay here like this all night. It was nice not hearing the constant whine of blaster fire or the screams of the dying. For a moment, it almost felt like he was back home, sitting with Dani and enjoying the warmth of her body against his, resting in one of Capriana's parks. Of course, there was no way in hell he was telling that to these bastards—they'd have a field day with it. But when he got home, maybe he'd make something of their relationship… if there was anything left to salvage.

"Did I hear your brother is joining us?" Flow asked.

Magnus looked over at him, surprised the news had spread so quickly. But with a last name like Magnus, he supposed it wasn't entirely out of the norm for intel to pass among the ranks. "That's what I hear. Fourth platoon should be pulling in sometime after midnight."

"He anything like you?" Mouth asked.

"A whole lot better looking." Magnus checked the time. "Well, it's getting late, boys."

"Aw, no, sergeant," Cheeks pleaded. "Say it ain't so…"

"I know, I know," he said, pushing them back with open palms. "I'm the life of the party here, and things just won't be the same without me. But you think this face pops off the pillow every morning looking this good on its own?"

The three men shared a glance. Then Mouth said, "Yeah, actually we do."

"Nice try, Franklin," Magnus said, using the man's last name. "But I'm leaving you three to enjoy the night air and free cocktails without me."

"Sounds good, sergeant," Mouth replied. Then he seemed to think of another question. "You're not waiting up for your little brother?"

Magnus shook his head. "I'm sure I'll catch up with him in the morning. If you see him, just stay away from his left hook."

The three men raised their eyebrows.

"He draws your attention in with all those right jabs and then —*bam!*" Magnus mimed the boxing combo, delivering the left hook with a vocal flourish.

"Sounds like you've been on the receiving end of that before," Flow said.

Magnus grunted. "More times than I care to count." He reached down and picked up his helmet, tucked it under his arms, and bid them goodnight. For their part, the three men sent Magnus away with farewell wishes for a good night's rest and dreams of big breasts.

Magnus walked toward the tents set up on a quad near the beach. Secretly, he'd hoped to obtain a bunk in one of the bungalows—*who wouldn't*—but all those had been reserved by the officers before they'd even taken the island. And why not? It wasn't like anyone here made enough scratch to come back in the future—that was, assuming the Marines or the Navy didn't blow this place to hell by the time this was all said and done.

WHILE MAGNUS WISHED he'd been in the middle of a dream with the blonde and the brunet on Cheeks' thighs—minus Cheeks—he was really in the middle of fitful sleep when the sound of blaster fire startled him awake. He could already hear glass windows shattering above him, evidence that the main hotel was being targeted by 'kuda anti-ship munitions. Magnus didn't even put on his armor. Instead, he grabbed his MC90 and stepped out of his tent wearing only his workout shorts and slip-ons.

Blue blaster bolts buffeted the building overhead, blowing holes in several floors. He knew that people were in there. Third platoon had been assigned a dozen rooms since arriving to the newly created and over-capacity COP. Fourth platoon had probably been pointed there as well. Like the officers who'd gotten the bungalows, Magnus had envied the two platoons. But not anymore.

Several people fell from the gaps in the windows. Most of the bodies were maimed or dismembered, but at least two Marines screamed as they fell to their deaths. For a fleeting second, Magnus wondered if one of those bodies was his brother's.

"Dammit!" Magnus yelled to no one in particular, then he reached back inside his tent for his helmet. As soon as the AI fired

Demons at War

up, a topo map appeared, lit with icons denoting Marines and Akuda forces not in the tens, but in the hundreds. The chat section was streaming faster than he could read, so he pinged Wainwright for a situation report.

"SITREP, LT?"

"We're getting three-sixtied! Get your ass to that hotel and start clearing Marines out! They're sitting ducks!"

"Copy," Magnus replied. Then he pinged the remaining Fearsome Four. Flow and Mouth were already standing outside their tent, reaching for their MC90. Cheeks stepped out of another tent, butt naked. He stared aloft as more artillery rounds pummeled the hotel.

"Cheeks!" Magnus yelled through his external speakers. "Get something on your ass! All of you, weapons hot, covers on. We're running exfil on the hotel!"

Cheeks ducked inside and returned fewer than ten seconds later with a pair of boxers, his helmet, and his blaster. The four Marines raced through the tent village, each wearing next to nothing, and headed for the hotel's main entrance. Far fewer Marines were leaving the building than Magnus had hoped, which meant they were dead, dazed, or trapped.

"Magnus," Flow said, "data shows the ground floor is storage, floor two is admin only."

"That puts barracks on three, four, and five," Magnus concluded.

"That's what I'm thinking," Flow replied.

"Then let's get a move on," Mouth said, bolting toward the nearest stairwell. Just as he was about to pull the door open, it pushed out. Two Marines limped through the doorway, one with a serious head wound and the other cradling the bloody stump of a forearm.

"Splick!" Mouth yelled, backing away so the two men could pass by.

Just then, another large-caliber round rocked the building. The chandeliers swayed, and bits of plaster and glass fell on Magnus's bare shoulders.

"Clear," Mouth said, barging through the door and up the first flight of stairs. Magnus and the others followed him. It didn't take long, however, for more Marines to appear, many suffering from severe injuries like the men they'd passed earlier. Those who didn't appear to be wounded were helping the least lucky Marines down the stairs. One woman had both legs blown off—two tourniquets were cinched around her upper thighs. Magnus stepped aside as she passed, then continued ascending toward the top floor. With every turn he took, he half expected to see Argus limping down the stairs missing one limb or another. Mystics knew the kid had a knack for being in the wrong place at the wrong time.

The line of Marines heading to the exit was becoming more constant now, which was a good sign. What wasn't a good sign was how bad the injuries were and how many more Marines Magnus knew were still in the building. If the warriors passing him represented the best conditioned Marines, he feared what they were going to find once in the rooms.

Magnus pushed the fifth-floor door open and stepped into a hallway filled with the shouts of Marines, the smell of fire, and the remains of broken walls. Another hit slammed against the building so hard that Magnus was thrown sideways against the hallway wall. His helmet took the majority of the hit—a flash of static fizzed out the display for half a second. But his shoulder and hip weren't without their own damage. He righted himself and saw two indentations his body had left in the wall. Feeling the pain of the impact and looking ahead to the patches of fire that emanated from several holes in the hallway, Magnus was beginning to regret not taking the extra minute to don his Mark IV armor.

"Look for survivors," Magnus said. "Focus on those who can't move themselves."

The three other men confirmed the order and started clearing rooms. Magnus moved furthest down the hallway, stepping into a room to his left. The large suite looked south toward the beach and had suffered a direct hit that blew out the main windows and toasted what he assumed had been a central living room. Two Marines in their underwear lay crumpled on the floor—one missing half his chest cavity, the other staring at the ceiling with dead eyes.

Magnus turned into the main bedroom and, aside from the sleeping bags on the floor and the upturned bed, found a woman leaning outside the bathroom wall. Her legs looked too burned to be used, but she was awake, clutching her left arm.

"Are you able to stand?" Magnus asked through his helmet.

"No," the Marine said. "I can't feel those burns. I think something hit my spine."

"I'm going to pick you up," Magnus said.

"Copy that, sergeant."

Magnus bent over and scooped her up, bringing her to his chest. The woman groaned as he moved her, but that was all. Whether or not she could feel anything in her legs, he knew she must be able to feel everywhere else, and from the looks of it, the pain had to be intense.

"What's your name, Marine," Magnus asked, trying to start a conversation that might take the woman's attention off the agony.

"Saba," she said. "Lance Corporal Melany Saba, with Fourth Platoon."

"Copy that, lance corporal." Magnus was back in the hallway, heading for the stairs.

"And you?"

"I'm with First Platoon. You can call me Adonis." Magnus was hustling down the first two flights of stairs, noting how the woman's lifeless legs slapped against his hip.

"That's your last name, Marine?"

Magnus shook his helmet, reluctant to say anything more. *But what the hell does it matter now?* "Last name's Magnus," he added.

"Well I'll be…" The woman seemed to blush as they descended, catching up to some slower moving Marines. "Never thought I'd actually get to meet Argus's big brother."

"You know Argus?"

"Course I do. Who doesn't know a Magnus when they're in your own damn—" Saba winced as Magnus landed a bit too forcefully on a landing. But he'd halfway tripped on his slip-on sandal.

"Sorry," Magnus said.

"When they're in your own damn company," Saba finished through gritted teeth.

"Know what room he was in by any chance?"

But Saba shook her head. "He was supposed to be two doors down from me."

"Supposed to?" Magnus rounded the last landing to the ground floor.

"He and a few of the others said they needed to blow off some steam before hitting the hay. Said they were sneaking off to the basement, I think. Then all this happened."

"You sure?"

"Pretty damn sure," Saba said. "Platoon commander sent…" Saba winced, then took a few short breaths. "Sorry. Sent another squad to look for them, but no one's reported back. Might be a good thing, for Argus's sake."

"How's that?"

"He and his crew take their playtime seriously."

"Don't I know…" Magnus was at least relieved to know that Argus hadn't been near any windows when the attack began. But he was apprehensive about what condition his brother might be in if left to his many vices. Chances were high that he was disabled during this firefight but for completely different reasons than being shot.

Magnus carried Saba across the lobby and filed out onto the hotel's front lawn. The sound of blaster fire behind the edges of the village had increased since Magnus entered the hotel just a few minutes prior. He gave his topo a quick scan and saw that even more enemy forces were driving toward the village, most gathering on the beach. He'd expected to hear the mortar's going off on the roof—the fact that they weren't meant one of several things, none of them good.

A medic raced toward Magnus and Saba. The man seemed to size up Saba's injuries fast, then said, "That way!" He pointed Magnus toward some more medics moving the wounded away from the hotel and toward a cluster of tents.

Magnus jogged toward the makeshift medical unit, careful not to jounce Saba too hard. But he needed to get back in the hotel and save more Marines… and find his brother.

"We'll take her, Marine," said another medic, insisting that Magnus lay the lance corporal on the grass. He did so, then removed his helmet to wish the woman well.

"Thanks, Adonis," Saba said, touching his bearded face. "It's not every day a Magnus saves you."

"Just make sure you live to tell about it," Magnus replied. He gave her a wink and was about to put his helmet back on when the lance corporal put a hand on his bare arm.

"Take care of him, okay?"

The gesture, as well as the comment, caught Magnus off guard. He opened his mouth to give her a quick reply, but she added more.

"People misunderstand him a lot. But I know he's a good man. Just… he's trying to meet his needs in the wrong ways, you know? And you're his big brother, so he respects you even though he doesn't always show it."

Mystics, is this lady a shrink or something?

"I'll look after him," Magnus said, doing his best to ignore Saba's comments. But the woman clearly had keen insight into the Magnus Family relationships. For all Magnus knew, Argus had bedded this woman on more than one occasion.

He replaced his cover and turned for the hotel again. "How we looking, Fearsome?" he asked over their squad comms channel.

"We've evacuated the last survivors on the fifth floor," Flow said. "Moving down to the fourth floor now."

"Copy that," Magnus replied. "I've got word there might be Marines in the basement. Going to check it out." He was back in the lobby, dodging the steady stream of injured Marines.

"Be careful," Flow replied. "Heard some chatter that supports are collapsing—they think some explosions went off down there when this first started."

"Copy that, Flow. I'll keep an eye out."

There was a moment's hesitation before Flow added: "You think baby brother's down there?"

Magnus swallowed, pulling open a separate door marked Basement. "I do, yeah."

"Be careful then. I know how thick-headed we can get when it's family."

"Roger that."

MAGNUS PLUNGED DOWN two flights of stairs in total darkness. He switched to thermal optics since the power in this section of the building had apparently been knocked out. When he got to the lower level, he scanned down the corridor to his left, then to his right. Increasing the sensor's sensitivity, he noticed movement roughly one hundred meters to his right. Several figures appeared to be inside the back room.

Magnus switched to night vision, relying on the light cast from small fires further down the corridor. Just as Flow had mentioned, several load-bearing columns had collapsed in the building's center. Magnus detected the sharp odor of synthetic explosives still lingering in the air. Black blast marks raced away from several flowering holes in the metal infrastructure.

When he got close enough to the fires, he switched back to optics and then double-checked that his air filtration system was operational. He also ran a finger along the soft seal around his neck. The last thing he wanted was to die of asphyxiation down below when there were far more heroic ways to die up top. Still, if it meant saving his brother's life, then he could think of few more meaningful ways to perish. *Mystics know I've saved his life a hundred times before… the ungrateful little ass.*

Magnus's skin prickled against the heat as he tried to skirt the damaged superstructure, before moving further down the corridor. Several pipes spewed water into a few-centimeters flood that his feet slashed through, but it was nothing to be overly concerned about. He did, however, wish he'd been wearing his boots—escorting injured Marines back this way with his slip-ons would be a pain.

He switched back to infrared to try and isolate an exact direction. Closer than before, Magnus noticed four… maybe five individuals a little further down and to his left. At least one of the individuals looked injured, lying prone on the ground. Another looked to be sliding off a table or crate—Magnus couldn't be sure. The remaining two or three Marines looked to be attending to the fallen. *Splick*, Magnus thought, *this is going to be bad*. But as he switched back to optical and approached the door, he wasn't prepared for just how bad it really was.

4

Magnus pushed open the door and stepped into the room marked Boiler. At first, he didn't know how to process what he saw. A young Nimprinthian woman was bent over a desk, her bare breasts pressed into the metal top while two half-dressed Marines assaulted her from behind. Neither man registered Magnus's presence—they were too busy with their conquest.

The third nearly naked Marine had a second girl's hands and thighs pinned to the floor while he forced himself on her. Between the sounds of battle and the women screaming, Magnus suspected none of the men had heard him enter. He pointed his MC90 at the ceiling, aiming as far back as he could, and fired three rounds.

The Marines looked around, seemingly less than surprised to hear weapons fire—which meant they were extremely desensitized, on something, or experiencing some sort of a psychotic episode. None of which were exciting explanations for Magnus.

"Step away from the women, now!" Magnus ordered over external speakers, feeling his blood flush his face.

"If you want in," said an angry-faced Marine with a thick neck and bulging shoulders, "you're gonna have to wait your turn."

"I think you misunderstand my purpose for being here," Magnus replied. He took two strides forward and then brought the butt of his MC90 across the man's face. Magnus struck him with such force that the man spun away from the table and collapsed onto the floor.

The second man at the desk watched his fellow Marine flop to the ground. He looked back at Magnus and then at last ceased his gyrating, though he failed to retreat from the girl who still wailed on the desk. The man on the floor, however, carried on, headless of Magnus's display of force.

Magnus raised his weapon at the man behind the desk. "Off her now, splickhead," Magnus said. The man put his hands up and backed away, rightfully more concerned with the weapon pointed at him than the limp one he was pointing at his victim.

Then Magnus turned toward the Marine still assaulting the second woman on the floor. "I said get off her, you son of a bitch!"

"Or what?" the man said. As he looked up, Magnus caught the familiar face of Argus. But this beast was a shadow of his baby brother. A wild sneer wrinkled his nose, and scratch marks along his neck and cheeks dripped with crimson tears. Argus' deranged face sent a chill up Magnus's bare skin. He reached for his helmet and ripped it off his head.

"Or I'm going to beat the living *splick* out of you, Argus."

Magnus's brother barely even flinched when he saw his brother. "Go tend to your own flock, Adonis. I'm busy here."

Magnus reapplied his grip on his MC90, fighting a battle of wills that caused him to lower and then raise the weapon's barrel on Argus. "Get off her, Argus."

"Or what, big brother?" Argus spit on the girl's bare chest. "You're gonna shoot me?"

Magnus swallowed.

This was a psychotic breakdown if he'd ever seen one. His little brother had always been the smarter of the two of them, painfully so. Where Adonis was a brute who solved most problems at the playground with a quick punch to a pain point, Argus had used more subtle ways of keeping bullies at bay—like convincing them their parents were watching from the cameras in the ceiling, or constructing fake bombs and putting them in their lockers at school.

When they both signed up for the Marines, Adonis had tried to convince Argus not to go through with it. While brilliant, he wasn't sure his younger brother could handle the violence. Even back then, he knew it did things to a person… things Adonis wasn't sure Argus was built for. And now the fear that those demons had whispered to him more than two years ago had come back to bite them both.

"Argus, this isn't you," Magnus said.

"Just get off her, bro!" said the second Marine still standing with his manhood out. The first Marine was slowly recovering from the blow Magnus had dealt him.

"Listen to your man, Argus," Magnus said, trying to talk above the young woman's cries. "Just get off her and we'll walk away from this."

"Nah," Argus said, then pulled a pistol from the rear waistband of his torn gym shorts. He placed it under the girl's chin, causing her to scream. "You were always the one in control, brother. But not tonight."

"Argus, put the—"

"Sounds like everyone's dying up there, and this… this right here… this is how we've chosen to go out. Not dying at the hands of a bastard fish just so some Senators can keep their precious vacation homes under Repub jurisdiction." Argus started shaking his head. Veins bulging. Sweat streaming. "Nah, not today. We get our share tonight. This is what we deserve."

"And what about them," Magnus said, indicating the two women. The first girl was holding her clothes to her chest and stepped behind Magnus, whimpering. "Is this what they deserve too?"

Even as he posed the question, Magnus noted that the first Marine was trying to stand. How the giant hadn't blacked out from the blow was beyond Magnus. Either the boy had the constitution of a starship or he was hopped up on something powerful. "Easy there, big guy. No sudden moves."

Magnus was beginning to regret taking his helmet off. If things got out of hand here, he wouldn't be able to call for backup, and he had no way of subduing three Marines without badly hurting them—which he would do if necessary.

"I'm tired of talking," Argus said. He pushed the pistol further under the girl's chin. She screamed. Magnus pointed his MC90 directly at Argus. "See there, Nos Kil?" Argus looked to the Marine, who was pulling himself up on a crate. "My brother is actually thinking of pulling the trigger on me. And isn't that just like family?"

Magnus noticed the Marine called Nos Kil look at something adjacent to him. It was another pistol. *Damn,* Magnus thought, *where are these guys getting officers' sidearms?* "Don't even think about it," Magnus said, nodding Nos Kil away from the pistol.

Suddenly, Argus yanked the young woman off the floor and pulled her up to stand in front of him. He used her body as a shield while keeping the pistol pointed at her head. Magnus swirled back to Argus. Nos Kil looked back at the pistol. Magnus aimed back to Nos Kil.

Splick. This was going sideways faster than he could have imagined.

"Listen," said the only compliant Marine of the three. "I don't want anyone gettin' hurt here."

"Shut up, Caldwell," Nos Kil said. Magnus glanced at the kid and wondered if he was related to the Major. He certainly had similar features. "You're such a disgrace."

"No, I'm not."

Nos Kil gestured to the man's loins. "Yeah, ya are."

Self-conscious for the first time since entering the room, Caldwell zipped up his pants and shuffled further into the corner.

"Coward," Nos Kil seethed.

"I'm getting tired of this," Argus said. "She dies…" Then he stretched the weapon out and pointed it at Magnus. "Or you die."

"Argus, stand down!" Magnus ordered.

"You're gonna shoot me? Over this?"

"I wouldn't have my weapon up if I didn't mean to use it. Now *stand down*."

"So… this is what it comes down to then." Argus looked to the side with a disgusted chuckle. "Figures. You never could stay out of my business."

"Argus, I'm not gonna ask you again. Put your weapon down and step away from the woman. This is your last warning." He moved his finger from the trigger guard and placed it on his trigger.

Nos Kil lunged for the pistol on the crate. Magnus pivoted and lined up a shot, but the Marine was fast. He grabbed the pistol and squeezed the trigger, but not before Magnus fired a round into the man's shoulder. Nos Kil's shot with the pistol went wide. He screamed, dropping the weapon, and reached for his injured shoulder.

A groan from the room's corner drew Magnus's attention. He glanced over long enough to see Caldwell slump against some crates. He'd been shot in the chest. Nos Kil looked up at Caldwell too—but where Magnus expected Nos Kil to show some sort of remorse for accidentally shooting his squadmate, the wretch displayed a look of curious satisfaction.

Magnus turned back to Argus and looked him in the eyes. But

in the time it took for him to refocus, his brother raised the pistol to the girl's right temple and fired. Driven by instinct, Magnus fired at nearly the same moment, delivering a blaster bolt to the center of Argus's forehead. The girl's left temple erupted in an electrical burst of gray matter and blood while Argus's head snapped back, tossing him into a cluster of crates.

The girl behind Magnus shrieked while Nos Kil dove for the pistol he'd dropped.

"You touch it, you die, Marine," Magnus said. The barrel of his MC90 hovered less than a meter behind Nos Kil's head.

"What the hell?" Flow asked, removing his helmet as Magnus emerged from the basement stairwell. Magnus held Nos Kil at the end of his MC90 while the surviving Nimprinthian young woman clutched Magnus's free arm like she might drown if she let go.

"Get an MP," Magnus said. "This one here needs court-martialing." He didn't bother mentioning that the man needed a medic for his shoulder too. Hell, the blaster bolt had cauterized the wound.

"Copy that," Flow said, waving at someone across the room. "And this lovely young—"

"Careful, Flow. I'm not in the mood."

"She needs a medic," Flow said, employing a sudden and wise course correction. "Miss, would you please come with me?"

But the young woman shook her head and clutched Magnus's arm all the harder.

"I'll take her," Magnus said. He breathed a small sigh of relief as two MPs put flexicuffs on Nos Kil. "Detain this one. If we last the night, Second Lieutenant Wainwright will have the charges."

"Understood," said one of the MPs. Then they hauled Nos Kil away… but not before the soon-to-be ex-Marine had something to say.

"I know what you did down there," Nos Kil said, spitting blood as he talked. His lips were swollen, and Magnus saw that his MC90's butt had broken a few of the Marine's teeth.

"And I know what you did, asshole," Magnus said.

Nos Kil sneered. The MPs jerked him away as more blaster rounds pounded the hotel's glass exterior.

"What was that about?" Flow asked.

"Nothing worth talking about now."

"Did you find your brother?" Flow asked.

Magnus's eyes went out of focus as he looked past Flow's face. "No," was all he could manage to say. That man down there… it may have been his brother by blood, but the moment Argus placed his pistol against an innocent person's head—hell, the moment he'd raped the poor girl—he'd stopped being a Magnus. "But let me know if you find him."

The building trembled and the girl held tight to Magnus.

"Come on," Flow said. "Let's get out of here. This place is going down."

"Copy that," Magnus said, moving toward the exit.

5

"Magnus," Wainwright said over comms. "I need a SITREP on the hotel."

"It's clear," Magnus replied. But his mind wouldn't let him forget his brother's body in the basement. Images of Argus's head tipping back, his body falling to the ground, kept fighting for prominence. If he wasn't careful, they'd distract him, and distractions meant more Marines dying. Instead, he pushed the emotions down and focused on his CO's voice.

"Good work, sergeant. I need you and the Four on the beach, double time."

"Roger that." Magnus liked when Wainwright used the moniker.

"Seems the enemy is breaking off its attack on the rest of the village and focusing all efforts—"

Magnus listened as muted blaster fire filled the comms.

"Focusing all efforts on the beach," Wainwright continued. "Take as many ammo crates as you can with you. We're running light. We lost some of our supply chains."

"Copy that, lieutenant. We're on our way."

"One last thing, Magnus."

"Of course."

"Word has it you and your squad are running around in your shorts and sandals."

"Didn't have time to get our armor on, sir."

"Make time, or else everyone on the beach might think you're showing up for a swim and not a fight."

"Copy that, sir."

It took five minutes for Magnus, Flow, Mouth, and Cheeks to suit up and move through the village to the south. Magnus was grateful that Wainwright had ordered them to suit up. He doubted he would have taken the time given how badly they were under attack. But Wainwright wasn't an idiot—a well-armored Marine could do more for the company than one roaming around in their underwear. So while Wainwright may have been concerned for Magnus, he was far more concerned with the entire operation.

"Looks like the most action is at the beach's center," Flow said over comms as they stopped outside a supply cache.

"Agreed," Magnus said. Without the mortar units on the hotel's roof, Magnus guessed the beach was going to be some highly contested territory. He stacked the ammo crates three high and latched them together, then pointed to Flow to take the handle on the other side.

"The 'kuda are trying to split us down the middle," Cheeks added as they departed the cache and stepped out from the village huts and onto the backside of the dunes. "Divide and conquer."

"So let's help stem the tide," Magnus said.

"Damn, sergeant," Mouth added. "You collect those jokes from the brass?"

Magnus smirked. He hadn't even meant to use the idiom while running onto a beach. "Nah. I did it just for you," Magnus said, lying to suit the moment.

"You really shouldn't have."

Cheeks shoved his side of the ammo crates as they ran, jarring Mouth to the side. "That's just the kind of son of a beach he is."

"You're killing me, Cheeks." Mouth readjusted his grip on the crates.

"Look alive, Fearsome, here we go…"

Magnus crested the dunes and saw a veritable sea of 'kuda emerging from the water and running for shore. They were moving fast, with fresh troops replacing downed ones as fast as the Marines could lay down fire. While the right and left flanks certainly appeared to have their hands full, the center boasted the largest concentration of 'kuda movement.

"Let's move these crates up as close as we can," Magnus said. "Get the lay of the land, and then kill us some fish for dinner." Everyone complied and then started down toward the strand.

Shortly after Magnus's company had secured the island, engineers had taken the liberty of deploying metal barricades along the beachheads. They were spiked on one side, facing the open ocean, but flat on the other, providing protective cover for Marines in situations exactly like this. The Marines had taken to calling them urchins based on their similarities to the aquatic lookalike.

Magnus slid down the dune face—his boots cutting long trenches along the embankment—before taking cover behind one of the urchins with Flow. Mouth and Cheeks joined them, toting their ammo crates. The heaviest fighting was still another two hundred meters toward the ocean at the place where the water stretched onto the strand. Magnus gave the order to advance, and all four of them made for the next urchin.

Several stray 'kuda rounds whizzed past their heads. "Careful," Magnus reminded them. "Eyes up."

The Four poured on the speed as they finally made it to their fifth urchin, one backfilled with several Marines who—apparently—had decided they couldn't advance further. According to the map on his HUD, Wainwright was still two urchins ahead. If Magnus was going to advance further and join him, he wouldn't be carrying ammo crates.

Magnus ordered his boys to set the crates down and then spotted another sergeant. He tapped the Marine on the shoulder and opened a channel based on the man's helmet ident chip.

"What'ya got, Sergeant Mendes?" Magnus asked.

The Marine turned and paused, probably registering Magnus's stats. "You're a Magnus too? Seen your brother anywhere? Cause right now, he's AWOL."

Magnus winced. His baby brother sure was away without leave—permanently. *Dammit, Magnus, keep it together.*

"Mendes," Magnus restated, "anything I need to know?"

"Just what you see. Damn fish won't stop coming. Whole ocean's full of the bastards. And without those mortar emplacements…"

"Copy that." Magnus pointed to the crates on the ground. "Got a birthday present for you. Make sure they get around."

"You shouldn't have."

"You can buy me a beer."

"Roger."

Magnus picked up one crate and asked Flow to mag lock it to his back. The crate would make running harder, but based on how close they were to the front, he wouldn't have to haul it far.

"Happy hunting, Mendes," Magnus said, tapping the man on the shoulder and making to move around the urchin.

"Hold up, where you going, Magnus?"

Magnus tilted his head at the other NCO. "To the front of the class, Mendes. Where else?"

"OTF, Magnus," Mendes said, his voice not without a sense of awe in it… and maybe an element of shame. Not all Marines were equal on the battlefield.

Magnus raised a fist and punched Mendes's knuckle. "OTF."

"Weapons hot, boys," Magnus ordered, back on their squad channel. "Take out any fish that puckers, and watch for IFF markers." The identify friend or foe icons appeared in their HUDs to separate potential targets from fellow Marines, and Magnus was diligent to remind his men about them. Firing on an enemy was easy when they were the only thing in your sight picture. But those opportunities were rarer than civilians thought. Most combat, especially the brutal splick, was fought in various degrees of confusion. Battle was a living thing that moved, constantly changing shape. If you got comfortable in one position, even for a second, it wouldn't be long before something doubled back to bite you in the ass.

Magnus rolled out from behind the urchin and charged toward the waterline some thirty meters ahead. Instantly, his squad's presence was marked by enemy blaster fire. Magnus crouched, took aim at the first fish he saw, and squeezed his MC90's trigger. The 'kuda doubled over from the blaster shot and slumped to the side. But it wasn't done. The fish eyed Magnus and raised its blaster. Magnus fired a second round, striking the 'kuda in the skull.

Flow, Mouth, and Cheeks took out several more Akuda as the four men charged for cover behind the next urchin. The fighting was getting thicker now, and Magnus could see Wainwright's icon another ten meters ahead. "One more urchin to go before we're in the worst of it," Magnus said.

"Oh come on, sergeant," Mouth said. "This is practically a school field trip compared to when your sister beat you up."

"And I still hold it against her," Magnus quipped. Everyone

knew he didn't have a sister. Hell, now he didn't even have a brother...

"Ready..." Magnus took a breath. "Go."

The Fearsome Four spun out into oncoming blaster fire, choosing targets and firing one round after another. Flow downed three 'kuda in a row, landing consecutive headshots as each fish fell away to reveal the next, standing in a perfect line.

Mouth pulled a VOD—variable output detonator—from his kit and lobbed it far out over the enemy. Magnus watched as the device exploded on the fragger mode, showering a swath of the Akuda with shrapnel. Several fish lost limbs. The enemy who was closest had its head split in two.

Cheeks switched his MC90 to three-round burst and began spraying the enemy with a short back-and-forth motion. Normally, such a tactic would have been deemed reckless and inefficient by Marine standards, but the 'kuda were so damn plentiful that he couldn't help but be accurate.

For his part, Magnus advanced methodically toward the waterline. His feet moved in a fluid motion, giving his upper body a stable platform to fire—pivot—fire—pivot. He delivered bolt after bolt, taking a slew of 'kuda down in a steady kill streak. The rhythmic pattern was Marine textbook as his legs, hips, shoulders, arms, and head worked together as a single lethal unit.

By the time the Four had crossed the distance to the farthest urchin, they'd downed a swath of Akuda that made the Marines upfront look back, double-checking just who approached from their rear. Magnus ducked behind the urchin and gave the onlookers a quick dip of his helmet. Over the platoon channel, he added, "Nice to see everyone."

"Bring me any ammo, sergeant?" Wainwright asked.

"We all know how you like your charge packs," Magnus said, turning so Flow could remove the supply case from his back.

"Cold and topped off," Wainwright said, opening the crate and removing the magazines. He passed them out as the rest of first platoon continued to unleash a withering assault on the oncoming 'kuda. "Thanks for joining us, sergeant."

"Our pleasure. Mind if we cut in?"

"Be my guest."

Magnus's squad relieved four Marines who, by the looks of their armor, could use a break. They climbed down the rungs in the urchin and let Magnus and the others climb up. Magnus looked over the barricade's edge, and his heart nearly stopped.

"Day-um," Flow said in two distinct syllables. "Would you look at that."

Spread from east to west, the entire strand was covered with oncoming 'kuda. They moved out of the ocean as if they were the waves themselves, flowing up and onto the beach like a force of nature. This was worse than he'd expected. Clearly, his helmet's AI and the Repub's orbital sensor array weren't keeping up with the sheer numbers of enemy combatants.

Magnus started firing, almost indiscriminately. He didn't need to aim—*just point and shoot*. No wonder Wainwright had called for more ammo. And, by the looks of it, they'd need a lot more than what Magnus had brought before the day was out. Hell, he

Demons at War

doubted if they'd even make it another fifteen minutes at this rate.

More explosions of sand and fire erupted from the strand as VODs exploded along the line. The sudden openings in the enemy ranks didn't last long, however. More 'kuda filled the gaps within seconds. By the time Magnus had gone through two energy mags, he realized this was a battle they weren't going to win, at least not here.

"I'm out," Magnus yelled, and then dropped down the rungs.

Wainwright caught him and turned him around. "Fall back, Marine."

Magnus double-checked the channel—Wainwright had opened a private line to him alone. "But sir—"

"I need you covering us when I give the order. I don't trust anyone else. Battalion has diverted some air assets our way, but they're still ten minutes out, and we need to clear the beach. Get the Four back there and give us covering fire."

"Copy." Magnus opened up the squad channel as he watched Wainwright climb up the back of the urchin. Regular COs weren't supposed to do what Wainwright was doing. But then again, Wainwright wasn't a regular CO—this he'd proven time and time again. "Fall back, Fearsome. We're going to rally covering fire to give first platoon a way out."

Flow, Mouth, and Cheeks replied with green affirmation pings and peeled off the urchin. Then they hunched over and followed Magnus back to the third line of barricades—two away from the dunes.

"You still got some ammo left, Mendes?" Magnus asked.

"Plenty, Magnus. You taking more up?"

"Negative—we're gonna spend it all to cover first platoon's retreat."

"Retreat?"

"We have air support inbound." Magnus checked the time. "Nine minutes. Gotta give our boys a way to clear the beach. Spread those mags out."

"Copy."

Magnus climbed up on the nearest urchin. He opened a proximity channel, and said, "Focus fire down the center. We gotta give Lieutenant Wainwright and first platoon a path back to the dunes."

Then, across all channels—probably from onboard an observation ship in orbit—Magnus heard the company commander say, "Air support inbound in eight minutes. All units, clear the beach. I say again, air support in eight, all units return to base. Command out."

"Open fire," Magnus said over the proximity channel. Suddenly, a stream of magenta blaster bolts focused around the urchin that hid Wainwright and the rest of first platoon. As soon as 'kuda bodies started dropping, Magnus watched his platoon start to fall back. They didn't waste time firing over their shoulders, they just put their heads down and started kicking up sand.

The Akuda must've sensed the change in tactics, however, because the enemy surge increased to the point that fish poured over the urchin. Several took blaster rounds square in the face, obliterating flesh and bone in pulpy sprays that covered those who took the dead fish's places. But the covering fire wasn't strong enough. The 'kuda were up, over, and around the urchin, driving straight into the Marine's blaster fire.

"Sweet mother of mystics," Flow said, swapping out mags. "These things just won't stop!"

"Try mooning them, Cheeks," Mouth said, to which the other Marine flipped him a middle finger.

"I mooned your mom and she didn't run," Cheeks said.

"Shift right," Magnus yelled, noticing a new push that was closing on Wainwright's icon. *The damn fool was taking up the rear*, Magnus realized. And that's exactly why he loved the CO so much.

The covering fire shifted to account for the new rush. Round after round drove into the 'kuda, covering the beach with corpses faster than Magnus's AI could update. He watched as Wainwright shoved his men onward, closing on Magnus's position.

"Hey, Magnus?" Cheeks's voice was an octave higher than normal. "What'da we do when—"

Cheeks was interrupted by enemy blaster fire that forced him to duck below the urchin's top edge. Magnus realized that while they'd bought time for first platoon to retreat, the enemy was rushing so quickly that Magnus would not have anyone to cover their retreat.

"Splick," Magnus said. He checked the topo map on his HUD and didn't see any Marines on the dunes. If they made a run for it, they'd be exposed until they got over the tops. But that was better than staying here and getting overrun.

He reopened the proximity channel, which now would probably include Wainwright and first platoon. "All units within square B9, fall back to the COP."

Magnus took out three more 'kudas before dropping back to the beach and backpedaling away from the urchin. Within seconds, first platoon had caught up, but slowed to turn around and cover their own retreat.

Up and down the central section of the beach, Marines ran backward, firing into the enemy ranks—in a few places, it was point blank. When Wainwright caught up with him, Magnus tossed up an extra energy mag.

"Thanks, Magnus."

"That one's a bit warm, sorry."

"We'll discuss it later." Wainwright ejected his spent magazine and inserted the fresh one. He charged his MC90 and started blasting away at three 'kuda that had gotten a bit too close for comfort in the time it took him to reload.

"Keep going!" Wainwright encouraged everyone.

Magnus checked the time. Five minutes remained. He felt the sand fall away under his feet, indicating the start of the dunes. His thighs burned as he marched backward up the hill, boots slipping and sliding. Still, he managed to keep a violent stream of fire trained on the enemy, hacking away at the aquatic bastards with trigger squeeze after trigger squeeze.

When at last they reached the summit, a new cluster of icons appeared with an arrow pointing off map. Magnus looked skyward and saw a cluster of ident tags in is HUD, indicating a squadron of FAF-28 Talons.

"Look who decided to show up," Flow said over the squad channel.

"Yeah…" Magnus took out a 'kuda who'd just nicked his helmet with a lucky blaster round. "But they're still three minutes out."

"Copy that, sergeant."

As soon as the rest of first platoon had crested the first dune, Wainwright ordered a full retreat back to the village. Fortunately, several Marines had set up mortar pits and laid into the enemy. The explosions were so loud, Magnus had to dampen his audio sensors even more than they already were. But he wasn't complaining. The big guns would buy them just enough time to get to cover.

Magnus pounded up and down the dunes until the edge of the village rose to meet their boots. The green grass seemed electrified under the glare of blaster fire, and he was happy to be on the grounds of the COP. But the village wasn't without its own destruction. Aside from the hotel—now a bleeding hulk of smoke and debris—several of the bungalows and outbuildings were on fire or razed to the ground. The Akuda's underwater artillery had done its job of softening the base.

Once inside the village, Magnus turned and ordered his men to take up defensive positions. He sighted in on three fish who had made it halfway across the dunes—apparently the fish's webbed feet made it much easier to skim along the shifting sands. *Bastards*.

"Outrun this, bitches." Magnus dropped all three with deadly accuracy.

"One minute," Wainwright called out.

If they could keep the Akuda confined to the beach, Magnus knew the Talons would take out enough to give the Marines an advantage—if not stem the battle's tide completely. They just had to keep any more 'kuda from getting across the dunes.

But that was easier said than done.

6

With only one minute remaining, the Akuda made a wild dash for the village. Magnus didn't know if they had some sort of sixth sense that warned them about imminent danger, or if their own ocean-based scanning tech had alerted them of the Talon's arrival. But either way, the push was monstrous.

Magnus fired alongside the surviving members of the platoons who'd been on the beach. They fired into the onrushing fish until their MC90's barrels glowed red. But still, the scaly beasts came, charging headlong into the relentless Marine fire. Like everyone else around him, for every two fish Magnus seemed to drop, another three took their places.

The hastily dug mortar pits were, perhaps, the only things truly keeping the Akuda from breaking into the village. They fired steadily, blowing holes along the dunes. Spouts of sand and body parts shot into the night sky, raining down on friend and foe alike. By the time the Talons arrived, however, Magnus was worried there wouldn't be enough Akuda left on the beach to make the assault effective. He double checked his HUD's topo map and breathed a quick sigh of relief as he saw a massive patch of enemy icons still clustered on the beachhead. It might not be the entire enemy contingent, but the fighters were certainly going to make a dent in the enemy's advance.

"Stand by for air assault," said the company commander over TACNET.

Magnus looked up as the Talons appeared, strafing from right to left. Their slender black fuselages and raked-forward wings made them look like midnight birds of prey skimming over the palm trees. They tore into the Akudas with their NR330 blaster cannons, nested on either side of the lower fuselage, while their secondary T-100 blasters in each wing tip shot high-frequency torrents that spit sand a hundred meters into the air.

The entire scene was lit up as if in broad daylight. Magnus could hear dozens of Marines breaking protocol and cheering over their open channels. But command let it go.

The final Talons to fly overhead must have been outfitted for bombing maneuvers as they dropped dozens of class-C torpedoes on the beach. The resulting explosions sent blasts rippling into the village, knocking scores of Marines off their feet. The concussions had been so loud that Magnus's ears rang even within his helmet.

"HELL YEAH," Flow yelled over the squad channel, pumping a fist in the air. Magnus could hear similar sentiments echoed up and down the line, many coming from Marines who were struggling back to their feet. A general sense of relief seemed to wash over the COP as the Talons powered up and away, their engines slapping the night sky with a blistering assault of heat and light.

"We ain't done yet, boys," Magnus said, calling his squad's attention back to the dunes.

"Son of a bitch!" Mouth said.

The Four watched in awe as a wave of Akuda continued charging the village. Whatever forces the Talons had hit on the main beach, they'd missed those on the dunes.

Wainwright was on TACNET next. "Look alive, Marines," he yelled. "Clear those dunes!"

Magnus leaned against a palm tree and opened fire, but it became clear that the battle was coming into the village. The Marines had lost precious seconds in observing the Talons' assault—seconds that the Akuda had used to advance in the coordinated absence of the mortar fire.

Magnus fired on a line of fish that were headed between bungalows and funneling toward his position. He dropped several 'kuda and then started backpedaling. The only thing left behind him were the tents. He double-checked his last mag's capacity—it was below ten percent. But based on the enemy's decreasing rate of fire, it seemed they were running low on ammunition as well.

Magnus continued to fire with his right hand while he removed the duradex combat knife from his hip with his left. He silently thanked the recon Marine who'd gifted it to him. And now that this battle was going hand-to-hand, there was no better weapon to have at his disposal.

The first 'kuda to close on Magnus when his MC90 went dry was a venomous looking creature who's serrated teeth and claws dripped with green fluid. He knew the stuff had infected more than one Marine's wounds, and he wasn't in the mood to be cooped up in a field hospital for weeks on end.

The fish swung at his head, but Magnus ducked. He jabbed at the 'kuda's soft underbelly in response, feeling his knife drive deep into the creature's gut. The fish screamed and threw back its head. Then it swiped at Magnus again but with the other clawed hand. Magnus blocked the blow with his MC90 and swiped his blade just under the 'kuda's chin. A dark fountain of blood splashed on Magnus's visor, but the beast was done, writhing in death throes as it curled up on the grass.

The next fish that assaulted him seemed more savvy. Rather than rush straight in, it juked one way and then another before leaping the last two meters. Magnus was knocked backward but was able to keep the animal's hands away from his body—knife stabbing the fish's left hand, and his right hand holding the 'kuda's other wrist. The two of them wrestled on the ground, plowing into several tents. The fish snapped at Magnus's helmet, its teeth cracking the visor and momentarily shorting out his HUD.

"Get off me, you son of a bitch!" Magnus used his legs to fling the Akuda over his head, which bought him just enough time to roll to his feet and lunge at the beast. He drove his knife into the fish's eye just as it tried to stand up. The creature dropped to the ground so quickly, Magnus lost his grip on the knife.

"Look out!" cried a voice somewhere among the tents next to him. Magnus looked back just in time to see a 'kuda break free from a tangle of Marines and charge him. Turning toward the dead fish with his blade in its eye, Magnus retrieved the weapon and readied himself for the oncoming 'kuda.

The impact rattled Magnus's head as the pair flew further into the tent village. They rolled into a grassy quad. Magnus felt them knock over several chairs and collide with the border stones of a campfire, embers still glowing from a fire earlier in the evening.

This particular fish was stronger than the others, forcing Magnus back and forth as it tried to dominate the Marine. But the beast had his hands immobilized, and it used its powerful jaws to try and pop his helmet like a piece of fruit.

"Kick it in the groin!" the same voice said from before. Magnus had no idea who would be watching his fight without coming to lend a hand themselves. But he also couldn't deny the strategic suggestion. Magnus focused on his free leg and then drilled his knee into the creature's pelvis.

The 'kuda produced a pitiful cry and lessened its grip on Magnus's knife hand. The release of pressure was just enough that Magnus wrested his wrist free and swiped the blade across the fish's neck. The loss of aggression was almost instantaneous as the 'kuda reached for its throat, attempting in vain to stem to loss blood that pumped from its veins into the open air. Magnus shoved the fish aside.

As soon as he gained his feet, Magnus looked to see who'd spoken to him. There, bound to a cement block on the far side of the campfire area, was a bare-chested young man in shorts and sandals. Magnus blinked in shock—it was the Marine from the basement. Nos Kil.

Magnus turned and started to walk away.

"Don't leave me here, man," Nos Kil yelled, a small whine to his voice. "Those things... those things gonna feed on me!"

"As well they should," Magnus replied over his external speakers.

"Hold up..." said the kid. Magnus turned halfway toward him. "That you, Magnus?"

"That's sergeant to you."

Nos Kil sniffed. "While I'll be. What a coincidence."

"Have fun feeding the fish," Magnus said, looking back toward the line of Marines and Akuda.

"No way, man. You gotta keep me alive. I'm a prisoner here."

"Like hell I do." But even as he spoke the words, Magnus knew he couldn't just let the Marine die here. Everything in him wanted to let the bastard get ripped apart by these devils—and he'd be happy to watch. But that wasn't protocol. That wasn't real justice. This kid needed to go to trial so he could rot in a cell till the Corps said he could go free—which might be never, given the testimony that Magnus would provide to Wainwright.

Suddenly, two 'kuda broke through the line and darted toward the easy target—Nos Kil cuffed to the ground.

"Son of a bitch," Magnus yelled to himself as he rushed to

meet the two assailants. He dove just as the fish were about to pounce on Nos Kil, who was cowering in a ball.

Magnus's right shoulder drove into the first fish, which not only knocked it off balance but caused it to slam sideways into the second 'kuda. Magnus reached around both fish with his right arm while jabbing the second one with his knife. A split second later, all three beings hit the ground and rolled to a stop. Magnus was on his feet first, challenging the two fish as they circled Nos Kil.

"Don't let me die," the Marine whined, panic covering his face.

"Shut up," Magnus ordered. "Or I might just let them kill you."

"You wouldn't!"

Magnus let out a low chuckle as if begging the kid to test him. "Just shut up, would you?"

Suddenly, one fish lunged at Magnus. Sidestepping the 'kuda's attacked, Magnus placed both hands on the knife and plunged it hard into the creature's back. The fish shrieked and twisted free, but the effort forced the knife to cut a deep gouge out of the creature's flesh. It backhanded Magnus in the helmet, flailing wildly, but Magnus ducked and stabbed the enemy again.

In the short time it took to dispatch the first 'kuda, the second dove toward Nos Kil. It landed on him with its claws open and mouth gaping. For a split second, Magnus pictured the kid raping the Nimprinthian girl in the basement and wondered if this wasn't the universe's bringing judgment on the Marine. But Magnus wasn't a vigilante. No matter how bad he wanted revenge, letting this kid die made him no better—that was the reason for the Corps, for standards, for code.

"Get off him," Magnus spat, then drove his knife into the side of the 'kuda's neck. The thing squealed, gills flapping wildly, as Magnus started hacking away at the neck meat like he was filleting a fish he'd caught off a pier in Capriana. The Akuda twisted on him, batting the knife away. In the next moment, Magnus was on his back, staring up into the creature's mouth. It lunged at his helmet, but the cover deflected the blow, sending it instead to his shoulder. Heat burst from his skin as the 'kuda's teeth made entry around his plate armor and sank into his muscle.

The fish pulled away, focused on something new. Magnus looked to see Nos Kil kicking the 'kuda in the side. Did this mean Magnus and the kid were now fighting side by side? The notion made his stomach churn… *or is that the poison in my shoulder?*

Filled with a renewed sense of *pissed off*, Magnus took advantage of Nos Kil's momentary distraction and rolled the off-balance fish to the side. The pair rotated away from the kid and toward the campfire. Magnus gauged the distance and threw the enemy around twice more until he rolled onto the fish, pressing the thing's back into the coals.

The fish shrieked, snapping its jaws at the air, and tried jerking Magnus off. But Magnus held fast, shoving the enemy again and again into the coals, forcing him to stay down as smoke and steam spit from the coal. When the fire pit had finally gouged a hole in the assailant's back enough to end its life, Magnus stepped away from the roasted carcass and looked at Nos Kil.

"You couldn't let them kill me, could you," the kid said. "I knew it. You're just as pathetic as your brother said you were."

Magnus didn't even hesitate. He took two steps toward Nos Kil and slugged him in the side of the face. The kid collapse into his handcuffs, lights out. Then Magnus retrieved his knife and wiped it on the Marine's shorts. "Have fun at trial, you piece of splick."

EPILOGUE

Magnus sat in a small anteroom on the Leviathan-class battleship *Emerald Victory* awaiting an audience with Major Caldwell. Contrary to what his men had claimed, this meeting wasn't Magnus's doing. It was one thing to talk a big game while stuck on a roof picking off 'kuda, but it was another to have the brass balls big enough to make the call. Magnus had too much respect for himself to go cherry-picking a promotion.

No, this meeting had been at the request of the major himself following Alpha Company's "near impossible defense" of T'io Mi'on's main village. Magnus secretly despised the term "near impossible" as every Marine knew nothing was impossible. Either you were successful, or you died trying, in which case you didn't know you weren't successful.

Still, he understood why the higher-ups were referring to the op that way. The Akuda assault had been relentless. Even after the Talon strafing run, which Magnus was sure would have ripped the will from even the most ardent enemy, three more waves of fighters had to be called in before the damn fish relented. As the conflict was drawing out, it seemed the Akuda were getting more desperate. *How many more of them were there in those oceans?* he wondered.

This was the first time Magnus had taken a shower on a starship in over ten months, and he wasn't complaining. He'd nearly forgotten what one felt like without sand under his feet. He also forgot what his dress uniform felt like—a whole lot easier to move in than armor, though he still hated the damn collar around his neck. But he was rather surprised that this meeting was happening in the major's office on a battleship and not a field office on Caledonia. That alone made him wring his sweaty hands more than once.

"Sergeant Magnus," said the secretary, stepping into the room, "the major will see you now."

Magnus nodded and stood. He smoothed his coat, took a deep breath, and walked behind the secretary in an administrative suite. Then, following the secretary's gesture toward a door with Caldwell's name on it, Magnus stepped forward until the door slid sideways automatically.

The major sat behind a large desk. He wore his gray hair tight on the sides and flat on top, and clenched a cigar in the side of his mouth. How the man had permission to keep the thing lit on a starship was beyond Magnus, but he wouldn't want to be the one to tell him he couldn't.

Despite his age and his years in the Corps, Caldwell hadn't

advanced as quickly as normal officers did. But by all accounts, he was far from normal. Procedure dictated that he should have been a general by now, only doing so would have taken him farther from the thing he loved most—being with Marines, not managing data pads. Of course, he'd already sealed that deal when he left the ranks of the enlisted years before. The man's legend of wanting to change the Corps' policies was known far and wide. And it was rumored that he was a pain in the ass for every colonel and lieutenant colonel he served under. Magnus had already seen the man in action several times. He guessed Caldwell was as much to handle on a battlefield as he was in a war room.

To his credit, Caldwell had the reputation of fighting for the enlisted Marines while negotiating in the hallways of the brass. No one, it was said, had the balls or the will to do it like Caldwell. Thus, he was respected—if not scorned—by the field-grade officers and generals, and worshipped by the enlisted.

Magnus saluted the major and then stood at attention.

"At ease, Sergeant Magnus," Caldwell said, gesturing to one of two leather-backed chairs. "Take a seat."

"Thank you, sir." Magnus strode forward and sat. He tried his best to get comfortable in the squeaky chair, but Caldwell staring at him for a few long seconds made it even more difficult.

"I'm told you did a damn fine job down there, sergeant."

"Thank you, sir."

"Your COs are recommending several commendations." Caldwell eyed Magnus as if he was supposed to reply to that.

"I'll be the last to question their judgment, but I was just doing my job."

"I'm sure you were." Caldwell puffed on his cigar and then eyed Magnus. Magnus wanted to adjust himself in the chair but knew the squeaking would make the long silence even more awkward. "You know, I knew your grandfather well."

"That's what I understand, yes."

"Did you know him?"

"Not well, no. He was committed to the Corps right up until—"

"We all know that part, sergeant."

"Right…" Magnus cleared his throat. "Anyway, my father didn't have much time for my grandfather. So we never saw much of him."

"Damn shame," Caldwell said. "He was the finest Marine I ever knew."

"Thank you, sir."

Caldwell nodded slowly, taking a long drag on the cigar and letting the smoke cloud his face momentarily. "You look like him, you know."

"That's what they say."

"Same eyes. Same jaw…"

"And same stubborn nature," Magnus added, suddenly realizing he may have just interrupted the man.

"That can be a blessing and a curse."

"A point that my father reminded me of many times."

"I'm sure," said Caldwell. "But I have to think your stubborn nature is what's landed you here in my office today."

"Sir?"

"I want to discuss what happened to my son."

Magnus swallowed. He'd suspected this was what Caldwell had wanted to talk about. Worse, he had no idea what he should say. *Best to not say anything unless asked*, Magnus thought. And then?

Then tell the truth.

"Word has it that he went missing," Caldwell said, eyeing Magnus. "Members of fourth platoon reported he went to the basement. They were looking for him just before the hotel came under attack, but found nothing."

Magnus held his tongue. He hadn't been asked anything yet. That, and the pain of losing his brother was still too raw. Hell, when would it not be raw? He knew if he talked about it now, he might not be able to control the emotions raging in his chest. The anger. The grief.

"They all said that he was friends with your brother, Argus."

Just the sound of his Argus's name made Magnus want to die inside. His kid brother may have been a traitor—may have even been evil—but he was still kin. And Magnus suspected that the major would probably wrestle with the same frustrations once he knew the truth.

"TACNET also has you going to the hotel's basement shortly before the building reached structural failure."

Dammit.

"Sergeant Magnus, you're in my office today because I want to know what you encountered down there." He sucked on the cigar, held the smoke for a second, and then let it out. "And I know what you're thinking, son. The warrior-half of your brain is telling you to measure your reply, while the survivor-half is preparing for countermeasures. It's calculating, strategizing. And trust me when I say that you do not want to make that mistake with me of parsing your words. Because one thing is for damn sure…" Caldwell leaned forward and emphasized the next words with his fat index finger on the desk. "I will find the truth."

A chill went down Magnus's spine. Whatever notions he had of being tactful with the major, they all went out the door. Call it the fear of the mystics, call it self-preservation—it didn't matter. As far as Magnus was concerned, he was face to face with his maker.

Magnus swallowed as he realized this was his day of reckoning. His sins hadn't even given him twenty-four hours before finding him out. On the professional side, if he wasn't tried in a military tribunal and sentenced to death for betraying the Marine Corps code, he was at least getting dishonorably discharged—probably after several months in the brig. Either way, telling Caldwell that he'd shot another Marine would be the end of his career. It didn't matter how right he thought he was in the moment. The fact was, he'd betrayed the Corps and betrayed a fellow Marine. There would be hell to pay, but that would pale in comparison to paying Major Caldwell first.

On the personal side, however, Magnus had to deal with the fact that he'd killed his brother. This was greater than betraying the Corps. He'd betrayed his own flesh and blood. And unlike the Repub, who would forget his crimes the moment he was thrown into a blackhole, Magnus would never forget staring into Argus's eyes the breath before squeezing the trigger. That was the event horizon the gravity of which he could never escape.

Magnus took a deep breath and then recounted everything that had happened from the time he left the lobby to the time he re-emerged. Despite wanting to leave out the grizzly details about the major's son—both in his deplorable actions and in his death—he didn't. He only spared the detail about the young Marine's manhood hanging out. There was injury, and then there was insult. Better to spare him the later.

Magnus kept expecting the officer to show some sort of emotion, but he didn't. He just sat there, chewing on his cigar, listening intently. The man's glare was withering. Magnus kept thinking that the major might lash out at him and dispense the penance due someone who'd committed fratricide. Maybe he'd shed a tear for his own son's death. Or grow angry at how the Corps had been betrayed by any and all of the Marines in the basement. But nothing came.

When Magnus had finished his account, ready to be escorted out of the office by some MPs, the major leaned back, folded his hands, and nodded. "Thank you, son."

You're welcome would have been the appropriate reply, but Magnus couldn't bring himself to say it. *What in the hell is the man thanking me for?*

As if in answer to his silent question, Caldwell added, "Your story corroborates that of the young woman's who we detained."

Son of a bitch. So his CO already had an idea of what went down. Magnus suddenly wondered what would have happened had he not been forthright.

"And I'm guessing you left out the part about my son's dick hanging out of his pants to spare me any undue embarrassment."

Magnus looked at the major, unblinking.

"I appreciate that as well." At the end of his cigar, Caldwell extinguished the roll of tobacco in the bottom end of a large-caliber energy mag. The metal magazine had been cut down, leaving a rectangular looking bowl that the man used as an ashtray. Satisfied the ember was out, Caldwell returned the stump to his lips and spoke out of the side of his mouth.

"Firing on another Marine with the intent to kill is a crime."

"I know that, sir, and I'm—"

"Shut up, sergeant."

Magnus sealed his lips.

"Killing your brother is another thing altogether."

Mystics, this guy knew how to stick it to him. But did he deserve any less than ridicule? Magnus literally wanted to be anywhere else in the galaxy but here. But this was the course he'd chosen. This is where his actions had brought him, and if it were anyone else, he'd tell them to own it and take what was coming to them.

"But raping two innocent women is a crime worse than those you've committed," Caldwell added. "Some might even say you delivered justice."

Magnus blinked.

"And I happen to be one of those someones, sergeant."

"Sir?"

"What happened down there was not the worst of the Corps

on display, it was the worst of humanity. And given the same scenario, I can tell you what I would have done."

A long silence filled the air, and Magnus wondered if he was supposed to inquire further. But he didn't have to.

"I wouldn't have thought twice about killing anyone else who was using innocent lives to protect their own." The Major leaned back and let out a deep sigh. "I wish neither of us lost family members yesterday. But they chose their fates, and it seems those choices have further intertwined our paths, Magnus."

Again, Magnus wanted to inquire as to what the major meant but felt he should hold his tongue.

"This episode will remain between you and me. The woman will be compensated to the greatest extent of my abilities and spared the pain of testifying in a tribunal. Instead, she will be informed of her assaulter's fate and left to live out the remainder of her life as best she's able.

"For his part, the sole surviving Marine will be tried and more than likely executed. I will see to it that he is detained in psychiatric solitary confinement. Even if his version of the story is heard, it will be immaterial."

"I understand," was all Magnus could think to say. He wanted to say more… to thank Caldwell for… *for what?* Magnus still wasn't off the hook.

"As for you, sergeant…"

Here it comes.

"I'm recommending we transfer you out of Bravo Company. In fact, I'd say we get you out of Second Battalion altogether."

"Sir?"

"Where do you want to go, son?"

Magnus didn't know what to say. *What the hell is happening here?* Just minutes ago, he was preparing to be court-martialed. And now he was being asked where he wanted to be transferred? This wasn't how a murderer was supposed to be treated.

"Sergeant?"

"Yes… I…"

Caldwell raised his eyebrows so far that his forehead turned into a mountain of ridges.

Before Magnus could keep the words in, out spilled, "I'd like to apply for recon indoctrination school."

Caldwell stroked his chin. "RIS…" Then he reached for a data pad and started flicking through several pages. "That's not an easy program. But you're not an easy going Marine."

"I understand."

"It might be made easier if you apply for officer training too."

"Major?"

"Says here you have enough schooling to make the jump if you want. And it seems to me we need more men like you at the top."

"Begging your pardon, sir, but I like being—"

"With the enlisted men? Son, who do you think you're talking to?"

Magnus knew not to answer that kind of question.

"The Corps isn't great because it has good generals. It's great because it has the best warriors in the galaxy. The generals just get the accolades because they tell everyone else what to shoot. But the best generals—they're the ones who know what it's like to bleed. And this…" Caldwell tapped the desk again. "The hell you just lived? That's what it means to bleed. To make the right call even though it's the hardest one to make.

"I know you came in here thinking you'd get court-martialed today. And damn straight: you should have been pissing your blues. But you also should never underestimate yourself when you do what you believe is right. I can't imagine the pain you must be feeling right now, son. I've never had to put down my own brother in defense of others, but I've had to do things close enough that let me know you won't ever outrun this one.

"So, I'm offering a chance to make the journey more bearable, more meaningful—to both join the recon and become a second lieutenant. But it's only a chance. No one's getting you through either program. That's on you."

"I understand," Magnus said, repeating the same phrase yet again.

"I won't lie. RIS is going to kick your ass, son."

Magnus almost said "I understand" again, but knew he'd be rebuked. No one knew what a school could dish out until they'd gone through it for themselves. And Magnus had heard stories about RIS.

"If I say yes, would you entertain a request?"

Caldwell chewed his cigar. "You wanna negotiate with me, sergeant?"

Magnus had the distinct feeling that Caldwell had suddenly switched from a family friend to a hard-nosed Marine CO. "Merely a proposal."

"Well, spit it out."

"I'd like to bring Lance Corporals Deeks, Franklin, and Chico with me."

Caldwell's face was stone cold. That wasn't a good sign. For a split second, Magnus swore he'd lost his chance at both programs. That sentiment was only reinforced when Caldwell said, "We don't do that, son."

For what he hoped was the last time today, Magnus said, "I understand. But these men are important to me. They may not have been in that basement with me, but they've been everywhere else. My success is their success, and if I go, they're going with me."

Caldwell frowned. He looked at the data pad again and tapped several screens. His eyes scanned the screen for the better part of a minute before he replied. "Seems none of them have any schooling that would make them eligible for the officer program. However, there's nothing preventing them from applying to RIS with you."

"So... that's green?"

"Consider it a favor for your grandfather, son."

Magnus hated the family favor angle, but he wasn't going to buck it either, not if it meant the Fearsome Four had a chance at remaining a unit. He knew it was unheard of, and he knew the odds were slim to none. But hell if he didn't at least try.

"Thank you, major. I'm extremely grateful."

"Damn straight you are." The major removed the stump from his mouth and said. "I'll let you know when your brother's funeral is scheduled and make sure you get leave for it. That is, if you want it."

"I would." Magnus nodded. While he would bear the wound for the rest of his life, there was no sense making it worse by missing his funeral.

"I'm thinking it will be small, as records indicate that you are his only surviving relative."

"That's correct, sir."

Caldwell nodded, then placed the data pad back down. "Well, pack your bags, son, before I change my mind and send you back to shoot me some more fish."

Magnus stood and saluted the major. The day's pain wasn't gone—he suspected it never would be. But it was being contested, and Magnus never backed down from a challenge. "Thank you, major."

To Magnus's surprise, the man stood up and returned his salute. The magnitude of the gesture wasn't lost on him. "Thank me if you graduate, son."

MAGNUS returns in GALACTIC BREACH, available now on Amazon.

For more updates on this series, be sure to join the Facebook Group, "J.N. Chaney's Renegade Readers."

Made in the USA
Middletown, DE
09 September 2021